PRAISE FOR *ISHA, UNSCRIPTED*

"Isha's struggle against family expectat[...]
prising turns, and readers will laugh a[...]

"Patel's fans will enjoy it."

"Isha's journey to stay true to herself is handled with care while still allowing this to be a fun, contemporary romance."

—A JILLion Books

"I have been enjoying reading about messy main characters. And Sajni Patel provides the perfect messy main character in *Isha, Unscripted*."

—Abigail Books Addiction

MORE PRAISE FOR SAJNI PATEL AND HER NOVELS

"Sajni Patel perfectly encapsulated Indian culture and traditions while giving younger readers such as myself an outlet to express our frustrations as Liya and Jay battle many of the issues we face."

—Jessica Reads It

"An endearing, feel-good rom-com celebrating love, heritage, and friendship."

—*Kirkus Reviews*

"A unique story about working hard to achieve your dreams."

—The Candid Cover

"Sajni Patel is a talented writer who is able to write about mental health, racism, and cultural issues with compassion and insight. She balances these issues with a healthy dose of humor and heart."

—The Bashful Bookworm

BERKLEY TITLES BY SAJNI PATEL

Isha, Unscripted

The Design of Us

THE
DESIGN
OF
US

Sajni Patel

BERKLEY ROMANCE
NEW YORK

BERKLEY ROMANCE
Published by Berkley
An imprint of Penguin Random House LLC
penguinrandomhouse.com

Copyright © 2024 by Sajni Patel
Readers Guide copyright © 2024 by Penguin Random House LLC
Penguin Random House supports copyright. Copyright fuels creativity, encourages
diverse voices, promotes free speech, and creates a vibrant culture. Thank you for buying
an authorized edition of this book and for complying with copyright laws by not
reproducing, scanning, or distributing any part of it in any form without permission.
You are supporting writers and allowing Penguin Random House to continue to
publish books for every reader.

BERKLEY and the BERKLEY & B colophon are registered trademarks of
Penguin Random House LLC.

Library of Congress Cataloging-in-Publication Data

Names: Patel, Sajni, 1981– author.
Title: The design of us / Sajni Patel.
Description: First edition. | New York : Berkley Romance, 2024.
Identifiers: LCCN 2023046661 (print) | LCCN 2023046662 (ebook) |
ISBN 9780593547854 (trade paperback) | ISBN 9780593547861 (ebook)
Subjects: LCGFT: Romance fiction. | Novels.
Classification: LCC PS3616.A86649 D47 2024 (print) |
LCC PS3616.A86649 (ebook) | DDC 813/.6—dc23/eng/20231128
LC record available at https://lccn.loc.gov/2023046661
LC ebook record available at https://lccn.loc.gov/2023046662

First Edition: July 2024

Printed in the United States of America
1st Printing

Book design by George Towne
Interior art: Floral Tropical Pattern © Anastasia Barre/Shutterstock.com

To all you lovestruck romantics. Take your shot.

ONE

Bhanu

I worked in UX. UX had always been, and still was, my techy passion. Most people had no idea what in the world UX stood for, much less what it was (user experience, BTW). It was simple, really. To put it humbly, I was the all-powerful bridge connecting creativity to technology, functionality to experience. Ever used an app or website and didn't find yourself frustrated with navigation or have any negative experience, then you, my friend, experienced good UX design and had an entire dauntless team to thank for the smallest clicks and details that made your browsing exploits so flawless that you didn't even realize you were having them.

That, of course, was oversimplifying. A great deal went into the tiniest things down to color specs. Tons of meetings and research and late nights went into every thought. Today was no different.

It was six in the morning, and even the sun hadn't peeked through the rain clouds on this Pacific Northwestern day. I'd buzzed around getting coffee and waffles in my elegant, flowing cardigan, feeling very much like a princess. Granted, one who was isolated in a tower but not-so-secretly enjoyed it. I spoke of . . . remote work. When else could a girl feel like a princess in baggy pajamas and no bra?

Fret not, I *had* donned a bra and shimmied into a meeting blouse to look the part, brushing my hair into a low ponytail as coffee cooled, and patted on light makeup while munching on waffles. I wasn't typically a breakfast person, but there was something about waffles that I couldn't shake off. So bad was my waffle addiction that I'd splurged on one of those heavy-duty waffle makers that made four perfect squares at a time. And yes, I was eating all four this morning. A few blueberries in the mix, smothered in butter, a dollop of whipped cream, and I was the happiest person in the world.

Odd-hour meetings were part of UX. Although my company was based in Seattle, we worked with clients from around the globe. Thus why hybrid work worked so well. No one was going to make me fight Seattle traffic and battle to the death for parking spots for this meeting.

Worldwide clients paid pretty pennies for us to collaborate with them on their next big tech designs. Typically, websites and apps. When I say websites, I don't mean WordPress. I mean industry giants with complex coding and hundreds of call-to-action buttons leading to a million user interfaces to push product and make sure their company rose above intense competition.

UX was cutthroat.

I prepped my slides for my segment, making sure the presentation was ready to go, and went over the hurdles clients were sure to toss out. They had a lot to say and seemed particular for no valid reason. Mainly because they didn't know what they wanted or what worked best.

Like, sir, why would you insist on that ugly shade when color theory clearly explained why it wouldn't work? It didn't fit the mood, the atmosphere, or the purpose of the app, and created horrendous legibility issues. And testing showed that 85 percent of users were either disturbed or distracted by said ugly color.

These were typical annoyances a UX team almost always had to deal with.

I sat down at my sprawling desk—made too small by all the items on it—with an oomph, careful not to spill coffee, and shoved another bite of waffle into my mouth. I'd love to say that I was extra careful with my desktop and laptop out, plus a tablet and phone because we were techy-techy, but nah. I enjoyed waffles with butter and sans syrup, so there was at least that. Less sugary, sticky mess to attract ants.

A hefty sigh left my lips. All screens up. Slide deck prepped and loaded. Virtual platform on. A few large squares showed the bright-eyed faces of coworkers blinking back at me as we prepared to go live. Those squares quickly multiplied as others joined.

My role as senior lead UX researcher meant I oversaw mind maps, extensive user studies, field tests, and more to make sure every aspect, every click and tap, every color, typography, size, responsive design, et cetera, was at its quality best.

As lead, I worked with the leads of other subteams, which made me Mama Duck, who pushed and protected her vast army of researcher ducklings while often butting heads with extremely particular designers and particularly overworked devs (coding developers).

But that was because we were passionate. And we made beautiful, thrilling designs.

I glanced up to see our lead dev hop on screen, but I was too busy enjoying this fine cup of cinnamon coffee to care. Sunny skimmed across his screen, a little wrinkle in between his brows as he focused, and then a smile cracked his uptightness. Probably looking at cat videos. He looked like a cat guy. An annoying cat guy.

I messaged my team in the private chat and then opened up a chat with the PM (project manager). Gabrielle declared all was a go.

My heart did a shimmy in my chest. No matter how many times I presented, which was at least once a week, it was a little unnerving when it came to presenting directly to overtly opinionated clients. Would they slash our research down to the nub, or would they let us do what they were paying us to do? It was always a shot in the dark as to what their mood would be. The men on our teams never seemed this stressed, which had me wondering if guys had it easier. What a dumb question. Of course they did. Clients probably respected male leads and took their word as gold. After all, what did I, a woman who'd worked in the field for over five years with a master's in UX theory, possibly know about some damn buttons?

Carol, the big boss overseeing multiple teams on various projects, started the show and handed it off to Gabrielle. She smiled, flashing dimples, and essentially looked like a doppelgänger of Gabrielle Union. She had a slightly deeper voice and made these wild facial expressions that promised nobody wanted to argue with her. She was, hands down, the best PM ever, and I'd learned a great deal from her. A shield against the higher-ups for us and a moderator between leads at times. She was a well-oiled organizing machine, and ever so eloquent.

Carol dinged me. I was up next.

"Thanks so much, Gabrielle," Carol said with an accent, for some reason rolling the *r*. It was funny until she announced, "And now let's hand the meeting over to Bhanu."

Damnit, Carol.

My name is Bhanu. Pronounced "Bon-oooh." It was almost always expected to have to correct someone on the pronunciation, to the point where it had become standard. But Carol—granted she wasn't my direct boss nor did she have a lot to do with me personally— and I had been working together at this company for years, and half the time she still said my name wrong.

She reminded me of an old classmate, Cathryn, who had once complained, "Ugh. I'm so sick of people misspelling my name."

"Try having people mispronounce your name," I'd countered.

She'd looked at me with big gray eyes and said, "Well, your name is a little hard."

"Bitch, it's two syllables."

Just kidding. I hadn't said that, but I was thinking it. I thought a lot of things that didn't actually come out of my mouth for fear of being labeled hostile, unlikable, et cetera. It came with the territory of being a woman, and even more so as a woman of color.

These days, with people being a little more considerate and "woke," many were prompted to ask for pronunciation, so they didn't butcher my name. Carol had asked more than once.

My name wasn't Ban-oooh or Bane-oooh. Yet here we were.

Behind some of those many on-screen squares were a few co-workers snickering at my immediate roll of the eyes.

Oh, Carol. This shouldn't still be a thing, ya know, the lack of respect to say a name correctly.

"Thanks, Cairo," I muttered.

She gave a confused look but there was no time. I dove right into my spiel. In between segments, I checked my image in the little box at the corner of my screen to make sure my blouse hadn't wandered down the front to expose my sexy sports bra. The fact that I even had on a bra was about the best anyone could expect from me, if we were going to be honest.

I adjusted my pajamas at the waist, tapping my feet in fuzzy, pink pirate socks underneath a throw blanket.

I offered a few visuals as I spoke. A couple of graphs, but not too many—otherwise I'd lose client attention. They could *try* to argue against data science, but look, numbers didn't lie. They couldn't keep saying they needed, for some unknown reason, a big-ass header on the landing page. God, we get it, you love your logo.

During our last meeting, we'd presented low-fidelity wireframes, which were basics. Boxes and lorem ipsum fillers for later text. This time, we had a prototype, which the UX design and UI (user interface) leads would go into next.

One of the hardest things for clients to grasp was how agile UX was. We worked in a constantly revolving circle. They couldn't just say they wanted this app and bam! We'd have a working high-fi prototype fully designed within weeks. No. We had to start with research, conduct testing, create storyboards and site maps, UI patterns for consistency, among a hundred other tasks, and then actually code the damn thing. And then we did it all over again, testing each element until we nailed the best version.

Data science was hard to argue against, but then I turned the presentation over to Juanita, the UX design lead, and that was when the clients essentially forgot everything I'd just said.

"What about offering more options in purchasing?" one asked.

I bit my lip, wishing Juanita could tag me back in so I could pull up the journey maps and storyboard slide showing how users moved through their app. I'd spent forever designing these! These weren't little stick figures with thought bubbles wondering how does one even open an app.

I retrieved my calm.

Gabrielle messaged me: **Bhanu! You have permission to jump back in!**

Aha! Back in the ring to reiterate, once again, after the clients had nearly dismantled Juanita.

I delved deeper into algorithms and pinpointed a few design suggestions that had particularly strong feedback. I then answered a few questions and, without thinking to hand it back to Juanita, handed the presentation over to the lead dev.

"Thanks, Bane," he said, and jumped right into his overarching structural gameplay for the code team, going through an actual functioning prototype.

I glared at the screen and blinked. Damnit, Sunny. Could we go one day without this?

My name was definitely not Bane. As in the bane of his existence . . . or even Bane from Batman. As hot as a Tom Hardy Bane had been, I just didn't think that was a compliment in any way.

But he wasn't worth my calm this morning. I was too chill to respond, which probably disappointed whoever had betted on today's pool of Bhanu vs. Sunny. He went through his segment, talking way more than he needed to. Sheesh, most devs in this business were known introverts, but here he was, loving the sound of his own voice. It was deep and gritty, more like Denzel Washington than a nerdy coder—ahem—but yeah, whatever, not my thing.

I lowered the volume and muted myself, wrapping my fingers around my warm cup.

The rain was a constant drizzle outside my Tacoma apartment, per usual for this time of year. The fireplace was going and added a nice, cozy warmth to the one-bedroom abode. I sat in the converted office corner of the living room, where the watery streams running down a frostbitten window had me feeling all sorts of ways.

Working remotely worked for me. A single woman, no kids, and approximately one year away from being a cranky old hag yelling at kids to get off her lawn. There was no traffic, no rushing in and out of the rain, no wearing uncomfortable clothes because they were "presentable" (what did sweatpants ever do to anyone except love them?), no starting fights when someone touched my lunch in the fridge, no being forced to sign cards for people I barely knew or being coerced to chip in for coffee when they never purchased the kind I liked, and best of all? I could mute anyone I wanted. It was essentially a superpower.

My thoughts drifted during Sunny-and-his-Denzel-voice's segment. Then our client-facing portion ended once Carol had thanked everyone. She disappeared, leaving Gabrielle in a breakout room with one lead at a time.

"Bane. Bane? BAAAANNNNEEEE," Sunny said dramatically, reminiscent of how movie heroes cried out in vengeful declaration against their archnemesis.

Ugh. Unmute.

"Yes?" I asked.

"Can we get the results of the CTA buttons ASAP? It may only take a day for you to get research done and about ten seconds to design, but adjusting any detail in code can cost us a week."

"I'm aware of that," I replied, swirling my coffee. He wasn't going to get to me today, no sir.

"Are you, though?" he asked, chin on his knuckles, elbow on a chair arm as he swiveled back and forth. Oh, that familiar, dry look, like he loathed talking to me.

The number of black squares on-screen had diminished, leaving a handful of people still on camera, all team, all muted. Except Sunny. Because he loved his Denzel voice.

His hair was disheveled, like he'd just popped out of bed to make it to this meeting. I'd like to say that was a side effect of remote work, but he always looked like that. Devs were like little workaholics stuck to their many, many windows glowing with a billion lines of code.

Back at the office, when we occasionally had to meet in person, I'd often walk into his section of the floor, a large room with cubicles and glass-walled meeting rooms covered in Post-its and scribblings, to find Sunny typing away while studying three gigantic computer screens filled with a dozen windows in alternating coding languages for various pages of any given project. My soul sort of died a little every time I saw it. While I understood basic HTML, CSS, and JavaScript, and could yes, in fact, create working, responsive prototypes from thin air, that stuff wasn't easy or quick.

Too many lines. Too many numbers and phrases and a hundred generational variants for one simple thing. Lord, I'd rather be working in a cubicle again. Spare me an even slower death.

I wondered if he had as many computers set up at home. Probably. And right now, he was glaring right at the virtual box my head was in. I smirked, imagining his bottled-up load of loathing and no Bhanu in person to unleash it upon.

Sarah, one of my researchers, came on video and unmuted herself to chime in. "Sorry about that! It's my fault. I'm uploading to the system now. Results are pretty solid, and I think the design team will lean toward keeping CTA buttons as is. Good news, right?" she added nervously.

I scowled. No team member of mine should be groveling at the feet of anyone. That was what I was here for. No. Not to grovel! But to erect barriers around my team so they could work without feeling the weight of others' demands.

"Thank you, Sarah," Sunny said at the same time I said, "You don't have to apologize."

Sarah opened her mouth but didn't respond.

Without missing a beat, Sunny added, "Bane's right. You don't need to apologize. It's the lead's job to make sure these things are on time."

"Thanks, Sunny," I replied bluntly, and then said in one breath, "And it's the lead's job to discuss this in private with fellow leads, which is the very job description of a lead, and not try to inflate an already gigantic ego that's about ready to burst and splatter brain matter on our screens in some severely traumatic, yet 'I told you so,' sort of way." I blinked. "Or did you bet in today's pool?"

His face dropped. His swiveling came to a dead stop.

"Oh. Didn't think I knew about the Bhanu versus Sunny office pool? You guys shouldn't be betting during work and on coworkers. But lucky for you, I'm a chill pill today." I toasted him with the coffee mug my sister had given me, making sure the decorative side faced the screen so he knew without a doubt that, just as the writing said: *It's Bad Bitch O'Clock.*

Besides, I'd also placed a bet on today's pool. I believed I'd just won thirty bucks.

"The research is live in real-time for the design team to look at and make their final decision." I glanced at the time on the upper-right corner of my screen, adding, "And with an hour to spare on its deadline, nonetheless. I'll be moving that Trello card to complete. Mmkay? Thanks. Hit me up if anyone has questions. Have a great day, teams!"

I went dark mode and muted myself but watched Sunny's look of exasperation.

After Gabrielle spoke privately with each lead in a breakout room, she spoke with all of us together.

"Are you still going on vacation?" she asked.

"Yes," Sunny and I said simultaneously.

She, and the other leads, eyed us like there was some naughty gossip to be had. Ugh. There wasn't. Trust me, never would I in a million years hook up with the Denzel-voice grump.

I immediately piped up, "I'm still going to visit my sister, but will be working."

Gabrielle frowned. "That's not what a vacation is. Or proper work-life balance."

"I'm sure I'll get bored. It's just my semiannual trip to visit my sister. She'll be working half the time, and it's not like we have a big agenda planned. Literally going to be sitting at a resort all week."

She sighed dreamily. "Must be nice."

"I guess." I didn't really feel like putting on "real clothes," much less leaving the apartment. In fact, with grocery delivery and food delivery and even alcohol delivery, I could go a month without setting foot outside. "I didn't know you approved two leads to leave at the same time."

"We're in a good place with the project. Junior researchers and devs can handle it for a few days."

"Well, I'll be—"

"Enjoying the beach," Gabrielle said pointedly. "I better not see you logged on or working." Then she said to Sunny, "You, either."

"Ah . . ." he started, looking both perplexed and anxious. "Sure," he conceded.

"Wow. For people going on vacation, you two sure seem to be dragging your feet."

I shrugged. I couldn't speak for Sunny—what with a name that surely indicated his cheery disposition—but I knew that I just wasn't in the mood for a vacation. I wanted to stay busy and keep my mind off the big in-house PM job interview I'd had a couple of weeks ago. Moving up in the company seemed like the best next step.

Honestly, it was in the bag for me with the only other serious competition being Sunny . . . rumor had it that he'd applied. But my seniority crushed his. He couldn't be *that* much of a threat. So then, why was I so anxious?

Except, while I loved my company, I'd kept an eye on bigger, badder game. Because Google could handle my big UX energy. And Google also had a position open, which was rare.

My parents kept hammering it into my skull that long-term stagnation was a slow killer.

"Do you want to become moss?" Mummie would chide. "Stay in one place for years, and you'll succeed in becoming one with the rocks that never move, quietly fading from life. Don't fade away, beta!"

Mummie could be a little over-the-top when we didn't listen to her.

I'd gone over Google's post for weeks, thinking that they'd surely have filled it the next time I checked. Hemming and hawing because I talked big game, but actual *change*? What was wrong with liking my life exactly as it was? I didn't need a man or a house or an ambitious job.

But Google's job posting kept calling to me. I met all their qualifications and then some. It would be a step back to UX design instead of advancing to PM. But their lead designers made up to two hundred thousand a year.

PM at my company was almost guaranteed, although not nearly as much pay, but staying close to my comfort zone. But Google was *Google*.

Sure. I'd applied to the tech giant around the same time as I'd applied for the in-house PM position. With Google, I'd interviewed nearly a dozen rounds over several months, from technical to portfolio presentation to whiteboard challenge. Two weeks had gone by since the team-matching round. So who the hell knew what was going on?

See what I mean? I had to keep busy to stay out of my head.

As soon as we'd finished our meeting, I logged off the chat, double-checked that my camera and mic were off, slid the cover over my camera, and went to the bedroom to change. Ah. Sweet T-shirt of mine. Even though I'd worn a blouse for an entire two hours, there was nothing better than getting back into pajamas.

I packed in between small meetings with my team and checking off work items. Hmm. What to pack? Tech was always a given. Undies and socks, sure. Toiletries, purse, wallet. Um . . . clothes? I wondered how many pajamas I'd have to pack for a week away, seeing that my sister didn't think a long weekend getaway was enough this time.

Speaking of that little sneak, my phone lit up with a text from her.

Diya: You better get your overworked ass to the airport on time. Don't try to ditch me. And for the love of all that is holy, please get out of sweatpants. It's Hawaii! Better trim up down there, because I expect to see you in a bikini by the pool. See you tomorrow! Love you!

Ah. To be blessed by such sweetness.

TWO

Sunny

I came into the company as lead dev, and there was no better way to get to know new coworkers than bonding over a common interest. Most were into soccer or football—this was Seattle after all—and it was easy to get into the Sounders or Seahawks. Some were into gaming. As for myself, I found my kind with bakers. We were a small but obsessive group. Get us together in a corner talking about leavening agents and cultural fusions, and whew! Might as well call me Captain America because I could do this all day.

Our unofficial "dev into desserts" club had decided to bake something for a coworker's annual party. I went with cookies. Yeah, basic as hell, I know. But cookies were easy, fast, and versatile. I could whip out a few flavors to feed a number of people, and most liked cookies. Plus, not only were leftovers easy to take home, but the amount being taken home was easy to hide in case no one liked my offering. I tried to spare myself embarrassments wherever possible, but if I were to be honest: No one could resist my cookies.

Ronny, a bulky redhead with a love for floral flavors, had arrived at the party right before me. I cocked my chin in greeting since we both had our hands full.

"What'd you bring?" I asked.

"Pistachio and cardamom bundt cake with a hint of rose in the frosting." He wagged his brows but deserved the applause.

"That's fancy. Where did you get the idea?" I probed at the very Indian flavors.

"Well, the host is, um, she likes Indian-inspired flavors," he added with a quickness that indicated he didn't want to assume our Indian host was into Indian spices.

"Hmm."

I hadn't officially met Bhanu, since I'd been allocated to smaller projects, and she worked solely on the company's more elaborate ones. But seeing that I had my eye on bigger clients, our paths were bound to cross at some point. So might as well get this over with. It wasn't as if we would be rivals in any way. She was a UX researcher, and I a coder. Our jobs went hand-in-hand (she was the eye-catching appeal of peanut butter and jelly, and I was the bread that held it all together) and the websites, apps, and programs we created couldn't have one without the other.

Ronny juggled the large plastic container on a pedestal while attempting to open the door.

"Let me get that." I slipped past him and opened the door.

"Thanks, man."

I waved him in first and we entered the top-floor apartment balancing our respective treats. We walked into a wall of thrumming music, conversations, and laughter. There were a lot more people here than I'd assumed there would be. Easily thirty, all packed in a spacious living room and open-concept kitchen beneath vaulted ceilings. Despite all the warm bodies, the AC and fans kept the apartment cool.

Ronny and I were met with warm welcomes from the few who noticed us, but pretty much everyone was already in small groups chatting away.

James, a junior dev on my team, waved me over to his corner of the kitchen. He was one of the friendlier coders who didn't seem bothered that I had come swooping in as a lead. Of course, I had no idea if he'd been aiming for the position.

I was six foot two and James was almost as tall as I was, making him easy enough to spot with his waving arm above everyone's heads.

I maneuvered through the crowds, hugging my tray of cookies against me like a football, and found a spot near the end of a full counter. I made space, pushing Ronny's cake pedestal down a little one way and the pan of Jell-O shots down a little the other way, and set my cookies in between them. It was as good a place as any other.

After pulling back the cover and getting a whiff of cinnamon, orange, and chocolate, I noted all the food my cookies were up against.

At one end there was a platter of various sandwich triangles leading into a nacho bar, salads, jalapeño poppers, and plenty of desserts. Not to mention a diverse collection of beverages from sparkling flavored water and soda to beer and wine.

"Wow. What a feast," I said, not having expected this much for a private work party hosted at someone's home.

"You made it!" James said, popping the last of his sandwich into his mouth.

"Might as well get to know everyone, right? Better here than in the middle of deadlines."

He handed me a beer and I took it, skeptical. Glancing around, everyone seemed to be on their best behavior. Adults could drink and not get stupid.

James, for all his shy qualities, was more relaxed than I'd ever seen him. He took a swig from his bottle, asking, "You don't drink, man?"

"I've just . . . heard horror stories of company parties with drunk employees."

"Nah, it's fine. These never get that bad. Especially at someone's house, you know? And . . . especially at *her* place." He pointedly looked past me at a woman holding a glass bottle of Fanta.

"Bhanu?" I presumed, opening the beer and taking a gulp. It'd been a long day, and this was, to my surprise, relaxing. At least she knew her drinks. This beer cooling my throat wasn't exactly the cheap stuff.

"No one would dare make a mess or start something at her party."

"Respect," I both asked and stated.

James hit the nacho bar next. It was a cool idea, to have a row of chips and dips and sauces and condiments to make the ultimate, personalized bowl of nachos. The smell of queso warming in a small crockpot and pickled jalapeños had my mouth watering, even as I surveyed and eventually took a sandwich triangle. It was labeled "Vegan ALT," or what I assumed was avocado, lettuce, and tomato with vegan mayo.

"Is she supposed to be the evil coworker?" I asked, biting into one majorly delicious piece of sandwich. "I wonder where she got these."

"Good, right? I think she made that one. But no, not evil. She's actually really nice and knows her stuff. Bhanu may be talking and eating, but she keeps an eye on everyone and will call you out if you get disrespectful of her space."

"Seems reasonable."

No wonder she was a lead on the big projects, able to take command and keep an eye on everything and still step in when she needed to without missing a beat. She sounded like the stuff leads were made of.

"You guys would probably get along great!" James said.

I deadpanned. "Because we're both Indian?"

His expression fell and he stuttered.

I clucked my tongue. "I'm just joking, man. Too far?"

"I almost peed in my pants."

I smirked and, taking another drink, surveyed the room. The kitchen, blocked off by a sprawling counter, spilled right into the living room. From here, everyone could be seen, including Bhanu. She was nodding, listening to a group of people. While her posture and attentiveness showed she was into the conversation, her eyes seemed distant.

I sneered. I knew that look. Our generous host was either bored out of her mind or just wanted to leave. The party hadn't been going on that long, but who knew how long she'd worked to put this all together. Maybe she had stressed over every detail for days. Maybe she was having a bad day or a bad conversation, but something other than this party was clearly on her mind, and I suddenly felt a need to slip into the circle and intervene.

"I should go introduce myself," I told James, who concurred with a raise of his plate of food.

The crowds subtly shifted toward the buffet, opening up space around the fireplace, where Bhanu was standing, an arm crossed over her stomach. I wasn't sure what I'd expected from the famous UX designer/researcher who headed most of the company's expensive projects. Was she an awkward nerd like most of the team, or eccentric like some of the designers?

As I got closer, the slightly dimmed light shone on her hair as she nodded, showcasing glossy purple locks. An ombré style from black roots to wavy lavender ends. A look that actually paired well with her light brown skin tone and eyes. While some were dressed up, she was all casual in black ankle-length pants that may or may not have been joggers paired with a dark blue blouse.

She turned to me as soon as I said, "Bhanu? Hi, I'm Sunny."

She barely looked at me but smiled anyway. "Nice to meet you! Glad you could make it. Sorry, I have to take this call."

And then she was off, sliding in between people to escape into a hallway and then a room. I could've sworn her phone hadn't rung . . . or that she wasn't even holding a phone.

I blew out a breath. Talk about anticlimactic. Well, I'd tried. I'd made an effort, which was something my ex had constantly gotten on me about. Sejal was the social butterfly, always at parties and gatherings and festivals, invited to everyone and their auntie's wedding and baby shower and gender reveals and whatever else people did. I was the "old for my age" guy wanting a smaller group of intimate friends, more meaningful interactions, and fewer late-night parties. And yes, Indian baby showers could last well into the night if the couple wanted.

Sejal was engrossed in what others were accomplishing, passively comparing. It was great that Arjun had bought a big-ass house, that Nina was engaged, Aditya was pregnant, or Neelish was planning a vacation across six countries in one go. It really was great for them, and I'd been ecstatic for my friends. But by the third or fourth mention, I found myself side-eyeing my ex and internally preparing for her look of both joy and envy.

She clearly wanted all of that, and I couldn't care less for those things. They simply weren't for everyone. Traveling the world sounded nice in theory, but exhausting. I wasn't ready for engagement or a house, much less kids. I'd never led her to believe that I wanted those things, and it didn't seem right to be pressured into them.

Her flicker of annoyance had turned into a raging wildfire, demolishing our relationship. She didn't want to discuss things from both sides. It always came down to . . . *don't you love me?*

Don't. You. Love. Me.

As if my entire worth, my commitment of affection, were based solely on what I could give her at any given moment according to her whims. As if my feelings didn't matter. I was never good enough, and she let me know it. And I'd accepted it. I wasn't good enough for Sejal; we parted ways. Much to the dismay of our families.

I never sat her down for a hard conversation, wasn't misty-eyed or on my knees begging for her to understand and stay with me. I spoke the truth. That was communication, right? Telling someone what was on my mind. We'd seen too many couples bicker, break up, or quietly combust from asinine amounts of repressed rage all because they didn't communicate. I'd seen my own mother silently crying in the kitchen because my father had done something. She was afraid that his feelings would get hurt or that he'd take it the wrong way if she ever said anything. Meanwhile, she was spiraling into sporadic episodes of anxiety for nothing.

No. I wasn't going to do that. I was straightforward with Sejal, as with everyone else. I didn't have time, nor did I care, for the bullshit.

Those conversations never ended well with her when she wasn't getting what she wanted. She'd even gotten my mother involved, convincing her that she was the one ready for the next step, and I was the one holding our lives up. And like many Indian mothers, Ma wanted to see her son married and rearing his own children sooner than later.

I huffed out a breath. I'd been looking forward to this party. Yet my ex's complaints were sprouting up. Was I being social enough? Approachable? Likable? Did the host know how much I appreciated the invitation to such a hospitable gathering?

If Sejal were here, she'd say: no.

Therefore, I spent the better half of the hour getting to know my coworkers, making a point to speak to everyone. I wasn't going to remember them all, and definitely wasn't going to recall all these backstories of who was married or dating or single or had kids or had just graduated, but they were going to remember me.

I was the guy who'd brought the cookies. Spoiler alert—they were a hit. Not a single crumb left. At one point, Terrance—a junior dev—held up a ginger chai spiced cookie and yelled over the crowd, "Hey! Who made these bomb-ass cookies?"

By then, because I had asked every single person, "Have you tried the cookies?" as an icebreaker, everyone pointed at me and called back, "Sunny!"

Guests started to head out. I checked my phone. It was almost eleven. Time sure did pass by quickly when a bunch of barely strangers came together for the love of cookies.

As we said our goodbyes, I figured it was a smart idea to hit the restroom before leaving, and hopefully find Bhanu to thank her in a way she felt appreciated. Maybe that was Ma talking. She always taught my sisters and me never to arrive at someone's house without a gift, preferably food, as a way to thank them. And of course, add specifics of what we'd enjoyed. Don't be generic.

Make yourself memorable.

I went to the hallway to find two closed doors and picked one to knock on and then open. There was a fifty-fifty chance this was the bathroom—it wasn't a large apartment—but I didn't expect to find someone sitting on the edge of the bed with her chin in her hands like she was bored out of her mind waiting for everyone to leave so she could make her grand escape.

Bhanu looked up, her eyes suddenly alert as if she'd been caught red-handed.

"My fault!" I blurted out, ready to fling the door closed, but curiosity got me. "Are you all right?"

She shrugged, her voice flat when she asked, "Why are you in my bedroom?"

"I was looking for the bathroom." Yet I didn't move. I couldn't move. I didn't know what was wrong with me. "Are you hiding? Have you been in here since I talked to you?"

Her eyebrows went up. "I guess so."

Another pause.

"Yes?" Her voice was soft yet cutting, annoyed even.

Well, shit. *Okay.* Maybe she wasn't the sprightly host everyone had made her out to be. For the past, what, two hours, she'd been sitting in her room during her own party and no one had bothered to find her? Was this normal? Or had no one noticed?

"You ditched your own party?" I intended that to be a joke, but apparently my execution needed some work because she retorted, "Yeah, so?"

"Okay," I drawled. "Well, I wanted to thank you for inviting me and say how nice of a time I had, but this feels as natural a moment as telling you three weeks from now if we actually run into each other at work."

"Email works, too," she replied with a hint of something. Was she amused or was she being facetious?

"Right. Email next time. Won't bother seeking you out."

We stared at each other. Her posture sagged and either she was exhausted or tipsy—maybe both. Maybe she'd been sitting in here drinking . . . well, by the look of the two bottles on her bedside stand, she'd had a few. But her room was dimly lit, and those could've easily been empty glass Fanta bottles. How was her bladder not bursting? Or had she snuck in and out of her bathroom, unseen, during her own party as well?

"All right. Well. Thanks for the invite."

"Thanks for coming," she replied, matching my dry tone.

"Right . . ." I mumbled, tapping the door before closing it behind me.

I took my empty cookie container and left.

THREE

Bhanu

Flights were a favorite pastime, said no one ever. Especially on a Saturday. Too many people and lines and layover drama, but bless the fact that I had a direct flight with a TV screen attached to the back of the seat in front of me fully equipped with every new movie and TV show that one could want. I might as well have been sitting in first class with how fancy this felt. But in sweats. Naturally. And compression socks because it turned out that my legs plumped to the size of watermelons when flying.

I'd forced myself to leave my devices alone and focus on relaxing instead of checking for any updates on the interviews. Let's be real—Google had probably ghosted me, and my company was taking their own sweet time on that PM position.

With the middle seat empty beside me, the hood of my sweatshirt over my brows, and my hands stuffed into my pockets, I shimmied into my seat to get nice and cozy for seven hours of Marvel movies. No one talked to me.

Complete bliss.

Before I knew it, we crested over turquoise waters and the

shoreline where an AC-less hub of an airport waited. We'd arrived in charming, albeit hot as hell, Kona, Hawaii.

The beauty of the various shades of blue in the water speckled with various shades of green, the dusty shores and lush vegetation lined with black lava rocks got me every time.

There was a saying that whatever happened on island stayed on island. I always thought of that when landing, and promptly chuckled. Nothing that exciting ever happened to me.

I removed my sweatshirt and took my time shuffling through the plane and onto a ramp that led down to the runway of the tiny outdoor airport. A wall of hot, dry air hit me, my sweat glands going from icy cold to pouring. The sweats were perfect during cold flights, but I was eager to hit the restroom and change into shorts. *Gym* shorts. Don't judge me.

Now changed into climate-appropriate attire with bags in hand, I waited on a bench for my ride. I took the chance to peel off my compression socks (listen, I wasn't here for puffy feet or a blood clot) and exchanged my sneakers for sandals. I wiggled my toes. Ah. Much better.

A gentle breeze swept through, cooling the sweat beads on my forehead as I guzzled down ice-cold water and texted Diya. How she could live on this side of the island was beyond me. The Big Island had eight climate zones ranging from desert to tundra. Guess which part I was likely to be in for the entire week? Thank the gods I was spending most of my time in a really nice hotel chain that blasted AC like electricity didn't cost an arm and a leg.

It was only a matter of minutes before Diya pulled up in her boyfriend's Jeep. For a corporate girl wielding a master's degree, she loved to go rugged. The island had changed her. She'd learned to live life by the day, slow down and be in the moment, and experience more of the amazing canvas the island had instead of being trapped indoors like most mainlanders. She'd lived on island for several years, so she was bound to learn to love the land and its people.

Which was ironic because she worked in tourism, a double-edged sword for the islands. But leave it to my little sister to take up arms on behalf of the employees, the majority of which were AAPI, including native Hawaiians. Every voice counted.

And speaking of voices, her high-pitched voice shrieked with excitement when she hopped out of the Jeep and ran toward me, arms out in the air, one holding a purple and pink plumeria lei.

"*Bitch* . . . you made it!" Diya attacked me with a hug as her boyfriend emerged flashing a giant grin.

"Oh my god." I laughed into the swells of her curly hair.

She cleared her throat and we paused, giving each other a knowing and calm look. I slightly bowed my head, allowing Diya to drape the lei over my shoulders so that it lay down my back and chest, not touching my neck, before she kissed my cheek.

"Thank you," I said, accepting her aloha.

"It's pronounced 'mahalo,'" she grunted.

"Hey, howzit?" Diya's boyfriend, Kimo, asked as he came in for a bear hug. Everyone knew I wasn't much of a hugger, including touchy-feely people at the office—god, we weren't that close—but family was different, and Kimo was essentially a brother. Diya's hugs were nostalgic. Kimo's were like a cuddly teddy bear.

I laughed. "Good! How are you?"

"Can't complain. You hungry?"

"Always. Also, ready for some AC."

"Tourist," Diya teased, but I knew she needed it, too.

Kimo placed my bags in the back, and we buckled in.

As I hugged the side of the car with the most shade, Kimo handed me a reusable water container and I gulped every last drop of icy water. I held out on a prayer that I'd make it to a restroom in time later, but for now, my Northwestern body, used to overcast and chill, needed the hydration.

"For you. Keep it. Refill it," Kimo said.

"Thanks!" I eyed the dark pink container, turning it over in my hand. A laser-etched design of my name above a honu appeared. "Aw! Is this from your shop?"

"Yeah. Got some new designs. Honu is inspired from my tribal tats."

"I love it. And I'm honored."

We were pretty much family at this point. I eyed Diya, wondering if my little sister would be getting married before I even found a man. Not that I wanted, nor needed, one. I didn't want anything crashing through my calm life and uprooting all that made me comfortable. Regardless, I was happy that my sister had found her happily ever after, and so quickly.

She'd met Kimo the first month she'd arrived on Big Island. She'd wandered into his laser-etching company storefront because she'd seen her coworker's cute coffee tumbler with Kimo's design. He etched everything from wood to metal, from plaques to flasks. She'd ordered a crimson water thermos with her name on it, and he'd talked about plastic waste reduction and protecting the land and ocean. It was love at first conservation conversation.

Diya came from prestigious degrees and international advisory boards. Kimo came from a deep connection to the land. Both balanced the other and each balanced the seemingly contradictory nature of their careers with their passions. But that was life, right?

Now, my sister, the general manager with an eye on VP of Operations for one of the world's largest hotel conglomerates, spent most of her time between supporting employee rights and protecting the islands. She was an all-around total badass wrapped in a dainty body.

We'd taken a left on Queen Ka'ahumanu Highway, which the

locals referred to as Queen K Highway, toward Waikoloa . . . one of the hottest parts of the island, but also one of the most luxurious resort spots. We passed the street for Costco on the right (because of course I knew where one of my favorite stores was located), the shopping centers and marina on the left, and then nothing for miles until a tour company appeared with its armada of metallic blue helicopters.

"Wanna try for an air tour?" Kimo asked, begrudgingly looking at one of too many tourist traps.

"I have better things to spend seven hundred dollars on," I replied. Nothing about sitting in a loud, tiny helicopter hovering over volcanos made me easy. "Plus, didn't one of their helicopters crash recently?"

Kimo clucked his tongue. "Decades of flawless flights marred by one tragedy."

"I don't want to die this time around. Not yet. There are other things to do."

"Like eat ube?"

Typically, as the elder (per my family and seemingly per my culture), I paid for everything. It was an essentially simplistic and presumed thing. Papa paid whenever we were with him. But without parents around, the price of every meal and hotel room and excursion fell upon me. Which I was happy to do. I wasn't here for freebies, although Diya's gigantic hotel discounts might as well be considered freebies.

Without Papa, this always turned into a little fight with one sibling trying to grab their credit card before the other could pay. I'd resorted to pretending to use the restroom and slipping the waitress our card. Which, in turn, evolved into Diya slipping the waitress her card before we even ordered. Which evolved into me making reservations with my card on file. I wasn't sure where we could go from there.

However, when it came to visiting the islands, it was the custom of the land to accept gifts. The lei was the first, embodying love and gratitude, and couldn't be denied unless, of course, the one receiving wasn't in the loving spirit. Diya made her own leis. She'd decided, once she moved here, that she would try to learn the culture. It wasn't too long ago that the islands had been colonized, and she wanted to help preserve as much as possible, or at the least, not stamp it out. So she'd taken classes to learn the language and arts, went out of her way to make Hawaiian friends, and tried to stay on top of local news that disrupted the sanctity of the people. I'd never seen her mature faster than at this point in her life, to see her go from privileged American to someone wanting to protect everything about the place she lived in.

When Diya picked plumeria off the trees at her condo, much to the HOA's dismay, and sewed them into a beautiful lei, she took it seriously. It was part of aloha, and the reciprocating part of aloha was graciously accepting. The same applied to other gifts from her while here.

But when it came to ube, I didn't mind that my baby sister had assembled a list of all ube finds so she could feed me until my belly was hanging over my sweatpants.

I steepled my fingers on my lap like a kid waiting for her parents to hand her an ice cream. Except the ice cream was a fluffy, dark purple ball of fried dough covered in sanding sugar.

Kimo handed me a reusable bag with a box inside. I squealed, my mouth watering. "Diya, you better marry this man!"

He laughed. "You won't say that when you see I've already eaten a few. Sorry."

"I don't even care. Thank you, Kimo!"

I bit into a sweet malasada with hints of . . . ya know, I could never quite explain the taste of ube. It fluctuated, depending on the dish. Ube was a sweet purple yam from the Philippines, which was often used in desserts ranging from ice cream to smoothies to cakes to turnovers to this version of a Portuguese donut. Everything I'd ever tried with ube was delicious. This was no different.

"Not that hard crap off the side of the road," Kimo promised, as if he'd ever get me something meant to draw tourists. "Not even from KTA."

"What! This tastes even better. Which bakery made this?"

"My mom made it for you."

I gasped—such affection—and immediately almost choked on sanding sugar.

"Calm down," Diya said. "His mom is thinking of starting a catering business and is giving out free food to everyone to get their thoughts."

Once I'd regained my composure, I admitted, "This is menuworthy."

"I think so, too," Kimo replied. "Her favorite is the li hing mui original, but I'm loving the ube and the lilikoi filled dusted with li hing."

My mouth, despite being filled with perfect ube, was watering over the anticipation of tart passion fruit fried dough covered in sugary dried plum powder. "Tell your mom that she can use me as a test subject. I'm happily volunteering."

He winked from his seat. "I'll let her know. She wants to have you over while you're here."

"Mm-hmm!" I agreed around a bite. Who doesn't love a mama's home cooking?

We'd arrived at the hotel Diya worked for, which covered nearly a hundred acres and featured a large golf course, four lagoons, many beaches, and three main hotels called locations (Queen's Land, King's Land, and Homestead). Yes, they were all the same hotel chain, but each was a level more exquisite/expensive than the last.

By the time we'd pulled up to fountains featuring marigold and ivory koi, surrounded by palms and orchids, I'd devoured all three ube donuts. I was sure they were meant to last a couple of days, but Kimo knew me, right?

An attendant hauled my luggage out of the vehicle while Diya checked us in and Kimo rode off with a wave for me and a kiss for my sister.

"Wait until you see this," Diya said beside a golf cart.

"Are we camping on the golf course under the stars? Sounds romantic."

She wagged her brows. "You ain't ready."

Diya was correct. My jaw dropped when we arrived at one of several private villas past the sprawling golf course, about a mini-yard, a short lava rock wall, and a sidewalk away from the water.

Island breeze swept over the ocean and, unobstructed, washed right over us. Sunsets here were going to be full-blown magical. It was so quiet, save for the waves and far-off chatter of passersby on the sidewalk, hidden beyond view thanks to the wall and the height of the property.

To each side, a row of thick, manicured shrubs created a fence separating one rental from the next.

The villa itself was the size of, well, a small home. A large sitting area with wall-to-wall sliding glass doors opened up to the lanai, equipped with a grill and a cushy lounge set with a fire pit. The fully equipped kitchen faced the living room and the sliding doors. To each side of the living room was a bedroom.

"Take the main, got a big bed in there and Jacuzzi tub," Diya insisted.

"You take it. You and Kimo can . . . um, never mind." I shook my head. No to that image.

She grinned. "I know you love baths."

"There's something gross about sitting in your own body oils like that."

"Maybe you'll meet a hottie who'll change your mind."

"Maybe I'll change a bath lover's mind, eh?"

I took the cozy king-size bedroom with private bathroom while Diya took the other room. I was sure it was just as nice, with maybe a queen-size bed or two beds.

"Wait. Is Kimo staying, too? Is your bed in there big enough?"

She waved me off. "Don't worry about us!"

Since their time together, she'd learned to enjoy both bougie beds and camping. She wouldn't mind camping on the floor of their room or even out in the backyard.

I dragged my bags into the larger room, amazed by the stunning gold-framed mirrors, tropical decor, and sturdy wicker and bamboo furnishings.

Once I'd showered the filth of airports away, Diya called into my room through the open decor, "Don't bother drying your hair! I'm treating you to a spa day."

I giddily went, taking comfort in the fact that Diya's enormous discounts worked their wonders.

We lounged around in plush robes surrounded by orchids and calming music. Soothing scented oils floated through the air as we enjoyed champagne and chocolates made from local ingredients like cacao beans, coffee beans, vanilla pods, teas, fruits, and nuts.

I was truly enjoying the start of my vacation. Nothing could break this serenity.

FOUR

Sunny

My first time on the islands was accompanied by a mix of astonishing and annoying things. First off, the views were fantastic, straight out of the highest resolution cinematic movie. Glistening ocean for miles hit the horizon and the slight curvature of the earth painted in clouds. Although a sobering thought. Looking out the plane window was a reminder of how much faith we placed in technology, in the engineering of this giant aircraft and these pilots, because one bad turn of events, one electrical glitch, and we would plunge to our watery deaths. Surrounded by sharks. There must've been a million of them underneath the glimmering waves, just waiting for a metal-encased meal.

So much for the beauty of the endless ocean. Now, all I could see were horrifying ways to die.

The water went from shades of dark blue to green and aquamarine and clear enough to see outlines of black rocks at the bottom. It was marvelous to see for the first time and had, ironically, made me incredibly thirsty. Or maybe it was the fact that the airline served us free mai tais as a welcome. They weren't individually made but poured out of Costco-size bottles and were sweet and tart with a hint of alcohol and enough to make my mouth dry.

Beyond the clear waters were serene coastlines and more black rocks with a sprinkling of trees and shrubs until we were flying over lush greenery and specks of houses. And still beyond that were massive hills, maybe small mountains, blurred out by fog and rising above the clouds like sleepy giants. According to the people excitedly chattering behind me, those were volcanos. Not as deadly as I'd expected a volcano to look, but dormant, which was preferable to a possible fiery demise.

I couldn't help but wonder if I would die here—sharks one way and molten lava the other, filled with poisonous centipedes in between.

We deplaned into a tiny outdoor roughing-it-in-the-wild airport, where a pall of humidity and god-awful heat hit the second we stepped off the plane and onto a ramp leading down to the runway. Hot as hell. I went from thirsty to parched, desperately fumbling to get a few bucks into the vending machine for water so expensive, I expected it to taste like heaven.

It didn't, but I drank it to the last drop.

I texted my sisters about Papa. His health had become a looming concern since his first stroke a few months ago. It had been mild with minimal long-term effects, but disconcerting nonetheless.

"I'm good," Papa insisted over the phone.

"Are you taking your meds on time? Drinking plenty of fluids, rest, exercises?" I pressed as I read my sisters' text responses.

Sheila: He's fine! We're here!
You're in HAWAII! Stop texting.
Don't call.

Sienna: Seriously, if anything
happens, we'll let you know.

"Beta," Papa replied firmly, "I'm doing everything the doctor in-
structed. Now, you relax. Don't worry so much about me, huh? Enjoy
your vacation."

Easier said than done.

Unlike my friends who'd flown in for this destination wedding, I
didn't notify them when I'd landed, or when I'd left baggage claim,
or when an Uber had picked me up, or when I'd arrived at the hotel
not only where we were all staying but where the wedding would
take place. Because that was too many damn texts in an already con-
gested group chat. I didn't need to read Maya's dissection of how
many sea turtles she'd seen while looting the beach for shells.

They're called honu. They're
endangered green sea turtles, omg,
they're gorgeous. OMG, they're
adorable! This one loves me. Look
at how it looks at me! I'm in love,
you guys! Can't get too close to
them. There are signs everywhere!

Followed by a dozen pictures that looked like either her camera
zoom capabilities were excellent or she'd gotten closer to the turtles
than she was legally allowed to.

More importantly, after a long day of traveling and cramped leg
space during a seven-hour flight, I wanted to shower before seeing
my boys. No matter how excited we were for this week, there was no
amount of bro love that could outshine the level of travel gross I was
feeling.

But fate had other plans.

"What do you mean there's no reservation under my name? Try it again," I said to the man behind the front desk.

The staff uniforms consisted of dark blue and green Hawaiian shirts in an open-air lobby that allowed optimal airflow from the ocean to the left. Granite floors, tall vases filled with fake flowers, large paintings on the wall, and water features everywhere gave this hotel an immediate welcoming calm. The gentle ukulele music over the speakers helped, too.

"Seems that you were supposed to check in yesterday," the man explained.

I showed him the reservation on my phone. "No. It's for today."

He typed away and I noticed beads of sweat gathering at his temple. It was humid, but also packed. The phones were ringing off the hook and the line behind me was getting longer by the minute, despite six staff members working furiously behind the counter. The place looked incredibly busy for a mid-October Tuesday.

I patiently waited another few minutes when the man excused himself and another person slid over to assist me. The manager. Which was never a good sign.

"I apologize, but it seems that we don't have any rooms available except for the luxury suites," he said with a worn expression, as if I wasn't the only snafu of the day.

I grunted. I just wanted to shower and change and maybe nap. "How much per night? Can I get it for the rest of my stay?"

"Eight hundred a night."

I balked at the price. The hell? Was it lined in gold?

"Although the only suites we have *may* be available beginning tomorrow night."

I blew out a breath, my chest tightening in the already humid air. "You don't have anything else?"

"I'm afraid not."

"But I had reservations."

"I'm very sorry. We had a hiccup in the system. Since it said your check-in was yesterday, we gave your room to those on standby," he tried to explain and imperceptibly nodded toward the secondary line full of impatient guests. "We're at max capacity."

I pressed my lips together. There was no point in arguing or yelling. This wasn't his fault, and the situation was what it was, but shit, this was bad. "Can you let me know if anything opens up tonight?"

Even for *eight* hundred a night. Damn, Sam and April were not a cheap couple.

"Of course. Please enjoy a complimentary drink at the bar for the inconvenience," he added, slipping a drink voucher across the counter.

The look on my face must've conveyed a much lower level of patience, or maybe just the right amount since so many were getting visibly upset around me. Some had even started muttering and one man became loudly irate. In any case, the manager slid a few more vouchers toward me.

I thanked him. He was kind and worked within his limits, and I *wasn't* a jackass. I was, however, going to break the bank at this rate. Easing away, leaving the crowded lobby, I was immediately met by a balcony-style enclosed lounge overlooking lush gardens with vibrant blooms, a manicured lawn with a generous pool beyond, and in the near distance, the ocean. The ocean breeze swept up and into my nostrils, soothing any irritation.

It could be worse.

Sitting at the bar and furiously looking up every hotel in the vicinity—which honestly wasn't a lot, but then again, this wasn't a city—I ordered a drink and began making calls.

One after another. Everyone was booked.

"Why's it so busy?" I asked the bartender.

"Ironman," he said simply, as if that explained everything.

"What's that?"

"The worldwide championship triathlon. Brings in thousands of visitors, athletes, and spectators to the island."

Talk about bad timing. The couple had been so careful to plan around holidays and times that were inconvenient for their guests and wedding party, yet here we were.

Not to worry. Surely someone wasn't coupled or rooming with another person and could spare some space. Maybe?

Who would I ask? Sam was definitely a no. He might've had his own room, seeing that the bride wanted the bridal suite to herself to relax in and get ready at before they met again as a married couple, but I couldn't crash with the groom. He was probably stressing out and had a detailed itinerary down to the minute. He was one of the most particular men I'd ever known, a perfectionist to heart.

Aamar, the best man, was here with Maya, his girlfriend and the maid of honor, and they probably wouldn't like having a third wheel during what was most likely a romantic getaway for them.

The only person left was . . .

My ex was here somewhere. Sejal, who always found a way to remind me that my emotional range was about as robotic as the coding I wrote. She'd wanted me to be a grand gesture type of guy. But she equated my level of devotion to how many roses were left on her workplace desk, the amount spent on gifts, or whirlwind surprise weekend getaways.

"It's social media; people try to look perfect," I'd told her. "Life isn't that romantic." (I'd learned that wasn't ever the right thing to say.)

"Romance takes effort!"

"Then tell me what to do and I'll try."

"I shouldn't have to tell you!"

I'd tried, although according to Sejal, I hadn't tried hard enough. What my ex wanted was a romance book lead: someone who knew what the hell he was doing and did it well.

"Ever think maybe she just didn't inspire you?" Sam had once asked me.

The thought had boggled my mind. But I'd loved her; why wouldn't she inspire me? And if she, a woman I'd been with for years who had woven herself into the very fabric of my family and life, didn't inspire me, then no one could.

Maybe she was right. Maybe I was dead inside. A robot better suited for typing out millions of lines of letters and numbers and symbols to make something from nothing, a digital hunter of 404s. Not a person meant to show affection.

I'd known all along she'd be here. Sejal was April's close friend and a bridesmaid. I was Sam's close friend and a groomsman. He'd checked with me to make sure I would be okay with the arrangement, but what was I supposed to say? *No, have the bride take her out of the wedding party?*

Bracing for her presence only added to my anxiety.

I threw back the last of my drink. The sour burned down my throat. I should probably eat something or else I was about to be drunk without a room to crash in.

Back to making more calls, this time with hotels in Kona. The closest, and largest, nearby town was a good forty-minute drive. Which meant I'd have to get a rental car of my own.

The few people around the bar shuffled out.

I groaned and glanced at the pool, my gaze drifting toward a woman two seats down the counter. I hadn't noticed her before because a behemoth of a man was sitting in between us, but I noticed her now. It was hard not to see her with her nose in her tablet feverishly reading away and sipping a tall, iced glass of what was probably water or clear soda.

That pulled-back purple hair.

Those sweatpants.

Bane. In the frumpy-ass flesh.

FIVE

Bhanu

I groaned underneath my breath, catching up on as much as I could with the real-time program we used for mind-mapping and assignment cards. Who was in charge of site-mapping in my absence? I couldn't find a single digital notecard. Also, where had the drafts gone for the new site page? Gabrielle wouldn't . . . would she? I'd never been blocked in my life.

Okay, whew! I was in, but why was everything moving so slowly?

In Asana (our project tracking program essential for agile methodologies), I checked for any assignment movement. The kanban board, where overall tasks were delegated in the form of digital cards organized by columns, hadn't changed, aside from adding Gabrielle in lieu of my place. There were about three to six oval profiles of each researcher assigned to a card. Some cards, more detailed or smaller assignments, had one or two profiles responsible for the task. The scrum board was similar, tacked on with additional labels and deadlines, although two assignments had been recycled for the next project. The roadmap, however, showed actual progress in the way of graphs. There was movement there. No red labels showing urgent attention.

All was good. The only problem, since this was a real-time program, was that others could see if I was live (aka logged in). If I made
a single change, my name/profile would be time-stamped in the
card's history. Here's hoping Gabrielle wouldn't actually lock me out
during my vacation. Still, I had to be careful. Hmm, maybe with the
time difference I should wait until later.

Slurping my ice-cold water after a tasty but overtly sweet coconut
concoction, I pondered on what to do with the rest of my day.

It had been a wonderful, peaceful five days of vacation filled with
different scenery across the massive lot of hotels, family fun and great
eats with Kimo and his family, and the usual going here and there
for my favorite foods. Since Diya worked most of her regular hours
and I had no intention of driving, I caught up on reading poolside or
on the beach, and worked up the nerve to swim in the lagoon. And
by swim, I mean get deep enough that my feet didn't touch the ocean
floor without freaking out. I could swim, but the current paired with
small waves and knowing there was plenty of marine life in the water
kept me on edge. I was *not* here to die.

A nap sounded nice right about now. I rubbed my eyes, nearly
knocking over my glass. I caught it just in time. I didn't care if my
clothes got wet, but not my device! Not today!

It was then, when I gingerly set my partially full glass of water
away from my tablet, that I noticed a man watching me. My heart
raced at the first flicker of recognition because no way. No mother-
freaking way was my work nemesis sitting two seats away from me
on *my* vacation.

That thick, disheveled hair, short-sleeved button-down shirt with
the top button undone, shorts, sandals . . . looking all kinds of nerdy
tourist. The only thing missing was a camera hanging around his
neck and a dollop of sunscreen on his nose.

The intensity of his dark brown eyes beneath perpetually furrowed brows settled on me in a way that said he'd made a point to

ensure I knew that he'd noticed me. My shoulders slumped forward, giving me that weird crane-neck look with my chin in the air. My eyes rolled into the back of my head. The devil was real, and he meant to torture me.

"Oh my god. What are you doing here?" I balked, hoping this very unlikely run-in was not actually with the man I thought I was seeing. There was a negligible chance.

He grunted, and in that Denzel voice, assuring me that he was real and that he was here, said, "What are *you* doing here?"

Damnit, Sunny. It was always him. Running into me at the office, bumping my chair during in-person meetings, glaring at me through virtual boxes, cap-yelling exchanges filling up my chat boxes.

"I'm on vacation," I retorted, although I'd asked the question first.

"Same," he said.

I dramatically looked around. "Of all the places to go on vacation, of all the places on this island alone, of all the places in this hotel itself, why are you here? Next to me? Now everyone's going to think we went on vacation together."

"Are you planning on blabbing on social media?"

I narrowed my eyes. "We work with smart people. They'll figure it out."

"No, they won't. I don't get into details. Maybe you shouldn't, either."

"Excuse me? How would you know? We've never had a personal conversation."

"I know," he said, turning back to his empty glass.

The stress of trying to get into work unnoticed had been replaced by Sunny's presence. He was triggering. We always, instantly, fought. It was like a dog and cat sensing each other. Primal. Uncontrollable.

I released a pent-up breath and slurped my water. He was *not* going to ruin this vacation. He was a tourist and would go out and do touristy things. We would not, aside from chance encounters at the large pool or the even larger beach at the cove, see each other, and even that was unlikely.

"Why are you wearing sweatpants in this heat?" he asked after a beat.

"Should I be baring my legs for just anyone?"

He stuttered as I gave him a "Well, what the hell?" look complete with jostling head bob that our people had mastered over the centuries. His lips twitched. "You look ridiculous."

"No one asked for your opinion on my appearance. And you're one to speak."

"What?" He looked down at his clothes.

"Epitome of tourist combined with the awkwardness of developer. I just can't with you. You stick out like a sore thumb. Well, not here in this hotel or in this area because it's filled with your kind, but go anywhere else and you might as well be holding a sign that says: 'tourist.'"

"And you're not one? At least I'm not baking in my own clothes."

"My sister lives here, and I hang out here so often that the staff knows me by name. I know all the local spots, and no, I won't be divulging such secrets to an outsider, and I know many of the customs and words and, ya know, culture."

"So basically, you come here to work at the bar in your sweats?"

I scowled. But yes, he was right. "Why are you vacationing here?"

His rigid posture slackened when he replied, "Here for a friend's wedding."

You'd expect someone attending a destination wedding at such a beautiful location to be more excited, but Sunny seemed anything but. Well, whatever issue he had wasn't my problem, despite wanting to know because, ya know, I was nosy.

I commented, "It's a bad time for a wedding here. Didn't the couple know about Ironman?"

His expression fell flat. "Apparently not."

"Wow. You're such a great conversationalist."

"I know."

I gritted my teeth. Sunny and his famous short, blunt replies. Why was I letting him get to me? I wasn't here for him, and again, we wouldn't run into each other often, if ever, while he was here.

His eyes flickered to something behind me, and the usually baiting deadpan of an expression he sported (yeah, try to imagine that one, but he'd somehow mastered it) morphed into tension with a sprinkle of irritation.

Something made his butt pucker more than me? This, I had to see for myself.

I didn't have to turn because the woman who'd caused Sunny's silence walked around the lounge chairs to stand several feet from him, enough that I could see her from the corner of my eye if I wasn't trying to be nosy. But, as established, I was nosy, so I swiveled my seat to face them better.

The woman was gorgeous. She was tall and slim with long, thick, flowing hair; fake eyelashes for days; and pouty lips. Sunshine shimmered on bronze skin shown thoroughly in her two-piece swimsuit with lacy cover-up. Shades sat on top of her head and a tote hung from the crook of her bent elbow.

"Fancy meeting you here," she said, her voice higher than mine and much sweeter.

"Not really," Sunny replied with a tic in his jaw. Hmm . . . interesting.

"Just trying to be nice. Meet Pradeep, my boyfriend." She hooked her free arm around the tall, built man beside her looking like a desi god. What gene pool were these people from?

"Nice to meet you," Pradeep said with a jerk of his chin.

"Pradeep, this is my ex, Sunny. He's also in the wedding party."

Oh. I watched while sipping water. This had just gotten even more interesting.

Sunny shot me serious side-eye shade, as if silently yelling at me to mind my own business, but these guys were making it my business because I was here first, and they weren't exactly quiet or subtle.

"Likewise," Sunny said to Pradeep, all surly.

Now I understood why Sunny was in such an uptight mood in one of the world's most leading vacation spots. If I saw my ex here, much less was in a wedding with him, I'd be pissy, too. No wonder he'd seemed less than excited to be off to vacation. Was this the reason he was the way he was?

Nah. Couldn't be. I couldn't see someone as hardworking, skilled, and assertive as Sunny being knocked down a few pegs by an ex. Or anyone for that matter. Seemed like any friction with another person only made him tougher, compelled not to let that friction take anything from him. It was actually one of the things I admired about the man. He was strong and hardly anything got to him. Well, except me. It was pretty much a superpower of mine at this point, one I wielded at every golden opportunity and with not great responsibility.

Unlike Sunny, Pradeep was the chillest about the entire ex thing. He was all smiles and just as happy as a clam being in Hawaii, noting the beautiful weather and cove at the beach where his girl had excitedly spotted a sea turtle in the distance. He even asked Sunny how he was and about his flight and what he did for work, et cetera, as if they were just two strangers meeting and on the road to friendship. The ex-girlfriend smirked, enjoying the entire exchange, her eyes never leaving Sunny. It was almost as if she were draining his energy, because his posture slowly wilted over the course of several minutes.

A tinge of annoyance hit me. I didn't care for people who acted that way. What had transpired between the two for there to be such palpable tension in the air, to the point where even *I* could feel the loathing? It was reducing any sort of peace I'd had. My soul might, in fact, be circling some dark, hellish hole at this point. Talk about toxic.

Sunny entertained the new man in his ex's life by answering his questions with as much friendliness as he usually toted, which wasn't much, but that meant he didn't loathe this guy.

Sunny even returned the questions out of sheer politeness, because no way was his indifferent posture relaying a single ounce of interest. Unless Sunny was actually this way with everyone?

I thought back to the times I'd seen him working in person. When he was focused, he was an animal with blinders on with zero spatial awareness outside of his many screens. But I'd recalled him blending in at my work party a year ago when he'd so rudely walked into my bedroom while I was in the middle of fighting a breakdown. We'd never been friendly, but Sunny spoke with kindness and understanding and interest with other coworkers.

All the devs under his supervision said he was tough, but easy to talk to. Sunny was *inviting*, if one could believe that. All the designers and researchers I worked with on shared projects said he was funny, a coding genius. I believed the latter but, the former? I had yet to see what the hell they were talking about.

"Excuse me, I have to take this call," Pradeep said after a glance at his ringing phone. "Nice to meet you, man. I'm sure we'll be seeing each other the next few days, right!"

He gave a hearty, good-natured laugh, kissed his girlfriend on the cheek, and took the call as he walked into the shade of the lounge. He paced the threshold between the indoor and the outdoor spaces, a large archway between pillars. Close enough to see but far enough to keep his conversation private.

"Nice boyfriend," Sunny commented, droll as usual.

His ex smiled. "Very nice. We've been together for almost ten months."

"So you got together only a month after we broke up?"

"Can't wait around forever. And timing."

"Yeah. Timing. He must be something if you bounced back that quickly after breaking things off with *the love of your life*." He said "the love of your life" with mocking.

"I really did love you, Sunny. But we would've never worked out. And once I accepted that, I broke up with you and pushed myself to move on. I deserve a romantic, sweeping love story, and you weren't it."

I grimaced. Ouch. Then I took another sip of water and continued watching.

Sunny curtly shook his head, his lips pressed, and I prepared for an explosive rebuttal. Instead, he said, "Congratulations."

Anticlimactic. But maybe that was Sunny. I'd never seen him get angry.

He swiveled away from her, but turned back when she scoffed, "That's all you have to say?"

"I'm happy that you're happy. Did you expect me to throw a fit? Be depressed? Challenge him to a duel?"

"Some type of emotion. But, oh, right, I remember who you are and precisely why we broke up."

"Because I should be run by emotion all the time? That's chaotic. I like calm."

She crossed her arms, extended one leg out, and tapped her foot, daring him with every fiber of her challenging expression. She . . . *wanted* him to be jealous. Ew. In my experience, when people wanted their exes to be jealous of a new flame, it was because some part of them was still stuck on the ex or whatever they'd once had. Or they liked the drama. Obviously, I didn't know this woman, and she seemed a bit scathing although alarmingly sweet . . . but she didn't look like drama-incarnate walking around in a red bikini.

"You came alone, didn't you? Have you even dated since we broke up?" she asked.

"That's not really your business, is it?" Sunny retorted, a flicker of annoyance in his voice.

"I worked really hard on you, and you just let all of that shrivel away?"

Eh? What sort of work was she claiming here? Now her tone was cutting edge, and I didn't believe I cared for it.

"I wasn't broken," he replied. *You tell her!*

She guffawed. "Sunny. You had so much to work on. I gave you so much and you did nothing. Your mother still messages me. If you're like this forever, you'll never find a woman, much less keep one."

Sunny's jaw stiffened and his posture returned to that hard, rigid line. He was suddenly twice as tall, took up twice as much space. The chair between us dwarfed in his shadow. The bartender had disappeared. The few other guests around us vanished. This felt like one of those Western showdowns . . . but in resort swimwear.

"You should probably stop," he said in that dark, commanding tone. "Don't mess with this wedding."

"Says the only guy in the group without a date. You're going to be the seventh wheel in all the activities and pictures. Couldn't even scrounge up a date with promises of Hawaii to even out the numbers?"

The tic in his jaw returned. Sunny got annoyed with me all the time and acted like he was upset, but he was never unprofessional, never actually angry. But right now? He was teetering on the verge of losing his cool, that leveled baseline he was so well known for having. He was hardly ever loud, rowdy, or irate. He was usually mellow as could be. I stilled with bated breath for his reaction.

"Focus on yourself and your new boyfriend," he said.

"I'm focused on us, don't worry. You're not that special."

"Then why are you talking to me when your boyfriend is alone?"

Resentment flickered in her large brown eyes. Like she was both vexed and hung up on Sunny. "Don't be such a downer all weekend, huh?" she said sweetly.

An actual vein appeared snaking down Sunny's neck. All right, listen, I needed this guy. He was a brilliant dev and our biggest project of the decade was going to fail without his specific expertise and insight. The way this man drifted between lines of code, no glitch escaped him. He was the last line of flawless user experience. All the work before him in various stages of research and design would mean nothing without those nimble fingertips typing away at the speed of light, those hawk eyes zooming in on the subtlest out-of-place symbol that could crash an entire program.

Error 404 was not happening on his watch.

"Did you mess with my reservation?" Sunny said out of nowhere, dragging my thoughts back to their conversation.

Her right brow arched. "You think I think about you enough to do that?"

"The hotel said my reservation was for yesterday. I'd made that reservation with you almost a year ago. They said it was a glitch . . . but I know I had the correct date. You had access."

She blew out a breath. "I needed a room. They were supposed to give us two separate rooms instead of the one."

"Did you check to make sure the original reservation would end up with a room for me on the correct date?" He fumed, answering without waiting for her, "Because now I don't have a room. This place is booked, every hotel is booked."

"I'm sure there's a room somewhere," she replied indifferently.

"Don't play this game with me."

"How dare you!" She began passively pulling Sunny apart, fault by fault. And he began lacing his responses with ice jagged enough to pierce souls.

I found my annoyance dissolving into temperament and I wasn't here to have my vacation ruined by drama or let someone tear down the most important dev on any of my teams. Sunny needed to return from this wedding intact and recharged to tackle the last phase of work projects, not end up a frazzled, incensed mess. He was, by far, the best dev ever. Despite our issues, even I acknowledged that our company had lucked out snagging him. Thanks to his speed, precision, and genius, we'd turned out more projects at staggering prices.

Crap. If Sunny had interviewed for PM, then he truly was serious competition.

This woman wasn't even my ex, but I could see how triggering all of this was for him. A wedding—happy couples everywhere. His ex with her new man, shoving it in his face and reminding him of all the ways he'd failed at their relationship.

Mr. Grumpy was about to turn into Mr. Aggravated. I didn't want to run into these vibes every time we happened to be in the same place this week, much less have him haul this crap back to work. More than that, I didn't think Sunny deserved this.

Maybe I was wrong. Maybe I didn't know a thing, I mean, I hardly knew Sunny in the first place. Maybe their rotting atmosphere was just getting to me, dismantling my chill. A headache teased at my temple, a sign of a sharper headache. But whatever the reason, it had me cutting through their increasingly heated exchanges.

"Do you mind?" I asked her.

She barely hinted at having heard me, spewing nonsense at Sunny while he paused to glance my way. His moment of ignoring her only made her angrier.

"Can you leave him alone?" I said, and not in a nice way. My tone came out surprisingly sharp.

She finally turned to me. "What?" The return of the sweet voice. Okay, so maybe she was just mean to Sunny. Exes tended to bring that out. Breakups were known to be ugly and even malicious.

But I wasn't having it either way. I sighed, crossing my legs, and swirled my almost empty glass of water. "Can you leave him alone, and maybe take your drama down a notch? I'm trying to relax. At this very splendid resort in what tourists call paradise," I added with a grand sweeping motion, as if maybe she'd forgotten where she was.

"Oh. Sorry. Didn't mean to bother you," she replied without any sign of leaving. In fact, she shifted so that she was turned from me.

"That's not going to make your argument any more private. Can you please, for the love of all the sea turtles you just saw, leave him alone?"

She gave me a quiet look. I gave her one, too.

At that, she replied, "I mean, you can leave."

Bitch, I was here first. Of course, I didn't *say* that. At this point, Sunny had stood, taking a step in between us to defuse the situation, but there was no situation. I didn't pick fights with strangers or get into woman pitted against woman escalations of cattiness.

I spoke calmly. "No. I was here first, and we were talking before you came over, blocking off the sunshine with all this shade." I gestured at her. Because she was the shade.

"Um. I'm sorry. *Who* are you?" she asked around Sunny's protective frame. I leaned around him, myself. He probably just wanted both of us to go away, yet here we were.

"Why are you getting defensive?" she asked, seemingly both hurt and jealous at Sunny's oddly protective barrier of me. "Wait, is she . . . no. No way. Not for you."

My head was going to splinter the way this headache was sprouting tentacles, and now I just wanted quiet, but I would be damned if *I* left. I was here first, in the perfect spot for the bartender, drinks, snacks, breezeway, shade, and minimal passersby with an even smaller chance of runaway kids zooming by. I just wanted peace, and for her to leave so that my lead dev didn't pop that giant vein now vehemently bulging in his neck. An incapacitated lead wasn't much use and I sort of absolutely needed him to help finish this gigantic project for the biggest client our company had ever had.

I blurted, "Yes I am."

"Yes you are what?" she said.

"His girlfriend. And don't worry, babe, you can stay with me. You think I wanted that big villa on the beach all to myself?"

Sunny swerved toward me, his eyes wide and his shocked expression all sorts of *what the hell are you doing?* Saving a man's ass, as a woman often does. He should be thanking me. Not only was I getting his snide ex off his back, but I'd essentially offered him a place to crash. Okay, so I hadn't thought that part through, but I, at the least, had bought him time.

They were both staring so hard, I was sure they'd frozen into place. I blinked at Sunny. He should really say something. Another second of silence and his ex was sure to figure out that I was a liar wrapped in loungewear.

Sunny pulled himself out of his stupor long enough to say, "Thanks. *Babe.*" His words were sort of soft, but his teeth were clenched. Wondered if his butt was, too. He needed a vacation more than anyone, and . . . well, crap, I felt bad for him.

I kept my eyes trained on him, calling forth all my hype-babe energy, and dragged my eyes back to the stupefied woman. "You must be the ex."

She harrumphed, her glare flitting to the edge of possessive. Yep. She definitely still had a thing for Sunny, but who was going to tell her that her approach wasn't going to win him back?

Before she crawled out of her sheer surprise to utter a response, I put up a hand and said, "Listen. I am on vacation and not here for the drama. I don't care if you guys are exes, were engaged or married or madly in love, or whatever else. I don't do the whole 'hate the ex slash hate other women' thing. You had your good and bad times but right now, in this *immediate* time, this is for *us*. And I'm not one for getting curt, because I'm typically a very laid-back, chill type of a person . . . but I'm not going to sit here and watch you berate my man, or anyone else. And I'm also not going to sit here while you demean and cut through my vacation vibes. As I mentioned, I was here first. So please take your anger or jealousy or irritation elsewhere, and find your peace. Hopefully we can be friendlier than this whenever we pass by each other, because we should be sunshine and rainbows and smiles, right? Look at where we're at. But most importantly, adopt the aloha spirit and chill the eff out. Don't be that tourist. No one likes them."

Her mouth had dropped to her feet somewhere during my monologue, but she didn't say anything. She looked like she wanted to unleash hell on me, at which point, I would just leave, dragging Sunny behind me. I didn't even have this much drama with the girlfriends of my own exes, much less a coworker's.

Maybe I'd lodged a ginormous foot into my mouth, because who knew what was going on in her head or what I'd gotten myself into by declaring Sunny as my man. But it got quiet. I liked quiet. Mission accomplished.

She straightened up and forced a smile, her voice chipper again. "Well, I apologize for the interruption. You're right, we should be enjoying this place. How long have you been together?"

"What is time, really?" I circumvented with a laugh.

She looked at Sunny. "I'm glad you've moved on."

I watched Sunny's entire body tense from the corner of my eye when she added, "Just don't make the same mistakes. See you at the get-togethers. This'll be fun."

If by *fun* she meant *cringey*, then yeah, probably.

She walked away. Lord, finally.

I hadn't initially taken her words to be cold or vindictive, but maybe they were? Maybe they weren't facetious or sarcastic, but her response kept Sunny on edge. Every muscle beneath his touristy outfit tightened.

I turned back to the bar and pushed my paper straw through the melting ice, softly asking, "Are you okay?"

SIX

Sunny

The last thing I expected, much less *wanted* to see, was Bane. Now she was turning one disaster into another.

I glared at her; her profile tinted a couple of shades darker as she must've been in beach mode from day one. Her vacation had started before mine by several days. I knew this because that was three blissful days of work without bickering, where her head in a virtual conference box had been missing. Such peaceful, productive days.

She had been reading on her tablet, probably sneaking into work and totally oblivious to the island breeze braiding through her hair, the taste of saltwater in the air, or the call of cold swimming water beneath a hot sun. Why was I not surprised?

"Bane."

"Yes?" she asked, not shifting her eyeballs a centimeter to look at me.

"What did you just do?"

"I made it quiet."

I leaned an elbow on the counter, tilting toward her. "You just told my ex that you're my girlfriend."

"Yes. That is accurate."

I pushed out a breath and looked skyward, noting how clear the day was. "You blurted that out to get some quiet, but did you consider that I have to deal with a storm now?"

She finally peered up at me through long, thick lashes. "You played along."

"In the moment so I didn't look like a pathetic jackass."

She frowned. "You're not a pathetic jackass. You could never look like one even if you tried."

"You call me a jackass all the time."

"Ass," she corrected, returning to her tablet. "I call you an ass, or the more popular variation of asshole. Which you are. Even if you didn't try."

"Funny."

"Thanks."

I groaned, pinching the bridge of my nose. "Listen. My ex is here because we were both invited to our mutual friends' wedding. Which means those friends are here. And my ex has probably group chatted the entire wedding party to tell them guess who's bringing an unannounced plus one."

"So?"

"They're going to expect to see you. What am I supposed to say? That you lied and I went along with it and then have to explain why? Because they're going to probe for an answer. And I mean, deep space probe. Then I'll spend the rest of my vacation not only grumpy because my ex is here and shoving her new boyfriend in my face as she passively tries to prove that I'm not relationship material, but now, let's add the awkwardness slash pity from my friends. I won't ever live this down," I ended in a snarl. "I hope you're pleased. You've finally succeeded in ruining me."

I shoved my chair into the bar, startling Bane as she gave me a deer in the headlights look of ultimate surprise and shock. I almost felt bad. Almost. But she did this.

She didn't say anything, making it clear that this woman truly was the bane of my existence. I pressed my lips together and nodded, like *right, this is how it ends because of course.*

We'd bickered since the day I found her drinking alone in her room during her own party. Our run-ins at work had been awkward, forced, the tension between us palpable. Maybe there had been a move to breach the topic of that night, an apology or explanation or some type of closure, but it never amounted to anything.

There was just something about this woman that made me want to clam up and be pissy for the hell of it. She wanted me to argue with her. Rile her up the way she riled me up. Sometimes our tempers got the better of us, but I swore to the coding gods she enjoyed it. Sadistic woman.

I was already at the elevator, not knowing where to go since I didn't have a room, when Bane called out, "Sunny! Wait!"

Bane had her tablet tucked against her chest, strands of purple hair slipping out from behind her ears, rushing toward me. The second I spotted her, she slowed down as if she hadn't just been sprinting at me like a leopard in hungry pursuit.

Coming to an abrupt stop, her cheeks flushed, she said, "Then let's just go with it."

"What?" I said, confused, and sidestepping from the elevator's path when the doors opened.

Four people spilled out and Bane pushed me inside, hitting a random floor number.

"What are you doing?" I turned to her, ignoring the residual heat that her palm had left against my chest. She was stronger than she looked, but just as aggressive as I knew she could be.

She pushed wayward hair from her face, brushing a knuckle against the sweat beading on her forehead. Her head dropped back. "AC. Thank god."

"What are you doing?" I repeated myself in case she hadn't heard me the first time. Of course, she had and chose to ignore me. "You're the one who pushed me into an elevator, remember?"

Bane swallowed, her gaze stuck on the doors like she was expecting an invasion. "We should just pretend we're dating for the duration of your stay."

"What are you, offering me accommodations like you work here?"

She scoffed, turning her worried expression to my gaze. "I didn't think of the implications. You have two options: tell them the truth and be ruined for eternity."

"Not exactly how I put it."

"Or play along."

I shook my head. "Appalling notion."

"Have you ever fake-dated before?"

"Well . . . no. I don't fake anything. Have you?" I side-eyed her. "You look like a faker."

"I will have you know that I've never fake-dated. But!" She dramatically held up one finger, her brows arched high.

"Big but."

"I *have* hammed it up," she added, and proudly at that. As if theatrically convincing someone of a situation was an uncharted gift of hers.

The doors opened and we walked out, slowly wandering the hall, where every so often, the building opened up to the beach and a breeze sent Bane's stray hair swirling around her face.

"You've had to convince people your relationship is better than it was?"

"No." She gave me a look so terse that it could glitch a perfect program. "It's called being a wingwoman. Hyping someone up. I have guy friends and there's nothing like me being all over them and loudly proclaiming their panty-melting assertion in bed to make other women turn their heads and want a piece."

"Of . . . panty-melting assertion."

"In bed."

"Right. There must be a difference there . . ."

We paused at a balcony overlooking a large water feature filled with pink lotus and surrounded by flowering shrubs. Bane closed her eyes in the gust of air. She really wasn't meant for hot and humid climates. But she was wearing sweats.

"I got you into this, and I will suck it up and get you through this," she stated.

"Excellent pitch," I said dryly.

"I'm willing to help. You can take it or tell them the truth. Just . . . let me know," she ended with a soft, almost hurt quality to her tone. Did she care? Or was she bored and had nothing better to do? "Also, you need a place to stay, and this place is probably booked for at least a night or two."

I looked past Bane and groaned.

She glanced over her shoulder at two men rounding the corner, deep in conversation. "Friends?"

"Yeah. Groom and best man."

"Wingwoman?" She offered with beckoning raised brows.

I grunted, but before I could even think long enough to find a remotely reasonable response, Bane had turned to me and adjusted my collar. It didn't need adjusting. Her touch glided across the top button and across my shoulders. The warmth of her hands seeped through the fabric, leaving a trail on my skin underneath. Her scent of floral hair products mixed with subtle sweat wafted toward me.

I cleared my throat. "What are you doing?"

"Jump-starting this whole thing in case you want to go all in. Why are you wearing a button-down shirt? Even if it's short-sleeved. Do you know what you look like? A dev. A nerdy dev. A nerdy dev tourist."

"You say that like it's a dirty thing."

"Are they watching?"

I checked. "Yes." With curious stares.

She focused on my hair like she was examining a pixelated header on a website project. Then she spread her fingers through it. I stilled. I couldn't look at her the way she was touching me, like we were friends or an actual couple. I forced myself to look past her at my friends.

Sam's and Aamar's expressions lit up right as Bane stepped to the side to face the hallway. Sam crouched low, all smiles, and ran at me like we were in a football game. He tackle-hugged me and tried to lift me off the ground, laughing.

"Bro, don't break your back before the wedding!" I said, playfully shoving him, grinning and then hugging Aamar.

Before they could ask any of the usual questions—how you doing, how was the flight, gonna be okay with the ex here—they turned to Bane and beckoned an introduction with smiles.

I groaned as Bane initiated. "Hi! I'm Bhanu. Who's the groom?"

"Guilty." Sam raised a hand and clucked his tongue. "Bhanu? Bhanu . . . hmm . . . sounds familiar."

What the hell was he talking about? I'd never mentioned Bane to my friends.

"Group chat. Ex ran into you two earlier," he clarified.

"Of course," I muttered.

Bane gave me a careful glance before asking Sam, "So you've heard all about me, then?"

"Well, not much and that's disappointing," Sam replied with an elbow to my gut. "How are you going to leave a girlfriend off the chat?"

I scratched my ear. "I thought you'd be more upset that I have a surprise plus one."

"Nah, man. We have plenty of room and food. When did you—"

He stopped himself, turning to Bane with a bow of the head. "I'm sorry. Sunny can be closed off sometimes. My bride and I are very happy to have you with us. You're in for a blast!"

"Oh, no," she insisted. "I'm just tagging along. I don't want to intrude—"

"Nonsense! You're Sunny's girl! He brought you all the way out here."

"Actually, I came to see my sister, and this is all a coincidence. I don't want to end up in your wedding pictures and forever memories."

"Okay, listen. I can stand here all day and try to convince you, but once you meet my bride, she's not going to let you go. I promise you."

Bane looked to me, silently asking, "Are we doing this or what?"

Maybe I could've tracked down my ex and had a private conversation, taking the brunt of the humiliation to keep this between the two of us, but damn, she'd already gone to the group chat and now everyone knew. And now Sam was excitedly insisting on having Bane present, which was a big deal. This wasn't a huge wedding. This would be small and intimate, and being my *girlfriend* meant he expected Bane to be at all the pre-wedding events. As in an entire vacation together. Dinner, drinks, outings.

I didn't have much of a choice, seeing that the awkwardness of the truth would be a low-hanging cloud over everyone anytime I was near. Seemed like a huge damper for a wedding week.

Damnit. I heaved out a breath and gave Bane a short, almost imperceptible nod.

In a matter of nanoseconds, she went from friendly stranger in our midst to fake girlfriend on overdrive. She batted her lashes and sank against my side, slipping one hand down to mine, and beamed up at me. "Are you sure? I want you to have time with your friends."

I swallowed hard, my mind blanking.

She turned to the guys and said, "He's being shy."

Aamar quirked a brow. "Sunny? Shy? This guy?"

She laughed and it sounded like angels blessing us with their presence. She'd never laughed like that in front of me before. Who was this woman turning on the charm so high that my friends were instantly eating out of her hands?

Bane shrugged and patted my chest. "Maybe he's just shy with me. It's very cute," she said with a sultry, flirty tone that had Aamar tilting his head and silently relaying in our age-old telepathic bro speak: *Damn, bro. You getting that?*

"Then it's settled! Sunny has a plus one! From henceforth, Bhanu will be joining us for everything. Right?" Sam asked, hopeful and a bit too eager.

Bane's dazzling smile was blinding. How often did she smile that big? She could stop entire worlds looking like that, but how much of it was genuine? The configuration of this ploy led to zero being the most probable answer. Because this wasn't real. She was faking it. But damn, was she good at this.

"What room are you in?" Aamar asked, pulling out his phone to take note.

With my lips compressing, my brain fidgeted with how to relay my answer without sounding like Sejal and I were at each other's throats, but also where exactly was I staying?

"The villas," Bane replied, looping an arm through mine while I stood in silence, dumbfounded and unable to add anything to her response, much less correct it. I didn't have much of a choice.

"Fancy," Sam said. "Like a honeymoon suite?"

Bane laughed that angelic laugh, a melody chiming in the breezeway. "Of course not. We're not on a honeymoon. No, just the quaint villas; a sister property of the hotel. It's on the other side of the golf course."

The guys jerked their heads at me. I shrugged. I had no idea what she was talking about, but apparently they did.

"The ones that look like actual houses?" Sam asked.

"Yes. Hence the name, I guess. Not very creative," Bane said, sounding like a designer. She had probably looked at the hotel's website and clucked her tongue, skimming down every page making mental notes of what she'd change in the overall UX design of it all.

Sam whistled.

Her shoulders scrunched up, a movement of friction against my arm. I'd never noticed how preferable our height difference was. She was on the taller side, but several inches shorter than me so that whatever little motions she made were brushes against unsuspecting places. Nothing dirty, or even remotely arousing—this was Bane after all—but surprisingly not irritating.

Her delicate shrug and innocent but overtly pleased expression said it all, and the boys seemed to catch her nonverbal exclamation.

"They look extremely nice," Sam commented, then whispered, "But, uh, don't tell my bride. She's going to wonder why I didn't splurge that hard."

I managed a chuckle. Sure. I could only assume these villas were expensive. Sam was well off as an engineer for Boeing back in Seattle, so for him not to splurge on the best room at this weirdly arranged multi-location-in-one-hotel was saying something. I had to remember to check out the pricing later. If I couldn't get a room, even for one night, and I had to crash on Bane's couch (presumably an expensive villa had a couch), then I should at least know what monetary amount to give her for my part.

Aamar's phone pinged and he told Sam, "The wedding planner is ready. Wants to meet at the beach gazebo."

"We better get going," Sam said, taking an awkward step toward Bane as if he weren't sure if he should shake her hand or hug her or . . .

She offered a fist. A fist bump. Of course she would. "I'm not much of a handshake or hugs type of person, so please don't take offense," she explained with that kilowatt smile that had disarmed my friends yet again.

When the guys had disappeared into an elevator, she slipped her arm out of mine and I said, "You don't have to cross your comfort zone by playing along."

"What?" She looked up at me with those soft eyes.

"The touching."

She waved me off and scrolled through her phone. "I know you, it's fine. Unless you prefer that I don't?"

I glanced at her. I had no qualms about her touching me.

Bane's lips slowly tugged up into a baiting smile. "In case the mere touch of my hand on your arm should make you combust?"

I groaned. "All right. Let's move on."

"Okay. What time and day do we meet for the wedding? Better add that to my incredibly packed schedule."

"Saturday early evening. They have this thing about sunset pictures."

"Cool. Guess I better acquire a dress? Is it formal?"

"Casual. But not like . . ." I swept a hand down the length of her body.

She deadpanned. "Joggers are in. Haven't you seen women wearing these with high heels? It's all the fashion rage."

"A casual dress or slacks and a blouse would be preferable. You're going to be in their wedding pictures."

She cringed. "I'll try my best to evade the cameras."

I wasn't going to argue on that one, especially when our fake breakup would happen shortly after we returned home. There was no need for someone to bring up Bane every time they saw her in wedding pictures.

What ever happened to Bhanu?

Why'd you guys break up?

How long were you two even together that you brought her to our wedding? She's in half the photos.

And so on. Seeing these choice pictures framed on Sam's wall every time I went over? Everyone loving her and constantly hammering me for answers on how I could let another good one walk away?

"For everything else, I'd say comfortable."

She blinked at me. "What everything else?"

"We're four days ahead of the wedding. The whole point is to turn this into a hangout. We have excursions planned."

"Like what? And am I supposed to actually attend all of them?" Her jaw dropped as if spending time together was the worst thing in the world, and it probably was. It was bad enough to have my ex in my space, but now Bane would be taking up a good portion, too. There was no place to turn without seeing misery.

I stuck my hands into my pockets and shrugged. "I'm not going to force you into anything, but my friends will wonder. I could always tell them you're splitting time between us and your sister. That's believable."

Her shoulders slumped. "My sister is working while I'm here, and she'll get on me if I don't actually leave the villa. Okay. What excursions and when?"

Bane dutifully entered dates and times for our outings: dinners, drinks, hiking, an afternoon on a boat, et cetera. At least there wasn't a rehearsal dinner. That was saved for the immediate family flying in.

She huffed, muttering, "Tourist things."

"Well, yes, we *are* tourists."

"Not even one cultural or local thing. Something that only this land can offer?" She tsked, as if it were a damn shame. It probably was, but the couple had set the events and we simply complied.

"I'm sure we can find time to wander off and be cultural," I added, not thinking she'd take my suggestion seriously.

"I have shorts and shirts aplenty for these excursions."

"And something to swim in?"

Her eyes flickered and heat rose to my face as I quickly added, "If you want to swim. I don't plan on swimming in the ocean. It's too . . . *unsettling*."

"It's dangerous for a dev. Sharks and sharp coral lurking, waiting for their chance to bite some of that coding off."

"Sharks?" I recalled how vast and deep the ocean was from the plane.

"Yes. There's a particularly territorial tiger shark in the dark water, but we'd never swim out there. I'm sure a bunch of tourists will want to see clear waters, not dark and murky straight out of *Jaws*. They can smell tourists like fresh chum, all bloody and gooey and ripe for snatching up."

"Noted." Not that I'd planned on it, but no way in hell was I getting into the ocean.

SEVEN

Bhanu

We hitched a ride on a golf cart while Sunny explained the dynamics of his friends' group. "Bored" wasn't exactly the word to describe this short soliloquy, never with that voice of his. To my chagrin, his voice was unfathomably pleasant to listen to, particularly when he wasn't demanding anything of my team or insinuating that my own work was behind deadline.

The gist was thus:

"You met Sam, the groom. He's marrying his college sweetheart, April. They've had many ups and downs between work, both engineers at Boeing. Her wanting to get her master's degree when he wanted to have kids led to a separation for a bit. Then there was drama when he considered leaving the company and she was briefly seeing someone else.

"His parents are a bit hard to please and her parents butted heads with his; therefore, they're flying in the day before the wedding for a rehearsal dinner that's more of a family calm-down dinner. The entire reason they're having a destination wedding is to keep the parents out of it, and to keep it small. Her parents wanted to invite everyone they'd ever met, and his parents wanted April to cut back on some things."

"Are they Indian?" I joked.

Sunny, to my shocked disbelief, actually hinted at a smirk. Gasp! Did his mouth know such things? It made his side profile attractive, if I were to forget what an ass he could be.

He replied, "You'd think. You met Aamar, the best man, also an engineer at Boeing. He brought his fiancée, Maya, who happens to be good friends with April and is her maid of honor. They're a relaxed couple, but Aamar's overseeing a lot of things for Sam, despite them having a wedding planner. Sam is a perfectionist, which drives April up the wall. And you met Sejal," he grumbled.

Ouch. Talk about a sore spot.

"She's a bridesmaid, for some damn reason, and here with her boyfriend."

Then he went quiet, but I wanted to know more. Strangely, I wanted to know about his life, these people I'd inadvertently agreed to sharing my vacation with, and this menacing former lover who appeared to be the archetypal ex.

"Is that all?" I pressed.

"Yep."

"Nothing else I should know about these people? Their dislikes? Points of discussions to avoid?"

"Nope. I'm sure they'll try to pry into you or us, but I'll be quick to cut them off."

"Speaking of us, what's our story?"

"Story?"

I sighed dramatically. "Yes. Basic facts. How did we meet? How long have we been together? Should we know each other's allergies, birthdays, tidbits about parents and siblings?"

"No."

I scowled.

"You don't need to know more about my life." And there was that clenched jaw again. The asshole was back.

"If this falls apart, then that's on you. I can only master the information that I have. Otherwise, I'll start making things up when they ask. And they *will* ask."

A few minutes later, he conceded. "We met at your work party a year ago, started dating two months ago. That's enough time, right? To bring you for a wedding but not long enough that they'd question why I didn't tell them? Besides, your sister lives here, so you were coming anyway. A last-minute coincidence."

"Sounds believable."

He continued to stew on other broad aspects of our fake relationship when we pulled up to the villa, the point being not to get too chatty. "It won't be an issue since you'd rather be doing your own thing with your own family."

If by "my own thing," he meant sneaking into work, then yes. Since I saw Diya on a regular basis, and this was a long trip for me, she couldn't take every day off. And I wouldn't want her to, not when I was content to lounge around. She was back to work, giving me time to relax without filling the void with conversation and plans.

Essentially, "plans" included me sitting on the lanai with an ocean view, sipping drinks, nibbling on cheese, and scouring my laptop. Diya would end me. Just like Gabrielle. Even if I didn't love my job, it was difficult to unplug. It was why I couldn't *just* watch TV and not be on my phone and tablet. And why it was hard to *just* read a book and get lost in the story. My brain had to juggle multiple things at once.

"I'm going to be a breath of fresh air," I told him.

"What?" He stared at me as if I'd spewed frothy lies at him.

"Your friends will only get off your back if you're deliriously happy. Especially with your ex there."

"*You're* going to pull off *deliriously* happy?"

I batted my eyelashes. "I make all my men deliriously happy."

He opened his mouth—knowing him, probably to inquire what had happened to all those men if I'd made them so content—but he, smartly, didn't say anything.

This might be fun after all. I'd always wanted to be an actor. Okay, well, maybe in high school during my Bollywood phase. I could ham it up. I could be the perfect girlfriend, if for nothing else than to occupy my time so I wasn't bored to death around his friends. Something to keep my mind off work and checking my messages every half second for interview updates. This was a vacation that had turned into a fake dating heist. I might as well be the center of my own best fantasy.

"I can tell this has already blown up in your head."

I snickered. "Your ex will be begging for you to go back to her."

"Not what I want."

"Then revenge relationship."

"I'm not vengeful."

"I'm sure whatever you want doesn't involve her pushing her relationship in your face all week and your friends pitying you."

He, again, opened his mouth, but snapped it shut. Instead, Sunny pulled his suitcase behind him as we strolled toward the sidewalk. He could act like he didn't care about any of this, but he wasn't a robot. He had feelings, and if I were in his shoes, I'd be annoyed, upset, hurt, agitated, anything except wholly joyous during my friends' wedding/vacation. Yet I found myself wondering if Sunny had feelings for Sejal, if they could work out in the end, and most importantly, what had happened.

Ugh. No. I wasn't here for the drama. But the tea? Yes. I wanted him to spill the tea.

"What happened between you two?" I asked as we walked to the front door and I unlocked it.

Sunny pulled in his rolling suitcase. "That's personal, and we're not that close."

I shrugged. "A current girlfriend would know what happened with the ex she's about to spend time with."

"No," he replied sternly, his voice gravelly.

I watched him take in the villa, adding, "A real girlfriend would be pretty upset with the situation if she didn't know."

He locked eyes with mine. "That's why you're pretend, and you can pretend to know and/or not care."

"We'll see."

"We should establish base rules."

"Okay."

"One, no prying into each other's personal lives."

I nodded.

"This is a ploy meant to last a few days. That's all."

"Of course. We'll return to bickering coworkers the moment we set foot on a plane."

"What happens on island stays on island."

I sneered. "As if anything should happen."

He dragged his gaze to me, and for the briefest of moments, those chestnut eyes challenged my dismissal. Until he clarified, "No one at work should know we even ran into one another here. Gossip can kill a career."

"Acceptable."

He watched me for a minute. "Do you have any rules?"

"Don't fall in love with me."

He shook his head, exasperated.

I grinned. "Try not to fight. If that's at all possible. I don't want drama on my vacation. Save it for the work pool."

"Agreed."

And that was that. There was no need to mention flirting or sex, et cetera, because that was, simply and hilariously, pushing the details a bit too far.

"This place is very opulent. Didn't realize something as easy as research paid so well. You must be doing nice for yourself," he commented.

And *here* we went. "Jealousy does not make for a good fake boyfriend slash last-minute houseguest."

He held his hands up. "It's just, your job does seem fairly easy in comparison to coding."

"We each picked our career paths. But I'll take that as a compliment; a testament, if you will, of how I make research look so easy. I do run a smooth ship." I blew against my nails. He didn't need to know that Diya had staggering discounts for this place.

"I meant to say . . . you run user tests all day. Show people designs and prototypes and observe them, ask questions, adjust as needed, and do it all over again until approval rating is high enough. It's not like coding, where you have to create working prototypes from nothing."

"Down to the last detail," we said in unison, Sunny scowling and myself mockingly rocking my head back and forth because I'd heard his mightier-than-thou spiel a dozen times.

"You ever consider that other people work just as hard as you do?" I asked, a hand on my hip.

"I know they might. You probably don't stay up all night fixing bugs and ignoring loved ones."

Did he mean exes? Was that why they broke up? He spent so much time glued to his many screens that he lost track of relationships? He vaguely reminded me of those couples who ate while watching TV, fell asleep to the TV, always had the TV on and never talked. They didn't discuss their days or problems or celebrations. They didn't cook together or clean together. Just closed mouths and a blaring TV. Days passing into oblivion without ever having done much to improve, much less enjoy, their lives together. It was sad. Was dating a workaholic like Sunny the same?

Aside from his good looks and Denzel voice, one might wonder why anyone dated him in the first place. Could he be that different with his relationships? Actually nice and generous and charming? I couldn't imagine he'd make a girl's toes curl, but who knew? Also, could a girl's toes curl? What did that even mean? Sounded painful.

"Maybe if you smiled more?" I suggested.

He turned to me, and I expected a big, fake smile. He did not smile. Sunny rarely smiled at me. I'd seen him smile before, elusive and legendary, but at me, for me? Nope. Not since we met a year ago had Sunny smiled at me. Like turning his frown upside down might sever his soul. But others really liked him. Coworkers respected him. Sunny was a mystery.

"Or not . . . hey, don't forget who's letting you crash here and saving you from awkward nights with your friends. Should be a little nicer. If you even know what that word means?"

"*Nice?*" he echoed, casting his eyes toward the ceiling. "Because you were so nice when we first met?"

"What are you talking about? How was I not nice inviting the new guy, whom I'd never even met, to *my* place for a party where I fed you and gave you at least six types of drinks?"

He shifted his weight onto his right foot. "That was all great, probably for show for the rest of our coworkers, but once we were alone, you weren't particularly welcoming."

I combed through my memories. That night was a blur, as was any event in which I was expected to be social for hours with a large crowd of people. All I remembered was biding my time before everyone had left and needing to sit in silence in my bedroom to recharge and escape from the energy-sucking climate of parties before a panic attack hit. I'd felt it coming when I was in mid-conversation. After that? I didn't remember much, probably because I was great at blocking out anxiety. Otherwise, I'd hem and haw for months over what could've been done to either preemptively avoid panic attacks or quickly defuse them.

"I don't remember what detail you're hanging on to, to think I was unwelcoming." I extended my arms in a grand gesture. "But take this into consideration?"

Sunny relaxed, his shoulders less tense and his face less . . . Sunny. "You're right. I do appreciate this. It's saving my ass and my entire vacation."

"Feel free to look around. You probably won't be spending much time here, but there's a fully stocked kitchen and a private yard overlooking the ocean."

He walked to the wide sliding glass doors that made up the back wall. The manicured lawn wasn't huge, but it was secluded. Past the rock wall, sunlight glimmered on the bright, blue water.

Pushing his fingers through his hair, he muttered, "Wow. It's going to be hard to leave this place once they find a room for me."

"You're welcome to visit."

"I've never been great at vacationing. I'm so tied to work, helping family, getting things done for the next phase, that it's strange to not do anything."

"If you're not going to do anything, then you might as well not do anything with that view."

"Yeah. I don't even think I'd ever come here if it hadn't been for Sam getting married. Maybe I'd come to Hawaii, maybe this island, but a cheaper place. A rental."

I knew what he meant. My family was on my butt to detach from work, and I would've never come here to this specific hotel, much less this often, if it hadn't been for Diya and her comically large discounts.

Sunny checked his watch. "I need to shower and get ready to meet the guys."

"Tonight wasn't on the agenda." A spiral of anxiety fluttered at the base of my skull. I hadn't expected there to be so many exursions because, well, I hadn't thoroughly thought this through. I could mentally prepare for later events, but tonight? Already? It was too short notice.

"No. It's just for the guys."

I sighed with great relief, noting how Sunny paused to give me a quiet look. He probably assumed I was simply overcome with relief for not having to be around him, which I wasn't going to correct. Let him stew for a second.

Instead, he asked, "Where should I put my suitcase?"

"Oh . . ." I looked to the right at my room with its lavish king-size bed big enough for three people and attached private bath, then looked to the left at the room Diya had staked claim on because "elder sis needed some luxury in her life."

She probably wouldn't want to walk in on Sunny undressing in her room. Kimo probably wouldn't want that, either.

Crap. I really hadn't thought this through. I indicated the room to the right.

"Thanks," Sunny said, pulling his suitcase into my room and promptly walking back out. "This is the room I should . . ."

Hmm. Had I left my underwear on an unmade bed? "Yeah. Um. My sister is taking the other room."

"To be clear: This is your room?"

"Yes. I'm sure she'll switch rooms with me. The other has two beds."

"Ah. That's okay. I'll take a quick shower and crash on the couch tonight."

"Sounds good. But word of warning, she wakes up at five thirty and is very loud."

"Why does she wake up that early?"

"She claims it's the equatorial sunrise. Always begins to rise around that time, so she naturally rises with the light. She hardly ever wakes up to an alarm clock."

He cocked a brow.

"I know, right! She's so weird. Anyway, she wakes up early, goes for a jog, comes back, and makes breakfast and lunch. Loudly. She lives alone—well, sometimes her boyfriend stays over, but he sleeps like a log—and anyway, she isn't used to keeping it down for others. You can try the couch if you're not a light sleeper."

"It's fine." He backtracked into the room, only to return. "Um, thanks. For this."

I nodded. I mean, what was I supposed to do? Ignore my co-worker's situation when we had so much space here? Had this been a typical hotel room, then no. I couldn't have helped much aside from storing his luggage and letting him use the bathroom. Unless we had double beds and Diya didn't mind bunking with me like old times.

When he disappeared to do what he needed to do, I called Diya.

"Hey! Sorry I've been MIA. It's chaos today," she said on the third ring.

"Oh, no. That sucks. Everything okay?"

"We'll get through it. It's like someone said, hey, your normal busy season pandemonium isn't enough this time, so here's more problems caused by the main booking site and now you can deal with it instead of the people who caused the issue! Yay!"

I groaned. "Sounds very stressful. Anything I can do?"

"No. I just wish that I could spend more time with you today. Hey, are you sure you don't want to take my car and go places?"

"You know me. I really like the peaceful alone time. I love walking the shoreline from here. I saw three honu already and dolphins! Had to tell someone to stay away from the honu."

"What is wrong with people? We have signs everywhere. Thanks for saying something."

"Of course. Hey, so while you're on the phone. Is it okay if someone crashes here? Just for a night or two? Promise he won't get in the way—"

"He *who*?"

"Oh. Yes. A coworker. His reservation got messed up and guess the hotels are booked."

"You better tell me more."

"Um. That's all."

"That can't be all. Who *is* this man?"

"Mmm-mmm." I clucked my tongue. "Don't get all excited for nothing. You'll only disappoint yourself."

"I will absolutely find out every detail about this man in person. Glad he's there. You shouldn't be alone."

I laughed. "It's okay. I'm not scared of the dark."

Diya tsked. "You know what I mean! You're here visiting me, and I feel like I should be spending every minute with you."

"Don't do that. You can't spend every minute with me when I'm here for over a week. And you have work. Besides, I'm not here for you, you know? I just came for this sweet villa and drinks and ube. Okay, so I just came for the ube."

Diya chortled on the other end. "Bet you finished all the ube malasadas Kimo's mom made for you at the get-together?"

"Yes. You know I did."

"I have to go and take care of yet another emergency. We have four key cards, so give your *friend* one if you want."

"Oh, boy . . ."

"That leaves an extra. Kimo doesn't have one. He wouldn't be going there without me anyway."

"Thanks! Hope work gets better . . ."

She groaned dramatically. I could practically see her throwing her head back in exasperation. I didn't know how she worked in the hospitality industry.

"Oh, by the way, I left you a book. In case you get bored or want to read, but seeing that you have a man friend, this probably won't apply. That one I was telling you about? It's pretty good. Saw it go viral, and typically, I wouldn't get into social media–hyped books, but all these readers were fawning over this book, particularly the love interest. And, girl, I read it in two sittings on my days off when Kimo was trying to get attention, and by the end, despite how amazing Kimo is, I was just, like, why aren't you a Jay Shah? Ugh. I had to slap myself back into reality."

"Sounds interesting."

"It's on my bed."

So it was. A little yellow book.

EIGHT

Sunny

Showering post-travel had to be one of the best feelings in the world, and much needed. Airports and long flights, germs, recycled air, disgusting restrooms . . . how could anyone love traveling?

I left most everything in my suitcase for now but hung up my suit. Considering how hot and humid it'd been already, I wasn't sure how any of us would survive wearing a suit for the wedding. Weren't Hawaiian destination weddings all about beaches and relaxed styles? Because April didn't want to risk bad weather or wind, the wedding and reception were in a large indoor room—with AC, thank god—that opened up to the gardens and ocean beyond. Half and half. Still, it would be a miracle if we didn't have pit stains.

Sam was the first to get married in our friends' circle and he was already setting the bar high for the rest of us. I imagined Aamar would cave to familial and cultural expectations to have a big desi wedding back home. Which sounded great to me. A long drive to a nice venue maybe; no planes. Plus, Indian weddings were amazing with all the food and dances as long as one was a guest and not the stressed-out couple. Not that I even had a girlfriend, much less a fiancée, but all I knew was that I wanted a small wedding and not all dozen events and traditions that came with an Indian wedding. *If* marriage was an option. But that was a big if.

Bane had clothes all over the place, strewn over the bed and floor. How did she live like this? She also had a nice view of the ocean from this room, mirroring the glass sliding doors from the living room. Must be nice to be able to vacation like this, which was another reason why I needed to get that promotion for PM. I was a great lead, but I knew I could be an effective PM. Besides, coding into the night was grating down my soul. It was one of the reasons why Sejal had left me. I didn't spend enough time on her. I didn't sleep the entire night in bed with her. I was too focused on work and getting to where I needed to be. Which was ironic because she wanted me to make more money but didn't like the amount of work I had to do to get there.

If only she'd stayed around for another year. She would've seen that I made lead dev, which was a bump in pay. And hopefully in a few weeks, I'd land that PM position to bump my pay even more. We weren't talking about a few extra dollars an hour, either. Enough to finally offer a sizable down payment for Seattle's expensive housing market. Enough to help my parents substantially with medical bills and mortgage, and to spoil my sisters. That was what I really wanted.

After a shower, I found Bane lounging on the back patio, a yellow book on the table beside her paired with water. For a second, I thought she was taking a break from reading to enjoy the spectacular view. But no. She was on her laptop working.

I leaned against the opened sliding door and folded my arms across my chest. "I'm pretty sure Gabrielle forbade you from working."

Bane jumped, then let out an exasperated breath, returning to work. "She doesn't own me."

"She's going to figure out you're logging in and lock you out. Then what?"

"Then I'll be forced to have a true vacation."

"Why don't you go to the beach or swim or golf or see waterfalls?"

"And get eaten alive by bloodthirsty mosquitos? These repellant candles are the only things standing between me and a swarm of vampiric bugs."

"I haven't been bitten once."

"You've been here all of three hours. Just wait until twilight, dawn, or when you're near a fruit tree. That's what they love. Lure you with the beauty of nature and then bam! Stick their little gross oscillating teeth into your flesh and drive you mad with itching. These mosquitos aren't like Washington mosquitos. Like most insects in Hawaii, they're huge. Monsters, really."

"Arbitrary excuses."

She rolled her eyes.

"I'm heading out. Should I . . . text you when I'm on my way back?"

"Sure. Probably a good idea to have each other's contact information since we're *dating*."

We exchanged numbers and I took the extra key card on the counter. But who was I kidding about not working on vacation? I planned on checking Jira for updated scrum boards, roadmaps, and repositories for DevOps the second I had extra time.

⌒〜⌒

I guessed that the golf carts weren't actually meant to cater guests to and from the many hotel buildings but were actually meant for use on the golf course. No matter, the walk back to the main building and the lobby of my actual hotel section was pleasant. This layout was a little confusing—this entire gigantic acreage was owned by one hotel chain, but had three different types of hotels/subnames, all separate, the next more elaborate than the last. Queen's Land (the least expensive but still pricey), King's Land (where the wedding party was staying and very nice), and the Homestead (sounded the cheapest but was the most expensive with entire villas to rent).

The walk was pleasant, full of fresh air and scenery of clear blue sky, sparkling ocean, gigantic palms and coconut trees, and endless flowering shrubs. Hot, but beautiful. An ocean breeze cut through the heat, making the walk across the golf course bearable.

April was the first of our small group to spot me walking through one of the hotel's many restaurants. She greeted me with a hug and then patted my face like my mother often did as if gesturing, *Poor baby*.

I knew what that meant; we all did. "I'm good. Seriously. Let's just focus on you and the stressed-out groom."

"Why is he even stressed? I should be the one stressed."

"As you've said: As long as the dress arrives safely and you get plenty of sleep, it'll be perfect."

"Then I guess half of perfection can be counted on thus far. Honestly . . . are you . . ." April eyed Sejal.

"She's your bridesmaid. I get it."

"She's not awful, you know?"

I didn't comment. Having to tell someone a person wasn't awful was often an indictment in itself.

"She had a difficult time after the breakup."

Because I hadn't? Sejal's words of how inadequate I was lingered around my aura like a dark cloud sending jolts of lightning. Unlike Sejal, I didn't expel all my heartache and issues and emotions into our friend group. It was easy to conclude that she'd suffered more, or that I, as she'd told me so many times, was part robot and emotions weren't in my vocabulary.

Of course, Sejal was wrong. Even if I'd expressed myself, she would've been quick to either dismiss me or say something along the lines of, "Where were these feelings before?"

I knew what she'd said about me. Everyone did. She'd told April and Maya, and they'd told Sam and Aamar, who'd then mentioned it to me. She'd cried for weeks over how much time she'd dedicated to us, how hard she'd worked on me, how I was never enough, how I'd never treated her like a queen on a pedestal, and how I was a hapless, hopeless, emotionless workaholic better suited for glaring at coding than being present in any relationship.

The transparency Sejal had maintained through the entire breakup and afterward, and the lack of rebuttal from me, made the entire situation one-sided and in her favor. It had almost created a rift between the guys and the women, until Sam and Aamar reminded April and Maya how I was the least destructive, least toxic person ever. Not to mention quiet as hell. I didn't think our breakup was anything to shout about, to discuss, to cause tension, or to get people to pity me or stand on my side. Even when Sejal had done it. Even when it appeared that she'd succeeded in turning everyone against me, including family.

As usual, I didn't make a remark on the ongoing conversation revolving around us. Instead, I said, "This is all about you and Sam. We're going to have a great time."

She beamed and nodded, as if she needed confirmation that I wasn't going to—what—make a scene? "Oh! I heard you brought a special friend." This, she said loudly, a call to arms for others to descend on the topic.

"Why didn't you tell us?" Maya asked.

"How could you keep that to yourself?" Aamar said.

"A new relationship," I replied. "Please don't make this a big deal. She . . . keeps to herself."

Sejal eyed me as she sipped her drink from across the veranda dinner table. Sejal could see through my BS, but I hoped my "robotic emotions" worked in my favor.

"She's really nice," Aamar told Maya.

"And cute," April said, shaking her shoulders. Sam had obviously told her, because there were no pictures of Bane to show. "Why didn't she join us?"

"I thought this was just for us," I replied, glaring at Sejal instead of the new boyfriend at her side.

Tension slowly built between us. She wanted to say something, wanted to start something. As she opened her mouth, I grinned at Sam and April and made a toast.

Despite my ex sitting across from me with piercing incredulity at my suddenly having a girlfriend, we enjoyed food, drinks, desserts, and views while catching up late into the torch fire–lit evening. About two hours later, April stood with a lingering graze across Sam's shoulders, mischief in her eyes. Maya and Sejal joined her and off they went for a bachelorette party. Sejal kissed her boyfriend, and he went on his own (despite being invited by Sam), while Sam, Aamar, and I headed for the bachelor party.

This island didn't have any cities, much less a big nightlife scene. But there was a shitload of drinking.

⤳⤳

I'd gotten back late. My friends must've mistaken our late twenties for our early college days when we could drink until 3 a.m. and be okay the next day. After many fumbling attempts with the key card, I crept into a very dark villa. I flipped on the kitchen light, noticing that both bedroom doors were closed. Pillows and blankets had been set on the couch.

I crashed. If the guys were expecting me to keep this up all trip long, they might as well leave me poolside with a lemonade. My throat ached and my head was on its way to pounding.

My eyes clasped shut, dreams may or may not have come, but the next thing I knew, the shrill sound of a blender and clanking pans and silverware had me awake and clutching the blanket over my head. This must be the generous, albeit early-riser, sister. She eventually went on her way, and I fell back asleep, waking up to nothing. No alarm, no texts, no calls, no impending meetings, just a clean, sunlight-filled room.

I looked up at the wide bamboo fan blades that matched the wicker furniture. My head felt like someone had tried to crush it and failed. In spite of a mild hangover, this finally felt like a vacation. For the first time in a long time. Not days off to visit family or nearby places or tightly packed itineraries through scenic destinations, but a vacation. Rest. Relaxation.

My mind drifted toward three things: family, work, and the urgent need to piss.

I texted my sisters to make sure Papa was okay, that he hadn't relapsed. They gave me a text full of enjoying my time without worrying over him; he was fine.

I used the bathroom next to the second bedroom instead of knocking on Bane's door. On the way back out, I stood at her door anyway and scratched my forehead. Well, shit. I needed to get in there for my luggage.

After several knocks, each louder than the last, I announced, "I'm opening the door."

She wasn't in the room. I took the opportunity to take a quick shower.

Tugging my shirt over my head and walking out of the bedroom afterward, I saw her.

Bane was sitting on a lounge chair, in the shade, reading that yellow book, her back to the sliding doors and to me, but far enough from the villa that she couldn't have heard me.

I should probably talk to her. At least say hello.

I pushed aside the glass door. She didn't budge. I stood over her. Her legs were stretched out on the lounge chair. She was wearing long shorts and a T-shirt, hair in a bun. Very much unlike my friends last night, who'd been all dressed up in flowing dresses, or like a lot of women in passing wearing dresses and floppy hats, as if visiting the islands mandated looking extra nice. But Bane was . . . *Bane.*

"Hey."

"Hi," she purred.

"Sorry, I forgot to text you last night that I'd probably be getting in late."

She flipped the page to her book. "Don't be. Your competition wasn't."

"Wait. What?"

She didn't bother looking up. "I come here several times a year. You think I don't have friends with benefits on island? Not wasting my time waiting around on you."

What the hell was she talking about? "Oh. Uh . . . good."

I didn't expect Bane to wait around for me, but I'd genuinely felt bad. Of course, my mouth didn't know how to formulate those words to tell her so. But she seemed fine. We weren't a couple. I shouldn't feel bad, and she shouldn't be upset. And I definitely should not feel any tinge of jealousy, yet . . .

"The fuck. How many benefits you got here, Bane?"

She peered up at me from over her sunglasses. "Language."

"Pardon me."

She pushed up her shades as if she'd resumed reading that yellow book with two Indian characters on the cover, arms crossed, side-eyeing each other. They were essentially us half the time.

"How many guys do I need to watch out for?" My words came out sharper than I'd intended.

"Why would you care?"

"I don't care. But if we're acting in front of my friends, it would be nice to know how many guys might interrupt us by sweeping you away with a kiss."

Her lips twitched. She wanted to smile and was holding back.

I clarified, "I'm not asking because I'm jealous. Just curious."

Her lips curled at the corners.

"Don't tell me." I turned to walk away but came back. "Are they in this area?"

"Don't worry," she finally said. "They're discreet. But if I have to suddenly leave, then you'll know why."

Don't suddenly leave then, I wanted to tell her.

"Is that an issue?" she asked.

"No. Good to know so I won't be caught off guard if some guy steals you away. Just try not to do it in front of everyone. My friends might have fallen for this ruse, but they're not going to believe we have an open relationship."

She pursed her lips. "Don't run off with my man-whores in public. Got it."

I groaned. "Okay. Now that that's settled—"

"You can't run off with anyone, either. To be fair."

"Who am I going to run off with?"

"A certain ex. Unless you want to?" Her tone went up on that last word, baiting me for information that I didn't want to give. Circumventing our rules.

"You have nothing to worry about."

"Oh, I'm not worried about anything. I'd just like a heads-up. Should I find out and be theatrically upset or just disappear when it happens? How do you want to play that?"

"I'm not telling you what happened with us."

"Should I be friendly toward her or cold? A real girlfriend would know the story. And if she didn't, it would be an obvious point of quarreling between the couple. How should I respond?"

"Try as you may, Bane, you won't get the details of my past relationship. Per the rules that you agreed to."

She pouted. "And here I thought I'd get to act out all my dramatic girlfriend fantasies."

"Not exactly what I'd consider a fantasy."

Bane tilted her chin into the morning sun. "What *do* you consider a fantasy?"

"I . . . don't know how to respond to that."

She squinted into the sun. "Well, feel free to order in breakfast while you think on it."

"Thanks. I'll pay for it instead of charging the room." I walked inside as she called to my back, "Order me waffles!"

Waffles were the least I could do. Just add them to my bill.

After checking my phone to find that Aamar had sent out a group chat reminder about lunch, I perused the hotel's breakfast service menu. There was too much time until then to risk not eating beforehand. The menu offered plenty to choose from and it all arrived on literal silver platters decorated with pink orchids and small vases of hibiscus and complimentary items of chocolates and 100 percent Kona coffee. Which, after Googling to see what that was, meant this coffee was grown on the lava soil slopes of the island and cost about fifty bucks a pound.

Was it worth it? For my salary, no. To my taste buds? Yes.

NINE

Bhanu

Out of all the things I'd imagine doing on a lovely Hawaiian Wednesday morning, having waffles with roasted macnuts smothered in coconut syrup with my work nemesis wasn't one of them. The open-concept room was quiet, awkward, with the sounds of chewing and gulping coffee and juice, and the swish of the fans. That was all. No talking.

At times, my eyes kept flitting toward Sunny out of habit, only to find him glaring at me. Ignoring him had failed. Offering a small smile had failed.

"What's wrong with your face?" I prodded.

He cut through his French toast smothered in powdered sugar and whipped cream. This meal couldn't be healthy for either of us. "What?"

"Is something wrong with your face? Because I know you can't be this upset to have breakfast with me. I mean, you could eat at the counter, the couch, outside, even leave."

He scowled. A line appeared between his eyes, making him

THE DESIGN OF US
89

appear serious and hot-tempered, the kind of person who needed to be in control at all times. But he was in control. He wasn't sleeping out of a rental car or floating in the ocean. Also, I'd never known him to be ill-tempered.

"You just seem upset for someone who got a posh, emergency vacation villa."

His expression softened. His brows unknotted themselves, his jaw less rigid, but that line remained in between his brows like it was fighting for its life. I almost laughed.

"I'm grateful," he said. "Truly. You're going out of your way for someone you don't even like."

I mean, he wasn't lying, so I did not correct him.

"Definitely true, then. You detest me," he stated.

"We're not friends. You're a bit of an ass. Can I say that? Yes. We're not at work."

"*I'm* the ass?"

"One of us is, and it's not me."

"Says every ass ever."

I nearly spat out the chilled POG (passion fruit, orange, guava juice) Diya had left for me in the fridge.

Sunny went to tip his cup of juice into his mouth. I snatched the glass.

"What are you doing?" he asked.

"My sister bought that for me. Go get your own POG."

He leaned back against his chair. "See?"

"See what? You can't just stay here, out of my good graces, drink my juice, and insult me. Be careful. You might get kicked out."

The Return of the Scowl should be the title of his memoir because there it was. "I better get going. We obviously can't be civil. I might as well come clean with my friends about you. But you should learn to ease up."

"I should learn to do nothing." Although I pushed his glass of juice back toward him. It was almost empty, and full of his germs. There was no point in wasting it.

He looked at the glass like I'd somehow poisoned it right in front of him. "You're always riding me. I mean, are you trying to make me look incompetent in front of others at work so I can't become PM?"

"First of all, did you apply for the PM position?"

"Inappropriate," he said without a fluctuation to his tone to hint one way or another.

"Coming from the guy who partakes of the Sunny versus Bhanu pool."

"So you admit to trying to make me look bad?"

"No. I'm not awful. You're not nice to me." I crossed my arms. "There. I said it. You're not nice to me, so why should I smile and pucker up for you?"

His brows shot up in surprise.

"Don't blame me for your inadequacies," I added.

"Wow. I was trying to nicely ask you to be a *little* more professional. It benefits you, too."

"Okay, first of all, you condescending jackass."

"Oh, boy."

"Don't sit here and tell me that I need to ease up or that I *need* to do anything professionally and slap on a label to call it helping *me* out. How much more professional can I be? I can't sugarcoat. I'm not telling you anything that our managers wouldn't tell you. I'm not yelling or demeaning. Sounds like you'd rather I tell you everything in private so you don't get your feelings hurt."

"A private conversation would help—"

"That's not my job. I don't have time to call you for every little thing. We all work together. We all tell one another what's late and what's wrong and what needs to be fixed and debugged and who needs to hurry up in front of others because someone is always waiting on someone else. That's UX. If we took the time to do it all privately, we'd never get anything done. And I've never had anyone tell me that I was being a bitch."

He put his hands up. "I didn't call you that."

"You're implying it." I gesticulated with my next words. "Woman equates to smiles and kindly relaying her thoughts so as not to offend others, particularly men with easily bruised egos, particularly in STEM fields; otherwise she must reevaluate her entire approach. Man equates to doing and saying whatever they feel is professional without regard to how others might feel because male leads equals automatic respect."

Sunny blew out a breath. "I apologize if that's how I came off. Not my intention. But I do think you're blowing this out of proportion."

"I've dealt with guys telling me all sorts of things since I could remember. I'm stating facts, not blowing anything up. If there's something serious or an issue that warrants discretion, I do that privately. The fact that I have to sit here and explain that . . . let me ask you. Would you be having this conversation with me if I was a man?"

He glared at me, and I glared right back. "Yep."

"BS."

"All right. Never mind. We can't handle this like adults."

"Deflection. Classic." I shoved another waffle bite into my mouth, pissed that it was cold and soggy now.

"Fine. You're not terrible."

"Amazing apology."

"Let's just leave it before this turns into some egregious debacle. You do your work. I'll do mine."

Some bitter, ugly little thing in me crowed. "You didn't answer my question. I heard you're going after the PM position."

"And I shouldn't? Or does competition worry you?"

"I don't worry about you."

Sunny finished his toast and ate a piece of fruit, then released a huge sigh. "Listen. Bane."

He didn't react to my RBF one bit, nor did he miss a beat.

"I support women in higher roles. I support women in STEM. I support whatever a woman wants to do with her life. But I also know my worth, my skill, my education, the results of my hard work. I aim to be PM, either with this opening or the next, or hell, even at another company. I know I'll be a good PM, and that's not to say you wouldn't. But I have to take my chance, too. It's a long shot because you've been there longer than I have, and I'm only assuming you applied for the same role."

We returned to cold, cutting silence while finishing the last pieces and final drops of our breakfast. In a matter of minutes, Sunny tossed his napkin onto the empty plate in front of him and bluntly said, "Thank you again for letting me crash."

"Thanks for the waffles," I pushed out, equally blunt.

"I'm going to check the front desk."

"You can call."

"I can, but I also want to get away from you. I mean . . . out of your way. I'm sure you have lots of vacation things to do and benefit buddies to call."

Was that a tinge of jealousy? All the anger left me like a heated pall drifting away. I smirked. "Good idea. Benefits sound nice."

Then he left. Silently, without a rebuttal. Without so much as a second glance. God, he was so grumpy.

TEN

Sunny

Bane had the uncanny ability to streamline straight to the raw end of my very last nerve without so much as trying. I hadn't meant to tell her what to do or how to behave, and sure, perhaps the wording and/or my tone had made it appear so, but she was so quick to jump on my ass about everything. She did it at work all the time. And while she ran a tight subteam, she wasn't the damn PM to treat me the way she did.

I'd applied, and interviewed, for our recent PM opening and was waiting on edge to hear back. No one had to tell me that Bane had also applied. Everyone knew she had. They wanted her to be PM, which would be great for non-leads, but not great for me. If she treated me this curtly now, how much worse would she be as PM?

She'd been at the company longer. Seniority played a huge part in the consideration process when it came to filling a role where multiple applicants showed strong skills, education, work ethic, effectiveness, and overall likability with teams, managers, and clients. My dev skills were beyond what the company was even paying me for. My presentations were effective and enjoyable. I'd even been given extra responsibilities by moving up to the company's larger accounts within the first two months.

But was I going to step aside without even trying? Hell no.

At least this wedding, and even dealing with the hotel situation, had left little time to stalk my inbox.

I went over the conversation with Bane. And groaned. I mean, shit. I guess telling her to be nicer wasn't the right thing.

Even as I walked the long path nursed by generous tree shade to get to the King's Land lobby, my blood was still simmering on edge of boiling. I couldn't get that infuriating woman out of my head. *Bhanu* had become the bane of my existence—Bane was a fitting name for her. Beneath that bubbly exterior was a deep-seated hate for me. I was shocked that she even offered me the villa.

I'd checked my phone for any updates—voicemails, emails, text messages, missed calls—but there was nothing aside from the daunting group chat. In a way, it was nice to be so far from the others. A long walk, sure, but not within the same building. They couldn't just knock on my door, show up unexpectedly, and the idea that I had a low-key girlfriend, well, it seemed that my friends now gave me extra space.

Shorts and a short-sleeved T-shirt allowed the breeze to cool my skin. Several people walked and jogged on the sidewalks, but the paved paths on both sides of the street were wide and extended as far as the eye could see so there were no crowds. Instead, plenty of space to take in the beauty of the island.

My phone rang and I answered on first call, hoping it was the hotel.

It wasn't.

"Hey, sis," I said into the phone.

"Hey, bhai! How's paradise?"

"Hot as Hades."

Sheila laughed.

"Is everything okay?" I asked, worried.

"Everything's fine. Just checking in, making sure that you're actually vacationing instead of remotely working."

"Sheesh. You think I'm that bad that you have to call?"

"Yes."

Fine, she was right. "Is Papa okay?"

"Yes."

Guilt riddled my bones. "I shouldn't be here when he's sick."

"You should. He's okay right now and we're here taking care of him."

"When that's my responsibility."

"Eh, spare me your gender norms."

"As the eldest."

"And your traditionalist norms. Besides, you're not really vacationing. It's your best friend's wedding, that you committed to nearly a year ago."

"Doesn't alleviate my guilt."

"Stop that."

But it wasn't easy to lessen the burden of shame. Traditionally, as the son and the eldest child, I was supposed to take care of my parents. My sisters lived closer and insisted on staying with our parents to help out. While they were counting out Papa's meds and making dinners so Ma wouldn't have to, I was in freaking Hawaii.

"When I return, I'll stay with them until he's better," I announced.

"No need. He's doing fine now."

"I work remotely. There's no reason why I shouldn't. Besides, it's been a while since I've stayed over."

"Sure, but don't think it's been too long a time since you've seen them. You were just here two weeks ago. Seattle isn't that far from Olympia. Stop being melodramatic as if you've abandoned your parents."

I nodded, squinting in the sunlight whenever it pierced the canopy.

"Have fun for once!"

I groaned.

"Wait, is that ex of yours there?" Sheila asked, her voice dropping to annoyed.

"Yes."

"She had the nerve, huh?"

"Let's not gang up on her."

"We were never friends, and you know I was always wary of her since that time she dated Yash. I dunno. Something about a person talking about their relationship issues to others is disturbing. Especially outside of their immediate circle. Anyway, she left you and had you believing you weren't capable of love. How am I supposed to react? You may keep your composure, but I say what's on my mind. She's lucky I'm not there."

"You know how I feel about holding on to resentment. There's too many other, more important, stresses to worry about. Resentment poisons the heart. Also, what if we got back together? Then what?"

"Then she'd better have changed her tune, first and foremost. And if you're happy and healthy, then I'm happy for you. But you can do better."

Could I, though?

We chatted for a few more minutes before hanging up. Knowing that my dad was doing better was a relief, and that my sisters were nearby to help. I should really take over once I returned. Staying with my parents would drive Papa up the wall. He'd insist that he was fine, that we were all overreacting.

But when he'd had to stay for several days in the hospital because of kidney stones or surgery or whatever the case, he was never alone. Someone would stay at his side all day and sleep over every night. We'd take turns. Even if he was coherent and moved around on his own. It didn't matter. For a few years there, we'd grown accustomed to hospital cafeteria food. We even had "picnics" in the dining area.

Sweat ran down my temples as I wiped the back of my neck. Ahead, the lobby was large with folding doors on either side, fully opened. There was no AC pumping through the open-air corridors here. Just the ocean breeze. And shit, it was sweltering.

The crowds made it hotter. The staff was inundated, even more so than yesterday, with three long lines stacked with annoyed or visibly upset people. The manager who'd tried to assist me was up front, hurrying between four front desk staff talking to customers and typing away on computers and two with their backs to the lines, on the phone.

He finished with a couple, gesturing toward the hall, where many others were waiting slumped against walls, pacing, or taking up every seat possible. Some singles, most couples or families. He looked up as he gulped from his thermos, eyes landing on mine as I stood near the long front desk, beside the lines, trying to figure out if there was a difference and which line I was supposed to get into.

"Ah!" He raised his hand and waved me over.

The manager was at the line closest to me. He was able to sidestep and allow someone else to seamlessly take over.

And here, I thought *I'd* been sweating. His round face was flushed, pink, and dotted with sweat beads. I hoped whatever he was drinking was ice-cold.

I ignored the scathing looks from those in line and said, "Thanks. You guys are slammed. The system error must've really screwed things over."

"Yeah," he said, out of breath. Maybe he was helping me to get a breather. Irate vacationers and system glitches were two of the many reasons I could never work in the hospitality industry.

"Is there an update on that suite you said might be available tonight?"

He scrolled through his tablet, swiping away sweat, muttering under his tongue as conversations got louder and phones rang. The staff were unable to keep up, and this was hard to watch. I honestly felt horrible. Had I been lead dev or PM on their reservation website, no such error would've happened under my watch. I would've seen a bug like this from a mile away. Okay, well not a mile away. Pretty close up and over many hours of test runs, but the point was, I couldn't imagine this happening on one of my projects. If it did, my entire team and I would be working around the clock to fix this. Surely a worldwide hotel chain as massive as this one had hundreds of people working on their sites. Surely they'd have fixed the problem by now. Woken up their top devs in the middle of the night. Said devs hustling to track and adjust.

But they had not, apparent by the level of raging tourist fumes. Many scrolled through phones or were on calls trying to find something. Tension thickened the air; grumbles were getting harsher.

Some were outright speaking loud enough for everyone to hear. "This is ridiculous. Been waiting in line for twenty minutes. I have reservations. Hawaii needs to get their act together."

"I've been waiting for an hour," another volleyed, as if out to win a game of who'd been angrier longer. He was with his family along a wall and his teenaged kids seemed severely disinterested.

And there it came. "Let me talk to the manager. I demand a manager. I don't want to talk to you!"

The manager in front of me side-eyed the customer, who was yelling at a short woman behind the counter, her face red.

"You don't need to yell," I told her, my voice rising over the commotion.

She glared at me. "Are *you* the manager? If not, mind your business."

"I'm speaking with the manager right now, so you'll have to wait.

No need to yell at staff who are obviously trying their best to fix problems they're not at fault for."

She huffed and glared at the manager in front of me. He plastered on a tourism smile, adding, "I'll be right with you."

Her hard stare swept back to me. "I was here first. He just walked over to you. I saw that!"

I replied, "Because I've been waiting since yesterday. Politely. How long have *you* been waiting?"

She grumbled her time in minutes. Not an entire-ass day.

I spoke to the staff, who had their heads down trying to find solutions on their computers. "Thank you for your help with this computer glitch that probably occurred on the umbrella website handled by someone on the mainland and had nothing to do with you."

I'd hate to work in tourism with so many entitled people who expected their vacations to be perfect while being completely unforgiving to staff. I appreciated my behind-the-scenes work even more, no matter the lack of upending excitement.

A younger woman walked through the lobby, parting the crowds with an authoritative presence, her dark hair pulled back into a bun. She wore a sleeveless white blouse, black slacks that ended a few inches above her ankles, and high heels. A woman in charge who immediately took charge, armed with a tablet to her chest and a formidable voice.

"Please don't yell at my staff, ma'am," she asserted to the customer. "We are trying our best to resolve the situation main servers created during an already hectic time of the year for the annual Ironman competition. I'd be happy to help you while the manager is helping another valued guest."

The woman scoffed. "I want the manager."

"I'm *his* manager," she replied.

"Then bring me your manager. I don't want to talk to you."

"But you wanted to speak with him?"

"I said bring me your manager! Ugh! This is asinine."

The woman with the tablet turned stoic and replied in a flat tone, "Here I am. You're not going to get someone above me unless you go to Oahu or the mainland. I'll try my best to help, but let me be clear: Please do not yell at me or my staff or you will be escorted off the premises."

"How *dare* you."

"Yes, how dare I. Now, may I offer you some refreshments while we work out your issue, or should I move on to the next valued guest waiting in line?"

"*Valued* guest!" She fumbled for the phone to record the manager of managers, who promptly snatched the device and said, "Security it is."

And the next thing we knew, security was escorting this woman off the property. Everyone else suddenly found the patience they demanded of others. The lines not only quieted but moved faster.

The woman swiftly helped break down the line while the manager and staff cast grateful glances. She looked a bit like Bane, had that commanding presence when she spoke, but more put-together.

"Sir," the manager said, drawing my attention back to him. "We still don't have any rooms. I'm terribly sorry."

"It's okay," I reassured him, feeling worse and worse for what the staff had to endure. "I'm here with others and able to stay with them."

"Oh, thank goodness. We will call you as soon as we have a cleared room. You're at the top of my list. And a full refund for the nights you were unable to get, plus complimentary meals and drinks."

"That's generous. Thank you. By the way, so I know how much to give my friend. How much is a villa per night?"

"Oh, you mean at our sister Homestead location?"

"Yes."

"Do you know what size?"

"Not sure. It was originally for two siblings."

"The smallest we have is eighteen hundred a night."

If I'd been drinking anything, I would've spat it out. I ran a hand over the back of my neck. "Shit. That's, wow, a lot."

He nodded. "Ocean views, sprawling yard with lanai and privacy, amazing amenities."

I let out a breath. "Okay. Thanks. Looking forward to that call, though."

I didn't think Bane went all out with vacations. *I* sure as hell didn't. Maybe we could work out a payment plan?

There was still some time before the group headed to our second excursion for the trip: a coffee farm in Kona. One of the many places that made the expensive-ass coffee we'd drunk this morning, which was admittedly good. On the slopes of lava rock–rich soil, we'd tour through the growing of coffee beans, FAQs, and roast and grind our own small batch. It was something April really wanted to do as part of our wedding party gift. She even had coffee labels made, complete with the couple's picture and wedding date, to mark the experience.

It wouldn't hurt to sit outside, in the shade, and enjoy a drink. Anything icy to cool off, but especially water. There were varying levels to this location, the largest building of three in a giant U-shape. Aside from convenience stores, gift and clothing shops, spas and gyms, there were several indoor and outdoor restaurants, bars, and lounges. The one farthest from these angry guest lines was past the gardens, almost to the pool, but not quite reaching the beaches.

I'd just grabbed an icy water and lemonade and wandered around looking for prime seating to catch shade, breeze, and isolation from others, when I spotted April waving me over to a cabana. I lifted my glasses in acknowledgment and walked past the pool, to the side, and wondered how the hell she'd spotted me from this distance.

Her cabana was on a bed of small black lava rocks and chunks of white rocks that might've been dead coral, fully covered, somewhat private and quiet, and attended to by spa and eatery staff.

I was betting that Maya and Sejal had sprung for this, since they were also here, appearing from around the corner of the open-sided tentlike cabana, lying face down on massage tables with the ocean shimmering in afternoon light in front of them.

"Come sit with us!" April suggested.

"No. This looks like bridesmaids time."

"Nonsense! We're almost done anyway. Have to get ready for the coffee tour soon. Two drinks?" She looked past me. "Is your mystery girlfriend around?"

"Oh!" Maya shouted from her position on the massage table. I had thought she was asleep. "I want to meet her!" She blindly flapped one arm at us, her head turned from us.

This would've been an excellent time to tell them the truth. While holding two drinks and explaining: *They're both for me, and that woman who claimed to be my girlfriend? Yeah, just a coworker who was annoyed with Sejal and wanted her to STFU.*

The truth would set me free. I wasn't a liar, had never been good at it. One lie created two, then three, then the next thing I knew, I was caught in a web of lies and had to follow each string to remember what I'd said before. Lying was exhausting when layers and details were involved. And the longer this lie went on, the more humiliating and hurtful it would be when the truth came out.

Besides, the truth would also set me free from Bane. She'd been pretty pissed when I left this morning. Being around Bane was bad enough, but being stuck with an angry Bane was far worse.

"Yeah . . . where is this mysterious girlfriend?" Sejal asked as she sat up from her massage, her adept scrutiny once again probing.

I'd wanted to end things quietly, although I'd been equally hurt. She didn't want to go quietly. Even now, she was obviously goading me into a corner, insinuating Bane was a myth, a lie. And sure, Bane was, but Sejal didn't have to call me out like this in front of everyone. The thing about my ex was that she could be kind and loving and the best person when she was on your side. She wasn't on my side, though. A broken heart and resentment meant that we could never truly be civil. I wasn't going to fight back. I never had and never would. We were over. She'd walked away from me, and I'd let her because she was right. I wasn't what she wanted, no matter how hard I'd tried.

She wanted me to argue. She'd even claimed that my lack of fighting meant I didn't care. I didn't understand her logic, but others seemed to agree. If you love someone, you fight to keep them. But . . . if they loved me, they wouldn't make me fight. Not like this. Not bickering and public arguments and pitting friends against me.

If Sejal had wanted to move elsewhere, I would've moved with her.

If she was having second thoughts about my commitment, I would've proven myself to her.

If she thought we didn't communicate well enough, I would fix the problem.

She wanted me to be more romantic, more doting, more public displays of affection. I tried to do all of those things, as unnatural and foreign to me as they were.

I fought for her in different ways, but she only saw that I didn't argue with her at the end.

Even now, she glared at me with a sweep of her eyes like she probably had known the truth all along.

"Where's your girlfriend? Or was that not really her?" she asked.

"Back at the room." Damn. Hadn't meant to carry the lie further, especially with such ease. Absolutely not the way I intended my confession to go, but maybe it was best to confess to my friends first, instead of my ex.

"Why haven't you ever talked about her? Shown her off? Brought her around? Let me see a picture of you two together. Or do you not have one?" Sejal asked casually, as if her intentions weren't laced with malice to undo my claim. "I wished that was one thing you'd done with me. Or really, another thing. It's like your girlfriends don't mean anything or stay on your mind long enough to mention them to others."

Tension erupted between us in the fastest, hair-splitting second imaginable. If she'd meant to claw into my skin and burrow so deep that I felt her presence eroding me from the inside out, then she'd wildly succeeded.

"Like how you seem to love mentioning me and all my faults to everyone and their auntie?"

"Damn . . ." Maya muttered.

Sejal spat, "It's just that I think you're lying about this whole girl-friend thing."

"And if I was, why the hell do you care?"

"I've only ever tried to better you."

"Have you, though? Like a pet project?" I asked calmly. "I'm sure April doesn't want this tension. Please save all that hate for after the wedding."

April sighed, her shoulders deflating. "Can you guys be nice? Se-riously, Sejal. How could you accuse Sunny of making up a girl-friend? You met her, the guys have met her. Besides, Sunny would *never* lie."

Oh, damn. April's glowing review of my morality wasn't going to make this any easier.

April went on, "We'll meet her soon." She looked to me and said, "The guys love her, by the way! I'm so excited to meet her, to hug her, to welcome her into our group!"

She squealed. Her perception of my ethics and her unfiltered ex-citement over this surprise guest twist put my resolve in a vise.

"What's got you so pale?" Sejal asked drolly.

"She doesn't like physical contact with strangers, so I'd chill on the hugs." Damnit, why was my mouth talking? Hadn't it gotten the memo from my brain?

"Oh, that's right!" April touched my arm, which had turned numb by now still holding two icy drinks. I couldn't feel my hands. "The guys said that. Fist bump, right?"

"If you must touch her, maybe."

"I'll be sure to ask first. We all look forward to meeting your new flame," April added in a singsong voice.

"Oh! Fantastic idea!" she went on with a clap of her hands, which meant her enthusiasm was getting the better of her. I braced for whatever she was about to say. "Bring her to the coffee tour."

"No." What excuse did I have? Ah! "She's spending time with her sister."

"Oh? Not taking advantage of a romantic getaway? She's really here for her sister, isn't she?" Sejal asked slyly.

"Her sister lives here," I stated. "Her plans included her usual visit here, and the wedding happening at the same time and location is a mere coincidence."

By now, Maya had finished her massage and sat up, taking a drink. Which reminded me that I should probably drink my own beverages before they turned tepid and unfulfilling, much like this conversation.

"Please bring her," April insisted.

"Or tell us where your room is so we can see her," Maya added. "I'm on edge wondering who in the world tamed you."

"No one tamed anyone," I assured her.

Before I knew it, the girls had convinced me to bring Bane or suffer their endless inquiries. "I'm sure she's busy," I said, desperate to avert.

"Call her right now," April said, hands on hips, that defiant boss look on her face. "Don't make the bride ask twice."

Crap.

"Yeah, Sunny. Call this mystery girlfriend," Sejal prodded.

April shot her a warning look. "Don't mind Sejal. She'll keep it cool, right, Sejal? Because no one wants a stressed-out bride."

Sejal nodded, turning away. April went to her side, muttering, "*What* has gotten into you? You're not jealous, are you?"

April was trying to mumble, but sound carried differently out here. I caught the question and Sejal's shocked expression. As if she'd gotten called out in the ugliest way. She couldn't possibly be jealous.

Jilted? Not likely. Annoyed? Pragmatically so.

ELEVEN

Bhanu

Since stalking unmoving kanban cards in Asana and sluggishly altered movements in Jira had been driving me nuts, I'd taken up walking along the beaches armed with my water bottle, shades, floppy hat, the highest mineral SPF sunscreen allowed that wouldn't kill the coral reefs, and this book. It was as bright as the day itself, and almost as hot. Diya, and all those social media readers, weren't kidding.

I occasionally stopped when I found shade beneath trees to fan myself off and let the ocean spray cool my skin. Or when a dolphin jumped from the ocean far away. Or when a honu beached to get some rest and sun. I was sure to shoo off tourists disturbing any, but most people exercised common sense today.

At some point, I found an empty, shady spot to sit on porous black lava rocks that seemed to sparkle wherever the sun hit. I dipped my toes into the crystal-clear aquamarine water, and sighed, my muscles going slack. Okay, this was *nice*. Tons of space from others, breathtaking sights of a vast ocean, palm trees to my back, little yellow fish darting around my feet, cold water lapping at my calves, a refreshing breeze, and peaceful solitude.

Quiet was the key to recharging. I was the first to admit that turning my brain off was the hardest thing to do these days. With my phone a protruding rectangular block in my cross-body purse, the temptation to check on work, calls, or texts was ever-looming. And let's not even think about interview callbacks. On the one hand, I was doing what Gabrielle had nearly begged me to do, which was minding my own nonwork business while away. On the other hand, I was waiting for a text from Mr. Sunshine himself to tell me he'd found a room and would be out of my hair and I'd be off the hook as far as this mad deception went. He'd come clean to his friends. They'd serve a round of pity drinks and solemn pats on the back, or whatever men did to express sympathy with these sorts of things. Then they'd laugh it off and tell him he'd find a woman of his own one day, but honestly not as beautiful and charming as that bewitching Bhanu.

No such text came.

Should I text him? No, then he'd know he was taking up space in my head and never let me live it down. He'd do that mocking smirk thing he typically did and bring out the fact that I'd been thinking about him every time we'd get into an argument. Which was essentially every day at work.

Plus, if I dared check my phone, I'd see a few missed calls, video calls, or texts from my mother. Whom I adored with all my beating heart, but she was desperate to see her daughters marry and start families or whatever nonsense she thought needed to happen for us to feel fulfilled and happy. I loved her for making us the focal point of her efforts, and she wasn't nearly as theatrical, pushy, or obtuse as some horror stories I'd heard from others about their mothers.

Instead, my mom worked with calculated calls. She was working with Diya to get information, while simultaneously encouraging Diya to lock down her man to start having little brown babies.

I understood. She wanted us to be stable and not alone. But I was still ignoring her. There was a 100 percent chance she'd corner me into a call at least three times this visit through Diya.

For now, I dove into this book. It had actually succeeded in getting my mind off everything else, even the interview waiting game. As the sun moved across the sky, shifting the shade until there was no place left to scoot without being in the water, my phone rang.

It was Sunny, and I briefly considered disregarding him. Except he was calling and not texting, so maybe this was important?

"Hello?"

"Hey," he said in that deep baritone voice.

I shivered, not realizing how cold the ocean breeze could sometimes feel. Because it couldn't be him. "Yes?"

"First of all, I apologize for this morning. I shouldn't have said that."

"Oh," I replied on a breath. A simple apology completely dismantled any lingering anger I had toward him.

There were some voices in the background when Sunny begrudgingly admitted, "I'm going to put you on speaker. My friends are with me, and they're being extremely pushy that I call you so they can invite you to a . . . coffee tour with us."

I stared at the striped fish near my foot, mouthing, "What?" But like most fish, this one didn't have an answer.

Guessing by the lack of enthusiasm in his voice, he probably didn't want me to actually attend. I was certain he wasn't planning on continuing this ruse. Hadn't he said as much this morning before storming out?

Confused, I jerked my head back and studied the phone. Okay. This was really his number. "My sister probably has plans for us."

"Oh, Bhanu! Bride here!" a sweet voice crooned. "I'd love to meet you today! Just a short tour."

Another woman's voice pitched in to agree.

"Oh, well. I should really check with my sister," I found myself saying instead of, "Thanks so much, but my sister and I have plans."

"Please join. Our treat," the first woman—the bride—insisted.

"Let me get back to you?"

"Okay! Soon! We're dying to meet you!"

"Aw, thank you." She seemed sweet, and I felt awful having to lie to her face.

With that, Sunny was sighing into the phone. "So yeah. My friends are eager to meet you."

"What happened to . . ." My voice trailed off in case everyone could still hear.

"We're not on speaker anymore." Yet his voice was calm and muted, so his friends were probably nearby. "You don't have to come. Spend time with your sister."

"She has to come!" someone yelled in the background.

"Stop deterring her!" another voice called.

"Why don't you want her coming around?" This one was a familiar voice, although not the first two. "Was that woman at the hotel just making it up?"

Ah, the ex. Man, she was acute if she could tell we were lying right off the bat. Or maybe she was poking the bear?

"Can you stop?" Sunny was muttering to her, his voice heavy with irritation. In a second, I saw this woman ripping him apart for no reason. I didn't want that for anyone, much less an integral part of my team. Forget that our company might be depending on this project to launch us into the tech giant stratosphere, but I needed this project to launch my candidacy into the PM promotion more than anything.

"Hey," I told him, my voice gruffer than I'd meant. "When do we leave?"

There was a pause before he asked, "Are you sure? You don't have to."

"Stop telling her that!" the bride called out.

"No, listen, I got you into this and I'll see it through. Just don't pop a blood vessel."

He grunted, "Not at all wanting to see me struggle, huh?"

"I'm not a jerk, unlike some people."

"See? That mouth of yours is going to get you into trouble," he said, his Denzel voice rumbling like a deep bass vibrating my insides. Oh my god, what the hell was wrong with me?

I stared at my phone for a second. I hated these things.

"Get a room!" the second woman from earlier said.

"Oh my god," we muttered at the same time.

"I'll meet you at the villa in about half an hour?" he asked.

"Okay."

Then we hung up. There were no thanks exchanged. But since I'd started this mess, going on a free coffee tour seemed like the least I could do. And sure, the tendrils of anxiety stirred, but they would calm. They had to. This wasn't a last-minute party. I'd been to plenty of coffee farms. Besides, how bad could his friends be?

So back to the villa I went. Boy, the walk back seemed much longer than the stroll out. I'd finished my water a while ago and my mouth was parched. First mistake was going out without enough water. My skin started tingling right as I cut across the gardens and rounded the corner onto the main street, where large flowering trees created much-needed shade.

As soon as I walked through the door, I ran to the kitchen for water, gulping it down until my stomach turned sick.

"Calm down! You'll throw up!"

I yelped, turning to face Diya and Kimo entering from the lanai doors. I choked on the last drops of water, but not so badly that Diya expressed any concern.

"This heat . . ." I mumbled, then went to the couch and fell onto my back beneath the ceiling fan and the air-conditioned air, pulling my shirt to just under my breasts. "Sorry, Kimo. Best look away."

Kimo was probably not even looking at me, but Diya knelt beside the couch and blew on my face as if that actually helped. At least her breath smelled sweet.

"Did you have cookies?" I asked.

"Yes. Work gave us cookies as a thanks for helping out with the crap show the reservation website left us in. So, naturally, I grabbed a few for you. Your fave: white chocolate macnut, you basic bitch."

"I thought that only applied to my love of PSL and all things autumn."

"It's becoming a more inclusive umbrella term."

"Ah. Good to know. Also thanks!" I inhaled two cookies as soon as she handed them over. Sugar and lots of water, plus shade and cooler temps, alleviated the borderline heat exhaustion that'd been stalking toward me.

"So tell me about this guy," she said, chin in her hand like a kid asking for a bedtime story.

"No."

"Why not? And why did he sleep on the couch?"

"Because it's not like that."

"He looked cute."

"Were you watching him sleep?"

"Yes. While I ate granola. He was passed out like a baby."

I groaned, wiping sweat from my brow and realizing how badly I needed a shower.

"When's the last time you got some?"

"Diya!" I squeaked. Pointedly looking at Kimo, who was on the adjacent chair surfing the endless channels.

"What? I tell him everything. He already knows."

Kimo nodded and shrugged, as if saying, "True, and sorry, but what can I do?"

"Oh my god," I muttered with a shake of my head because little sisters sure thought they had liberty with everything.

"And our parents call me every day for an update."

I cringed. "On me getting some?"

"No! Ew. On you getting a man. Although I'm sure they know what that entails at some point."

"Everyone is in my sex life."

"Everyone except you because you ain't getting any. Bitch, you better make use of that 'there's only one bed for the both of us' situation. None of this couch business because he'll find out in the morning that I watch him sleep while eating breakfast."

"Wow. The language on this one," I said to Kimo because I couldn't handle Diya for another second.

He responded, "I'm sorry. She's been hanging around Keanu, and Keanu can't have a conversation without cursing."

"Aw. How *is* your sister? I didn't even ask. I'm so rude!"

He lit up. "Keanu's good. She has one more year at U of H over on Oahu. Keeping it local, even if she's off island, ya know?"

"I bet your parents miss her."

"They couldn't wait to get her out of the house because of her language," he replied, grinning.

I nodded. The few times I'd met Keanu, her sailor mouth had floored me. Having to watch her language in classes and study groups and in any sort of professional environment had probably helped curb that habit. Or it meant she'd been bottling it up and it exploded the moment she got back. Just a young, cute volcano spewing out profanity.

"Oh! I gotta shower." I hopped up and hurried to my room, almost forgetting about first impressions with the friends of my fake boyfriend.

After a quick douse, I opened the bathroom and bedroom doors and called out, "Hey! Diya! Something came up!"

Returning to the bathroom, I hurried to dab on a light layer of foundation and mascara, did my brows just a little, maybe lip gloss, and . . . did I need bronzer, highlighter, blush? No. I'd been in the sun long enough to have a glow by now.

"What are you doing?" Diya asked from the door, her arms crossed over her chest as she looked me up and down.

With a bobby pin in my mouth, I pulled my hair into a ponytail and said, "Remember that coworker who crashed here?"

"Yes. The *man*. Whom I need to meet, but go on."

"He's here for his best friend's wedding and they invited me to a coffee tour. I bet it's that place in Holualoa. Good for them for getting more visitors."

She smacked her lips, her gaze studying the low front of my tank top and my short shorts—by which I meant not knee-length gym shorts. "Looking kinda cute *and* putting on makeup?"

"Don't go there. Anyway, is it okay if I bail out for a bit and go with him? Also, he might need to crash another night or two. Guess he's one of the guests who had their reservations screwed up."

"Well, I'll make sure to hurry on *that* one," Diya jested with a wink. "Let me help. This is crooked. How about a low bun? Make you look like a classy, sexy woman in STEM begging for him to undo your hair while he talks dirty into your ear."

"Been reading too many rom-coms? Also, not sure if I should be offended that you just reduced my entire career to what could possibly be the beginning of a porno?"

"No! And it is a good idea for a rom-com. You know? I think I'll write a book one day. How hard can it be?"

"I'm sure it's easy and fast and will yield loads of cash and fame," I replied dryly.

"I think so, too."

There was a knock at the ajar bedroom door. Assuming it could only be Kimo, I replied, "Come in!"

It was not Kimo, but Sunny led by that Denzel voice that had

Diya pausing in mid–bobby pinning to swerve her head toward the bedroom. Just his voice. That was all it took.

"Hey, I'm a little early. You have time, don't worry. Just came by to say . . . can you please . . . um . . ."

"I'm not wearing sweats!" I yelled. What the hell was wrong with him? Was he seriously telling me to dress nicely for his friends? Well, shorts and a tank top were all they were getting.

"Damn," Diya muttered. "He sounds fine as hell. Voice certainly matching that face."

I rolled my eyes and pointed at my hair. She unrolled the bun and went for two French braids, saying, "Forget classy. You need to look more like, come hither and pull on these braids, Daddy, but still talk dirty because, damn, that voice."

"Shut up," I hissed.

Diya grinned at me through the reflection of the mirror, where my face was getting redder by the second.

"Thank god." He sounded as if he was going through his suitcase, sounds of lugging it out of the closet and the zipper opening.

"Why are you so obsessed with what I wear?"

"I always notice what you wear."

"*Obsessed*," Diya whispered. "*Yes*, Daddy."

Sunny went on, "I thought about what you said, and let's agree to two months? We've been dating for two months and it's nothing serious; that's why I didn't tell my friends."

Diya tugged on my braid as she worked, her eyes giant circles through the reflection as she mouthed, "*What?*"

Oh, no. This was not happening.

"Everything else is the same. Separate cities, work, keeping it discreet, and—" Sunny's last word ended abruptly as he came to the slightly open bathroom door, his eyes first landing on Diya, then on me. Then on my cleavage. Then down my legs. Everywhere his gaze swept left a rising fire. Probably sunburn, though. I needed to make sure I kept up with my sunscreen here.

"Oh. Sorry. I thought you were alone."

"No," I said flatly. "My sister, Diya. Diya, this is Sunny."

A flicker of recognition hit his features. "Ah. I think I saw you at the front desk earlier?"

"Yes," she said sweetly as she quickly finished my hair. "I'm the GM and was helping with our reservation glitch. So glad you could join us! I've heard nothing about you, but need to know everything." She hooked arms with his and led him away as he glanced back at me with so many unspoken questions.

"So you're the boyfriend, you said?" Diya was asking as I finished up and hurried after her.

Kimo was nowhere to be found; he'd probably headed out. Diya was practically fawning over Sunny as they sat on the couch.

"Boyfriend?" He curiously looked to me and all I could do was blankly blink.

"You just said you two were dating."

"Oh." He was still looking at me, silently asking if our ruse had spilled over to my family.

Of course not! I intervened with, "Diya. Don't get all excited for nothing. We're not—"

"Oh, look!" Diya squealed with her buzzing phone in hand. Before anyone could blink, she had our mother's face on the screen waving at me before turning the screen back to herself. "Mummie! What a surprise."

I nearly lunged for the phone, but not before Diya slipped away, telling our mother, "Did you know Motiben has a boyfriend?"

Mummie's shrieks of joy catapulted out of the phone. Diya had to lower the volume *and* hold the phone away from her.

Mortification enhanced by deep regret crashed into me like pounding waves. This must've been what Sunny felt when I opened my big mouth to his ex, who then told his friends, who now believed the same thing my sister and mother believed. Turned out, karma was real because what went around came around. By my own execution.

If I could go back in time, I'd tell that ex of his to watch her tone and be kind to my lead dev instead of: *Shut your face, he has a girlfriend, now everyone be quiet.*

"I just met him!" Diya was talking this entire time while I stood stunned into place.

"Let me see, let me see," Mummie insisted with unbridled joy.

There was no humanly possible speed at which I could block or snatch the phone before Diya flipped the screen toward Sunny so he could see my mother grinning like she was meeting her future son-in-law for the first time. The way she lit up, you'd think Sunny had just succeeded in giving her the first grandchild.

Crap.

"Oh. *So* handsome," she said.

I was speechless, even when Sunny glanced at me for some sort of indication to the direction of this entire thing.

His shock had worn off by now, and his face had returned to its usual stoic expression, which had somehow, at some point, slowly evolved into a charming look. He smiled, showing teeth . . . how had I never noticed those perfect teeth before? Oh, yes, because he didn't smile at me like that. Well, he had amazing teeth and an amazing smile that had Diya and Mummie silent. Silent! Did he know what sort of power he wielded? What great responsibility came with great charm?

Charm and Sunny weren't two things I'd ever associated before, but they paired seamlessly when he not only generously conversed with Mummie, answering the beginning of what was sure to be a long line of biodata inquiries to be followed by his family, religious and cultural background, how often he prayed, if he had a house and where, the number of children he planned on siring, and his blood type. And he did so . . . in Gujarati . . . in that Denzel voice.

Every ovary in my body was popping, every excited hope in my sister went off, and every prayer my mother had ever uttered was being answered.

Damnit.

Diya gave me a look that pretty much said, "You better lock him down with a ring. Don't wait for him to propose!" Plus a hefty dose of, "Damn, sis. *Get. It.*"

Sunny's Gujarati was fluid and far better than my, what we called, village Gujarati. I sounded uneducated and from the poorest villages when I tried to speak my parents' language because, well, our family was from a poor village. He leaned in on his elbows, hands clasped, giving in to the auntie whims my mother was throwing at him, and *laughed*.

Something warm spread through me, seeping into my gut and deeper into my bones. I had to shut that down quickly because this wasn't real and I would have to deal with the aftermath later.

Finally stumbling out of my stupor, I grabbed Sunny's hand and yanked him away. I pushed against his back as Diya and her phone followed me, Mummie scowling and crying, "Ay! Where are you going?"

"We have time-sensitive plans!"

"Prevent the mossing!"

"Talk to you later! Bye!"

I didn't release Sunny until we were speed-walking halfway down the street. I was still tugging him behind me. He was actually chuckling.

"This isn't funny!" I belted.

He laughed so hard that his eyes squinted up and the sun glinted off his canines. "What goes around!"

Sexy canines? *What* was happening?

I had to stop staring at his mouth, but there was so much goodness to behold. He could absolutely destroy entire worlds with that smile.

"What does she mean by 'mossing'?" he managed to ask in between all that amused chortling.

"She thinks I need to move forward in life at a faster pace or my stagnation will lead into me devolving into moss."

When Sunny found his composure, he nudged my shoulder with his and said, "I guess we're both in it now?"

"I had no idea what to say," I confessed, my face too warm to be considered healthy.

"You froze. With a deer-in-the-headlights look. I've never seen you like that."

I groaned as I texted Diya to calm down. I'd typed out that we weren't dating, and this was all a misunderstanding, but then she replied with a: Guess I won't have to bug you to get out during your stay and Mummie will leave you alone. At least until you get home.

Hmm. Maybe this wasn't a total disaster? I'd explain to them later and add that their current and previous prodding and pushing me into being more extroverted and finding a man had led me to this falsehood. Yes. Sounded like a great plan, which started with no one breathing down my neck for once.

Fine. Ruse extended.

TWELVE

Sunny

While we walked toward the meeting point, I checked my phone for any sort of update from my sisters, just in case something had happened between now and the last time I'd checked in. Their updates were enough to ease my worries and be in the moment. A moment that involved Bane standing beside me at the front courtyard water fountain waiting for the others to come down.

"Your sister and mother seem nice," I commented, meaning to be sincere, but somehow, the words came out as a filler to cut through the silence.

"Thanks. They are."

More silence.

Bane's shoulder deflated as she turned to me. "Okay. We need to get some things straight if your friends are going to believe this. My family desperately wants to believe that I have a boyfriend, but your friends are probably more intuitive. Especially when we look like strangers together."

I pulled my hands out of my pockets. "Better?"

Her brows went up. "Should I call one of my lovers to show you how it's done?"

Something rancid nipped at my gut. The idea of Bane having other guys on her was . . . nah . . . it couldn't be jealousy. It had to be disdain. "How many do you have again?"

"Not important. Just play the part. You need them off your back and I just want some peace. But also, this is a little fun, showcasing some acting skills."

"If you say so."

"I think you like messing with people, too."

"I've given no indication to lead to such an assessment."

"You were so wonderful with my family."

"I'm not an ass, Bane. I'm a decent guy."

"Are you sure?" She poked my chest. "Because you've fooled me."

I took her hand so that her little pointy finger was still against my shirt. "You obviously don't understand people."

She leaned into me, her eyelashes thick and dark and her skin bright with a sun-enhanced glow. Had she always looked this nice, or was this the effects of the Hawaiian sky? "I know people better than you."

"You talk. I observe."

She took her hand back. "Okay, Mr. Observant. What do you call me?"

"Bane."

She hit my arm. "No. A sweet nickname befitting a girlfriend. You cannot call me Bane. What the hell? Also, you shouldn't call me that anyway."

"Babe?"

She furrowed her brows, studying me like she knew this was a word that I would obviously never use. "Is that what you called your exes?"

"I called them by their names."

"No term of endearment?"

"Not really. They have names for a reason."

"*Babe* sounds juvenile, silly even. It reminds me of Barbie, for some reason."

"You're the one who called me babe earlier," I reminded.

"I clearly wasn't thinking," she retorted.

"You set a precedent."

"No," she grunted.

"What should I call you? What have your exes called you?"

"Sweetie. Sweetness. Sugar. Pumpkin."

"So . . . food."

"I guess so."

"You must be edible."

Her cheeks flushed, and mine probably did, too. Wasn't sure why, or how, those words came out of my mouth. And now we were staring at each other again. Like idiots. Like anything other than a couple. I lost in this game of awkward chicken, my gaze flitting away and down, catching a glimpse of her low tank top. I swallowed, my eyes dropping lower to a pair of nice legs. She was toned, like maybe she jogged. Was that why she was always in joggers?

"So—why pumpkin?" I asked, not understanding why I insisted on knowing more. "Sounds like something a parent would call their kid."

"Because I love fall and pumpkins."

I groaned. "Don't tell me you're one of those girls who lives for PSL season."

"I'm that basic white girl everyone jokes about." She beamed. "I'm not ashamed."

"Ah, to be that confident."

"Big PSL energy the same way I bring big UX energy. Okay. I guess just call me by my name? My actual name. Can you do that? Or is that too much acting for you?"

I pinched the bridge of my nose. "Bhanu. Bhanu. Bhanu."

"Sunny!" Sam called from behind me. He had an arm wrapped around April's shoulders.

The second April's eyes landed on Bane, her entire face lit up. She even did a jump while clapping her hands once. Hurrying over, she nearly tackled Bane before she suddenly paused and extended a fist. "So wonderful to finally meet you!"

Bane looked utterly confused, and a little adorable, as she blinked at April before granting her a fist bump.

"I told her you aren't comfortable with physical contact," I explained. "This is April, the bride."

"Oh! So lovely to meet you!" Bane replied, her entire demeanor a personified rainbow, all glamour and color. She looked so normal when she talked with others. Maybe she just had a thing against me? Maybe I'd find out by the end of this trip so we could be civil toward each other upon return.

"So nice to see you again, Sam," she said to the groom, who didn't try to physically greet her this time.

Before we knew it, the rest of the group had arrived, and April and Maya had gathered around Bane. I didn't catch most of their conversation, but snippets led me to believe that they loved her hair and top . . . the very attractive top that made even Bane look sexy.

Sam and Aamar went to retrieve the cars, leaving Sejal and Pradeep off to the side by themselves, although one could tell that he wanted to talk to me. Sejal kept a grip on his arm and eyed me, then eyed Bane, who seemed wonderfully oblivious.

"Pradeep. Sejal," I said.

"Hey, man! How's it going?" Pradeep asked, moving away from Sejal's hold. Poor guy. He seemed nice, and Sejal was probably going to ruin this trip for him because of me.

In a matter of minutes, the guys brought the cars around.

"Bhanu's with us!" April declared, leading her to the "bride's car" with Maya driving. Seemed that April aimed to sit in the back with a blatantly annoyed Sejal.

April gave Sejal a warning look, but Bane must've noticed. She frowned at me, like I was throwing her into the lion's den.

"We'll go together," I said, wrapping an arm around Bane's waist in a weird tug-of-war with April hooking arms with her.

"Nonsense. It's a short drive. It's fine," April insisted.

"April . . ." I said, looking her dead in the eye, and she knew exactly what I meant.

"Oh, right." She released Bane. "Sorry! I just love getting to know new people, but we have plenty of time for that! I didn't mean to touch your arm without your consent." Nice save. Except I'd touched Bane without her consent, but now she was nestled into my side of her own will.

"That's okay. I appreciate the welcome," Bane said with a generous tone.

We filed into our cars, and since we were part of the "groom's side," we now had one extra person. But the car was big enough for us.

"I'll sit in the middle," Bane offered.

"No, that's okay."

"You really want to sit with your legs squished in the middle car thing? It's fine."

No, what I really wanted was for her not to be sitting next to Pradeep. While he seemed like a nice person, I didn't know him. But Bane was already scooting into the car.

Once in, we kept our hands to ourselves as the guys asked Bane all about her work and where she was from.

I let the conversation go for as long as Bane seemed comfortable. She gave vivid, energetic answers but never delved into many details. I clenched my fists in my lap as I watched Pradeep's widespread knees inch closer and closer to Bane's bare legs with every turn and bump, until his knee touched her.

I gritted my teeth and she tensed. I looked at him, my lips parting to tell him to move the hell away, when she scooted closer to me and politely told him, "Oh, do you mind?"

"Ah! Sorry about that."

"Thanks." She was much sweeter and nicer than I would've been.

Pradeep didn't look at me. He kept his usual friendly smile on his face and paid attention to the information Sam and Aamar were throwing at us about the coffee farm.

With our thighs and arms smooshed together, I muttered in Bane's ear, "Are you comfortable?"

"Yes, why?" she whispered back.

"We're touching?"

"I don't mind."

I tried to make myself smaller, but that was impossible in this car. "I'm sorry. I didn't think about the cramped seats."

She looked up at me, her face extremely close, her smell and warmth consuming. She gave a reassuring smile. "I know you. It's fine."

"Okay." I would make sure we went in couples next time because Bane didn't need to subject herself to this.

She also didn't need me staring at her mouth like I'd never seen one before. Her lips twitched and I swallowed hard, dragging my gaze away and catching Aamar watching me from the rearview mirror with an amused smile.

Shit. But I supposed the game here was to convince my friends we were dating.

When we'd finally arrived and parked at a small parking lot adjacent to the farm, I couldn't get out of the car fast enough, pulling Bane out after me. I kept glancing at her, searching her face for clues of discomfort. But she seemed to be fine, just as she'd said. If there was one thing I knew about Bane, it was that she spoke her mind. She'd tell me.

We spent the next half hour learning about the coffee planting, picking, cleaning, drying, parchment peeling, and roasting processes. Then we roasted our own beans in little roasters, where April giddily slapped on a label with the wedding date, names, and picture.

Then we stood at the top of a sloping hill covered in coffee plants. Bane and I stood off a short distance while the others, in pairs, took pictures and videos.

"Thanks for coming," I began to tell her.

"Since it's my fault? Yeah, yeah."

"Yes, but I was going to say even though you had to be touched in a car."

"Sounds much worse than it was. It's okay."

"I'll make sure it doesn't happen again. We'll go in couples from now on; otherwise you don't need to come."

She pouted. "Don't break up the bride and groom cars."

"You'll either be touched or in the bride's car without me."

"I'm a big girl. I'm sure I can handle myself."

"Or we can Uber."

"No. Hang out with your friends. I do not mean to take you from them."

I wasn't expecting her consideration. In fact, she hadn't complained once.

"Shame you guys didn't come around February or March," she said, looking down the slopes of endless rows of short coffee trees.

"Why? Less people? More available rooms?"

"Yes, but the Kona snow."

"Snow?"

"All the coffee plants flower these tiny white blooms, and it looks like the plants are covered in a dusting of snow."

"Ah. Sounds pretty."

"Your friends are watching."

I hesitated to look over my shoulder.

"Don't tense up. Are you always this weird with your girlfriends?"

"I'm a grown-ass man who doesn't know how to do this."

"Lower your voice." Bane smiled, twisting back and forth at the hip, taking the hem of my T-shirt and tugging.

Something rumbled in my gut. "What are you doing?"

"We're supposed to look cute," she muttered. "Mr. Grown-Ass Man is going to blow his cover if they hear you. You have to make it look believable when all eyes are on you."

"Ah. They're still watching?"

"Not at all inconspicuously."

I tensed anyway. They probably all knew the truth and were exchanging expressions of sadness over my pitiful life. "So what should I do?"

"What do you mean?"

"To make this look believable." I gestured with my hand, indicating the air in front of us as if it had to create the bulk of our illusion.

She shrugged. "How should I know?"

"You seem like you'd know."

"What is that supposed to mean?"

I shrugged. "Don't you know? What do you do when you date?"

"The better question is what do *you* do when you date?" She pressed a hand against my stomach. My stomach automatically clenched at the touch. What the hell was happening to me?

"Um. Maybe this?"

Bane kept her hand right where it was and looked up into my eyes. She said, "You're in capable hands. If anything, we'll just look like a bickering, awkward couple. And one of us is definitely awkward."

"And one of us definitely bickers."

There she went jabbing a finger into my chest. "You're both, you know? A bickering, awkward dev."

I took her hand, dropping it to our sides. "Yeah, yeah."

We ended up walking on a dangerously narrow pathway alongside the road to a café up ahead. This wasn't a sidewalk at all, evident by the lack of cement, but Sam and April wanted to try this place that made lattes with coffee grown from this farm. So we went.

We ordered in pairs, which quickly turned into the theme of this trip. I didn't know what I wanted except something local. A quick decision. No one thought this hard on a coffee order. So lavender and macadamia nut it was.

It was a small place and Bane and I took our drinks outside.

"Don't you want to spend time with your friends?" she asked.

"It's crowded in there." There was barely enough room for Sejal's glares.

"Thanks for the coffee," she replied with an appreciative smile, which fell flat as soon as we were outside, at a small metal table for two. Because from the corner of my peripheral vision, Bane's little expression of confusion turned to realization, and was promptly followed by her signature smugness.

"Don't start," I warned her.

"Did you just get lavender coffee?"

"Don't even say it."

"Sunshine and flowers *do* go together." She laughed in that devious way of hers, chin turned down, eyes raised to lock gazes dead on like a slightly aggressive way of saying: *Behold my outright amusement at your expense.*

"Yes. I like fruity, floral things. Get the jokes out of your system."

Bane simply smiled. "It's freaking cute."

"Matches my personality perfectly, doesn't it?" I asked drolly.

She leaned across the corner of the table and tugged on my sleeve. "You must think it's somewhat adorable of your parents to name you Sunny because you have a little, teeny smile there."

"I absolutely do not."

She tapped my lips. "Boop. Must be a muscle twitch, then."

For some reason beyond any sound logic, I found myself wanting to lick my lips where her touch left prickling specks of embers. Instead, because that would send the worst signal, I watched the door just behind her.

"My name means 'sunny,' you know?" she was saying while the breeze swept through her hair, sending her floral scent crashing into my skin. That was why I always smelled her when she was around, even before I saw her. Bane smelled like flowers. Gardenias, to be exact.

She readjusted some loose strands, tucking them back into her braids. I never thought anything of braids on a woman, but she made them attractive. I focused harder on the building, on the screen portion of the withered old door, willing Sam or April to come out and break this tension rising in my stomach.

Bane was still gabbing away about her aunt naming her and then asked, "Did your parents name you, or . . ."

My brow quirked up. "Who else would name me?"

She deadpanned. "A relative? A guru? An astrologist?"

"My mom named me. All by herself."

Bane stared at me, not quite in the eye but somewhere near the vicinity.

"What?" I scowled as she smirked.

"I just want to iron out that little wrinkle between your brows."

"There's no wrinkle there. My face is as smooth as a baby's butt."

Bane took another sip, the half-melted ice sloshing around. "Did she have high hopes for your personality?"

"Watch it, Bane," I replied with a hint of appreciation because that was pretty good. I had to hand it to her when it came to her jabs, delivered with accuracy and just the right mix of expression and tone.

"What? No smart-ass comeback?"

"If I had one, I would've already given it."

"True." She studied my face like she was reading code. "Dark. Brooding. Sure. It makes sense. Your mother must've seen it on your face the moment she laid eyes on you."

"I was an adorable baby, the sunshine of her life. I don't mind the name."

"Because Sunny is pleasant. Unlike Bane."

"Since Bhanu means 'sunny,' we can't have two Sunnys, can we?"

"You're right. That's too much sunshine in the world."

"I'm essentially saving the world from combusting from all this heat. You're welcome, world."

She rolled her eyes, but she'd never admit that my nickname for her bothered her, even a little. Or was in any way annoying. "As perplexing as you are, you're a grump named sunshine. Ha! Get it!" She cackled.

"Smart-ass to the end. That wasn't even funny."

"Then why are you smiling?"

"You must have that word confused with 'unimpressed.'"

She looked up from over the rim of her cup, her thick lashes fluttering. She didn't have a comeback but held my gaze. And . . . well, maybe her face wasn't hard to look at. All right, it was pretty easy, like the flash of a spectrum of colors with the movement of indented lines when scrolling through perfectly written code. Mesmerizing. Satisfying to watch.

What . . . the hell was I thinking? And why was I staring?

Bane blew out a breath. "So impassive. Do you even have emotions? Better yet, do you even know what emotions are?"

Ah, excellent. My stoicism was finally working in my favor. She couldn't tell I was admiring those thick, dark lashes framing rich brown eyes, the sparkle of her nose stud on her petite nose, or those full lips stained with pink. Lips that puckered every time she took a sip.

Strange. When Sejal accused me of being robotic, it was a verbal stab, a brawl, a call to arms that both angered and ridiculed. When Bane said it, it was just her jesting, a way for us to keep volleying quips. And I didn't mind it one binary byte.

THIRTEEN

Bhanu

Sunny and I parted ways after we'd returned. His friends had been very nice and welcoming, and it was different to see him relaxed. But there had been thinly veiled animosity with his ex, which led me to needing to know what had transpired between them.

No! No! Don't fall into the drama trap! Or break any of the rules of this arrangement.

On the car ride to the farm, Sunny had taken me away from the bride's group and it was a no-brainer to know why. He didn't want our ruse to fall apart. But I'd joined the ladies on the way back, and it had been fine. Sunny had insisted to no end to go couples or Uber, but I'd somehow managed to talk him down off his weird ledge. The deception wouldn't fall apart, and I'd had a nice time.

Maya sat in the back seat with me, Sejal drove, and April navigated the conversation from up front. Every time they aimed to get more details about me, my life, or my relationship with Sunny, I expertly maneuvered back to them. I honestly wanted to know more about them. My energy may have been drained being around strangers, no matter how much effort I put into my pulled-back shoulders and smile, but people were fascinating. Which helped keep my anxiety at bay; no sudden need to hide in another room, no socially overstimulated brain shutting down, no withering posture wishing to fade away. Sunny's friends had made me feel as comfortable as being one of their own.

For example, April kicked ass in a field dominated by men. She was a manager, didn't take any crap, and made a point to wear some shade of pink and/or shimmer daily. Aside from pink being her favorite color, she loved to see how uncomfortable it made some men in STEM.

Maya was Gujarati, just like Aamar, Sunny, and myself. She spoke seven languages that she'd learned just because, and had a map of the world with a hundred pushpins indicating where she'd been. Her goal was to reach every continent, including Antarctica (apparently tourists were allowed during the summer months, most likely staying put on a boat), and as many countries as possible. The idea of traveling exhausted me, but it brought her to life.

Sejal was . . . not interested in talking. Which made me want to know even more!

Aside from the standishoffish vibes from her, surely it must've been strange for her to be in the same car with her ex's current girlfriend, but sis had nothing to worry about. In fact, if she wanted Sunny back and he wanted her, I'd be all for it. I sort of wanted to tell her that.

Honey, if he's the love of your life and you want him back, take your shot.

But that wasn't my business. Even though I would help them.

Once we'd returned to the hotel, the groups went their separate ways. More bonding time for friends, which was great. Being around strangers who wanted to know everything about me had depleted all my energy. I was tuckered out.

I returned, alone, to the villa for a quick nap, only to be awakened by Diya jumping into bed with me.

"Ugh. What time is it?" I groaned, prying open my eyes.

"Almost six, Sleeping Beauty."

"The original *Sleeping Beauty* has horrific underlying tones of assault."

"Don't sour the mood when you know what I'm here for."

"To feed me?"

Diya tapped my belly and I flinched with a giggle. "Surely your man fed you while you were out."

"Just coffee."

"Nah. He needs to do better than that. Can't ever let your loved ones be in want of food."

"No one said anything about love."

She snuggled up against my side. "Maybe not yet."

Pangs of guilt plucked away at my conscience. I should probably tell her the truth before she created some fanciful future for us. I didn't want her upset with me later on, much less disappointed.

"Are you going to have a big fat Indian wedding?"

And . . . there it was.

"Because I need to know ahead of time to get outfits. I haven't been to an Indian wedding in years. I miss getting extra, not to mention the food. Kimo doesn't want an elaborate wedding, and neither do I. Sounds stressful to plan one."

"Wait." I turned my head toward her, bumping my chin against her forehead and rubbing her head with an apology. "You and Kimo are discussing marriage?"

"We've had chats. Nothing saying we're ready for the next step, and who knows? Maybe the next step for us is to move in together."

"Oof. Don't tell the parents that. Speaking of parents, don't get them all excited about Sunny. You don't get excited, either. Trust me."

"Too late. Trust *me*. And what do you mean? You sound like nothing will ever come out of this."

"We're . . . newish."

"Well, if he has any common sense, he'll put a ring on that finger and a baby in that uterus."

"Oh, hell no. No kids. And engagement is the furthest thing from my mind. I'm just not interested. I'm good where I'm at."

"Same."

"Solidarity, my sister, against the parents' wishes for us to be *moving forward* before we're too old."

Diya sat up, running her fingers through my hair, the braids having been undone before I crashed. "Speaking of family, is it cool if Kimo's comes over for dinner?"

"I would never say no!"

"That's because his mom cooked for you."

I laughed. "Among other things. I adore them, you know? I'm glad his family is as wonderful as he is. They must really like you if they can put up with you."

"Right!"

"What did his mom make?" I asked, suddenly alert and hungry.

"She made mochiko tofu with greens and butter mochi for dessert. Knowing her, and you, she probably added ube."

My mouth was already salivating.

"Luau stew, I think Kimo said. And that taro leaf and spinach dip that you liked last time, with the coconut milk."

My heart pattered with all the feels. "Wow. I love her. She didn't have to go through all this trouble. My goodness! Why are they coming here with so much food? Why don't we just go to their place? Make it easier."

"Because they want the view," Diya explained with a giggle. "They stay at the hotel all the time with my discount for staycations, but usually the other building because it's cheaper."

"Definitely should share this view."

"Kimo's brother is picking up beers from the brewery."

"So it's just going to be a party?"

"Not loud or crowded. Just like how it was when we went to their house a few days ago. Will you be okay?"

"Of course. They're family. It's different," I reminded her as if she weren't aware that my social anxiety didn't scream during small gatherings with close friends and family. "I was making a joke. Ya know? Food and drinks with an ocean view . . . gonna get lit."

"Oh my god." Diya pushed off the bed. "You have to work on your execution if you ever want to make it as a comedian."

She untucked her blouse, and honestly, I was surprised she hadn't changed already. She usually kicked off her shoes and had her clothes off by the time she reached her room. "Where's Sunny?"

Oh, right. That was probably why she hadn't stripped down by now. "With his friends."

"Will he be back soon?"

"I don't know."

"What do you mean, you don't know? Call him. Invite him. He can't say no to food. What else is he doing?"

"He's here for his friend's wedding."

"That's right! You're a wedding date!" Diya giddily screamed. "Bitch, you need a dress."

She promptly went through the few clothes I'd managed to hang in the closet and mockingly looked back at me. "You didn't bring a dress?"

I sat up, rubbing my eyes. "It was a last-minute surprise."

"Don't worry. The hotel has fancy boutiques, but there are some nearby shops, too."

"Don't get carried away."

"You need shoes. But we're the same size, and I can bring you sandals. Unless you brought some?"

"Do hiking sandals count?"

She dropped her chin and deadpanned. "You're hopeless."

"I'm low-maintenance, but yes, a dress and your sandals sound fine."

She squealed with a clap of her hands. "Tell him to come back for some amazing dinner."

"No. I really want him to enjoy his time with his friends. The entire wedding party is here, and the guys grouped together to do . . . whatever it is guys do before a wedding."

"Ah. That sucks. He doesn't know what he's missing! Eh. We'll save some food for him. Will he eat any of it? Is he vegetarian or vegan or keto or diabetic?"

"I don't know."

"How do you not know?"

I shrugged. "I'll ask."

I texted Sunny, mentioning the food and Kimo's family and left-overs if he couldn't make it. He never responded.

FOURTEEN

Sunny

Okay. Okay. So I know I'd said we couldn't possibly keep drinking and staying out late like we were in college where weekends started on Thursday, but here we were. I'd somehow made it back to the villa, stumbling the entire way. It had to be at least two in the morning, and I should've just asked if I could crash on the floor of Sam or Aamar's rooms, but their SOs probably wouldn't want to be stumbling over me. Knowing April, the girls had probably gotten a bit wild, too.

The villa was dark when I arrived, except for the corner of the living room, near the TV, where a lamp had been left on a dim setting. I went straight for the couch, looking forward to passing out and putting up a fight next time the guys wanted to drink their weight in alcohol.

Upon closer inspection, there appeared to be another body asleep on the couch. It wasn't Bane or her sister, but a man. He had his face against the back of the couch, no shirt on, and a blanket to his waist.

Hmm. What was I supposed to do now?

Maybe sleep outside on a lounge chair?

I turned toward a noise behind me. In the dark kitchen, Bane had opened the fridge and stared into its depth like she was either trying to cool off or was maybe sleepwalking.

The next thing I knew, I was standing behind Bane, my body going slack as icy air hit me. I groaned. What relief.

"What the hell!" Bane yelped, turned around, and was practically in my chest.

I flinched, my hand racing to my temple. "Shhh. Please?"

She let out a rough breath and took a step back toward the still-open fridge as we both absorbed the frigid chill. "What are you doing?"

"It's hot."

"You scared me."

"Who else would be here? Also, who's on the couch?"

She looked past me. "Oh. One of my lovers. There's another one in my room."

"What?" I was suddenly a little less tipsy and more awake.

"Kidding. That's Kimo's brother—Kimo is my sister's boyfriend. He had too many drinks, so he just crashed here." She rummaged through the fridge and pulled out a plate.

I was leaning toward the pleasant call of the fridge, practically bent over her.

"We saved you food. Because, one, despite your false observations, I'm nice. Two, Kimo's mom's cooking is bomb. Three, you're never going to get authentic food like this. But the hard seltzers and beers are gone."

"Please don't mention alcohol."

She straightened up, turning toward me with an enclosed container in her hands, and nearly jumped. In my near-drunken state, it took seconds too long to realize that my nose was practically in her chest. Because I'd been bent over her, and now, she was standing upright and had turned around. Yes. That was how movement worked.

I hadn't moved. But Bane had moved, shifting so that her breasts aligned with my face. Hmm. She was wearing a thin tank top. Not as low as the one she'd had on earlier, but I, unwillingly, had noticed some fine curves that maybe I sort of wanted to run my tongue over.

"You gonna do something while you're down there, or . . ."

I grunted and stood upright, towering over her, and then catching myself on the counter behind me when the motion made me dizzy.

Bane grabbed for my waist and snatched my shirt in her fist. "Whoa!"

She dropped the container onto the counter with a soft thud, her other hand at my waist to steady me. I found enough composure to steady myself between her and the counter. I had to get myself together. She couldn't see me drunk. She would hold this over my head for years.

Oh, remember that time you were drunk in Hawaii and I saved you from hitting your head on the floor and dying?

Bane would absolutely exaggerate.

I explained, "I had one too many. My friends think we're still twenty-one."

"Clearly. Do you want to eat to slow down that alcoholic descent?" She hadn't stepped back, hadn't removed her hands. She was so close to me that I could smell every fragrance on her. Soap, shampoo, lotion, and something spicy. Maybe remnants of dinner?

Hmm. Smelled like I'd missed something really good.

She gave a half laugh. "Are you sniffing my neck?"

"You do smell edible, *pumpkin*."

"Well, we had very tasty food."

Every time she breathed, her chest grazed mine. Damn. I must've had way too many if Bane was turning me on. Very dangerous territory if my brain cells could misfire this horrifically.

"Do you want to eat this or not?" she asked softly.

"Eat what exactly?" To be clear.

"Leftovers from dinner."

Ah. Right. "You ever seen babies fall asleep in their food?"

"Did you eat at all while you were clubbing it up with your boys?"

"This place has no clubs," I muttered into her hair. Did she taste as good as she smelled?

"Were you expecting a stripper for the bachelor party or something?"

"Nah. We're not those kind of guys."

She pulled away and patted my chest. "Okay, Drunky. Sit down before you fall. And eat to soak up some of that alcohol."

I did as she commanded. "Oh, man. This is good."

She watched me from a kitty-corner chair at the dining table as she drank water, pushing a glass on me every other bite, and nodding. "At least you get leftovers. They taste much better heated up."

"Microwaves cause cancer."

"Says the guy who gave his liver a hefty shot of overtime."

I scowled. "I don't usually drink, and definitely not like this."

"Mmm."

"Think what you will, but the circumstances allow it."

"Sure."

I let out a huge sigh. "Ugh. So. Question."

"Okay."

"Where should I sleep? Outside?"

She gave a soft chuckle. "Where there are mosquitos, giant moths the size of bats, red ants that will leave you in pain for weeks, and probably scorpions? At least it's too hot for the centipedes. I think . . ."

I cringed. Hell. No one was man enough to sleep in that death zone. "I'll take the floor."

"With your messed-up back?"

"How do you know about that?"

"You complain often when you think no one is listening."

"Ah."

She groaned and looked me dead in the eye. "Can you handle sleeping in the same bed as me?"

I barked out a laugh. "You think so much of yourself."

Bane dramatically rolled her eyes, and I wondered if that ever hurt. "It's a king-size bed and large enough for the two of us with plenty of space. There will be a pillow barrier that, if crossed, you will get knocked the hell out."

I laughed. "I would not risk crossing pillows."

"It's me you should be worried about crossing."

"Thanks. Do I get the couch back tomorrow?"

"Yes. Sorry about the intrusion."

"He's like family, right? Besides, can't turn someone away when they've had too many."

She shook her head and took another sip of water, pushing my glass into my hand. "I don't know why so many people are getting drunk on a Wednesday."

I finished my last bite and drank the entire second glass of water.

"You've got something on your . . ." she started, tapping at her lips.

I rubbed the corner of my mouth.

"The other side," Bane corrected, reaching up to rub something off the corner of my mouth right as my tongue darted for the spot, hitting the tip of her finger instead. She sucked in a breath, drawing back.

My gut clenched just from that minuscule, fleeting touch, from that sexy little gasp. Damn, it must've been a while since I'd gotten some because no way. Not Bane.

I stared at her, like an idiot, my eyelids hooded, heavy.

She smirked. And here it came . . . "Did you just lick me?"

"You're imagining things," I muttered.

"I'd almost believe you if I wasn't here when it happened."

I shook my head.

She teased a smile. "It's okay, you know?"

"What?" I grumbled.

"That you want to lick me."

I sucked in a breath, my jaw hardening among . . . shit . . . other things. "Don't joke about things you're not ready for."

Her smile slipped. "So confident, huh?"

I leaned toward Bane. She boldly did not back away. She was frozen, immobile. And not because she was being her typical smart-ass baiting me. Nah. Because the sarcasm in her expression had wilted into something else. Her lips parted and she swallowed. I watched it all. I watched her nerves come undone as I inched toward her. I watched the skin on her arm pucker with goose bumps when I swiped my finger across the back of her hand, the hand on the table that had been trying to drown me with drinking water.

I held her gaze so intensely that it left her speechless. For once. My eyes dipped to her mouth. "Bane," I said, my voice thick, guttural, sleepy. "How are you going to handle me licking you when you can't even handle me looking at you?"

At that, Bane audibly gasped, and I wondered what else made her breath hitch. What else made her speechless? What else made her look at me this way, with heat burning in her eyes?

And why, for the love of god and all that was holy, was I so interested in finding out?

FIFTEEN

Bhanu

I vaguely remembered having drunk so much water that my egregiously small bladder had dragged me out of a dead sleep to pee two, maybe three, times.

I stomped back to bed in the dark. It wasn't pitch-black. Light seeped in through the gaps at the edges of the curtains. With a burp, I plopped into bed and rolled onto my side, hitting a fortress of pillows.

I shoved them back. They didn't budge. Another shove, a much harder one after that, followed by an annoyed, throaty, "What, Bane?"

I almost shrieked as I shot up in bed. "Sunny?"

"Yes?"

"Why are you . . ." Oh, right. Kimo's brother had crashed on the couch and Sunny had come in late. Drunk. And . . . had been flirting with me?

I groaned. Whatever. I was too dang tired, and by the silence, Sunny was, too.

But there *was* a man sleeping next to me. Not a boyfriend. Not even a friend. Not quite a stranger, but a coworker nemesis. I peered over at him. Sunny was hidden behind the fortress of pillows. He'd had at least followed the one rule I'd given his drunk butt last night.

"Are you watching me?" His voice was a low, gravelly grumble. And it did some funny things to my insides, tying them up into knots constricting and releasing in slow, pleasant tugs.

"You're protected by the fortress," I replied.

"I didn't want to get knocked the hell out."

I bit my lip. "Good memory for a drunk."

"Almost drunk," he corrected.

"Seemed pretty much there to me."

"You've not seen many drunks, have you?"

"No."

"What a protected life you lead."

"Do I have to deal with you stumbling in, in the middle of the night, almost drunk again?"

"Hopefully I get a room."

"You probably won't. Might as well just stay here."

Sunny poked his head up from behind the fortress, his hair adorably disheveled and his eyes as low and brooding as they had been last night. "Why wouldn't I get a room?"

"You're not the only person needing one, and you have a place to stay . . . so . . . let someone else have a room."

He watched me, perplexed. "You're inviting me to stay the entire trip?"

"Yes. I doubt you'll get a room as nice as this." I lay on my side and watched his expression turn from sleepy to wary to thoughtful.

"You don't even know how long I'm staying."

"When do you fly out?"

"The wedding is on Saturday, and I leave on Sunday."

I shrugged. "It's a couple more days. You're not in the worst situation. The invitation is there. I'm more concerned about some poor family or an actual couple who has no place to go."

"That's considerate."

"You're welcome."

The corner of his mouth twitched. "Thanks, Bane. You're all right."

I shoved the pillow between us into his face. "I thought I was pumpkin and edible."

He laughed into the pillow, pushing it away in a quick game of back-and-forth until he pulled it away. There was a breach in the fortress, and no barrier between our top halves. Not that the bed was small by any means, but a gaping reminder that, holy crap, a man was in my bed.

"I don't think I said that," he replied.

"You definitely did, *almost* drunk Sunny."

His eyes closed. "What time is it?"

"Time for you to get a watch."

"Funny."

"Why should I move to answer your question? Where's your phone?"

He fumbled around, slapping his butt, then his side, slipping his phone out of his pocket. The screen illuminated his face. "It's past nine. We're supposed to meet up at eleven to go hiking."

"In your post-drunk state? Don't they know you're an old man?"

"Screw me."

"Am I still expected to go?"

He pried open one eye. "You don't want to?"

"You sound disappointed."

"My friends like you."

I pushed myself onto my elbow and tapped his nose. "That's because I'm freaking lovable."

"Right. It's just me . . ."

"You're the only person on this entire island who doesn't like me, so you do the math. I know you're good at it."

"Smart-ass."

I sat up and stretched, acutely aware of Sunny watching me. And for some unknown reason—because, one, I wasn't trying to show off, and two, this wasn't on instinct—I raised my arms above my head and arched my back.

Sunny grumbled something inaudible.

"What?"

"Nothing," he muttered, rolling away and heading to the bathroom. "I . . . need to shower."

"I'll heat up leftovers."

"I thought those were for me," he said as he passed through the opened bathroom door.

"You snooze, you lose."

While Sunny took a speedy shower, I had leftovers heated and was plating up.

"That was fast," I told him when he emerged from the bedroom.

"Didn't want you to eat all the food."

He grabbed a plate and helped himself. "Where's everyone?"

"They must've all left this morning. It's Thursday . . . so at least two of them have work."

Kimo was likely to have left with Diya, which meant Kimo had dragged his brother out, too.

"This does taste better heated up," he confessed, which had me wondering how drunk he'd been to remember our conversation last night. And if he remembered everything. What he'd said, the way he'd looked at me, like he wanted to try some of this edible pumpkin.

My skin tingled. It was just the thought, not the man. No one had paid any special attention to me in a while. No one had spent this much time in close quarters, alone, in a while. And maybe I was reading too much. That book Diya lent me was a rom-com, and rom-coms had some great sexual tension and provocative imagery.

Alas, Sunny was not it. He couldn't be, and if he somehow was, he could never know.

He constantly checked his phone and I asked, "Trying not to work, huh?"

"Yeah, but not just that."

"Wedding stuff?"

"Some of it."

I watched him until he finally put his phone away. "Is everything okay?"

He scratched his forehead. "Checking in on my family. They say I worry too much, and that's one hundred percent true."

"Tell me about them, your family."

"You don't need to know."

"What if someone asks: How's so-and-so? And I have no idea to whom they're referring. Your sister, mom, aunt, cousin, child?"

"I don't have children."

"Now we're getting somewhere."

"We should get going." He washed the dishes and I put away dwindling leftovers.

We were several minutes down the street when I asked again, "Your family?"

"No. Respect the rules."

I squinted up at him. Sunshine rained down on his profile, which was a pleasant one to look at, not going to lie. He had fluffy, wavy hair that kept falling over his forehead, a straight nose, attractive lips, and one firm jaw. His neck was thick and fit perfectly onto a pair of broad shoulders.

He side-eyed me, never missing a step. "Admiring my presence?"

"Would you rather I tell you about my many lovers . . . in case someone asks who so-and-so whisking me away is?"

His jaw hardened, the muscle at the joint contracting. "Do you seriously have benefit buddies here?"

"Would you like to know? I can tell you about all seven of them. Current ones. The past ones don't matter. But only if you tell me about your family."

"The hell?"

I smirked. "Are you bothered that your nemesis gets so much more than you?"

"You're obviously lying."

"You're obviously bothered."

"I'm unbothered."

"Hmm," I hummed, merrily walking alongside this tall, brooding giant who noticeably side-eyed me every other minute.

He grunted. "Fine."

And then he proceeded to tell me about his family in Olympia, all superficial but helpful details to know should anyone ask, and not knowing more meant we weren't that serious. Plus his sisters, Sheila and Sienna. What they did for work, their ages, and how they weren't married but may or may not be dating at any given moment.

"You haven't met them, and I haven't told them about you. So if they happen to call while we're all together, or someone brings it up, it won't be a surprise. And to show we're not that serious, so when we *break up*, it won't be a shocker. And your family?"

I matched his details, but of course my family knew about him, and we were all hanging out apparently.

"So you're more into me than I am into you," he stated.

"My heart is more open than yours. You've been hurt in the past, not ready to love again."

"Fair enough."

We walked in silence after that, and all the while I wondered if his sisters and parents were like him, quiet and sarcastic but brilliant in their field.

"Where are we hiking?" I asked when we met up with his friends at the water fountain. "One of the valleys? Sure your legs can take it before the big day?"

"We're going to a monument, I think."

By "monument," he meant Puʻukoholā Heiau National Historic Site, where I hoped he and his friends would be respectful of the ancient land or otherwise I'd be that vocal, and therefore unlikable, person telling people to calm down.

Before that, we walked along Lapakahi State Historical Park. I should've advised against trekking these areas during the hottest parts of the day. While other parts of the island were cooler, even cold or rainy, this side was not. The lava rocks only intensified the heat.

I slathered on more SPF—coral reef friendly—and offered the bottle to Sejal, who gawked at me.

"Trust me," I assured, "brown people sunburn, too."

"I've never sunburned."

"You'd think that, but this sun will have your skin blistering and peeling and little sweat blisters popping all over the place."

She cringed.

I wagged the bottle. "Don't risk it right before a wedding."

April agreed, pulling her bottle out of her purse. She held a typical cream-colored version that matched her lighter skin tone.

I said to Sejal and Maya, "Mine is pigmented for melanated skin with a matte finish. You'll love it."

At that, they took the bottle.

I offered it to Sunny. He shook his head.

"Sunburn is essentially your cells self-destructing to protect the rest of your cells from radiation-inflicted DNA mutation. Don't neglect cells willing to die for the rest of you."

Sunny stared at me, and I stared back, neither of us willing to budge.

"Babe . . ." I said sweetly.

He grunted and relented and applied SPF. "Happy?"

"Extremely." I swiped a smear off his chin, ignoring his annoyance.

The girls were all prepped out with floppy hats, and I kicked myself knowing that I should've taken the time to bring my hat, a cap, a scarf, sunglasses . . . anything. Why hadn't I?

"Are you okay?" Sunny asked as we ventured along the dusty paths between rocks and sparse shrubs.

Despite the ocean being right there in front of us, it wasn't enough to keep me cool.

My mouth was parched by the time we walked back to the trailhead to go down the other path. I'd already drunk all my water.

"Hey." Sunny had slowed down to meet my even slower pace.

Here I was, big sister to a local who came here all the time and was always in tourists' faces about this and that, and yet, I'd failed the most basic thing. Cover thyself and always have water.

"Umm . . ." Yet I didn't want to spoil their adventure or make him worry. "You go ahead."

His friends were getting farther ahead of us. He looked at them and then at me. "Bane?"

The sudden chills, the unholy level of burning coursing through my body, the way my skin felt singed, the parched mouth, and the slowly, but surely, bit of dizzy spell that would come. Heat exhaustion. It was coming. Even at eleven in the morning, it was too hot with the sun blazing right on this equatorial region.

I gulped hard after drinking the last drop of my water, my steps slowing down even more as my legs turned jellylike. The goose bumps came, the shivers, and oh, no . . . it was too late. It was here.

I immediately sought shade, but there was very little shade beneath scant, short trees that were more gangly branches than leaves.

The group was taking pictures and looking around, leaving us behind. So I just turned around and went back up the path. No need to bother them.

"I'm going to go sit down," I announced.

"Bane! Where are you going?" Sunny called out, jogging after me.

"How are you not hot?" I wheezed.

He shrugged. "I am, but it's just for a short while."

I smacked dry lips and hobbled back toward the parking lot. "Give me the keys . . . to the car . . ." I rasped.

"What's wrong?" He stopped me by the shoulder and bent down to look at me.

I rubbed the goose bumps from my arms, every word labored. "I'm getting heat exhaustion. I need shade, AC, water."

"Okay. Okay," he said, sounding panicked. Oh, boy. He'd never make it in the medical field.

"It's fine. I just need to sit in the car."

He called back to the others, "We're going back to the car!"

I flinched.

"Sorry," he said, touching my back. "I'll text them when we get you settled. Are you okay to walk?"

"Yeah. I'm just slow. My body temp is probably rising; I'm getting achy."

"Bane." He looked me dead in the eye in the most devastatingly serious manner. "Is it okay if I pick you up?"

"Wha-what?"

"To take you to the car faster. Because you don't look good and you're barely moving, and I don't know where the closest hospital is."

"Oh." Here I thought I was moving quickly enough. I wanted to decline, truly, but without sufficient shade in sight and the degree of my symptoms, pride had no room to make decisions for me. I nodded.

He swept me off my feet in one fluid motion, carrying me through the trail and deftly zipping past a few onlookers, as I wrapped my arms around his neck and buried my face against his chest. I didn't welcome the extra heat from his body, but I welcomed the shade, or what little there was to be had.

"We're here," he said in a matter of minutes, or hours. It was hard to tell when I was just trying not to pass out.

He set me down by the car, unlocked the door, and let me in on the shady side. Of course, the car was blazing hot. Sunny ran to the driver's side to turn on the ignition and ran the AC full blast with the windows down. He rummaged through the trunk for water and handed it to me. It was tepid, but I took it.

I drank and drank, my stomach rolling with nausea, then I dabbed some water against my face, neck, shoulders, and arms, not caring that my top turned damp and sticky.

Sunny, sitting in the driver's seat, quietly watched me as I leaned my head back and closed my eyes, worry oozing off him and filling the car. Once the AC was blowing cold air, the windows went up. After about ten minutes, my body had cooled down and the goose bumps and shivers subsided.

I pried open an eye and looked at Sunny. He was turned toward me, frowning, and watching my every move. "Crisis averted," I assured him.

He sighed, as if he'd waited with bated breath for my assessment. I hadn't seen him look so relieved since that time he thought he'd butchered the master copy of code but had really been working on a local branch and his error was totally fixable. Actually, this level of genuine concern was sweet. Beneath all that surly smugness was an honest-to-god kind person.

"Thank you."

He nodded once. So serious with that wrinkle between his brows.

"I usually never forget to bring a hat and extra ice water and account for every source of shade," I explained, tamping down the tinge of embarrassment. "Ever since I realized on my first trip here that I'm prone to heat exhaustion, I try not to go to places like these during the hot hours." Or during my period, because, boy, that only intensified matters.

"You're fine?"

"Yes."

"Bane," he said, dead serious in that commanding voice. "Are you sure?"

I cracked a smile and brushed a finger against his forehead. "You know you get these wrinkles in between your brows when you're so serious?"

He let out a breath, his expression relaxing. "I'm glad you didn't pass out. I have no idea how to explain to work that your demise wasn't my fault."

"Quite suspicious. I'll probably need a restroom soon though." I drank more water.

"There's a port-a-potty." He cocked his chin at the nearby facilities.

"I'd rather pee under a tree."

He cracked a laugh.

"Were you seriously worried?"

"I honestly don't want our coworkers to hear of you dying out here and thinking I had anything to do with it."

"Jerk," I teased, pinching his side.

Sunny flinched away, smirking. "Careful. You might pee on yourself."

"I'm not cleaning it up."

He pulled out his phone. "Was so busy watching you for signs of further distress that I forgot to text the group."

A warm sensation rose in my chest, and not the heat exhaustion kind. His worry was utterly sweet. Maybe Sunny had a sunny side to his doom and gloom after all.

"What do you want to do?"

I pulled away from my thoughts. "I can call Diya. You go back to your friends."

He seemed genuinely perplexed the way he looked at me. "Isn't your sister working? I'll take you back."

"Ubers exist here. Go enjoy yourself and be with your friends."

He glanced past my shoulder. "Nah. I didn't want to come anyway. Now I have an excuse to leave."

I snorted. "Am I your scapegoat? So your friends can blame your girl when you ditch them? Savage. They're going to be rooting for you when you tell them about our breakup."

"First of all, it will look disconcerting on my part if they know you left because of getting ill and I stay out here instead of taking care of you. But more importantly, I need to make sure you don't relapse."

"I won't. As long as I stay away from intense heat and sun, I'll be fine. Look, no more goose bumps."

He eyed the arm I was holding out as evidence. "So those bumps are normal?"

I looked down at a hundred tiny water blisters created by my sweat when the sun was trying to cook my flesh. I cringed, retracting my arm, embarrassed. I, however, refrained from popping them so little pockets of water oozed out. "They'll go away."

Sunny texted again before buckling in. I followed suit when he eased out of the parking lot. "Even if your sister drove you back, you'd be left alone. Not taking that chance."

I watched his profile. I never had the chance to just look at him. Usually, we saw each other in passing or during brief conversations or at meetings when I was focused on important things. Sitting here in silence while he drove was surprisingly pleasant. Might as well enjoy it while it lasted, because it would be short-lived. "You're not annoyed that you have to leave?"

"I'm annoyed they dragged us out there and you got sick."

The right corner of my mouth went up. Was he actually mad *for* me instead of *at* me?

He side-eyed me. "What are you staring at?"

"You have a nice side to you."

"You think I look nice from the side?"

"That's not—you know that's not what I meant."

He focused on the road.

I clapped my hands. "Let's get shave ice."

"You almost passed out."

"And ice helps. So does sugar."

"Were you faking it?"

"Yeah. I faked water blisters. Witness my powers."

"Fine. Where do I go?"

I gave him directions. We could go only one of two ways on the highway, and we took a right, toward the villa, to a little shave ice shop tucked out of the way in Kawaihae. There was enough shade on the stretch of restaurants, shops, and convenience stores to stand outside and not pass out.

"What are you getting?" I asked when Sunny parked mere feet from the front of the shop.

"Nothing."

"Why not?"

"Seems like a lot of ice." He indicated the sizes with his chin. They had one size: extra large.

"Okay. Let's share?"

He gaped at me as if sharing shave ice would send his soul into the ether to be pulverized.

Naturally, I ignored him. "What flavors? I like blue Hawaii, mango, cherry, blood orange, and lychee."

"Hmm . . ." There went those forehead wrinkles while he contemplated sugary syrups as if decoding a secret.

"It tastes best with ice cream and a snowcap."

"What the hell's a snowcap? Ice on ice?"

"It's sweetened condensed milk drizzled on top, tastes way better than it sounds. Trust me."

He pressed his lips together.

"Just one bite?"

He sighed. "Whatever you'd like, I'll try it."

I beamed.

"Just . . . calm down. Don't pass out."

"I won't pass out. You saved me."

With that, I slipped out and ordered a scoop of ube ice cream buried beneath a dome of shave ice, drenched in three flavors of syrup with a snowcap and a shake of li hing mui on top for a little tartness.

Sunny was suddenly behind me, or maybe he'd always been there, and slipped his card out to pay before I could dig through my small purse.

"Saved me and paid for a shave ice? What a day."

He grunted, "I'm beginning to think this *was* all a ruse, Master of Water Blisters."

I nudged his shoulder with mine as another wave of chills started, which didn't go unnoticed by him. "Go to the car and I'll bring it."

"Thanks."

Within minutes, we were enjoying a giant colorful shave ice surrounded by the cool comfort of the car's AC, and blessed by sidewalk awning shade. I was feeling 80 percent better and giddy.

Sunny took tentative bites, his lips puckering at the sweet and tart li hing mui.

"Dried plum powder," I explained. "Get down to the ice cream. You'll never be the same."

I watched with great interest as Sunny shoveled through the

layers of shave ice and syrup to hit a jackpot of purple ice cream. He examined it the way he examined pixels on a prototype. When he took that first bite, his face went from curious to alive.

"Good, right?"

"What is this masterpiece?" Sunny shoved aside the ice and dug out the ice cream. He could've just ordered a scoop of ice cream.

"It's ube, bey-bey," I said in a singsong voice, unable to help it, because in my head, I was singing to the tune of Salt-N-Pepa's "Push It" hookline that went, "Ooh, baby, baby." But of course as, "Ube, bebebaby . . ."

I explained, "It's purple yam from the Philippines. Used in a lot of desserts. Life-changing, right?"

"Damn, Bane. You're passing on your addiction."

I grinned. Because even ube couldn't negate that stupid nickname he had for me.

SIXTEEN

Sunny

Bane was giggling like a kid eating the rest of her melted shave ice. She offered the last drops to me, but I let her drink them. Her lips were plump and red from the icy treat, her tongue equally red when she stuck it out.

I didn't know why, but I wasn't particularly interested in getting back to the group or even to the villa.

"You ready to go?" Bane asked, licking her lips. I wondered if they tasted sweet, if they tasted like cherry syrup and ube ice cream. If her tongue was cold like the ice she'd just consumed.

I cleared my throat. "Whenever you're ready. Do you want to go to the villa or . . . a hospital? Although they'd probably wonder why you had time to stop for shave ice."

"No one wonders that."

"Hmm. Tell me where to go."

"We have to pick up your friends anyway, right? They can't all fit into the other car."

"Sure they can."

Bane twisted in her seat. "Why don't you want to spend time with your friends?"

Could it be being surrounded by happy couples, including my ex? Seeing Sejal reminded me of how perfectly she fit into my family. And how crushed I was knowing that my parents still talked to her, called her, chatted with her about everything. Although she hadn't gotten into details with them the way she had with her friends, I'd never felt so abandoned. All I'd heard for months from my parents was why not her? Why couldn't I make it work? Why couldn't I do better? Why had I ruined things?

It was never her fault. Always mine, and always mine to amend.

It made seeing my parents hard when all I wanted was for them to be happy.

The smart thing would be to say something. Tell my parents the truth and how things would never work out with her, how them bringing her up every conversation killed me a little each time. But therein lay the initial problem that had triggered Sejal. I didn't speak. I let things float away because I couldn't figure out how to express my emotions. But if I couldn't chat freely with my own parents, then how could I do so with anyone else?

Speaking of which, I checked my phone out of habit. No updates on Papa.

"Why are you always on the phone?" Bane cut through my thoughts. "Can't be work. They don't call me."

"You sound offended."

"That you're always on the phone or that work doesn't call me?"

"Well, it's you . . . so the latter."

She shivered and for a second I panicked, thinking her heat exhaustion had returned, when she turned the vents toward me and crossed her arms.

"Are you cold now?"

"You're not?"

I turned the AC down from full blast. "I was freezing, but you needed it."

"Aw, you do care about me."

"It's more about how to dispose of your body in the case of your demise . . ."

She faced forward again. "Fine. Don't tell me about the text slash call that you're waiting for, or why you don't want to be around your friends, or your breakup. I get it. We're not friends."

It wasn't that. It was me. It really was; just ask Sejal.

I pulled out of the parking lot, remembering the two turns it took to get here along long stretches of highways, and returned to pick up half the group.

After Aamar and Maya slid into the back seat, since I was *not* allowing anyone to displace Bane, we headed to the monument.

"Are you feeling okay?" Maya asked, clearly worried.

"Yes, thank you. Much better," Bane replied.

She explained heat exhaustion to them and how imperative it was to always carry water.

I pulled into one of many empty parking spots and touched the scorching dashboard. I looked at Bane and silently asked if she was okay to go out in this blistering heat with one rise of my brows.

She shook her head. "You go ahead. I'll sit under a tree at Spencer Beach, right there."

She cocked her chin at the bottom of the parking lot where it curved into a different parking lot leading to a small beach with plenty of shade.

"Are you sure?" Maya asked from the back seat. "We don't want you to feel like we're ditching you."

Bane laughed. "No, it's fine. I've been here plenty of times and I don't want to slow you down or worry anyone. But it will be hot. I don't remember there being any trees, so be careful."

Aamar placed a hand on my shoulder, as if indicating it was

understandable if I stayed with Bane. "Why don't you park down there so Bhanu doesn't have to walk?"

"I'm fine, really," she began to say as I replied, "Was planning to."

She watched me, her expression pleading with me to go with my friends. Instead, I told Aamar, "Text me when you're ready to go and I'll drive back over."

"That's okay. We should walk down to the beach. Didn't realize one was so close."

"I know!" Maya added. "Would be so nice to get into the water."

"Maybe we can make this quick?"

She grinned at him. "They don't *need* us, right?"

"Don't forget your waters!" Bane called after them and then said to me, "I forgot I needed to use the restroom. Be right back!"

"Be careful!" I called after her, not wanting her to pass out in the heat between the car and the restrooms.

Aamar waved at me from the sidewalk as Maya walked with Bane to the restroom and back.

She plopped into her seat. "You guys act like I'm still in danger."

"We don't know." I shrugged and found a spot in a shaded area closer to the ocean.

I followed Bane to the beach, letting her pick out an area. She sat down right on the sand, covered in shade, and a few feet from lapping water. The breeze, paired with the shade, was enough to stay comfortably cool. And isolated. The crowds had sectioned off into clusters of couples, families, or small groups.

"Are you going to sit? The ocean won't snatch you from here."

"Haha," I replied dryly and sat beside her.

She removed her shoes and dug her feet into the sand, water lapping closer and closer to her feet.

"You're fine now?"

She nodded. "So tell me about yourself, Mr. Sunshine."

I groaned. "Why?"

She looked at me from over her shoulder. "We shared shave ice. We're practically one being now."

"Tell me more about your family."

"Do you really want to know, or are you just wanting me to fill up time so you don't have to talk about your family?"

"Both."

"I'll tell you something, and you tell me something?"

"No."

She turned to the water. "Then may the ocean swells snatch you whole."

"Oh my god."

"And may you suffer in your watery tomb."

"Fine. But just so you're aware, you're breaking the first rule."

"What are my consequences?"

I looked skyward before replying, "Being bored."

She grinned, moving windblown hair from her face. A wave hit farther up her leg than before and she yelped. "My shoe!"

I jumped to my feet and stomped into the shoreline, grabbing it before the current snatched it away. Water was frighteningly powerful. In another second, her shoe would've been gone. Imagine if that were a pet or a child! This was why I didn't mess with the ocean.

I jogged back, thumping her shoe in the air to get the water out, and sat in front of her. She'd moved away from the water's reach, her cheeks flushed in anticipation of her nearly lost shoe . . . or from the sun.

"I thought you put on sunscreen?"

"Is my face red?" Bane gently touched her cheeks, frowning. "I better not peel."

"Beautiful imagery."

She stuck out a red-stained tongue. I bet it still tasted like cherry syrup.

"Careful with that tongue."

She pushed my hip with a foot. "Or what?"

"Or put it to use."

We both stilled with nothing but a stare in between us. Her cheeks flushed redder than before and mine grew hot. Hmm. Shit. *That* was definitely not something I'd meant to say aloud, and now all I could think about was what the hell her tongue tasted like. Cherries. Cherry like the color of her plump lips, like the sweet flavored shave ice. And ube. A *potato dessert*. Why? Because I was beginning to like something that I'd never thought I'd like.

"You're so full of it. Can't even think of a better comeback," she snickered, breaking the tension.

"Like you have one?" I watched the waves.

"Yeah. Watch it. Or *I'll* put it to use. Ha!"

I looked Bane right in the eye, cocked a brow, and asked, "How would you like me to put my tongue to use?"

Her mouth hung open. A strangled stutter.

I smirked. "Checkmate."

Except now my entire thinking capabilities were drowning in images of using my tongue on her. How *would* Bane like me to put it to use? Kisses? Licks? A lot of licks? On her mouth? Her neck? Her chest? Her stomach? Lower?

No. Oh, hell no. Brain, get your act together. We are not *going there. Not with Bane.*

"Think you're so smart," she muttered, pushing her foot against my hip again.

I grabbed her foot and swiped my thumb across the arch. "You better watch it."

I glanced back at Bane when she didn't respond. She was biting her lower lip and staring at the water, her fists clenched around the sand. I immediately released her foot. "Sorry."

"What?" She stared at me, almost stunned.

"Your foot. Didn't mean to touch you . . ."

Her eyes were dazed, her chest heaving with a pant. "Oh . . . no. That's . . . fine."

Hold on. Was she blushing? No, couldn't be. Logically, the sun was causing that rosy glow. Therefore, as deductive reasoning would conclude, Bane was simply sunburned.

Bane was *not* turned on.

SEVENTEEN

Bhanu

Mummie has been blowing up my phone for updates," Diya had been telling me later that day while I stole glances at the closed bedroom door. It sounded like the shower might still be on, but who could tell through two solid doors and a wall?

"Please, do *not* get your hopes up."

"*You* tell them to calm down."

"I have and I will again. But can you, for your part, tell them as well?"

Diya winked. "You mean like how you kept it low-key when they wanted to know all about Kimo?"

"I fed them enough to keep them calm. You're spoon-feeding every detail that isn't even there. I'm telling you . . ." I lowered my voice, adding, "I really don't see things working out with him."

Diya frowned. Behind her, Kimo was minding his own business in the kitchen.

"I'm being realistic. Just because he's here, by coincidence due to this wedding, doesn't mean much. Okay? None of this was planned. It's all very circumstantial."

Diya pouted.

Sunny opened the door and we all turned toward him. He was shoving his fingers through damp hair as he paused, skimming the room. He was probably seeing an apologetic woman who was more trouble than this was worth, a grinning fool of a sister wanting to bring up two unnecessarily excitable parents over video call, and a curious bro watching this all go down from the safety of the kitchen.

My sister immediately fawned over Sunny, throwing out ridiculous variations of handsome and questions of family, work, his island experience, and what . . . a wedding? How romantic! Was he getting ideas? Et cetera into oblivion.

Sunny, for his part, had promptly hurdled out of a stupor and entertained Diya as if he were the one boyfriend above all others. Complete with a smile flashing sharp canines (*I mean, damn* . . .), a shallow dimple in the ridge of laugh lines, crinkles at the eyes showing off the genuineness of his responses, and volleyed questions. He casually stood there with arms folded over his chest, his T-shirt tugging at those biceps and pecs that had me cradled against him several hours earlier, chatting away as Diya gave me a not-at-all-subtle impressed nod of approval.

Sunny was welcoming and friendly and unbearably handsome like he was a whole other person.

I could still feel his strong arms carrying me to the car, his instant love for ube shining on his face, the hint of protection of not wanting to leave me alone, the jolt of pleasure ricocheting through my core when he touched the arch of my foot, and the tingles of lost thoughts when he'd mentioned putting tongues to use.

It was going to be difficult looking at the virtual box of his head during work without thinking about any of this, much less during in-person meetings.

"Okay, that's enough. Let him breathe," I interrupted.

"What?" Diya asked innocently, but she was far from it.

"I don't mind," Sunny insisted, a hand at the low of my back, his Denzel voice scraping my cheek and sending shivers down my spine.

Either I was getting way too caught up in the fantasy of us or his acting skills had skyrocketed.

Sunny, to my surprise, helped me set the table, accidently brushing my arm as he leaned past me with plates and glasses.

"Are you sure that you want to skip dinner with your friends?" I inquired.

"Yeah," he said. "Would be suspicious if I left you alone to party after today."

I frowned.

"It's fine. Really. I need a break from them anyway. I can't handle their level of partying."

Diya brought over the sides and Kimo walked over the main dish. We oohed and ahhed over the decadent fried fish on a bed of choy sum with a heaping sprinkle of his homemade furikake seasoning.

As Sunny and I took our seats next to each other, eagerly awaiting mouthwatering food, Kimo explained, "I hit the farmer's market this morning down in Keauhou and they had the greens you like."

"Ah, thank you!" I said. "You're so sweet."

"No worries, yeah? No white pineapple, but . . ." He cocked his chin at Diya, who brought over a pitcher of beautiful fuchsia liquid. "They had a few pitaya."

I squealed, wiggling in my seat as my sister handed me an ice-cold glass of water turned purplish pink by the juice of fresh, pink-fleshed pitaya. Slices of the dragon fruit floated at the top of the pitcher.

"Enough to make dragon fruit piña colada?"

"*Bitch*," Diya drawled, "it's the after-dinner drink by the pool."

"Ugh. Yes." I turned to Sunny, adding, "Please excuse my sister's vulgarity. She doesn't know how to act in front of decent company."

"Bitch, don't be ashamed of me," Diya said, plating veggies and fish for us.

Kimo sighed. "It's my sister's doing. I take full responsibility."

"It's endearing," Sunny said.

When he looked at me, I retorted, "If you ever call me that, I'll end you."

"I would never," he said in all seriousness, and now I felt bad for even joking about it.

"No. Of course, you would never."

He leaned toward me and whispered, "Smart-ass, yes."

I pinched his side before he could elbow-block my attack.

Kimo plated the fish for Sunny first. "You'd said you liked fish, yeah?"

Sunny did his best to show the utmost appreciation. "Most people in Seattle do. Fresh salmon and all."

"Ah, nah, brah. You don't like fish? Here, give me that. I'll make you something else. Everyone stop eating."

"No, wait," Sunny said, tugging the plate back from Kimo. "I like halibut. I like the fish that doesn't taste fishy . . . if that makes sense."

Kimo relinquished and grinned. "Ah, we good then. My cousin caught this yesterday. It's ono . . . which is ono."

We had a chuckle and I explained to Sunny, "Ono is the name of the fish but also means delicious. And it's very mild. Doesn't taste like fish."

Sunny nodded, thanking Kimo, who added, "Bhanu doesn't like fishy fish, either. She's good with ono and mahi-mahi. But my cousin didn't catch any mahi."

"That's good to know because I've seen mahi-mahi on menus," Sunny said, driving a fork into his perfectly flaky fish after we'd all been plated.

He leaned down to take a bite. We watched with bated breath.

He glanced at each of us, his mouth hanging open in front of his fork.

"Sorry!" Diya said, elbowing Kimo.

I went for the soy sauce when Kimo shot me a glare and said, "Don't be salty like your sister."

I scowled. "I'm your elder."

"It's perfectly seasoned. The greens have shoyu on them; don't add more. Here, have some chili crisp." He pushed a container of a semi-spicy condiment consisting of crushed, fried red chili and crunchy soybeans in chili oil.

I took it, the taste adding a depth of flavor that tasted a lot like the dried chilis my mom made at home, the ones she fried with each meal. Although those chilis were brown and spicy.

"What do you think?" Kimo asked Sunny, the cook eager to hear his thoughts.

Sunny's brows hiked up with appreciation and he said, before taking one big bite after another, "My man, this is really good!"

Kimo beamed, nodding at Diya and at myself, as if anyone had been arguing against his culinary skills.

Sunny enjoyed everything and took heaping seconds. Kimo urged me to take more.

"I have to save room for these drinks," I contested. The drinks would be filling in themselves, seeing that they were made from coconut cream with farm-fresh pineapple and dragon fruit.

"Tonight, my cousins are swimming for bugs, so maybe we'll get a good lunch tomorrow?" Kimo mentioned around a bite.

"Bugs?" Sunny asked.

"Lobsters," I explained.

"Yeah, we free-dive and usually catch a few, makes for good eats," Kimo said.

Knowing how averse Sunny was to being in the ocean, I added, *At night.*

Sunny stilled. "Don't start with me."

I silenced a laugh, although, to be honest, being in the ocean at night, much less free-diving, was especially terrifying. Even Diya stressed out whenever Kimo went for night dives, because anything could happen in the water, especially in the dark. As she'd often vented, how would they find his body, much less save him? She, much like everyone else at this table, had absolutely no intention of dipping one toe into a dark ocean.

Dinner was a hit, per usual whenever Kimo cooked. "You pau?" he asked my sister.

Diya nodded, confirming she was done eating. All of our plates were empty and Kimo deftly took them out of our way.

My little sister entertained us with stories of tourists and work, of her experiences in wildlife preservation and supporting Kimo and his family in local protests to protect the land and its people.

As she spoke about all the great things she was doing, I leaned my elbows on the table and steepled my fingers, watching her with awe and admiration and such a deep sense of love. We were wholly two different people from the same womb, the same household, and yet so far apart. I was happy for her, and I was happy with my own life. Sure, there were ambitions and goals on the horizon, but I wasn't miserable or envious of Diya. In a world where jealousy and hate ruled, this baseline was a huge win. I couldn't see us being otherwise, ever.

Kimo leaned back in his chair, draping an arm over the back of Diya's chair as she related another story of the feral cats on the property. He looked at her the way a king looked at his queen, powerfully loving, and I wished I could somehow covertly get a picture of this moment.

Kimo cringed when Diya ended with, "So a tourist found a dead feral cat and yelled at the first staff he saw, calling them a murderer and how he was summoning PETA. And I happened to be walking by, and you know me, I don't play with that mess. Yelling at my staff like some entitled asshole. Like, sir, did you see my staff kill this cat, who happens to be feral and destroying this part of the island with out-of-control numbers? I mean, if you want to get into it, let's talk about the amount of fuel it took for you to fly here, the trash you've accumulated by being here, and all the touristy stuff you're doing destroying the reefs, polluting the air, and damaging the land."

Sunny shook his head. "I had no idea tourists were that bad."

We gawked at him. I muttered, "Seriously?"

"I mean, I know American tourists are an international joke and entitled everywhere they go. But I didn't think they were this bad going to another US state."

"A brown state," Kimo reminded. "Recently colonized, recently stripped, recently scattered people. It might as well be a foreign country."

"Feels like it," Diya added. "We're in a drought but this area uses up a lot of water to keep it green; the state encourages hotels to keep using water for tourists while locals have to ration. Had a woman complain about not having hot water during the entirety of her twenty-minute shower, and I was like, ma'am, do you understand locals can't even use up that amount of water in one day?"

Sunny nodded, frowning, as if he might be reevaluating his entire presence here.

Kimo sighed. "We could talk all day about the inequality here and then to have tourists shove it in our faces, but! This is a happy evening with family." He raised his empty glass, and we followed suit on instinct, only for him to laugh and nudge Diya. "Woman, where's these delicious drinks you said you were making?"

Diya feigned insult and dramatically pushed out of her chair, muttering, "I work all day only for you to cook a great meal and then expect me to deliver on the drinks I already said I was going to make with all the ingredients prepared by you."

Sunny chuckled as Kimo grinned, even as he was checking out Diya's backside. Sigh. Okay, to have a man look at me like that every time I walked away would be nice. Wasn't going to lie. My sister really was out here in the middle of the ocean living her best life and I loved it. I loved this for her.

I leaned toward Kimo and said, "A woman who can make you drinks. You better put a ring on that."

He simply smiled. And I wondered . . . wait, was he considering proposing to my sister?

I gave him a curious look before helping Diya with the fancy drink glasses. She was deftly dropping chunks of pineapple and dragon fruit into the blender, dousing it with coconut cream, and plopping in a handful of ice.

"With or without alcohol?" Diya called out across the bar counter.

"With!" everyone concurred.

She added a splash of rum, closed the lid, started the blender again, and leaned against the counter with a hand on her hip.

"Are you and Kimo thinking about getting married?" I whispered, even though the blender was doing a fine job at keeping our conversation private.

We glanced at the guys chatting when she shrugged. "I wouldn't mind. We've talked about it, tried to work out the logistics of different cultures, languages, and religions . . . but I don't think anything too serious. Like I wouldn't call Mummie and tell her."

She stopped the blender while I arranged the glasses for her to pour a beautiful, thick mix of pinkish-purple drink. The color was the most amazing shade I'd ever seen, and I loved it. It was the type of color one could get lost in, of rich Hawaiian sunrises, orchid leis, dramatic lipsticks, and lush silks that complemented my skin tone in the best ways. It was the type of color that one could see, taste, smell, and feel.

"But would you say yes?" I asked quietly, watching her add whipped cream and then going to the fridge to pull out a small bag.

A smile swept across her face, the kind a person couldn't hold back even if they tried, the kind that said the answer as clear as day. My little sister would marry Kimo in a second.

She plucked out purple and white orchids from the bag, already washed and wrapped in a paper towel, and arranged one flower to each glass.

"I want to live inside this color," I told her as she handed me a drink. I held it up to the light before taking a second one to Sunny.

Diya took hers and one for Kimo. We retired to the lanai, where large string lights added ambience so we could enjoy the sunset.

Even though there were four lounge chairs, Diya curled up alongside Kimo, who wrapped an arm around her and thanked her for the drink. They clinked glasses, and ugh, if they could stop being adorable for a second, that would be great because Sunny and I were as far from snuggling as a "new couple" could be. In fact, our chairs weren't even touching.

I took a sip of the slightly sweet, slightly tart, slightly alcoholic, fully creamy drink. I threw my head back. "This is so good! I missed this so much!"

"Better than ube?" Diya teased.

I shot her a look. "I saw ube paste at KTA. Do you know what we could make with that?"

She rolled her eyes. "I know damn well you didn't go to the grocery store."

"But I did go to their website."

"To see what UX you'd improve on?"

"Yes. Always. But also to see if they have ube anything. Which they have lots of."

"Enjoy *this*."

"This is perfect. I don't think ube could elevate this any more than what it already is."

"Shocking statement!"

"This is very good," Sunny agreed, raising his glass to his hosts. "Thank you for this. I . . . wasn't expecting so much."

"Hospitality?" Kimo asked. "You're dating Bhanu, so you're pretty much like family, and we have lots of aloha for our fam."

Sunny and I gave each other a quick look, and I was beginning to feel bad again. Kimo and Diya were being so hospitable for a lie. I was sure they'd understand once I explained, but why ruin the moment? Not that I had to try, because the world's biggest moment blocker was blowing up Diya's phone.

"That better not be work," I told her, nodding at the glorious shades of orange and pink brushed across the sky as the sun descended and set the water on sparkling, golden fire.

"It's Mummie!" she said with cheer.

"Don't answer."

But it was too late, to which Diya shrugged and mouthed, "Sorry."

"Eh, why haven't you answered your phone?" Mummie said through the speaker.

Diya pointed at her phone and mouthed, "See?" then cheerfully said, "Hello, Mummie!"

She, knowing why Mummie was really calling, turned the screen toward us.

Sunny and I froze, staring at my parents through the miraculously annoying trap known as FaceTime. I shifted to hide Sunny behind me, but Mummie immediately swiped her hand across the air and said, "Let me see this man who has captured my beta's heart, huh?"

EIGHTEEN

Sunny

I wasn't going to lie and pretend that watching Bane squirm under embarrassment wasn't entertaining as hell. She groaned, sinking into her chair so that her parents had a full view of me on video call. By now, I'd had enough practice acting the part in front of friends and getting acquainted with Bane's sister to turn on the charm. My exes probably hated me, but their parents loved me.

Draping an arm on the back of Bane's chair, I smiled. "Hello again."

"*Oh*. Such a nice voice!" Auntie crooned.

I chuckled. "I get that often."

Bane shot me daggers from the corner of her eye, which prompted me to give her shoulders a gentle squeeze.

Diya was holding the phone toward us while leaning against Kimo. They were a very lovely couple, and knowing this side of Bane would make it harder for me to continue giving her crap when we returned to work. They were all ear-to-ear grins, which had me wondering if carrying out this lie on them was harmful. My friends would be annoyed, but family? That was different. Or maybe they were as surprised by the idea of Bane being in a relationship as I would be.

"Oh, hah, he *is* handsome. Look!" Auntie said to a man beside her, whom I presumed was Bane's father.

"Oh my god," Bane mumbled, her hands covering her face.

I tugged down on her wrists and replied, "Thank you! May I return the sentiment? I see where your daughters get their lovely features from. What a beautiful family."

Bane peered at me from between her fingers, but not with death glares as I'd expected. She seemed . . . confused? No *suspicious*. Ah, normal Bane-ish tendencies.

She returned her hands to her lap as her parents engaged in further conversation.

Auntie had been asking, "Beta, where do you work at? What do you do? What are your parents' names?"

"Mummie," Bane warned. "Let's not."

She pouted. "What, you think I'm going to research him?"

"I know you already have."

She smiled sheepishly, her focus returning to me. "He's such a smart man. Why didn't you tell me you work together!"

"That hot office romance," Diya said.

"Oh my god," Bane muttered beneath her breath while I stifled a laugh and proceeded to answer her mother's biodata questions. This had become a thing that typically happened when I met the Indian parents of anyone around my age, and most especially the parents of single women. And my parents had done this to others, ambush and all.

Diya mentioned how I'd helped Bane during her episode of heat exhaustion, and suddenly the word "hero" was being thrown around.

"What fresh hell is this?" Bane grumbled.

Tamping down laughter was getting exponentially harder. I caught Kimo's amused look when he shook his head. He'd probably gone through the same thing. He got it.

"So, so. How long have you been dating and why am I only now learning of this, huh?" Auntie asked, although she could've been talking to either one of us. "And how serious are you? My daughter isn't getting younger, you know?"

"Okay," Bane said, holding up a hand and shifting to face me . . . a practically hysterically laughing man.

While Diya and Kimo partook of the laughter, Bane was watching me as if she were studying an alien.

She slapped my thigh. "Don't laugh! You're only encouraging her!"

I flashed my best impish expression and said, "But, babe, we should be polite."

She fumed.

"You met my friends with such gusto, I have to return the favor," I teased.

"How many children do you plan on having? Where do you live?" Auntie was asking.

I opened my mouth to respond when Bane shot to her feet and pulled me up, pushing me ahead of her and shoving my drink into my hand while she grabbed hers.

I played deadweight, unmoving, as she pushed against me. Her breasts suddenly pressed against my back in her momentum, her hand at my waist, her touch searing through the fabric of my T-shirt like a fire. I was fine right where I was until she muttered, "You better move."

"Can't miss the sunset! Talk to you later, Mummie, Papa! Love you! Smooches!" she called behind us.

"Goodbye!" I told them with a wave, noting that Diya had turned the phone so that it was still trained on us as Bane dragged me to the rock wall across the lawn to watch the rest of the sunset.

"What are you doing?" she demanded.

"Being friendly," I said, my smile slipping but my wink teeming with amusement.

She poked my side and I flinched. "Not with my parents!"

"You did with my friends." I grabbed her hand and kept hold.

"Okay, but your friends will get over it once you break the news. My parents might be devastated."

I frowned. I didn't want that. "They're very nice."

She looked back and groaned. "They're still watching. Probably making up a big fat Indian wedding checklist for us. I'm going to end you."

"More like making plans to have me over for dinner when we get back." I released her hand and took a sip of creamy, tart, semisweet drink, my focus affixed to the sunset. Wow. It was glorious and soothing and breathtaking all in one.

She poked my side again. "So you better be ready for that, because I'm not telling them."

The thought of being with Bane and her loud but hilarious family eating home-cooked meals didn't suck. "I wouldn't mind."

"What? Breaking my parents' hearts?"

"Dinner. With them."

Bane was staring at me as if discovering I was indeed an alien. The last rays from the sunset hit the side of her face in a deep, orange glow as the sun completely dipped beyond the horizon, sinking into the ocean. She blinked up at me with her incredibly long, thick lashes framing chestnut eyes. My gaze skimmed down her nose to full lips bathed in pink from the drink. I'd always noticed when she walked into a room, even when I was ignoring her. I'd never denied how attractive Bane was—no one could, even when she was stomping around my last nerves—but god damn, those lips.

"Too far?"

"Are you joking?" she barked.

"No?"

"Is that a question or an answer?"

"Both?"

"Don't mess with my parents."

"I would never. But dinner does sound nice. Maybe?" I asked, hopeful. What was wrong with me? Why in the world would I want to spend *more* time with her?

She scowled. "Seriously? This isn't some dumb joke?"

"I would joke about you to you, but I wouldn't joke about your family."

"Oh . . ."

The ocean breeze picked up as she took a sip. Goose bumps skittered over her skin, and she shivered.

I draped an arm around Bane's shoulder. "Are you cold? It's like eighty degrees, weirdo."

She swallowed her drink, but didn't move away, even when I mindlessly rubbed her arm and subtly pressed her against my side. Bane was still shivering.

"It's not another episode of heat exhaustion, is it?" I asked, panicked.

"Oh! No," she assured.

"Is . . . that okay?"

"Yeah," she whispered. "Wait. Do you mean touching me or meeting my parents?"

"Both. We could tell them we're just friends?" I suggested. "This was all a misunderstanding. I think that's a good way to break it gently to them."

Bane nodded. It was a good way . . . although it wouldn't work on my friends. That was going to be an awkward conversation with no other way around it.

"Would be nice not to argue at work for once," I added.

"You're the only stress I have in my life. Would be so much better without the back-and-forth."

"See, you don't stress me out at all. But useful to know that I get into your head and stay there all day."

"You wish you were that important."

I squeezed her shoulder, inadvertently pressing her against me, feeling every curve on point of contact. "I know I am. It's okay to admit it. The truth will set you free."

We broke apart when Diya promised she'd hung up the phone, and we sat with her and Kimo on the lounge chairs around a crackling fire pit encased in a curved, grated metal cover. The evening filled up with more decadent drinks, conversation, laughter, and watching two sisters hilariously poke fun at each other.

For a while, hours longer than I'd anticipated, there was no nagging pinch at the base of my thoughts to constantly check my phone about work or the interview, wonder how Papa was doing, or dread having to be around Sejal again.

For a while, I was content.

For a while, I found myself watching Bane. In all her irritating beauty.

"It's late. I have to work in the morning, oh my god. I don't want to deal with these bitches," Diya crowed.

Bane squawked, "Language!"

Diya pointed at me and clucked her tongue like she was giving me a thumbs-up.

"Okay, you've had enough," Kimo said, swooping her up and throwing her over his shoulder. "Gotta put you to bed."

"*Byeeee!*" she called back to us.

Bane shook her head. "Please forgive my sister. But yeah, she made some strong drinks. That's why I only had one." Bane held up an almost empty glass before slurping the rest.

"Should probably get some sleep, too," I said.

"Yeah."

"On the couch, I guess."

Bane rolled her eyes, her shoulders slumping. "Diya will be all in my business wondering why I kicked you out."

"You want me to sleep in your bed again?"

"Rules of the pillow fortress apply."

"It's more like a pillow barrier, but okay."

"Can you manage not to get snarky with me? Or is that an impossibility for you?"

I rose to my feet and offered a hand. "Should I throw you over my shoulder, too?"

"You mean carry me like a princess, so I don't have to walk after nearly dying out in the scorching wild today?" She stood. "It's the least you could do."

Bane pointedly glanced at her feet as if I should actually swoop her into my arms again.

I shrugged. "Okay." I took a step toward her, and she backed away.

"No. Like earlier," she commanded.

I smirked. "Sure."

"Sunny. No," she spat, as if she were telling me to sit, promptly followed by a squeal when I ducked down and nearly tackled her.

Okay, so this wasn't going as smoothly as when Kimo had done it, but Bane was over my shoulder, clutching the back of my shirt so that night air whooshed up my back.

"Calm down! I almost dropped you!"

"Don't blame me if you can't even carry me," she bit out, kicking the air. "Don't smack my head against anything, Sunny!"

"I'd never hurt you, Bane."

I carried her, wobbly because of course I'd had a few of Diya's strong-ass smoothies, and somehow made it to the bedroom without smacking any part of Bane's body against the doors *and* without dropping her.

She must've pushed the door closed when we walked in, because it slammed shut behind us. "Okay! Let me down!"

"Shh. Your sister needs her sleep for work," I chided.

I meant to gently lower her to the bed but the amount of alcohol in me had me losing an iota of balance. Bane went toppling into bed, her hair everywhere, her tank top halfway up her stomach as she heaved through an onslaught of laughter.

I dropped down beside her, out of breath. "Damn, you're heavy."

"You're tipsy, jackass."

Pushing myself onto my elbow, I realized how closely I'd fallen next to Bane. She shoved hair out of her face above me while I looked eye-level at her stomach. Shit. How was she so perfect beneath all her frumpy clothes?

What did her skin taste like? Was it as smooth as it looked? What would she do if I kissed her stomach? If I licked her navel? Bit her hip? Slid lower? Licking and kissing. Would she clutch my hair? Push me down? Arch into me? Moan my name?

Fuck.

I rolled onto my side of the bed, crossing the barrier separating us, and smashed my face into my pillow. And *not* into Bane.

⌒⌢⌒

The next day, Bane and I walked the back route to the usual meeting point on a warm Friday morning. This was a longer way, but scenic and serene between sprawling golf courses and the ocean, dotted with small, rocky beaches. The morning hours were pleasant and cool, but that didn't mean I wasn't constantly checking on Bane to make sure she wasn't suffering from another episode of heat exhaustion.

"I'm fine," she promised.

"Got plenty of water this time." She had her bottle and I carried three more in my backpack. Plus sugary snacks because she'd mentioned sugar helping.

"You sound like my mother."

"Water, snacks, SPF, shades, floppy-ass hat. Good."

She ignored my quip. Bane hadn't mentioned last night. Either she hadn't noticed that I was about to lick her as if she were the last scoop of ube ice cream in the world or she didn't remember. Either way, good. Excellent. We didn't need a lapse in judgment affecting the rest of our working relationship.

"I'm surprised you haven't asked if I'm wearing a swimsuit," she said. "You'd seemed so concerned with me looking nice for your friends."

"Please don't wear sweats to the wedding is all I really asked for."

She shimmied in her short shorts and long . . . I dunno . . . was that a silk cardigan? Was she wearing a swimsuit underneath or a tank top, or was this thing a top?

"It's called a cover-up," she explained, as if reading my perplexed expression. "I'm wearing a swimsuit beneath this just in case, but there is a less than one percent chance of any of it showing."

"Are you wearing a bikini?" I mused aloud.

A sly smile curved her lips and I wanted to kiss it off. Damnit. Not even one hour around her and my brain cells were frying themselves. Must've been too much sun. "Why are you asking?"

"To be prepared."

"Nothing will prepare you for seeing me in a swimsuit. In fact, your eyes might melt from the sheer glory."

"I bet," I mumbled.

"*What?* What are you possibly trying to mutter under your breath? Because nothing you say will burst my self-esteem."

"I'm not arguing. I bet you look fine as hell in a swimsuit."

She studied me pensively. "What new angle of snark is this?"

"It's not snark. I believe I'm not ready to witness you in a bikini."

"You're not." She side-eyed me in the shade from underneath the bouncy rim of her giant hat.

"Agreed."

"All wet and wild."

"*Okay . . .*"

She shoved me with her shoulder, although without any weight to it, I didn't budge.

"Don't start with me, Bane."

"You're the one wondering what I look like underneath my clothes."

I bit the inside of my cheek to keep from saying anything because I wasn't just wondering, I was imagining.

"So your friends rented a boat for a few hours?" she asked.

"Yep. At least there will be some shade for you, or we can shove you into the water to cool you off."

"Don't you dare!"

"Can't swim?"

"I can swim but there are deadly things in the water. No thanks."

At least we could agree on that.

When we met the others, they greeted Bane like she was the missing link to our circle while Sejal kept a cordial distance. We drove out to the marina and excitedly stepped onto a good-size boat large enough for all of us with plenty of space to spare.

Aamar and Maya had splurged on the couple by renting a boat to take everyone out into stunning turquoise waters. I wasn't a water guy, but the intensity of these colors in clear water was tempting.

Even Bane was leaning over the railing, holding her hat on her head as the boat sailed out. Sun glistened on her skin, speckled with ocean mist kicking up from the side of the boat. She beamed at the water, on her tiptoes and so close to teetering off that I almost grabbed her before she could fall overboard. The silky belt of her cover-up flapped in the breeze. What would happen if I caught it? Tugged at it? Would that open her cover-up and reveal her swimsuit?

How the hell was a piece of clothing so interesting? Was she wearing a bikini or a one-piece? Just a top to go with the shorts? What color was it? Red? Black? White? How did white hold up when wet? Shit, now I needed her to get into the water.

"So beautiful," she was saying.

When I didn't remark, Bane looked to me and said, "Don't tell me you're thinking about work instead of enjoying this."

"I was actually thinking about how to get you wet."

Her mouth dropped, cheeks flushed.

"Um . . . in the water. The *ocean*, Bane."

I walked away before I said anything dumber, only to find one chair left, kitty-corner to Sejal and Pradeep. I had every intention of standing when Sam slapped my shoulder, inadvertently sitting me down. At least Sam had placed a cold water in my hand. Others had beers or iced coffee.

Minutes went by and my body relaxed, melted into the chair with the breeze whipping through my hair. I tried to stay in the conversation, mainly wedding things and snorkeling information, but my focus kept wandering toward Bane. The wind kept raising her cover-up higher and higher, the long ends fluttering up and away, revealing sneak peeks of light brown skin. Ah. So, a two-piece?

"Did you hear me, Sunny?"

"Hmm?"

Leave it to Sejal to interrupt me. She was wearing a string bikini clearly seen beneath a lacy dress and sitting on Pradeep's lap. He placed a hand on her thigh and kissed her neck. Even though I didn't check, I knew the others were watching me. Waiting for a reaction that never came.

I expected to have one. Jealousy. Annoyance. Pain. Anything.

Maybe Sejal was right that I didn't have emotions, at least not enough or the right kind a girlfriend needed, because I felt nothing. As long as she was nice to Bane, her presence floated by unnoticed.

"Where's your girl?" Sejal repeated.

"My woman," I corrected, "is doing whatever she's doing." She was obviously on the boat, so why was Sejal asking as if Bane had jumped ship and swum off? Although it wasn't a horrible idea. If Bane fled, I'd follow her.

Bane pushed away from the railing and walked past us on her way to the nose of the boat in her floppy hat, short shorts, and sneak-a-peak cover-up giving me all sorts of glimpses of skin. Cute, awkward, kind of hot. My eyes followed her. Damnit, what was she wearing?

"Bhanu! Why don't you sit with us?" Sejal crooned.

"Oh, okay." Bane looked around for a chair. Before I could give her mine, Sejal suggested, "Oh, you can just sit on Sunny's lap."

I stiffened, and so had Bane. Her expression went deadpan, and the others had quieted to watch our little weird interaction of current and ex-girlfriend. Were they expecting something to happen? They seemed ready to jump in to douse any situation that might arise, but I wasn't having any said situation get that far.

I shifted to get up when Sejal said, "I'm sure Sunny won't mind. Since you are his girlfriend, aren't you?"

I lowered my feet off the footrest and began pushing myself up when Bane calmly replied, "That doesn't seem comfortable."

"Oh, it's fine! I'm doing it."

"I need more space for all this, I guess."

My brows shot up and I imperceptibly leaned back to conclude, that yes, Bane had a nice, full backside.

Sejal stuttered, like she didn't know how to respond.

Bane twisted toward me. "Were you just checking out my butt?"

I nodded with grave appreciation. "It is nice."

Bane rolled her eyes, trying not to smile, and told Sejal, "I was on my way to look at the water. There are dolphins out."

She smiled and walked around my chair to lean down from behind, running a finger up my arm, setting every inch from her touch on fire. She whispered in my ear, "You're welcome to join me . . ."

And with that, I jumped to my feet and announced to my now silenced friends, "Yep. Dolphins."

I hurried after Bane, my hands on her hips. She didn't hurry, and now I had my chest pressed to her back, vaguely feeling the curves of the nice backside I'd just been admiring. She fit so perfectly against me.

"Look!" She pointed out at the water where two dolphins jumped into the air, spinning.

"That's pretty cool."

We leaned against the railing, and I kept an arm around her, pulling her to my side, my hand precariously low on her back. She stiffened and I was quick to ask, "Too much? Should I move?"

"Are they watching?"

I stole a glance over my shoulder. "Yep."

She snaked an arm around my waist, inadvertently twisting into me so that two things simultaneously happened: My hand slipped lower, nearly groping the top of her butt, and her breast grazed my side. In response—I swore to the gods I hadn't meant to—my hand twitched, an imperceptible squeeze where it rested much too low on her backside.

I braced for her reaction. It didn't come.

Where was Bane's shove? Her pushing me into the water? Her quick remark to put me in my place? Or was she . . . was she so uncomfortable that she couldn't move? I should move.

From this angle, I caught her profile. The rim of her hat hid her eyes, shaded her nose, but left her mouth to my hungry gaze. She was biting her lip.

Did she . . . like it? Did she like me touching her?

Because I was bold or stupid or really wanted to get slapped into the ocean . . . I gave a slight squeeze.

Bane heaved, her petite fingers clutching my shirt over my hip. If she bit her lip any harder, she was going to bleed. But damn if I'd ever been more turned on.

NINETEEN

Bhanu

The air sparked around us. Was Sunny . . . touching my butt, and more importantly, did I like it? I did not, could not, be attracted to Sunny. Ludicrous, unsound, to feel this way about a grump who'd made it his career goal to irk me at work every single day.

However, twisted insides and roller-coaster thrills and a fired-up body were telling my brain to shut up. If the chemical reactions raging through me could be a voice, they would collectively say, "Sunny is getting your dried-out wheels lubricated. You need this."

Ugh. The obvious explanation was that this stupid fantasy tied up into the fact that I hadn't been touched by a man in a long time had finally unraveled any good sense.

For however long this interaction lasted, I allowed myself to enjoy it. But never would I cave. I would never melt into him, never squeeze him back, never flirt, never let him know what his touch did to me, never act on these ridiculous impulses. Never, ever, ever.

At some point, we had to part. Sejal had brought a basket of breads, sweets, fruit, and cheese onboard. We hadn't had time for breakfast this morning, and this was a welcome treat.

"Please, help yourself," she told me. "And I'm so sorry. Truly."

Sunny, even while biting into a croissant, seemed suspicious.

"Perhaps I didn't respond well," I began to say when Sunny wrapped an arm around my waist and pecked my hair, stirring butterflies in my belly. But I had to remember that he was playing a part, and maybe he was even acting more for his ex.

"You responded correctly," he said.

Sejal's shoulders deflated, and here I was truly expecting her to snap. I really wanted to know so many things that no well-mannered person would ask in this moment, but . . . what the heck happened between these two and did they still have feelings for each other? Was Sejal jealous? Was Sunny playing her game? Slowly, the idea of him wanting her back turned sour.

I chewed on decadent goat cheese and rustic bread knowing this was going to make me bloat in a matter of minutes, but I didn't care. It tasted so good. And I needed something to do.

"I did not mean to manipulate anything," she confessed, then said to Sunny, "But I'm glad that you've moved on and are doing . . . better."

"Better" didn't sound like a compliment, not the way Sunny tensed.

Maya and April, who wore cover-ups shaped like short kaftan dresses, joined us with effervescence and excitement about breaking out the bubbly. I'd learned that Aamar and Maya had sprung for the boat and Sejal had brought all the drinks and food.

Sunny excused himself to find the restroom, and shortly after, April took a call and Maya had to calm her down from a possible "flower disaster." I didn't envy brides, but somewhere in the back of my mind, I mused over how Indian brides got through planning multiple events and days of traditions and parties.

Sejal didn't slip away to calm her friend. She must've seen my curiosity because she explained, "I'm backup. I have no idea how to fix wedding things. Honestly, Aamar and Maya have taken that role and they've been pretty good at it. I might keep them in mind when my wedding arrives."

"Are you and Pradeep considering marriage?"

She shrugged. "That was my hope, but he's not there yet. There was only one person I'd gotten that far with . . ."

Her voice trailed off as she plucked a grape from its stem and popped it into her mouth.

I quietly observed.

She said, "He must've told you our history?"

Ah, so she *did* mean Sunny was the one she'd wanted to marry, the one who got away.

I didn't respond; instead I watched her through my polarized shades. My dad had often dealt with people who talked their heads off, liked to argue or shove their privilege down others' throats, and what he'd learned was to stay quiet. If a person was trying to argue or push a point and the other person refused to argue back, it deflated their antagonization. If he let that person argue until they had nothing left to say, he found that they'd often shut up and realize that he didn't care and/or they didn't have much of an argument in the first place. Those people eventually stopped arguing with him, stopped trying to push their narrative onto him, and grew less assured about their stances.

Papa had said it was interesting to watch people with pointless views unravel themselves in the quiet.

Maybe I'd learned my take of no-drama from my father. And this was a brilliant tactic. It worked every time.

Sejal had been saying, "We dated for a long time, were thinking about engagement, you know? Of course you know. Our parents are good friends, and everyone was expecting him to propose, but well, things weren't at the level they needed to be."

I didn't move or utter a sound, yet my body was relaxed.

Sejal, on the other hand, fidgeted with the stem in her hand and her expression subtly changed every couple of sentences. She'd started with haughty, then a tinge of annoyance, a pause for jealousy, annoyance again, and then her confidence eventually broke into uncertainty. Not about the story she was telling—it was probably true—but about my reaction. Or lack thereof.

"We were serious, obviously. But Sunny is a workaholic. All he cares about is work. I wanted more, needed more. He kept saying he was trying, but he wasn't. Finally, I'd had enough." She scoffed, as if Sunny had deeply traumatized her. "It wasn't my fault that I went to someone else who understood."

At that, I reacted, my brows coming together in a scowl. She'd cheated on him?

"Oh. I mean I left him for someone else, not Pradeep. It was a fling, but I don't cheat. Anyway. I worked on Sunny for so long, and he improved. I'm sure my work must've paid off; he's come a long way. You seem happy with him."

No response. Was she expecting me to . . . thank her?

She shifted under my impassive glare, as if my silence was making her uncomfortable. She tucked hair behind her ear, her once confident gaze flitting to her feet. She swallowed. All signs that she was losing her conviction, questioning herself, maybe even questioning her motive for telling me all this, whatever that might be.

"Was that right?"

I wasn't sure what she was referring to. It wasn't right for her to take credit for who he was today.

"I didn't have a choice. He forced my hand. But anyway. Here we are. I think he's still mad at me. But it worked out! I hope all the work I did on him doesn't unravel on you. He's the type you have to keep after."

I still hadn't budged more than the in and out of my chest in regulated breaths.

"I guess . . . I'm telling you all this because if you want him to be attentive in any way, you really have to work and stay on top of it. And if you don't mind, then good. But you should have a clear expectation with him."

On the surface, none of this was cruel or malicious. She wasn't trying to break us up, I didn't think. But there was an underlying tone of something. Warning? Passing on intel?

"Oh, I hope that doesn't affect how you feel about him."

I smiled. "We seem to have had two totally different versions of Sunny."

Her expression fell, if only for a second.

Her phone rang and her lips tipped in a smile. "How awkward. His parents are calling me. I have to answer."

She held up a finger, as if I'd been talking or even interested in this one-sided conversation, and just like that, all her hubris resurfaced.

The video call was on full display for everyone when Sunny reemerged.

Sejal exclaimed, "Hi! . . . I'm good! How are you? . . . It's been an entire two weeks since we've talked! . . . Look at where we're at! . . . Yes, of course, Sunny is right here!"

She'd turned the camera to him, and he waved, albeit confused.

"The entire gang is here! Sam and April, Aamar and Maya." She went around showing his parents everyone. Except me.

It shouldn't have bothered me. It didn't. I was the outsider to their college gang. His parents had no idea I existed, nor should they.

Sejal focused the camera on everyone, one by one, as they returned the greeting with waves and cheers and wishing how they could have made it.

Sunny glanced at me almost apologetically. With my shades on, he couldn't tell if this bothered me. It didn't. I wasn't part of his world or hers or theirs. But as a fake boyfriend, shouldn't he say something about me?

No, of course not. He wouldn't want his parents involved in our little charade. Still, there was a touch of isolation and feeling wholly left out when his ex's current boyfriend was waving back at his parents like he knew them, too.

And just like that, the tendrils of anxiety sprouted at the base of my skull. This small group that I'd been around long enough, who had made me feel welcomed, became a blur. Suddenly, the heat was rising, my shoulders were deflating, and my gut was turning heavy. My brain knew this was nothing to get panicked over, but my body caved to the throes of social anxiety. I was typically prepared to battle it going into a party or a crowd, sometimes even a movie theater or a concert. Other times, the unrelenting slide into obscurity came from nowhere, for no reason, and I wanted to fall through the floor of this boat and let the ocean swallow me.

"Yes! Let's get a picture!" Sejal exclaimed.

She faced me, holding the phone out to capture everyone smiling behind her.

"Wait! What about Bhanu!" April exclaimed.

"No, don't pressure her," Sunny said as I shook my head and waved them off and even flashed a smile, despite resisting the urge to escape into a corner.

I didn't want this lie encapsulated in any of these wedding memories, much less to meet Sunny's parents this way. Fortunately, the call ended shortly afterward, when it was time to snorkel. I gulped water in an effort to chase off anxiety before it became a full panic attack, and I offered to be the unofficial photographer to, one, have something to do; two, avoid being in said pictures; and three, not get roped into getting into the water.

Besides, taking pictures of a happy couple and cheerful friends was fun. It focused my thoughts and actions, allowing me to gather full control over any lingering bits of anxiety.

Sunny was quietly watching me when he walked toward me. He didn't touch me, and I was surprised by how much I wanted his hand on my waist, a reassurance and grounding. How strange. While I didn't like most people touching me, I'd never been bothered by Sunny's touch.

His brows were narrowed, worried, and I immediately told him, "No heat exhaustion. It's early enough in the day and plenty of shade and water. I promise."

His look of concern didn't wane. "Is there something else that's wrong?"

"No," I replied with a smile, neither wanting to share nor wanting to dampen his fun. "Go! Stop using me as an excuse not to party."

"Okay. Just . . . tell me if something is wrong."

I nodded and off he went, but only after Aamar had yelled for him.

I snapped shots of the bubbly—best to be served after water activities—and of everyone getting ready with gear, hugs, and sneak kisses, peace signs, heart signs, and everything under the sun when I noticed Sejal slurping the last of her iced coffee.

She had brought a Starbucks drink onboard, one of the few places on island still phasing out plastic straws. When she pulled the straw out to lick a remnant of whipped cream at the bottom, it slipped from her hand and fell into the water. My heart dropped as I lurched for the straw. My body nearly dangled over the edge before Sunny grabbed my waist and hoisted me back.

"Whoa. Are you okay?" he asked.

Sunny had my back flush against his chest, an arm around me as if I were trying to jump overboard into a frenzy of sharks. He peered over the edge. "What did you lose?"

"Oh, it's just a straw," Sejal replied.

"That could hurt an animal," I corrected her.

"Don't worry about it." Sejal waved us off and sashayed away.

I bit back my words, pressing my lips together, but no amount of tension could ease the fumes sprouting out of my nostrils. I'd helped Diya and Kimo on many of their eco-volunteering passes. I'd already loved honu, but once I saw Kimo pull out a bloody straw from one's nostril, watching helplessly as the turtle yawned in pain, in quiet screams, I'd never loved an animal so much. Every plastic straw gave me flashbacks of that sea turtle.

"You're shaking. Are you sure you're okay?" Sunny asked, still holding me like I might jump over.

I dragged in a breath and pushed him off. "It's not just a straw."

I walked away when I could no longer see that clear piece of deadly plastic floating around. Ooh, the confined rage. I wanted to curse Sejal out so badly, but I didn't want to make a scene. These weren't people in passing on a beach where I could tell them to leave honu alone like the signs said as I walked by.

Sunny approached me, touching my arm, letting his hand slip down to my wrist. "What was that all about?"

"Nothing," I grumbled.

"Don't do that. You're going to be in a corner fuming over some shit no one knows about."

"Oh? Would that exasperate you? Embarrass you?"

"No," he said pointedly. "I don't want you having a bad time here, not when I dragged you along."

"As if you really care?"

"I mean, *you* started this domino effect, but yes. It would weigh heavily on my conscience."

"It'll pass."

"But it was something. Obviously triggering. I've . . . never seen you pissed."

"Really?" I asked, surprised. Had I never been upset in front of him? Wow, did I know how to keep my crap together at work or what.

He was still holding my wrist, something we both seemed to glance at but neither of us let go of. "Did she say something?" The cut of his jaw turned into a sharp line.

Was he angry? Because Sejal said something mean, or because she'd made me upset? "Not exactly."

"Tell me."

I let out a rough breath and looked at the railing where the straw had fallen from. Others were tiptoeing toward swimming, waiting for someone else to go in first.

"She let a plastic straw fall into the ocean and didn't give a crap."

Sunny arched a brow. "Okay. I'll talk to her about pollution."

"It's not that . . . it's . . . here. Watch this."

I pulled out my phone and showed him the very graphic video I took of Kimo extracting a straw from a honu's nostril with pliers. The amount of strength it took to hold down the terrified animal, the amount of delicate skill it took for Kimo to pull out the straw without hurting the turtle, the way one could hear my sobs in the background.

Sunny looked at me. I blinked away, realizing how on the verge of tears I was. Maybe that straw wouldn't end up hurting marine life. Maybe it wouldn't get stuck inside an animal or get lodged in a nostril or a throat or a stomach. But chances were, it would. Sejal didn't care. Was she even aware these things happened?

"Let's go!" Sam called at the edge of the boat, diving in after Aamar and Maya.

Sunny grabbed the hem of his shirt and tugged it over his head. He handed it to me, and I didn't know whether to stare at the shirt in my hands in all of my confusion, or at his defined chest, ridged abs, and a very delectable V-shape at the hips where his trunks sat a little too low. And now I was utterly pissed because he'd ignored me and all it took was a shirtless Sunny for me to momentarily forget about dying endangered sea turtles.

He walked away. So he *didn't* care. Wasn't sure why that surprised me.

He jumped into the ocean. Wait. Hadn't he mentioned how he would never swim in the wild? Did he think I was overreacting so much so that he literally leapt into his worst fears to get away from me?

I nearly collapsed against the wall of the cabin behind me, exhausted. I couldn't wait until we got off this boat. This deal was so over. He could keep up the lie or not, but I wasn't going to spend one more second around Sunny or his clueless ex. Maybe all his friends polluted and didn't give a flying crap about how their actions hurt others.

April was at the railing, waving me over. I abided, but only because she was the bride, and it wasn't her fault she got caught in the middle of this emotional fiasco.

"What are you doing way over there by yourself?"

"Taking a breather," I said as cheerfully as I could manage.

"Are you going to get in?"

"Not my thing. Floating around in the ocean is terrifying. Aren't you going?"

"Oh, I wouldn't leave you alone."

"No! Go! Please. Don't hang back for me. This is all for you."

April smiled and then drifted her attention to the water, where Sejal was complaining, "What are you looking for? We're supposed to be snorkeling and having fun! Let it go!"

To the right, Sunny, Sam, Aamar, Maya, and Pradeep were looking for something. My guess? Manta rays or something that came out at night, so they weren't ever going to spot them.

"Found it! Thanks!" Sunny called back, clutching something in his hand as he swam back to the boat. He hurried up the ladder and went for a towel. He wore a look of shock edging toward trauma when he wiped his face and arms.

"I thought you hated the water," I called out to him.

"I do. Here," he said, holding out something.

"What?" I asked, annoyed but walking toward him nonetheless.

In his hand, Sunny held a plastic straw. My brain, my body, froze before jerking back to life. "Did you . . . just jump into your worst fears to find the straw Sejal dropped into the ocean?"

"Yeah," he said, out of breath. "Can't endanger any more endangered animals, can we?"

He licked his lips. I could freaking kiss this man in all his sultry, water-beading-down-his-naked-torso glory.

My heart spasmed and then filled with so much bubbling gratitude and hope for humanity that I swung my arms around him and crashed into his cold, hard, wet body. I held on to him as if he'd saved *my* life. "Oh my god. That was so sweet of you. Thank you."

He'd gone rigid, but an arm fell around my waist as he muttered into my hair, "I did it for the turtles; don't know why you think everything is about you."

I laughed into his slippery neck.

Sunny's hold tightened. Both arms were now wrapped around me. He was hugging me, gently holding me against him. And not in passing seconds, but what felt like long minutes. He felt incredibly solid, slick, welcoming. Were we having a moment? No bickering, no snark, no tension, just a kind embrace. Maybe even more than that as his chin tilted down. I could very well kiss this man, swept away in this moment.

But it was just a moment.

All right. We'd been hugging for way too long, and when I pulled away, my clothes were damp in the front and clinging to my body, revealing the bright colors of my swimwear underneath.

Sunny glanced down appreciatively (or was that in my head?), before dragging his eyes back to mine. His skin flushed.

"Don't say it," I muttered.

The corner of his mouth slowly arched up. Sunny leaned down, brushing his lips against my cheek when he whispered, "I got you all wet, Bane."

I practically growled. Ugh. Way to ruin a nice moment, but also, holy crap, way to relubricate my dry wheels.

He went to the edge of the boat, held up the straw for all to see, and yelled, "Don't trash the water again. I'm not going back in there!"

There he was, ardently warning his friends, beaded skin glistening in the sun like a sheath of diamonds, his hair slicked back, his muscular back and shoulders on full display with rivulets of water skimming his taut flesh, and his trunks hugging him in all the right places.

I drew my lip in between my teeth, devouring the sight of him as he stood over the railing like some water-soaked saver of sea turtles. And that was, without a doubt, the hottest thing a guy had ever done for me.

TWENTY

Sunny

For a good part of the boat excursion to now, there had been two things battling for attention: Bane and the fact that Sejal was still so close to my parents that they'd called her. Not me. That was a painful twist of the knife already thrust into my chest. But at least Sejal hadn't announced Bane, for whatever reason. Maybe she wanted to isolate her from the group or purposely ignore her. Maybe she knew better than to assume my parents would know about a new relationship if my friends hadn't known.

"Hey." Bane elbowed my side as we walked toward a new restaurant to try at the hotel for a late lunch post boat excursion.

"Hm?"

"Are you okay?"

"Why?"

She brushed a finger over my brow and my gut clenched. "That frustrated wrinkle between your brows."

"I'm not that easy to read."

She cackled, drawing curious looks from my friends ahead. Bane clamped a hand over her mouth.

"Almost ruptured my eardrum."

She flicked my ear. "Big baby."

I grabbed her hand. "You seem to like touching me. Careful."

"Or what? You're always threatening me. Talk so big and never follow through—"

I stopped dead in my tracks, spun Bane into me so that she hit my chest, moved one hand to her waist and the other to her jaw, and leaned down toward her mouth. I let out a rough breath, every muscle in my body tight. Every concern and pain caused by my ex vanished. Bane incinerated Sejal's presence as if she'd never existed, as if she'd never hurt me, as if she'd never left a trail of ashes in her wake. More than that? Everything and everyone around us melted into oblivion.

Bane grunted, gasped, some sort of soft, surprised, sexy noise that had me wondering what she'd sound like beneath a flurry of kisses. That sound, whatever the hell it was called, made me want to make her make those sounds again. And again. Tiny puffs of breath that slowly unraveled me.

"Who never follows through?" I asked, my voice dipping low.

She gulped, staring at my mouth. Her nostrils flared. She clutched my hips, digging her nails into my sides. And if she wasn't careful, I might just toss her back into bed.

Damn. It. Bane was really out here tempting the hell out of me without even trying.

"You keep touching me, Bane, and we might get into some trouble."

She sucked in a long, deep breath so that her breasts rose up my chest. *Fuck.* My gut clenched and I nearly, almost, pushed her into me. I wanted to feel more of her, all of her.

She whispered, almost labored, "Still talking, I see . . ."

"Does me touching you like this bother you?"

"No," she said on a breath.

"What about now?" I ran a thumb across her bottom lip. Bane never moved away. She never told me to stop. Her body always reacted, like these little pants escaping her right now, and the way she imperceptibly tilted toward me. Was she . . . into me? Did she feel a fraction of anything I was feeling with her?

I yearned to know. But what if she didn't? What if she was simply playing the part because my friends were nearby? That seemed to be the only reasonable conclusion.

"Ya'll going to make out right here in public, huh?" a voice announced to my right.

Bane jumped and stepped back, and I dragged my eyes away from her to see who the hell had interrupted us, but softened when I saw it was Diya.

Diya was standing a few feet away, a tablet clutched to her chest, and a dopey grin on her face. "You have a whole villa for that."

"Oh my god," Bane grumbled, her cheeks turning a delectable rosy glow.

"I can crash at my place, don't worry." Diya double-clucked her tongue.

"Okay, bye." Bane walked after the group, who'd been seated and had probably been watching our interaction based on the approving winks from Sam and Aamar and the expression of unfettered glee on April.

"I have a favor to ask," I said.

"Oh?" Diya replied.

"Bhanu loves ube, right?"

"Like it's the only dessert in existence."

"She'd mentioned this place had ube cheesecake, but I noticed a couple of other ube items as well. Which one is her favorite?"

"She loves them all, trust me."

"But which one is the most amazing? The one that will . . . make her ditch my friends with me?"

I didn't imagine Diya's smile could get any wider, but it had. "Ah! Now that's an entire mood! Let me see what I can do."

I went to our table and dropped my backpack on the floor, taking a seat beside Bane, somewhat proud of myself for creating a hopeful escape. I enjoyed my friends, I truly did. But I saw them often, and this lunch wasn't a mandate like the excursions. Right now, I just wanted to be with Bane in this bubble of pleasantness we had before it broke.

"What was that about?" she asked me.

"You'll see."

"Hmm. Very suspicious, you talking to my sister alone and her wicked little devilish expression. I saw that."

Draping an arm around the back of her chair, I promised, "I think you'll thank me for what's coming."

I watched her get quiet as conversations rose around the table. She imperceptibly glanced at the others, who were busy perusing the menu and recapping the boat adventure. Bane had seemed a bit drained since we left the marina, quiet. Even now, she stared into the distance, uninterested in the untouched menu in front of her. I'd seen these signs in my mother to know that maybe she needed a recharge.

"Are you okay?" I asked.

"Yes, why?"

"You seem bored."

"Being 'on' for so long wears me out."

We'd been with my friends for hours now, and even I was tired. "Do you want to get out of here?" I whispered.

She ran a hand down her neck, letting her arm hang, and nodded.

"Okay. Give me a few minutes?"

The waitress arrived and took drink and appetizer orders from everyone except us.

"Are you not eating?" April asked.

"No. I think I'm okay for now," Bane said right on beat, patting her stomach over her cover-up. She'd crossed her legs and my knee tilted to touch hers. Magnetic. Automatic.

"Are you sure?" Sam asked, and I nodded.

Right as the drinks arrived, Diya appeared at the bar. I told Bane, "Be right back."

"On the house," Diya said with a wink as she handed me a drink.

"I appreciate it."

"Just so you know . . . I won't be back to the villa until late evening. Or . . . not come back at all?"

Heat flushed my face. "Um. That's okay. It's really not . . . it's fine."

She raised her brows and lowered her chin as if saying, "Yeah, right. I got you anyway."

I took the tall to-go cup of light purple drink topped with whipped cream and a cherry with a pineapple wedge on the lip. I returned to the group, but I hadn't even made it to my seat when Bane's look of wide-eyed surprise, perhaps awe, stunned the others in our group into silence.

Standing over Bane, who had been eyeing April's tray of sampler mai tais like she wanted to try them, I asked, "What are you doing?"

Bane stuttered, fixated on the drink in my hand.

"Babe, I already got the good stuff."

She squealed! "You brought the ube?"

Bane jumped to her feet like a kid on the last day of class and took the drink, slurping up sweet, purple goodness.

"What's ube?" one person after another asked.

"If you gotta ask . . ." Bane said around muffled slurps, waving them off. "You don't even know. You're not ready."

I grinned triumphantly.

"Oh!" Bane offered me the drink, looking up at me with those big brown eyes, so willing to share. "Did you want to try it? You have to try it!"

"It's for you."

"You already tried it!" She held up the drink, noting the lowered quantity.

"How could I give you something that I already drank? That's all you."

"Not like we haven't exchanged spit."

I gave a sheepish smile. "Fine. Let me try and see what all the damn fuss is about."

I lowered my mouth to the straw, keeping our gazes locked, and sucked.

"Don't drink all of it!" She poked my side. "And?"

"And . . ." I gestured with a hand as if a gesture explained it all, but very little could explain the smooth, creamy, subtly sweet, robust flavor of an ube smoothie. There were notes of pineapple and banana and maybe strawberry?

"If you tell me you're not in love with this, then you have no taste buds . . . much less a soul."

"It's amazing," I said, deadpan.

Bane gently slapped my chest. "Amazing? That's all. I knew you had no soul."

I took another sip and handed the drink back to her. "You already know I love ube ice cream. I am an instant ube fan."

She took another sip as I swung my backpack over my shoulder and handed Bane her purse before draping an arm around her shoulders and leading her away with a wave to the group.

"Where are you going!" Sam called after us.

"Ube!" I called back, but we were already out the door and spilling into the gardens.

When we were surrounded by flowering shrubs far enough from the restaurant, Bane said, "Saving me from having to spend more time with people I don't know *and* feeding me ube? I'm not mad. Was this what you and my sister were plotting?"

"Yes."

"Scary how well you're getting to know me."

"Is it?" I reluctantly retracted my arm.

We didn't slow down until we'd passed the pools, making our way to the cove and beaches.

She offered me the drink every once in a while, and as tempted as I was to partake—damn, I really should've asked for two—I let her enjoy it. "Thanks for the drink."

"I didn't know you had so much nice in you, Bane."

"What? Are you still calling me that!" She shoved me.

"I meant *babe*!" I chortled.

We meandered in the direction toward the villa. "I don't know about you, but I'm looking forward to a shower and a nap. A nap. Wow. Haven't had one of those in years."

"Yeah." She slurped. "You stink."

"No. Because I actually got into the water, smart-ass."

"Because you stink."

"Because I was doing my part to save sea turtles."

She inhaled the last of the drink surprisingly fast. "I appreciate that. Look at this straw. It's already deteriorating. It'll be mush before it hits the trashcan and never stand a chance of hurting honu."

"You care a lot about an animal that comes from a place you hate getting into."

She nodded.

"Maybe we should change that?"

"I'll always love honu!" she said, appalled.

"I meant the water . . ."

She stopped. "No. Don't you even dare think it."

I glanced past her at that glistening ocean surface. "Seems fair."

"I'll bite you."

"I look forward to it." I leaned down and snatched Bane off her feet, throwing her over my shoulder as she half screamed, half laughed, and half kicked, half punched.

"Stop! Sunny! No!"

I dropped her feetfirst into the water. "There."

Bane glared at the water lapping at her ankles. "My shoes are wet."

"They're sandals. They're fine."

She rolled her eyes, and we walked along the shoreline as long as possible before having to cut across lawns to get to the back of the villa.

"Since you threw me into the ocean—"

"Not quite what happened."

She went on, "So tell me: Have you heard back about the PM position?"

I arched a brow. "Sounds like a breach of confidentiality."

"Why?"

"A conversation with direct competition? Are you trying to get intel? Sabotage? Spy?"

Bane scoffed. "Please. It's in the bag for me."

"So sure?"

She nodded. "Skills, education, years of experience, *seniority*. I'm just trying to plan for my future and make plans if this doesn't work out."

"Am I your biggest threat?"

"Aren't I yours?"

I frowned. Did she see me as the enemy?

TWENTY-ONE

Bhanu

Sunny had taken a shower and consequently passed out in bed, on his side, of course. I was on the couch reading another chapter from this riveting book, avoiding the heat and the bugs outside, when my phone lit up with a text.

> **Diya:** Saw something at the
> boutique earlier and snatched it for
> you since it's perfect. Last one, too!
> Should fit. It's on my bed.

Aw. That was awfully sweet of my sister.

I knocked out of habit, also just in case Kimo was here for some reason. There was a wide, rectangular white box—tied shut with a yellow ribbon around it—sitting on her bed. The hotel boutiques had very nice, expensive items, but Diya had a sizable discount that she'd surely used.

Tugging the ribbon off, I lifted the cover to find a lace dress so gorgeous that it stole my breath. White lace overlay on silky fabric dotted with a pattern of small, bright lemons and jade green leaves. I pulled it out of the box, running my fingers across the rough, textured lace. It wasn't a light dress but had some considerable weight and thickness to it. Holding it against me, I figured the knee-length, strapless dress probably fit. Diya had an acute sense when it came to sizing things up, typically needing to only pull one size off a rack and knowing it worked.

I stripped down and tried on the dress. And true to Diya's accuracy, this stunning dress fit perfectly. How did she manage that with a strapless dress! The bust was snug enough that I didn't worry about it slipping; even when I bent over, my breasts were never in danger of spilling out. There weren't any weird bulges, either, with just a hint of cleavage. The waist was snug but breathable and the skirt flowed as I twisted one way then another. There was a pinkish-purple grosgrain belt in the box, probably optional, but I tried it on anyway. And wow, did it enhance the entire look, adding a burst of color and a flattering line to my silhouette. Not to mention, it brought out the purple in my hair.

I texted Diya.

Bhanu: This is gorgeous!

Diya: Did you try it on? Does it fit?

Bhanu: It's perfect! How much did you spend!

Diya: You know I used my discount, so it wasn't much. Don't worry MOM. I knew you'd forget about the dress!

Ugh. She knew me so well. I *had* forgotten all about needing a dress.

Diya: Bitch, were you just going to
go in shorts or something?

> **Bhanu:** A pair of your slacks,
> at least.

Diya: You're hopeless.

I typed as I swirled back and forth, giddy with the swishing of
the dress. I typically preferred the comfort of joggers and slacks, but
this dress felt absurdly opulent and beautiful. *I* felt beautiful. I might
just wear this around the apartment.

> **Bhanu:** I appreciate this,
> really. It's so sweet of you, but
> the wedding isn't a big deal. I
> just met these people.

Diya: One: I checked, and this
couple is dropping a lot of money
for a fancy wedding/reception, and I
cannot have my sister representing
my family in shorts. Two: Bitch a
man is taking you to a wedding that
HE'S IN, a wedding for his BEST
FRIENDS . . . it's a big deal. All
of it.

I sighed, but there was no point in arguing with her, not without
telling her the truth, in which case my parents would blow up my

phone for a whole other reason and I'd never hear the end of this. A few more days of quiet would be nice.

Diya: I brought some shoes for you
to try. In the closet. Borrow whichever you want.

Bhanu: Thanks, sis. Love
you!

I opened the closet to find six pairs of dressy sandals, some with short heels, and the ever-daunting high heels.

After trying on, and walking around in, each pair multiple times, going on the tiled living room floor and outside in the grass to really test them, I decided on a pair of strappy sandals with a small heel. Let's be real, high heels weren't my thing. I didn't have the best balance for them, my weight distribution resulted in sore feet and tender calves within minutes and terrible calf cramps later, and I'd probably slip and break an ankle.

Besides, no one was going to be looking at me.

Changing back into a pair of shorts and a T-shirt, I carefully put away the dress, keeping it in Diya's room so as not to disturb Sunny, before plopping onto the couch and sneaking into work. Because, of course, neither Google nor my company had delivered an offer email.

"Where were we?" Verifying all the cards that had been checked off, I was glad to see the steady progress being made in my absence.

"What are you doing?" Sunny asked, suddenly leaning over my shoulder.

"Oh my god!" I yelped. How was he so quiet?

I closed my laptop as Sunny sat beside me, rubbing his eyes. "Not working . . ." I lied, even though I couldn't get into the server or lure information from coworkers.

He grabbed my laptop, slipping it behind his back.

"Hey! Rude!" I went for my device, reaching around him as he played keep-away just by twisting his torso. He was all broad shoulders and solid chest.

"No working. Gabrielle will behead you."

"As if you haven't checked in, Mr. Workaholic. Always on your phone."

He pressed his lips together. "I already got blocked from the server."

"See?"

"Which means I'm not in Hawaii on a beautiful day with my nose buried in work."

He relented, placing my laptop on the table as I sat back on my haunches. Sunny looked exhausted, but in an adorable sort of way with his hair mussed and a pillowcase crease indented across his cheek. He'd changed into joggers and a T-shirt after his shower, so simple and basic yet unfathomably sexy. They weren't too snug or too loose, just the right fit to enhance the broadness of his shoulders and chest, lend a little imagery to his abs, and um, lower.

STAHP. I had to stop.

Sunny lay back on the couch so that his head rested on the arm, cushioned by a pillow, his hands folded over his chest, and his body twisted at the hips, bent at the knees so that he wasn't touching me with his feet. He watched me with hooded, drowsy eyes.

"I check my phone because of my parents, not work," he clarified.

The same parents who'd called his ex? Why hadn't they called him? Was he avoiding his parents like I was mine?

I replayed the boat excursion in my head, how Sejal's video call with his parents seemed as if nothing bad had ever happened between them, like they were still easily a couple and obviously a match that both families preferred. Which was important in our culture. Indian parents typically thrived on being included in their children's big decisions like colleges, careers, and spouses. It was beneficial to understand the wisdom and tradition of older generations, to view things outside the scope of one's life experiences by seeing them through their parents' eyes. Usually, those types of families were close, which meant there would be a lot of future interactions. It was helpful to have good relations.

I turned toward him. "Is everything okay with them?"

He watched me without a reaction, but there was something in his solemnness that said maybe there was something wrong.

After a long minute of silence, as if deliberating on answering, he replied, "I worry about my dad being sick, or rather, getting sicker."

"Oh. I'm sorry to hear that. Do you want to talk about it?"

He shook his head.

In my family, we took care of our parents. It wasn't a strange concept that he wanted to make sure his were healthy.

"They seemed nice. On the video call," I commented.

"Yeah. They're excited about the wedding."

He'd spoken with incredible ease with my parents and didn't bicker with his own. They'd all been so natural with one another on the video call. It was good to see this side of him. Sunny other than a grump, other than a coworker who spent dauntless hours on projects, Sunny who had a life where he was loved, where he thrived with others. He'd never been one-sided, and it was nice to see those other sides of his world come to life.

"Do your parents call Sejal often?"

"What?" he asked, his voice gravelly, still full of sleep.

"She was so comfortable with your parents."

"My parents are nice to her, hers to me. They're not the type to hate us because our relationship didn't work out. They were friends before us and stayed friends after."

"That's good. What happened? With you two?"

He kept that intense, solid gaze fixed on me. Not one of anger or annoyance or amusement. Sunny was so difficult to read sometimes, and I wondered if this signature expression of his was purposeful. A poker face.

I should've told him never mind and remember the rules, but he could decide if he wanted to share or not. Maybe it was just me, but it seemed that Sunny and I were finally getting to a place where we could be, dare I say, friends.

TWENTY-TWO

Sunny

I sat up and ran a hand down my face. "Let me get some water first. Want some?"

"Yeah."

I brought over two glasses of ice water.

"Thanks," Bane said, and took a drink as I guzzled down half my glass.

Instead of looking at her, I stared at the condensation. Words had never failed me when I needed them for anything other than explaining my relationships or emotions. Work, classes, presentations . . . sure. I could speak eloquently, quick on my feet. Admitting aloud that I'd failed my ex, even having a side to the story, had never left my lips to most people. Even when telling Sam and Aamar why Sejal and I had split had been short, sans details.

My brain knew Bane would get an even shorter version, but those words, once so difficult to bridge between thought and spoken, fell out of me. It was as if Bane weren't here. Or perhaps Bane had become someone who made talking easy.

I told her everything, from our parents being friends and growing up around each other in the community, being friends with Sejal in high school and college, being pushed into each other by parents and finally dating because we liked each other, to the accusations and fights about me not being romantic enough, not being attentive enough, not being communicative enough, social enough, or enough of anything really in the end.

Bane listened wordlessly, a calming presence, which just encouraged the words to keep flooding out of me. Part of me felt like an idiot, unleashing all of this on her, but there was undeniably a larger part of me that had relaxed. Only because of Bane. Only *with* Bane. And hell, it was scary. My voice quivered. Why were things so different with her?

"So . . ." she finally said after I'd finished. I expected her to agree with Sejal. She knew me that well, had called me robotic, even. Instead, Bane said, "Your ex manipulated you into a toxic relationship?"

"What?" I swerved my head toward her.

Bane had a pillow on her lap and leaned toward me, furrowing her brows to understand. "Sejal claimed you don't communicate enough, and I can see how one might think that, but she in response didn't communicate on her end and instead used passive aggression, silent treatment, ultimatums, and deflecting tactics to make you feel bad enough to do whatever she wanted, even if she wasn't willing to understand or work with you?"

"I . . . no. That's not it."

"Did she ever ask why you didn't want to go to parties, why you worked so much, why you have a hard time expressing emotions?"

"No."

"Sunny." She deadpanned, giving me a dose of the many looks I'd given to her over the past year. "She wanted everything from you and wasn't willing to consider your side. She wanted communication, but she wasn't hearing you."

"You make her sound like a villain."

"You're defending her for making you feel bad. You tried, and it still wasn't good enough."

Hearing someone say those words cut deep. I flinched from the physical pain in my chest. If Sejal had taught me anything, it was that I wasn't good enough for a relationship.

"It was one-sided. Seems like there was a reason for her to be unhappy, but you tried to fix it. Believe it or not, you're not actually a jackass."

"Such kind words," I replied flatly.

Bane leaned toward me even more. "You're not. I've seen you with your friends and with coworkers. People genuinely like you. You get on my last nerve, but you do that on purpose. If you didn't try to annoy me, we'd probably have a barrel of laughs, and I would honestly feel somewhat terrible winning that promotion over you."

"As one would."

"All I've known of you is our constant bickering, but when I see you with others, you're a good person. Likable. Lovable . . . You are who you are, and instead of Sejal trying to work with that, just like you had to work with who she was, she wanted someone entirely different, and it wasn't right, or loving, of her to force you into a box that you didn't want to be in."

"Nothing she said was wrong."

Bane twisted her lips, studying me like she could read down to my DNA coding. "She really got into your head, didn't she? Open communication is important, expression is important, but not to the point where it's demoralizing. You should feel complete and supported and loved in a relationship, and vice versa. It's always going to be work, some type of effort, but it shouldn't be draining or one-sided."

"Toxic, demoralizing . . . these are very strong words, Bane." I just wanted us to move on and not have animosity between us. I wanted peace.

"Did she make you feel like crap? Did she make you second-guess yourself? Does this still linger in your head? Detrimental effects? I mean, Sunny . . . if we were in a real relationship, would you be happy with yourself, confident in us? Or would you constantly wonder if you're good enough for me, if you're being open enough, if you're making me happy at all? Or would you just be happy with me?"

I glared at Bane—not exactly the conversation I wanted to have— but her disposition remained soft.

"She did all that and then has the nerve to say she worked on you."

"I see you two chatted about me?"

"She's lucky I didn't toss her overboard."

I smirked.

She took in a big breath and released. "I don't think you weren't good enough for her. I think . . . it was her. She wasn't in it. She wanted something different and blamed it on you. I also feel like maybe she still wants you or is jealous or something. Something is there."

I looked ahead at the palm tree art on the wall. I licked my lips, folded my hands, and admitted, for the first time ever to anyone, "I'm not sure about that. I do feel like my parents loved her so much that they talk more with her than with me, that they blame me for not working it out. And that shit hurts."

There was a rustle beside me, then a gentle swoosh of air as Bane hugged me. At first, I was immobile, confused as to why she was hugging me. But having her warm body nestled against my side melted away bits of trauma. I relaxed, muttering, "Thanks."

"I'm going to feel a little bad when I win that promotion over you," she mumbled into my neck, her breath skittering across my skin.

I wrapped an arm around her waist, tugging her into me. God, she felt so good. "Just a little, huh?"

"Yeah . . ."

Despite having told Bane so much already, I couldn't find the words to tell her about my dad's health issues and how a promotion, and the considerable pay raise that came with it, would help. I talked about my parents with my sisters sparingly, to build them up, to help out as much as possible, to keep appointments and medications and progress orderly and efficient. But I didn't want to burden them with worry. I was supposed to be strong, resilient. Just like my father had taught me to be. But perhaps it was okay to ask for help, to know limitations, to speak up.

"Okay. Enough pity," I mumbled.

"This isn't pity," Bane insisted, hugging me tighter, her soft body fusing into my side, her floral scent overwhelming me. I could practically drink her. "You deserve to be happy with who you are. You're not that bad."

"Coming from my work nemesis, that means a lot."

"As it should."

She lifted her chin to look up at me as I tilted my head to look at her. A guy could get lost in those eyes. But those lips? Consumed.

I spent all my energy on not tilting another inch toward her mouth, but I was damn near staring at those lips. They parted ever so slightly, inviting, tempting.

Bane was going to destroy me if she didn't move away. Because I was losing this game. And if I kissed her, and this was all a temporary, fake moment, our working relationship would be ruined.

Neither of us budged.

Until her phone pinged from the coffee table, and she pulled away to check it, leaving my side suddenly cold and lonely. "Do you have to get back to your friends?" she asked, her voice strained.

The wedding wasn't so big and detailed that we had the typical rehearsal. Just show up early at the venue onsite and follow orders from the wedding planner. Walk down the aisle. How hard was that?

There was dinner and drinks somewhere tonight for the couple's families who'd arrived throughout the day, but honestly, I couldn't think of a better place to be. "No."

She bit down on a smile. "Hope you're hungry, because Kimo is cooking again tonight. They're on their way."

TWENTY-THREE

Bhanu

Diya and Kimo were making a commotion in the kitchen, assuredly about cooking. Kimo required control when it came to cuisine. He'd learned from his grandparents, parents, and aunts and uncles and cousins and so on how to live off the land and work with fresh ingredients. His style was subtle but precise.

Diya, on the other hand, was like our mother, who threw in all the spices and salt without ever measuring. Kimo hip-pushed her out of the kitchen and she shoved him.

"Eh! What you doing? That's hot oil!" he said.

"This needs more salt, it's so bland," Diya argued.

"Both you and this dish need to be less salty," he shot back.

Sunny leaned against the couch as we both tried our best to pretend they weren't arguing. "Are they always like this?"

"If you mean loud and in love, yes."

"Ah. So this is love?"

"Yep. They are unapologetically themselves and can raise voices and throw opinions and disagree without fighting."

"That's not a fight?"

"Nope. I don't think I've ever seen them fight, and never anything major. They're both hardheaded and stonehearted," I said with a laugh. "I mean, they're not sensitive when it comes to taking things too personally or the wrong way."

"Ah . . . must be nice," he said with a hint of envy that had me wondering if Diya and Kimo reminded him of his ex. Had they fought lots of real fights? Or had they been silent fights? Both seemed terrible in their own ways. And I hated knowing that someone hurt Sunny as much as Sejal had.

I was a loud fighter, just like Diya. I got it all off my chest and then went quiet because fighting exhausted me, leeching more energy than work, conversations, and parties combined. But maybe fighting was part of relationships, part of communicating, part of passion. Because I didn't remember having too many of them. My exes mistook my lack of throwing down in more than one or two fights as a lack of interest in them when really I just didn't want drama.

"The wedding is tomorrow," I said, saddened by the idea that our fantasy time was almost up. I really hoped we could return to reality as civil coworkers, maybe even friends.

"Yeah."

"Should we stage a fight in front of your friends for maximum couple effect?" I asked.

He winced. "I don't want to fight with you more than we already do."

"But isn't it realistic?"

"I don't think my friends would want to remember us fighting instead of the actual wedding."

"But we're so memorable," I jested.

"You're just full of yourself and your hype-woman skills."

"Aha! So you admit it. My skills are incomparable. Magnificent, even."

"I absolutely did not say that."

"It's in your tone. I read subtext very clearly."

He scoffed. "If only you brought this level of confidence to meetings."

"Only if you can tone yours down a notch. No one likes being smothered by that much arrogance."

"I just happen to be confident, charismatic even."

I laughed. "Yeah, okay."

Sunny pushed himself off the couch, his chin elevated so that he was looking down at me with brooding intensity. "Where's the lie, though?"

Had his voice dropped? It seemed to make its mark, darting straight to my core. Ugh. I hated what his Denzel voice did to me.

I took a step to meet him before realizing something. "Wait. Are we expected to dance?"

He pondered as if this was an actual question.

"Sunny! Of course we are! It seals the whole illusion, or do you not dance? Do you just code and dive into the ocean to save sea turtles?"

"Don't start."

"What?" I asked, baffled.

"You better not start your shit with me."

I smiled innocently and shimmied a little dance. Sunny groaned, pinching the bridge of his nose. "You're starting with me."

I grinned, making subtle dance movements as I glided toward him. "We'll have to dance, *babe*."

"Stop," he said, his voice a little lower, less its usual dry harshness.

"I'm not doing anything to you," I teased, turning my back to him before our chests could touch. I may have accidentally slapped him with my ponytail.

From behind me, he let out a ragged breath. I imagined him standing akimbo, glaring at the back of my head, exasperated with me as he often was.

"Don't we need to practice dancing so we look like a romantically involved couple who's touched before? It's okay, you know? You're not going to combust. I know I'm sizzling, but . . . Do you even know how to dance?"

Sunny was probably more awkward than I was at dancing.

I imagined him stiff and unyielding, needing someone to literally drag him onto the dance floor, and even then he might just, barely, rock back and forth and call it a success. I giggled at the thought of Sunny, so commanding and in control, being hilariously cumbersome and out of his element.

My giggles were quickly stifled when his hands landed on my waist, the sheer warmth of his touch burning through my shirt and branding my skin. My breath caught in my throat. My body stilled, but not in a statue sort of way, where every muscle tensed and warning bells sounded . . . but in a melting, pleasant, never-let-go-of-me way.

I had to actively tell myself not to make a sound, not to flutter my eyes, not to tilt my head back, not to arch into him, not to sink into his chest.

My heart was beating so wildly that I was certain Sunny could hear it, could feel my pulse pounding against his palms where his hold had tightened.

The heat from his body intensified like solar flares, telling me that he was mere inches from pressing against my back, quite possibly centimeters. I was heady and hot, my thoughts swimming and my legs thrumming. Oh, boy. I was in so much trouble.

His voice was deep, guttural, a rumble in my ear when he spoke. "You started with me . . ."

I swallowed. Oh, lord. He sounded like he was about to flip me onto a bed and plunge deep into my soul until I didn't have a coherent thought left. And curses to my body because it was responding with a sudden clench, an unfathomable need. These damn wheels were getting lubricated. "Oops . . ."

"Is this the plan?"

I swallowed. "It-it should be. Don't you think?" Damnit, why did I sound breathy? He shouldn't know what he was doing to me. It wasn't right, not when we were coworkers vying for the same promotion. Not when this was a dumb fantasy ending tomorrow.

"So we don't look like a fake couple," he clarified, his lips so close to my ear that I could almost feel them brush my skin.

"Exactly. Wouldn't want to make it to the finish line and get caught."

"Do you know how to dance?" He gently squeezed one side of my waist and I almost catapulted out of my skin. Who told him he could be this sexy?

"Dance? Yes? Dance well? No . . ."

He chuckled. "And *you* were making fun of *me*?"

I shrugged, only to have my right shoulder bump his chin. Oh, wow. He was standing so close. A shiver ran down my spine when he began to sway, taking my body with him. "I don't think this is one of the dances . . ."

"Huh," he grunted. "Thought couples danced like this at weddings?"

"Usually they face one another—"

He spun me, casting my breath right out of my lungs like some supernatural force. I, ungracefully, collided against him, chest to chest. A hard chest, yes, one that had probably formed with some type of exercise. Solid. Hot. Oh, my. Was I running a hand down his biceps and forearms? Yep. I remembered these carrying me.

Sunny's biceps stretched against his T-shirt, and good lord, how was that simple flex so sexy? His hands were at my waist, like before, but now we were facing each other. His height enabled me to fixate on his throat, which was utterly mesmerizing when he swallowed. Enticing my tongue for a taste, maybe even to nip the rigid angle of his jaw.

His hand fell on the small of my back, a soft and pleasant sensation. His hand slipped even lower where my butt began to billow out from my back—because, yeah, I was thick right where I wanted to be—and a warm flutter eased up from my stomach. It was a whole other level of subtle touching, an entirely new layer of nerves that lit up and threatened to ignite.

Sunny leaned down and whispered, "Is this believable?"

I was staring at his lips and the flare of his nostrils, but mainly his mouth. This was a fleeting vacation fantasy disguised as fake dating to help a guy out, but I just wanted to kiss him.

I swallowed and nodded. "Very." So much so that even *I* believed it.

The corner of his mouth curled up and my knees almost buckled. "Okay. Good."

I'd never thought my grumpy, nerdy coworker could be so damn fine. Ugh. Like bite-my-lip kind of fine. Which had me thinking about all the places he could bite me. Which had me realizing that I *wanted* him to bite me.

My skin flushed and I took in a big breath, a giant heave. That inadvertently stretched my torso muscles, drawing his attention to my breasts. Even if it was a fleeting glance. He could bite there, too, if he wanted. Sunny was quick to look away, as uninterested as a guy could be. Well, hell. That hurt. But it was for the best. We weren't here to get caught up in sultry moments and big mistakes.

It took a minute to realize that we were still swaying.

"How's this?" he muttered.

"Better." Ugh, nothing like being shown disinterest to halt the fantasy building in my head. My body followed suit. Shut that down.

"I don't think your hands are supposed to be clenched into fists against my stomach?"

"Oh!" I relaxed my hands as they fell down. Oops! They didn't need to fall that low. "Sorry," I mumbled, fumbling to get my arms around his neck.

"Don't strangle me, Bane."

"Haha," I said sarcastically.

"Why are you so tense?" he teased. "Are we fighting at the wedding dance?"

"We're always fighting."

"But this is a fake dating, fantasy vacation, wedding destination thing. No fighting in public."

"Are you telling me how to act like a couple? You, who didn't know how to act *all* this time and asking *me* what to do?"

"The smart-ass is back."

"With a vengeance."

He chuckled, his chest rumbling against mine, the friction so light against my breasts but might as well have been a jackhammer. Oh my lord. Did Sunny even realize he was touching my breasts? I mean, this wasn't a sexual embrace and there were better ways to grope a woman, but technically, his chest was rubbing against mine . . . so technically his chest was groping me. Sunny was getting second-base action and he didn't even know how lucky he was!

I took a step back, just enough to give the girls some breathing room. He should at least take me on a proper date first.

Sunny was sort of smiling. I wished he would stop that. It made him endearing and attractive and deliciously delectable.

My brain kicked in the second I registered the absolute silence around us. As in, there was no bickering, no sounds of frying or pots and pans or utensils or any movement coming from the kitchen. How could I forget where we were? Without looking, I knew my sister was watching us.

"We're not alone," I mumbled.

Sunny and I immediately took a huge step away from each other. He scratched the back of his neck and let his hand hang there. I'd never seen him flustered. It was a cute look on him.

"Dinner almost done?" I asked, swinging my gaze toward the kitchen, only to find Kimo leaning against the counter and Diya with her phone to her face.

I cried, "Were you videoing us? Delete that!"

"No!" she refuted, tapping away on her phone.

I rushed toward her, practically tossing aside the couch and entire chairs. "Don't send that to anyone!"

She gave her screen a final, dramatic tap right as I reached her. "Oh? What did you say?"

My phone pinged. Damnit, Diya. She'd WhatsApp'd that video to our family chat. Within seconds, our mother was going to be gushing and asking for details so she could work through the mighty desi auntie network and find every ounce of information on Sunny and then proceed to plot out our entire future. By the time I responded to the chat, my mother would have found out Sunny's complete biodata down to his height, income, and how many vacation days he had left so he could best utilize them for a big fat Indian wedding.

There was no point in arguing with Diya. She couldn't retract that video any more than either of us could stop our mother from pressuring us to get married every single time we talked to her.

I shook my head as Diya innocently shrugged. Around us, a dozen WhatsApp notification pings went off like musical notes in the background of a thriller.

"Really?" I asked.

"Really," she replied.

"Are you actually so invested in us, or are you deflecting?"

"Both."

"Watch it, little sister, or I'll be sending Mummie videos of you smooching Kimo."

Diya narrowed her eyes. "You wouldn't dare."

I smirked. No one out-bested the elder sister. Our mom was

pretty liberal with us dating. Obviously, we were grown women, living on our own with our careers and lives, but that didn't mean Mummie hadn't retained some tradition when it came to Indian dating. She didn't care about the race or religion of our boyfriends, as long as they respected ours and made us happy and indulged Mummie in a giant desi wedding with grandchildren soon after.

If she saw a video of Diya and Kimo getting cozy, she was sure to swoop in with marriage talk, focusing on the child who'd been in a happy, loving, committed relationship much longer than the elder child, who had just, seemingly, hooked a guy. It was basic logic. Marriage was much closer on the horizon with a long-term relationship in hand as opposed to a brand-new guy out of the blue.

Diya deflated. "I'll behave."

"Good. Is dinner ready? What can I help with?"

We had an enjoyable dinner on the lanai watching the sunset cast magical colors amid a cool ocean breeze, and where I'd never been more aware of Sunny sitting next to me. Instead of drinks into the night, Diya drove Kimo to pick up his Jeep from the shop—turned out driving a vehicle all up and down lava rocks and rough terrain required more maintenance than the typical paved-road-only car.

Sunny had swung his feet down from the lounge chair, checking his phone for the hundredth time, leaning onto his thighs, stretching the fabric of his shirt over his shoulders. With the sunset rays cast over him, he looked quite handsome.

"You look so serious. Or is that your ate-too-much face?" he said.

"So funny for a guy who never got his own hotel room and is shacking up in my bed."

He laughed so that his smile reached his eyes, setting them aglow like I'd never seen them. His teeth flashed, a few pointed at the ends and undeniably attractive.

I didn't know if I wanted to slap that smile off his face or kiss a mouth that could do some naughty things to me.

TWENTY-FOUR

Sunny

N ow that you've succeeded in getting so much personal, and embarrassing, intel on me, it's your turn. Why aren't you dating anyone?" I asked Bane, who was lounging on a patio chair, basking in the last remnants of sunset glow.

"Rude. You never ask a woman that."

After a moment of her signature simmering, she replied in an unexpectedly lively tone, "Okay! So let me preface this by saying I'm happy where I'm at, okay?"

I nodded. Clear indication she wasn't looking for a relationship. Noted.

"I don't need a man or a house or a family to be fulfilled."

"Of course."

"Just like buying a house, I have standards. Why waste the time and energy and money on anything less? I'm not going to buy a place just because society or family says I should, or any reason aside from knowing it's the one, the house that makes me happy and makes me excited to go home every night. Similarly, I want a man who does the same and makes me feel loved."

"You've never felt loved before?"

"My exes have said they loved me, but it was more that they really, really liked me. I want . . . romance; unbridled passion would be nice."

"Same thing Sejal said." I spoke before thinking.

"I mean, look at you. Why did she expect you to be something you're not?"

My chest spasmed. Talk about a hard-hitting jab.

"Oh, no. I don't mean . . . Sunny." Bane swallowed her words and gnawed on her lower lip. "That was insensitive of me."

"It's true."

"But you're not that guy, and that's okay."

"Yet you want what she wanted."

Bane shrugged. "I don't mean flowers and dates and candles and parties and vacations. I want to feel like I'm meant for him, and he's meant for me. Like rom-coms."

I eyed the yellow book haphazardly left on the foot of her lounge chair. "Rom-coms are cheesy and unrealistic."

"Rom-coms remind me of what real love can be. Not simply feeling adequate in a relationship, but feeling amazing, thriving, belonging. Maybe that's not the norm, but no one should have to settle for something because it's common. I'm not dating anyone because I'm not settling for anything less. But I wouldn't force anyone to be that way. Defeats the purpose."

"Tell me what you want."

She watched me for a second before calmly replying, "I want hugs from behind."

Now I was the one waiting for her to go on, to know more.

"Kisses on the forehead. Little things to show that he cares and thinks of me. Texts or calls during the day to tell me dumb jokes. When he knows I'm not feeling well and brings me something to cheer me up. Sees my social anxiety and takes action."

Ah, so I'd guessed correctly. Bane *did* have social anxiety.

"Looks at me like there's no one else. Makes me feel alive, happy to be around him, miss him when we're apart. Someone who misses me when he's gone, like really, truly, deeply misses me. Someone who makes my stomach lurch, my skin tingle, my toes curl."

"That's impossible. What the hell are you going to do with curled toes?"

She glared at me.

"Continue. Please."

"Someone who helps with cooking and cleaning because he knows I'm not his maid. Who holds conversations like an adult and does not throw tantrums or make assumptions. Someone who supports my career ambitions."

"Even if it takes time away from couple things?"

She nodded. "Because I would support him if he wanted to do something to become better or change course to be happier, fulfilled. We both need growth."

I mulled over her words. "So . . . let's say if we were dating and I chose to study new coding languages instead of going to a party with you—"

"You know me, right? Parties exhaust me."

"Okay, not a party. A family dinner?"

"I think family time is important. I'd ask if you could come for a little bit, and everyone would understand why you left early. They'd also understand if you missed dinners once in a while and would make extra for leftovers. It couldn't be missing every family dinner, but if you did, we would discuss why. There has to be a reason other than you having other obligations. I'd hope that you would be happy to have family dinners and try to make them. If not, then there's something bothering you about them and we should approach that."

Hmm. Definitely not a Sejal answer. I leaned toward her, my elbows on my thighs. "What if I stayed awake all night to work?"

"I'd encourage you to have better work-life balance, but I do the same thing. Just be in the other room with sufficient lighting, and make sure you're hydrated and exercising and eating healthy. Munch on a salad while you're working."

"So we'd just enable one another?"

She thought for a moment, pensive. "I'd say, maybe we can work out a system. Limit ourselves. No work after midnight. At least seven hours of sleep. No extra screen time one hour before sleep or within thirty minutes of waking up, preferably longer times on both ends. And . . . let's read together. Or walk. Whatever. Build heathy habits, but together. But mainly, I'd want to make sure you're in a healthy place."

I cracked a smile. "And hold each other accountable?"

"Yes. As long as you bring me treats."

"Treats?"

"Didn't you make cookies when you came to my apartment for a work party last year?"

I laughed. "You remember those?"

"Yes. They were amazing cookies."

"Now you're just flattering me."

"I'm being honest."

"And yet you don't remember where things went wrong that night?"

"Wrong? Aside from you barging into my bedroom? Felt like an unwarranted violation."

I groaned, rubbing the bridge of my nose.

"Ah, our time of civility must be up. Back to bickering already?" She looked at her wrist as if she were wearing a watch. "And here we were having such a normal time."

I took her wrist, lowering her hand. "All right, smart-ass. Tell me what you think happened that night."

"What I know happened?"

"Sure."

I was still holding her wrist when she explained, "I put on a work party every now and then for fun and morale and a way to meet people outside of work all in one go. Plus drinks."

"They were good."

"And the food."

"Divine."

"But being around people in social settings for too long drains me. Being at a party that large sucked my energy dry that day. Other people are like . . . energy vampires. Oh! That's another thing I need in a man: someone who doesn't suck my energy."

"No vampires. Got it."

"Are you taking notes?"

"Extensive ones."

"Good. I'd already been at my limit when you introduced yourself to me. I should've been more present, and I apologize that I wasn't. That was probably a bad first impression, but I was on the verge of having an anxiety attack."

"That's when you ignored me?"

She nodded. "Not intentionally. Everyone started to blur together, and the only thing I could focus on was how to get out, but it was my party at my place. I faked an important phone call and escaped into the bedroom, where it was quiet and dark, and just stayed there. I didn't know how long it had been, and I physically couldn't move. Not even to say goodbye to people. I knew they were leaving. I heard them, people were looking for me, texts on my phone, but then someone thought I was outside, so more people shuffled out. And then you came barging in, but I was still having an anxiety attack at two percent battery on my way to shutting down."

I stole a breath. How often did misunderstandings happen because both views were dramatically different? How many ruined moments or failed relationships or failures to become more? A hell of a lot. We were a prime example.

"Then you said something about me ditching my own party and I wanted to cry."

My heart fractured. "I . . . had no idea. It was a joke. To break the awkwardness of me walking into your bedroom. I know. I have to work on my tone."

"It wasn't you. Tack on a panic attack and exhaustion and worries over career and work and life and failed relationships and . . . a lot of things snowballed into that one moment. I wanted to cry, but you were there, so I couldn't."

"I'm sorry I made that moment worse. Had I known . . ." I rubbed the back of her hand with my thumb. "So that's why you snapped at me?"

"Did I? I didn't mean to. It was a blur. And I hadn't even had alcohol."

"I figured you didn't like me, and you were short with me afterward at work to seal my assumption."

"Short? No. No. We were swamped with huge projects and major deadlines, and everyone was asking me for everything, and I was giving everyone direct answers that were . . ."

"Short?"

She smiled, her shoulders relaxing. "They had to be quick if I was going to respond to everyone. But then you got snarky with me."

"Because you gave short, irritated answers."

"So that means you had to shove it back at me?" She shifted to face me so that our knees were almost touching. Annoyance flashed across her features.

"If that was a moment or days or weeks of stress, then how the hell did this last a year?"

"Because you were giving it to me!"

"Only because you started it!"

"Real mature."

"But that means you kept playing this short, annoyed response game in spite of me, huh?" I arched a brow in challenge.

Her irritation faded. She clamped down on a smile.

"Don't try to hide it." I nudged her knee with mine.

She leaned onto her elbows, matching my posture. "I always assumed you were this grumpy, snarky, stoic person."

"I am. But okay, it'd become a game with you. I admit it. To know that I could get under your skin is fun." The corner of my mouth twitched.

"I started doing the same with you because I could tell you enjoyed annoying me."

I tapped her fingers hanging close to my hands. Her skin was so soft. I couldn't stop touching her. "What do you think of me now?"

She peered right into my soul with those beautiful, dark eyes. "I think you're kind of nice. Maybe even rom-com cheesy."

"That makes me boyfriend material, you know?"

"I thought you *were* my boyfriend."

In all this fraud dating, I found myself wishing it weren't so fake. That these sensations coursing through me were real reactions. That these moments were true, and that these sparks between us were everlasting.

"And what do you think of me now?" she asked.

I touched her bare knee, daring but irresistible. Her gaze darted to where we made contact, but she didn't move away. "I think you're still an effervescent smart-ass."

"Lovely," she jested. "Quite romantic."

My thumb stroked the inside of her knee. Her breath hitched. Her eyes flashed to mine. "I love your reactions to me."

"When you're pushing my buttons?"

"Yep."

My hand glided higher up her knee, moving to her outer thigh until I felt the underside of her chair and dragged it toward me. Bane squeaked, grasping my biceps as my right knee slipped in between her legs. Her eyes fluttered. Her chest moved in and out in mesmerizing bursts.

I leaned forward, touching my forehead to hers, my hands finding their way to her soft, warm thighs. Her hold on my arms tightened.

"I really want to kiss you," I muttered against her cheek, where I could hear her panting. "So I need you to tell me not to."

"I will do no such thing." Her hand moved to the nape of my neck and clutched my hair.

"*Bane*," I groaned.

She turned her head slightly, our mouths closer to alignment. "Yes?"

I dug my fingers into her thighs. "To be clear: You want me to kiss you."

"To be clear: You want to kiss me."

I chuckled, my lips grazing her jaw. "Smart-ass to the end."

"All talk . . ."

"Yeah?" I dragged my lips down her jaw.

She gasped. "Yep."

Until our mouths met. A slow, burning caress. A soft, tender kiss. It seemed to be something I'd waited my entire life for.

Her lips tasted like cherries, sweet, succulent. Her presence consumed me.

My left hand slid up, underneath the hem of her shorts, my other hand at her neck as she released a sigh against my lips. She was so damn perfect.

I opened her mouth with mine, darting my tongue inside, eager to find out what her tongue tasted like when she let out a moan.

And then her phone pinged in three rapid successions.

Flustered, Bane pulled back. "We . . . um . . ."

"Shit," I mumbled.

"Right." She jumped to her feet and hurried inside.

I dragged a hand down my face. I was such an idiot.

We weren't really dating; that much was clear. We were coworkers returning to our real lives in a matter of days, to our bickering rivalry and competition for PM. This was all a fantasy, and we both knew what reality was like.

I was *not* her rom-com.

TWENTY-FIVE

Bhanu

Oh my lord, what was happening? Why was my body on fire, my skin burning, my goodies aching, my wheels lubricated like they were trudging through a monsoon? I didn't even know what to do with myself . . . I mean, sure, I *did* know what I'd do to myself if I were alone, or better yet, let Sunny finish what he'd started.

Ugh! Stop this!

I frantically paced the living room. What would that be like? His hands all over me, pulling, tugging, groping, squeezing, exploring. His mouth all over me, kissing, licking, sucking. Was he a biter? Oh my god, I wanted him to bite me. I didn't even want gentle caresses. I was at the point where I just wanted everything hard and fast while he slammed me against the wall. Could I ask that of him? Would he do it?

Oh my god. This room, with its many fans and AC, was much, *much* too hot. I needed to strip off my clothes. I could barely breathe.

Sunny slipped in through the back doors, keeping his distance as we met halfway. His face was flushed, his eyes imploring. "Are you okay?"

"Hmm? Yeah." If by "okay," he meant desperately needing a release.

"Was I misreading?"

I shook my head. God, no. I wanted him to kiss me. I just . . . ugh! *What* were we doing? How would this impact us at work? Especially if I ended up being his PM? What if anyone at work found out?

He took a few strides toward me as I lowered myself to the couch. Anything to keep from pacing, to stop the anxious jitters.

Sunny sat next to me, twisted at the hip so he could face me, and never once took those dark, intense eyes off me. "Did I make you uncomfortable?" he asked carefully.

"No." At least not in the sense he was asking. My body was raging, practically squirming. Oh, my. When had a man ever made me feel this untethered, like I could drift away at any moment?

He exhaled, his gaze skittering down to my throat, leaving a scorching heat. And oh, how I wished it was his mouth instead of his eyes surveying my flesh. "Should I . . . not have . . ."

His voice was devouring, smoothly entering my body, a body that wasn't prepared to be devastated by how it reacted. The tightening of muscles, the tenseness, the wave of rampant desire that could be felt down to the bone. It was a vibration causing an acoustic wave against my eardrums, as simple as that, yet reverberating through my entire being.

"Can I?" I rubbed my neck, unable to hold back.

"Anything," he growled, not waiting for my request.

Before I knew it, before he could blink, I crawled toward Sunny and straddled him, lowering myself onto his lap, our eyes locked, his hands on my waist guiding me. I was becoming undone. He felt so incredibly sensational between my legs, so close to those very well-lubricated wheels. I hadn't meant to rock against him, but it happened. He furrowed his brows in wanting, his chest moving in and out. By the way his arms tensed, I suspected he was trying very hard to control himself. Which, of course, turned me on even more.

"I've been dying to try this . . ." I confessed.

Unleashing inhibition, I moved to his neck and licked his throat as he swallowed, panted out a breath. How I loved his reaction to me. His hands gripped my waist a little harder, rocking me against him. And this time, I felt his readiness. A pleasant surprise of solid girth.

A kiss up to his jaw. A grind against his lap. My thighs tightened around him. Oh, boy. I wasn't going to last long. How embarrassing would that be? And how little did I care?

I bit back my moan. He kissed my cheek. Oh my lord. Here he was being gentle and sweet when I wanted him to pound me into oblivion.

Sunny slowly, methodically kissed me and nipped my lower lip. Grazing his teeth over my skin, sucking. It did all sorts of chaotic things to my insides.

Then he bit me. *Finally.*

I kissed him fervently, like a madwoman who couldn't remember this would have consequences, to which Sunny promptly responded. He returned my kisses with a passion I hadn't felt in a *very* long time, if ever. Lightning bolts of pleasure razed through to my core, heating my body by several degrees, setting me on fire. When his tongue met mine, when he bucked up into me, I couldn't fathom the sorts of noises coming out of me.

Sunny's hands skimmed up my sides, beneath my shirt, undoing the back of my bra like a snap of his fingers. At this point, he could give my clothes one look and I was sure they'd just disintegrate.

"*Bane,*" he muttered, pressing one hand against my butt, encouraging me to ride him, and another hand skimming across my side to cup a breast.

I let out a squeak of pleasure. Every touch, every movement, incinerated the consequences.

His kisses wandered down to my jaw and throat, nipping at my neck. He dragged that masterful tongue across my collarbone and down my chest, darting it lower, underneath my shirt. And lower, beneath my bra. And lower.

I clutched his hair, arching my chest, willing him to get to the right spot. How could he be close and so far? Was he teasing? I didn't need teasing. What I needed was his mouth fully on my breast. I'd have told him if I could form any actual words right now.

My shirt was now halfway up my breasts when the front door opened.

We parted so fast, my head spun. Sunny grabbed a pillow for his lap, and I tugged down my shirt because my breasts weren't about to be hanging out for Kimo to see. Except it was just Diya at the door, one foot inside, one foot still outside. Her eyes were as big as lemons, but then she snapped to herself and squealed, "Get it, girl!"

"Oh my god," I muttered, my fingers at my temple.

She smacked her lips. "You go ahead. I'm going to crash at my place. Byeeee!"

Diya had already spun on her heels and closed the door behind her before I could protest.

I let out a grunt, casting a glance at Sunny. He draped an arm over the back of the couch and watched the door, unbothered. He asked, his voice rugged, "Did she really leave for the night?"

"Yeah."

His chest rose with each deep breath as he dragged those dark eyes to me. His lips twitched. The brooding intensity lingering on his face, his breaths as ragged as my own, well, it wasn't far-fetched to assume that he wanted to keep going. After all, Diya's departure shouldn't be wasted. Her sacrifice of time, of having to drive through island traffic on one-lane streets to get to her condo, the bonding time lost between sisters . . . shouldn't go to waste.

I drew my lips between my teeth, and Sunny's focus immediately dropped to my mouth. I liked to think that I was forward enough. I went for what I wanted. Degrees and grades and jobs and projects and promotions. Those were typically things I needed. And sure, maybe I needed this more than I cared to admit, but men were a different nature.

And Sunny? Well, having known him for almost a year, he didn't seem like the type of guy who just went for things like this, either. He could talk his way through presentations, charm the pants off clients and bosses alike, and code like it was his breath of life. He seemed more like the kind of guy to bicker with me than the type who'd throw me into bed.

I prepared to resign the heated anticipation of going any further with him when he said, "Then we shouldn't waste the night."

My breath hitched. His gaze was scorching and his voice . . . damn that Denzel voice . . . had me squeezing my thighs together. Nerdy, grumpy, not-so-sunny Sunny had me tingling in all the right places and he knew it.

"Unless you don't . . ." he began, but his intensity never waned. He wasn't seriously questioning himself or this situation because he knew. He'd always known.

In case he wasn't clear, he added, "If you'd like. Or we can take a walk on the beach, and you can call Diya back."

"Do you want me?" I found myself asking.

He swallowed, leaning toward me, his hands practically balled into fists, the knuckles digging into the couch. "What kind of question is that?"

He pushed away the pillow, took my hand, and guided me to the very clear, hard answer. I wrapped my hand around the length of him, my breathing escalating, my body quivering as he leaned his head back and sucked in a breath.

"I don't have protection. Do you?" I asked.

"No. Don't need it."

"Excuse me?"

"I mean . . ." He settled a knee in between my thighs, gently pushing me back. "I want to make you feel good. Don't worry about me."

"Oh?" My skin flushed hot. I was *not* expecting this side to him. "Um. Just to be clear . . ."

Sunny slid his palm down my stomach, relishing, appreciating every inch, and undid the button of my shorts. "To be clear: I want you to enjoy yourself."

He unzipped my shorts, splaying open the waist and exposing the top of my black-lace-hemmed panties. Thank goodness I'd only brought brand-new underwear.

"To be clear," he continued, "I'm only using my mouth."

The room tilted on its axis and all I could see was Sunny watching me as he lowered himself over me with a raw desire sparking his eyes. He kissed my neck at the same time he swiped a finger under the hem of my panties.

He was definitely teasing. He knew damn well that there was no way he could be that close to the right spot and still be so far off.

He nibbled on my collarbone, gliding his tongue down to my top and kissing lower to the loose, undone edge of my bra. "Maybe my hands, too."

He flattened one large palm over the top of my shorts and slid down, underneath the fabric of my panties. Exploring, teasing, undoing.

I held my breath for fear of combusting. How could he feel this good when he'd barely just begun?

"To be perfectly clear," he added, treading kisses over my breast, "I've been dying to taste you for days, Bane."

I grabbed a fistful of his hair and nudged him lower. "Then taste me."

"*Fuck* . . ." he muttered.

"Language . . ."

"In about two minutes, I'm going to have you screaming worse than that." He nipped at my breast and I let out a lewd sound.

"Is there a word worse than that?"

I pressed a hand against his stomach, beneath his shirt, unprepared to feel the hard flatness of a toned body. My hands greedily felt every inch of smooth, warm skin of his chest and back and shoulders as he said, "Let's find out."

I didn't want him to move, but he took my hand and walked me to our room, stripping me down on the way. Before we even made it to the bed, Sunny had dropped to his knees in front of me.

I had never unraveled faster. I had utterly come undone.

⌒◈⌒

We lay heaving and sweaty, the pillow fortress demolished, the sheets to Sunny's waist and my chest. He drew me into him as we stared at the ceiling fan, which couldn't possibly churn air fast enough to cool us off.

"Guess there isn't a word worse than that, huh?" he asked.

"Guess not."

He bit my ear. "Now who has a filthy mouth?"

Heat crept across my face. I'd never used the F-word. Just wasn't my thing. But apparently that had been the only coherent word coming out of my mouth.

Part of my brain sparked to life, pushing around the obvious questions of: What did this mean for us when we returned? How were we supposed to work together? What would we be? Did we need a label? Was this just a fling? Did it all end once we left the island?

Sunny drew languid figure eights on my back to my stomach and down to my inner thighs . . . promptly shutting down my brain.

Eh. It wouldn't hurt to just enjoy this for tonight. Right? The wedding was tomorrow, and Sunny would leave the day after. Suddenly, our end was too soon.

As he slipped the sheet from my body and his mouth slowly followed the trail of figure eights, my breath caught, my eyes fluttered closed, my fists clenched his hair . . . and no thought was left in my head except how incomprehensibly amazing this man had me feeling.

Oh, boy. I was going to be in trouble when this fantasy ended, wasn't I?

TWENTY-SIX

Sunny

Waking up next to Bane was like waking up to a new day. No lingering pain or worry, just contentment. I was well aware that it wouldn't last. We'd be back to reality in two days, bickering at work, vying for the same position, and depending on who got the promotion, one of us might be the other's boss soon enough.

I looked at her as she slept snuggled into my side. I gently pushed back hair from over her face, gliding my thumb down to her lips. Damn, she was so fucking beautiful. It was going to hurt later, but I couldn't stop myself. Seeing her, knowing that we'd never be together because why would she want someone as messed up as me? She always said she didn't want drama, and drama had somehow become synonymous with my personal life.

It was already starting to hurt, a crack in my sternum, knowing that our "goodbye, it was fun while it lasted/what happens on island, stays on island" moment lurked around the corner. Common sense said detach now. But every other part of me told me to savor every second with this woman. I'd never wanted to protect someone as much as I wanted to protect Bane, to make her feel good and safe and loved.

Bane stirred beside me. "What time is it?"

"Late morning."

She groaned, her back to the light prying through the edge of the curtains. The room was still mostly dim and cool. "Are you watching me sleep? Creeper."

"The creepiest." I grazed her cheek with the back of a finger.

I kissed her temple, hating that I had to leave, but Sam and April would kill me if I was late to all the pre-wedding stuff they had planned. "I have to shower and get ready for this wedding thing."

"Nothing cock-blocks like a wedding," she said, then proceeded to laugh at her own joke.

The joke itself wasn't funny, but her reaction was the cutest. I kissed her softly.

"You're going to be late, Mr. Groomsman," she mumbled against my lips.

"They don't need me," I said against her mouth.

"They're going to be so upset if you miss this."

"I couldn't care less right now."

"Sunny," she moaned.

"*Fuck*, Bane. You can't say my name like that."

"Like what?" she teased.

"Like you want me inside you."

She made a little mewing sound, and god damn, she was going to break me.

Her leg rose over mine so that my knee automatically slipped in between her legs. I hooked a hand behind her knee as she slowly moved her leg higher. She was going to end me. I could barely stay in control, but that was why I had kept my shorts on. We weren't about to mess around without protection.

Bane's knee was against my side now, and I leaned down to kiss it.

"You should get ready," she said, even as she tempted me to stay in bed all day and forget the reason for this entire trip.

"I don't have to actually be there until two. We have plenty of time."

"For what?" she baited innocently.

Moving down, I kissed the inside of her thigh. "I have a few ideas . . ."

I pushed Bane onto her back, triggering a delicate moan from her lips, and took my time. I wanted to adore her like she deserved, like she was meant for me and I for her.

I loved the smell of her, the taste of her, the feel of her. The way she grabbed my hair to show me her need. The way she writhed and gripped the bed above her when she was close to the edge. And the way she screamed my name on that very last wave, bucking wildly into me.

Bane crashed back against the pillows heaving, her entire body glistening with sweat. And while I was so very tempted to lick every bead off, I had to get to the bathroom.

"I thought you had a couple of hours?" she protested, pushing back her untamed hair but leaving her fully naked body to my ever-appreciative gaze.

Grinning, I replied, "I have to take care of something first. But don't worry, I'll be right back."

I turned into the bathroom with a heave, tempted to finish myself off in the opulent, large-enough-for-three shower.

"Hey," Bane said, hugging me from behind.

In the mirror I watched her press against me, still naked. She smiled and tucked her face against my back as I placed a hand on her thigh.

"What are you taking care of in here?" she asked.

"You want me to spell it out for you?"

The next thing I knew, Bane was shoving me against the cold shower tiles, water on, and a bar of soap in her hands.

"What are you doing?" I rasped, pushing my wet hair back and wiping water from my face.

"If you need to *take care* of something on account of me, I should probably help."

"We shouldn't be in a shower together—" I began but choked on the rest of my words.

Bane's soapy palm was down my shorts and around my length, stroking. Her full, round breasts against my chest, her mouth against mine, and damn if I didn't just lose it right then and there.

Well, shit.

If we only had today left, then we were going to make it count.

TWENTY-SEVEN

Bhanu

I wasn't expecting to be this delectably sore trying to put clothes on while Sunny finished getting ready, yet here I was. Practically wobbling.

I put away dishes from our lunch of leftovers, dreamily reminiscing of last night. And this morning. Several times over.

Whew! I guzzled ice water to cool down but nearly spat it back out when Sunny walked out of the bedroom wearing the heck out of black slacks and a white button-down shirt. Even though it was hot out. Surely the venue would be indoors with AC cranking and save the entire section of groomsmen from suffering pit stains.

Pit stains or not, Sunny looked pretty good dressed up. His slacks weren't too baggy or tight, like they were tailored, which meant they showed off a nice butt when he turned to grab his jacket. Ugh. A jacket in Waikoloa was like having to walk into a hellishly hot death.

His shirt was equally tailored so that the threads were just the right amount of loose at his sides but a little snug at his arms so that the outline of his biceps showed while holding his jacket.

A tie hung around his neck.

"I can't believe they're making you wear a suit here," I said as if I didn't have water dribbling down my chin.

"Fuck me, it's already hot." Then he winked at me and said, "Language. Sorry."

I clucked my tongue. He wasn't sorry at all. "Not going to fix your tie?"

"I'll fix it there."

"Let me see how you look with a tie. Here, I'll take pictures."

"What the hell for?" he asked quizzically.

"I dunno . . . to commemorate this momentous day?"

He rolled his eyes. "For the social media I don't use?"

"Or for yourself? Memories for later?"

He shook his head. "They have a professional photographer. One of the reasons I have to get there so early."

"What kind of knot are you doing? Are you all doing the same?"

"Um. Basic knot?"

"Basic?" I crossed my arms, visually studying the single twist in the tie at his shoulder. "Do you know how to tie a tie?"

He scoffed.

"Well? Mr. I-Can-Do-Everything. Let me see your technique."

"No." He walked around the couch, and I went around the counter, blocking his path to the door. He heaved out an exasperated breath. "Don't start."

"I'm fascinated with ties. Show me."

"I'm going to be late."

"You should've thought about that before you pinned me in bed."

He groaned like he wanted to relive this morning, and my legs went weak. No! He didn't have time for this.

"You still have about half an hour before you have to meet with the others." I took the jacket and tossed it onto the back of the couch.

He dropped his head to the side. "Bane."

"Sunshine." I deadpanned.

"You're starting, and I'm pretty sure I asked you not to start with me."

"You didn't ask at all, and I don't take orders."

Sunny raised his chin so that he was looking down at me. Boy, he sure seemed an entire foot taller when he did that, and oh so attractive. "I don't have anything to prove."

"That's right. The basic skills of tying a basic tie don't prove a thing."

I knew him well enough to know that he didn't like backing down. When it came to me, he definitely didn't like me getting the last word.

Sunny fumbled with his tie, not even adjusting the twist on the shoulder, much less adjusting the ends correctly. I snickered when he just about slapped himself with one tail. His face flushed, his jaw tight, but not once did he say anything, much less ask for help.

As amusing as it was to watch him struggle with basic tie skills, I couldn't take much more. It was like watching a puppy trying to get up that very first step after learning how to walk.

"Just going to stand there laughing?" he grumbled. Not exactly a request for help.

I finally gave in to pity, took hold of the solid blue tie, and helped him. Sunny grunted but relented, his chin high, his gaze fixed on the ceiling as if looking at me would set him on fire in a painful death. His entire body stilled as I dramatically swept one end of the tie over the other, the fabric almost slapping his face. He winced but didn't pull back.

I stifled a giggle. "Oops."

"Sure you know how to tie?" he muttered.

"Yes." I tugged, jerking him forward.

"Funny . . ."

He still wouldn't look at me, so he couldn't see the stupid smile on my face or how much I was enjoying toying with him before taking this seriously. The tie had to be even, the lines of the knot just right, the length of each tail, and the tightness so it wouldn't look bunched or off-kilter or sloppy in any way.

"How do you not know how to tie?" I asked.

"Do I look like a guy who wears ties?"

"Not even for your job interviews?"

"For devs? No. At best, a button-down shirt and slacks, maybe a jacket. Never a tie. Where'd you, uh, learn how to do this?"

"Oh, you know. Just tying ties for guys all over the place. I'm pretty easy that way."

He grunted. "I honestly wanted to know, but since you brought it up—what happened to all your *benefits*?"

"I was joking. You think I have multiple lovers? Wait. Did you think I was serious? Were you jealous?"

"The idea of another guy all over you?" he grunted, as if that was an answer.

"So you were jealous?"

"I do *not* like the idea of someone else getting to touch you."

I bit down on my smile.

He peered down at my skills and asked, "YouTube?"

I sighed, recalling fond memories as a kid who thought she was a huge help to her hopeful Superman of a father. I focused on the tie, adjusting it in the smallest ways, as I said, "My dad went through a lot of interviews when we first moved to the States. All that racism and stereotyping and discrimination, et cetera, set him back. His English wasn't perfect, but he had a degree in civil engineering and a strong work history, but from India. Would never get the job. He'd take smaller gigs, whatever he could get, multiple jobs at once. Janitor, burger flipper, county clerk. But he kept applying and thought he should start wearing a suit for interviews. He had trouble tying. So I learned how to tie and tied all his ties, sometimes pre-tied so he could slip them on, adjust, and go."

There was a pause before Sunny asked, "And . . ."

"And what?" I fiddled with the ends, but the tie was just right.

"Did he get the job he wanted?"

"Yes," I said with a big smile. "Not the job he'd have for the rest of his career, but one that got his foot into the door and provided a better income and benefits, got us out of the ghetto, saved my mom from having to work two jobs. He was at that company for a decade, got promoted. Then he was fielding offers from companies who came after him and ended up working at his dream company. Near the top. His ambition wasn't to make it to the top. This was more than he ever wanted and he's in a good place. But whenever he has to attend tie events, like work parties or weddings, I always tie his tie and I feel like that little girl again helping her big, protective, hardworking papa. I knew tying his ties was a small thing, but he made it sound like it was the best help in the world, magic. He told everyone he got the job because his daughter tied the best tie."

I patted Sunny's chest but neither of us stepped away. I looked up from my great tie-tying work to find him watching me. How long had he been watching me? He was slightly frowning, enough to create that cute little wrinkle in between his brows.

I brushed that wrinkle and said, "This is going to end up being permanent."

Permanent or not, it wouldn't matter. That wrinkle worked for him, adding a degree of personality and intensity and a myriad of emotions without him ever having tried. Hm. Maybe my theory that Sunny didn't know the meaning of emotional expression was flawed. That little wrinkle said it all. And in this moment, it said that he—maybe—found me interesting and tolerable and maybe even gravely attractive with my hair in a messy bun and in pajamas.

"What?" I asked on a breath, realizing how warm his body heat was in this proximity, enough to glide over my skin, reminding me that Sunny was the very definition of scorching when he looked at me like that.

He leaned down, lifting his hand to brush wayward hair from my face so that his fingers grazed my cheek. My knees went weak. My legs were actually shaking, and I was now questioning reality. This must've been a dream because there was no way he, of all my nemeses, could make me feel this way when very few others had. Come to think of it, had any other man made me feel things that I'd once laughed at in rom-coms? Seriously, knees buckled because of arthritis and ligament damage, not because of feeling swoony from a mere touch. No one had that power, at least not in my experience.

But this? Lord, I needed to fan myself.

"What are you thinking so hard about, Bane?"

"One, if it's socially acceptable for me to eat cake as soon as I get to the wedding venue because I think my blood sugar is low. Two, call me Bane one more time and see how vindictive I can be."

He smirked. "Not what I was thinking."

Damn his Denzel voice. It was doing all sorts of weird things to my body, things my body knew better than to do for him. But the truth was, we were way beyond this surprise. I knew, and had known for a while, that Sunny got to me in the most fantastic ways.

"Can't possibly be thinking about anything sultrier than cake," I teased.

His right brow shot up while I was silently ordering my cheeks not to flush because we both knew the alternate meaning to the word "cake."

"I'm all for the . . . cake," he said.

"Right. I mean, that's the only real reason I'm attending this wedding."

"To be clear: for the cake?"

I nodded. "Yep. I love cake."

Sunny leaned down and spoke in my ear, his voice dropping. "Bane?"

Damnit. Why was he making his stupid nickname for me sound incredibly hot? "I thought I warned you."

"Yet I'm still waiting for a punishment."

"What is it, *sunshine*?"

He flinched. Ah, so he didn't like my new nickname for him, either. How convenient for me. He sighed, his breath crashing against my neck and sending shudders down my back. "Please tell me that you're not attending in sweatpants."

He was mocking me? So freaking smugly, at that!

He laughed when he started to pull away. I grabbed his tie and pulled him back. "Don't make me undo this tie."

His amusement vanished faster than a blink. Sunny's crooked half smile now a straight line of pressed lips; the laughter in his eyes melting into intensity. There was a need there, deep and ruminating.

With that sultry gaze locked on mine, our chests only inches apart, my hand still wrapped around his tie, Sunny said, "Don't start with me."

I scowled. "What?"

"Don't say things you don't intend to do."

I bit my lip.

His gaze dropped to my mouth, then eased down to the fist around his tie.

I released the tie and smoothed it down over his chest. "Too bad you have a wedding to get to."

He grunted, "I'm about five seconds from ditching this wedding."

I kissed his cheek and stepped aside. "You don't want to be late, sunshine."

TWENTY-EIGHT

Sunny

I hurried to the venue, briefly considering picking up protection. But I thought better of it. If we didn't have protection, Bane and I wouldn't cross the line. Well . . . another line.

My phone rang, and Papa's name flashed across the screen.

"Papa?" I answered on the second ring, my heart spasming. "Are you okay?"

"Yes, yes, beta! No need to worry so much over me."

I blew out a breath. "You're doing well?"

"Yes. Everyone is fussing over me, but I'm doing everything the doctor told me to do. I just wanted to say, please give Sam and April our congratulations on their big day."

"Ah. Yes, of course, Papa."

"Are you there?"

"On my way."

"You sound like you're hurrying."

I was walking faster than I had all week. Once I knew my dad's affirmative update, we hung up and I focused on the wedding. There wasn't much to do except keep the groom calm and know when to walk down the aisle.

Yet despite the whirling conversations around me and the flurry of excitement, my thoughts kept meandering back to Bane. No matter how hard I tried to stop myself. There she was. Implanted in my memories like a delicious treat to savor for eternity. Her smell, her kisses, her skin, her dumb jokes.

Damnit. I was so fucked.

TWENTY-NINE

Bhanu

Despite having a good amount of time before the wedding started, I didn't risk taking too much time getting ready.

A thorough shower, hair washed and dried, shaved, and in my robe, Diya arrived armed with a box in one hand and a friend just outside the door talking on the phone.

"Oh, hello," I said, ignoring the mischievous grin on my little sister's face.

"How was last night?" She wagged her brows.

"Amazing . . . just like this morning."

"Yayes! Hey, FYI, I'm going to crash at my place tonight, so ya know . . ." She double-clucked her tongue.

"I only have a couple of days left. I didn't mean to ditch you! I'm such a horrible sister."

"Shut up. I love you and we see each other throughout the year, but you haven't had a man in a while and it's *Sunny*. I will never cock-block my sis."

"Well, we didn't actually, ya know, the whole thing."

"Why the hell not? What were you two doing all night, then?"

"Other things. We didn't have protection . . . which is for the best."

"You better get some. He leaves tomorrow, right?"

I nodded, ignoring the depressing sensation in my gut.

"We'll have some time to chill afterward. To be clear, after you get some."

"Mm-hm . . . What's all this?" I asked as the other woman ended her call and walked inside.

"Remember my good friend, Leilani? She owns a hair salon that also specializes in special day hair and makeup."

I waved off Diya and hugged Leilani. "I know this woman! How are you, girl?"

Kimo's cousin laughed. "Good! So glad I got to see you. It's been so busy, and I wanted to stop by sooner."

Leilani always looked perfect, tall and curvy, wearing an off-the-shoulder pink top and skinny ankle pants. Her hair flowed over one shoulder in dark waves with bronze highlights. Her makeup was done professionally down to the eyelash extensions. If I recalled, because she owned her own beauty salon, she went in a little early every day and fixed her hair and makeup there. She'd once said she had to look the part so her customers could see that their stylist knew what she was doing.

I told her, "No worries! Not when you're hustling and your business is booming! Glad to see you now, though. Are you here for a wedding?"

Leilani looked puzzled before Diya swooped in, ushering me to the counter. "She's here to help you."

"What? That's too much effort. Diya, this isn't my wedding. I barely know these people."

"So you're going to go looking like how you always look?"

"First of all, this isn't a mainland wedding. It's going to be relaxed if it's partly outside. I think." Despite the guys wearing suits. "And second, it's not like I'm going to be in any of the pictures. I'm really and truly a last-minute guest because I happened to be here."

Diya set down the box on the counter, plopped me down onto a barstool, and said, "But you might. The point is, doesn't matter about knowing the couple. You got a man who's going to be there."

I grunted, "So I need to look fancy, is that it? He's lucky I shaved."

Leilani stifled a giggle as she opened her own box. The box to the left was full of hair tools from blow dryer to curler. The box on the right was full of makeup and brushes.

"What is my sister paying you? I'll double it for your time," I told Leilani.

She waved me off. "If I could get some pics of you for my business social?"

"Of course," I said. Even if I'd never consider putting in this much effort for a stranger's wedding, the idea of getting made up by a highly sought-after professional didn't totally suck.

"Yes!" Diya said, jerking her fist down like she'd won a battle.

"Diya, don't be that Indian. You should compensate her," I said even as I reached for my purse.

"Don't throw around stereotypes. Of course I paid! Don't touch your wallet!"

I flinched. "Oh my god. Okay. Chill. Can I at least tip?"

"Fine."

"What are you wearing?" Leilani asked.

I brought out the dress Diya had gifted me.

Leilani gasped.

"I know, right? It's so pretty!"

"Can I add a purple orchid to your hair?"

"I don't need an excuse to wear flowers in my hair. Of course!" I said, suddenly very into attending a wedding.

"I know exactly which color palette to use."

Leilani worked her magic on these slightly frizzy waves so by the time she was done, my black, purple, and lavender hair had texture, definition, and oh so much shine. I was practically taking notes on a style that looked so easy to obtain but I knew there was no way I'd be able to replicate this on my own.

She then went to work on my face, when I reminded her, "You know that I haven't mastered winged eyeliner, much less contouring."

"I got you," she replied and talked through every step, every layer, and the techniques she was using and why. Talk coding to me or research, and we would be fine. Talk makeup application, and I was totally lost. This was an art I'd never wrap my head around.

"Leilani!" I squealed when she'd finished, oohing over my reflection as Diya oohed alongside me. "I look like a freaking princess. Thank you!"

"Thank you for letting me play with your style!"

I fluttered my lashes. Oh, they were so long and thick and dark. And yes to every chance at wearing glitter, like the gold and pink shimmer on my eyelids. But the lipstick stole the entire show: a soft, floral-oil, pinkish-purple shade that matched the belt and the orchid in my hair.

"You look, and smell, like paradise," Diya said.

"That's so cheesy!"

"But true! Ugh, that man is going to take one look at you and tell the groom he needs to get out of there the second the wedding is over!"

My cheeks flushed. I could only dream for a man to see me that way. Sure, I'd had boyfriends and sexy encounters—and Sunny gave looks so scorching that my knees went weak—but none of them ever gave off the particular vibes of them falling to their knees with one look at me. Maybe that was an unobtainable fantasy, only happened in movies and in books, taught to us by poetry and impressed into our minds by raunchy TV scenes. But I'd seen the way Kimo looked at Diya like she was a fabled queen who'd mesmerized him with her presence. So I knew that kind of attraction existed. But I was also aware that it didn't exist for most.

Which was one reason why I hadn't settled down. I wanted that. Maybe it was too much to ask for, to be seen and treated like a queen, for everyone to recognize how my man adored me, but maybe it also didn't seem like too much to ask for. Sweeping, epic.

Once I'd dressed, which was easy in a strapless outfit without messing up my hair and makeup, I checked the time to realize I was running late. My adrenaline kicked in. I wasn't sure why; not as if I was part of the wedding or had even been cordially invited. But I wanted to see Sam and April's wedding, or maybe just see Sunny in his suit again. And that was perhaps the only thing keeping my social anxiety at bay.

"Why are you smiling?" Diya asked in a singsong voice when I'd emerged from my room fully dressed with purse and sandals in hand.

"Huh? Oh, am I?"

Leilani whistled. Warmth tinged my neck. Already armed with her phone for pictures, she strutted around me. "Girl. This entire ensemble is gorgeous."

"I know, I know . . . I don't even look like me."

I shrugged, twisting back and forth at the waist and feeling ever more like a princess. I knew why I didn't get fancy more often—thinking about the time and skill involved was exhausting—but also, where would I go? To my desk in the corner of my living room?

Looking down at my dress, practically startled by how in my face my plump breasts were, I imagined wearing this dress to work meetings. Wouldn't that be fun? Who, alongside myself, would be distracted by this massively effective, strapless push-up bra?

As if this were prom, both Leilani (for her salon's social media) and Diya snapped pictures of me. My sister fiddled with her phone when the familiar FaceTime chime sounded.

"Hah, she's right here," Diya said, turning the screen to me.

I sighed, slouching as my parents gushed over me.

Mummie was misty-eyed and cooing, "So beautiful, beta! What a nice, *sexy* dress, huh? Get Sunny's attention in a second."

"Oh, lord . . ." I muttered.

"Easy to take off?"

"Mummie!" I cried, almost slapping a palm over my mouth but stopping short because I wasn't going to ruin this meticulous makeup.

"No one is undressing my daughter!" Papa bellowed in the background. "Where's my champal?"

Oh goodness. My father was ready to beat Sunny with his sandal.

"I'm joking. I'm joking!" she said to Papa, but then turned to me as Diya stepped closer, whispering with a wink, "He's handsome, no? Don't get too wild. Oh! Glitter eyes. And what beautiful lipstick and hair. Who did this?"

"You can't believe I did this?" I asked, planting a hand on my hip as Diya lowered the camera and then brought it back up so Mummie got a full view of me.

Mummie said, "It looks like professional work."

Leilani gave a thumbs-up when Diya directed the camera at her, announcing, "The master artist. Mummie, you remember Leilani? Kimo's cousin who owns the fancy salon you went to?"

And then my mother proceeded to praise Leilani over her work. It was very good work, and for her to take my dull, boring self and turn me into a princess was no easy feat. But I was running late.

"I have to go! They're going to start before I get there! Thanks for everything!" I called back from the front door, slipping into the sandals, and making a mental note to electronically send Leilani a tip or drop by her salon with a tip and treats.

"We won't be here tonight!" Diya shouted after me.

The walk to the venue wasn't terribly far, even in dressy sandals. Utilizing concrete sidewalks most of the way helped. With the heat and humidity, I slowed down and walked in the shade wherever possible, beneath towering palm trees and flowering trees alike. There was no reason to sweat and ruin any part of my look, and if I was late, then late I would be. No one would focus on me.

When I walked through the lobby, I paused, throwing my head back to enjoy the chilled air before getting a complimentary water and following the gorgeous sign displays leading to the wedding. I was welcomed by the scent of fresh flowers and lingering perfumes as I turned the corner and wandered into a semi-open room full of people chatting and laughing and taking pictures. Light music hummed in the background.

Oh. There were more people than I'd expected. A pall of heaviness swept down my body, gathering at my legs and turning them into stone, telling me they didn't want to walk into this.

"Oh! Sorry!" Sejal had appeared from nowhere and nearly doused my dress with water.

I jumped back just in time. From the corner of my eye, staff members hurried to bring something to clean the floor. "I'm fine."

She gave a nervous laugh, her eyes darting across my chest and down my dress. Sejal looked lovely in a pink and beige dress. Suddenly, I felt way overdone. "I have to get back to the bride. Again, so sorry. Um, beautiful dress."

It took a second to realize what I'd done. I'd worn white to an American wedding. Crap. It wasn't uncommon for guests at Indian weddings to wear their own wedding outfits again, much less whichever color . . . but what was the appropriate etiquette here? Maybe if Diya and Leilani hadn't noticed, it wasn't a big deal?

"Love the hair," Sejal added.

"Hmm."

And off she went.

I shook off the interaction, but couldn't help wondering if she'd meant anything by her words, or had meant to get water on my dress.

Well, there was no turning back now. I mean, I could and only Sunny would notice. Otherwise, my absence wouldn't make a difference. I willed my deadened legs to move, my brain to shut off, and I swallowed my nerves and went ahead. For some reason, I didn't want to disappoint Sunny.

The archway stage was covered in red roses and white lilies, immediately capturing my eye. So breathtaking. Everything from the white bow chair coverings to the vases of flowers to the ribbons cutting the aisles off from the walkway to the stage set a romantic ambience. When the breeze snaked through, it sent the petals on the walkway scattering.

The walkway meant for the wedding party and the bride.

The walkway where I was standing, only a few steps away from disturbing it if I didn't move to the side.

The walkway where I looked up from the floating pink and white petals and realized so many people were watching me. Whispering, smiling, wondering.

I sucked in a breath, forgetting that large breaths probably reamped my already ample bosoms, and wrung my fingers together at my lap. So much attention, like they could tell I didn't belong, that I was a walking lie literally wrapped in a pretty bow.

As I decided which side to sit on, not that it really mattered as long as I sat in the back, my eyes fluttered over onlookers, following them down a line until my gaze landed on the groomsmen.

My breath caught in my throat when Sunny appeared in the crowd. He was talking to Aamar and Sam and a couple of others when Aamar cocked his chin toward me. Sunny's gaze followed. He was adjusting his tie and I'd have to redo it if he kept messing with it. The wind had blown some of his hair astray, but it looked intended and perfect. We hadn't been separated for long, but I'd almost forgotten how handsome he was in a suit and in that tie, which I now desperately wanted to undo.

I shook the thought from my head. Absurdity! No, brain! Don't go there! This was all an act, remember? To end very soon.

The cut of Sunny's jaw tightened. His eyes, even from this distance, bore into mine. That little wrinkle in between his brows appeared, as if he were scowling, but his look was as far from a scowl as it could be. A look of intensity, of longing, of undiluted need.

My lungs burned right along with my skin.

Sunny looked at me the way Kimo looked at Diya, but with a level of yearning that probably shouldn't be witnessed in public. Was I reading too much into this? He was probably trying to send me a telepathic signal to get off the walkway. Yet I couldn't look away. We seemed to be tethered and neither of us was able to break off.

I was still acutely aware of those staring at me. Part of me wanted to back away and get out of this room of strangers engrossed in this lie we'd been spinning. Part of me wanted to go straight to Sunny and . . . well, I wasn't sure what.

Kiss him. *You want to kiss him.*

The truth bubbled up the back of my thoughts, the declaration I'd been trying to stave off and yet was so achingly aware of.

I wanted Sunny. Badly. Unequivocally. Devastatingly.

This man was going to destroy me.

THIRTY

Sunny

Aamar was calming Sam down from his "oh, shit, I'm about to get married" panic surge. The guy had known this was coming, right? He'd planned this and had paid for it. I didn't understand why some people got cold feet or panicked about exchanging vows in front of others. He obviously adored his bride; he had no regrets. But I was one to talk. Me and commitment seemed to be polar opposites.

Sam chuckled and exhaled as if things were suddenly all right. Maybe they were. Maybe this wasn't about huge life changes or eternal commitments, but the emotion. His eyes were glistening, and Sam would most likely cry when he saw April walking down the aisle, which was going to make her cry, which was going to make everyone in the audience cry.

Aamar patted Sam on the back and laughed with him, looking up at me and then past me. His mouth almost dropped. He cocked his chin and I turned to see what all the fuss was about. Because Aamar wasn't the only one gawking at the woman at the entrance. One would think the bride had made an early appearance. This wasn't the woman of the hour dressed in a white gown.

No.

This woman was far more captivating, and I wasn't the only one thinking that. Not when so many seemed stuck on her, whispering, "Who is that?"

"She's gorgeous."

"She's sexy," a man nearby uttered, and I rolled my eyes. But there was no lie there.

"Breathtaking dress."

"Stunning hair."

"Purple hair? How dramatic."

"It works for her."

"Her skin."

Her presence was a force to be reckoned with and had stunned me into place.

I'd always noticed Bane when she walked into a room. There was a soft yet immediate knowing. I think everyone noticed her, really. She lit up the place with either her bubbly aura or her work ethic or her skill. Here, in this surreal moment where time had stopped, she was lighting this place on fire with her looks, an all-commanding presence, so powerful that it stole the breath right out of my lungs.

Bane was a fucking goddess.

I *almost* expected to see her in sweatpants or, at the most, unassuming monotone slacks. I always noticed what she wore. Solid colors, nothing too eye-catching, comfortable clothes. Nothing could have prepared me for Bane in a sultry strapless white lace dress. It had a subtle design of yellow and green, and ended at the knees. A vibrant purple belt tied into a little bow made her stand out even more. It matched the purple flower in her hair, which complemented her hair. Purple and black waves cascaded down over one shoulder.

She seemed uncomfortable with the attention, wringing her hands in her lap as she approached, her gaze darting left and right. Once our eyes met, her body relaxed. Her hands fell to her sides, and she offered a soft smile. Just for me. She made me feel as if I were the only other person in existence and everyone around us were ghosts fading away.

My heart was hitting my ribs. I'd never felt this before, this rush in my blood and excitement in my chest. I could see why people got off on adrenaline and craved more. I didn't want this thrilling sensation to end. Probably not great for my blood pressure, but who cared?

"Wow, Bane . . ." I said on an exhale.

She stopped in front of me, her eyelids speckled with glitter and her lips—god damn those lips—a vibrant pinkish purple matching her belt and the flower in her hair. She scowled and I put my hands up in silent apology, whispering, "Babe. I meant babe."

She rolled her big brown eyes, her lashes twice as long, twice as thick, twice as sexy beneath shimmering eyelids. Bane was, without a doubt, the most beautiful woman I'd ever had the honor of breathing the same air as. Her look was everything: complementary and beauty and art.

Maybe I was staring. Maybe a few extra seconds or a few extra minutes had passed without a word. I had no idea. She warped time. I was completely enraptured by her. Nothing else existed.

Bane swallowed, her gaze breaking as she adjusted a segment of hair, and I wondered if it was as soft as the skin it touched.

I brushed the hair aside, my fingers gliding over her collarbone. Her breath hitched and I said, "You look amazing."

She scrunched her nose as if to ask, "Really?"

I clucked my tongue and ran a hand down my face. "You look fine as hell, and you know it."

"It's what happens when I get out of sweatpants. Which is why I don't do it often. I could bring down entire nations. It's obviously enough to distract you."

"I can't argue with any of that."

She tugged on my tie and adjusted the knot with the slightest pressure, but it might as well have been a punch to the gut. A light floral scent crept up from her hair, and I just wanted to lower my face to her neck and see if her skin smelled as good.

"I'd say you look pretty good yourself, except I'm the one to thank for that."

"Is that so?" I asked, my voice rumbling out of my throat. Could she even see what she was doing to me? Part of me hoped not, because how embarrassing to give her an upper hand and fodder for future teasing. But part of me wanted her to know, to explore what her reaction would be, what her next move would be. If we'd tiptoe around this with jokes and banter, or if we'd near a continuously blurring edge until there was no coming back. I needed to know.

"The tie is everything. Without it, you might as well be in your touristy shorts."

"We both know what happened to my last pair of touristy shorts." Her cheeks flushed.

I cracked a smile. "Thanks for completing my look."

Her hand slid down to the end of the tie. The warmth of her touch seared through my shirt, to my abs. I had to focus, to remind myself that we were in public, in the middle of a crowd.

Not alone where I could place one hand on her waist, drawing her near, the other at the base of her neck, stroking her throat with my thumb as I kissed her. Where I could press her body against mine, eradicating this annoying space between us so that she was clutching the sides of my shirt, tugging it out of these slacks, letting bursts of chilled air hit my skin to cool me off but in no way actually cool enough. Probably nothing would cool me off at that point unless someone shoved me into a freezer.

We weren't alone, so I couldn't skim my hand across the exposed part of her chest and down her arm, to her hands, which would be unbuttoning my shirt. But first, the tie. Her fingers slipping into the knot and dragging it off me, her eyes locked on mine so that I could see the need in them the way she could see the need in mine.

Off with the tie and the shirt before I hoisted her onto my hips, my hands underneath her dress to hold her in place, feeling the roundness of that backside that I'd admired way too much this week. She'd gasp against my lips and . . .

Bane snapped her fingers, and I came back to reality with a jolt. Shit.

"Where did you go?" she asked, then gave that smart-ass smile of knowing. "Good thing I don't dress like this all the time. You'd never get anything done."

I tilted my head. "No, I'd definitely get something done."

She shook her head, her skin still flushed. "Can I ask you something, and you be honest?"

"Of course."

"Am I not supposed to wear white? Is that why everyone is looking at me?"

I glanced around and promised, "You are wearing the perfect dress. People are looking at you because they weren't expecting a fucking goddess to walk among them. They can't help but stare. And I stand by them."

She bit down on a smile. "You're so corny."

"Where's the lie?"

She lifted her chin. "I'm a goddess, huh?"

"Every inch of you."

Chattering pierced our bubble of solitude, and a soft melody began to play; a signal that we would begin shortly.

Bane looked around as people began claiming chairs. "I better find a seat."

"Sit anywhere you'd like."

She spotted one behind me. "I'll take that one in the back."

"Sure you don't want to sit closer? You can fawn over me in a tie with a better view."

She rolled her eyes, the sparkle of her eyeshadow catching the light. "So full of yourself."

A few rows away, Aamar motioned for me to meet him.

"We're about to begin," I told her. "I have to go. Try to enjoy yourself. It's an all-expenses-paid wedding, you know?"

"Lucky me."

"Which means reception afterward."

"I know."

"If you'll be okay. I know it's a lot of people, but if you're drained or bored—"

"I wouldn't ditch you." She smiled and walked past, brushing my arm with hers, her hand gliding across my stomach, which had me instantly clenching my abs.

I had to calm down around her. As much as I enjoyed teasing her, I was pretty sure she was teasing me back, trying to get to me in order to win some unofficial game we'd been playing, to best me at something we were both so good at doing.

Bane took a seat in the very back, adjusting her dress as she sat. Damn, it was hard to peel my gaze away from her as we moved into place. Sejal grunted at my side as if having to be paired with me was her worst nightmare. But it was easy to ignore her when Bane had established herself so fully in my headspace.

I even found myself smiling.

Aamar gave me a look.

"What?" I asked, clearing my throat.

"The sparks between you and Bhanu could start a fire."

"You're imagining it," I replied. Bane was just very good at playing girlfriend.

He wagged his brows to stand by his claim.

The intro music picked up and we walked down the aisle, each groomsman with a bridesmaid. Then everyone stood to welcome the bride as she walked down the petal-laden walkway behind the flower girl. April looked radiant, grinning and eagerly looking at her groom. Sam looked infatuated with her, and I got why he wanted me to have something similar.

Sam had it all. Looking around at our friends, they had it all, too. I was the odd one out, even if they didn't know it. In these past few days of faking a relationship, my loneliness had become nonexistent. Not because I was literally never alone, but because this fantasy vacation was burrowing deep into me. To the point where I had to remind myself that none of this was real. None of this would last. As soon as we set foot off this island, everything we "had" here would dissipate like Seattle morning fog.

I staved off the pain from knowing such a thing. At least until I had to leave.

The ceremony was short and sweet. That was the great thing about destination weddings. Everyone wanted to come together, watch an official union be born, and then get back to the vacation.

An explosive applause went off when the couple exchanged vows and Sam swept his bride into his arms for that first kiss. We whistled and hollered. My eyes skimmed over the pleased crowd, landing on Bane. She was the most collected, awkward in her little corner with a smile. She was gawky in a crowd that wasn't hers, but she was here for me.

I shoved that thought out of my head. No. The truth was, Bane was here because she got us into this mess and felt she had to save me from an atrociously grumpy time around my friends.

Bane caught me watching her. She gave a thumbs-up, as if I were a kid who'd just had the best recital of my life. I shook my head at her. She was so damn cute.

Aamar elbowed me in the side. "Haven't seen you cheese like that in a while."

Ah. I was grinning like an idiot, wasn't I? "I haven't heard anyone use the word 'cheese' that way in a while."

"You seem really happy with her, man."

Either our acting skills were impeccable, or . . . nah, we were being great liars. There was no other explanation as to how we were pulling this off. "If you say so. Thought we bicker too much."

"Maya reads lots of rom-coms. She calls your guys' antics as classic sexual tension."

The blood drained from my face. "What?"

He elbowed me again. "You better be making the most of coupling at a romantic place like this."

I cleared my throat. "No way I want to discuss that with you."

"Ah, right. You like to keep that to yourself. But a bro can tell."

Was it written all over my robotic face?

The wedding planner called us over and off we went to take a million pictures on the beach.

"You should bring Bhanu," April insisted, seeing that everyone would have paired off for the few non-wedding-party-only pictures.

"No," I said with a shake of my head. "We just got together."

No way in hell was my fake girlfriend going to end up being in their perfect wedding pictures only for me to tell them weeks from now that we'd split. I was not set up to have to hear about Bane for the rest of my life every time my friends showed these pictures.

But April wouldn't hear of it as she waved over Bane, who reluctantly eased toward us. She slipped up beside me, our arms touching, and I'd never wanted to get out of a suit faster. Not just the heat, I wanted to feel her skin against my skin.

"You look so beautiful!" April exclaimed.

"That's what I'm supposed to be telling you!" Bane replied. "You looked gorgeous during your nuptials, truly. You're glowing and it's everything."

"Oh, you're so sweet! Thank you. I was just telling Sunny that you should come be in our pictures. We're going to the beach to take them."

Bane hugged my arm, sending me a whiff of the floral scent that was trying harder than ever to get me to my knees. If she kept pressing against me, I'd be ditching the rest of my duties, taking her back to the villa, and more than happy to get on my knees.

"No, I couldn't possibly be in your pictures," Bane argued in that sweet voice of hers.

"You must!"

Bane shrugged, moving her arm up mine. It was a mistake glancing down, because the movement only brought attention to her swollen cleavage. I bit my lip and looked away. Damn that dress.

"No. I can't. My cousin got married years ago and another cousin had brought his girlfriend because there was serious talk of engagement, which is a huge deal in my family, almost a done deal if you mention engagements . . . anyway, the couple included her in the family pictures, but then they broke up a few months later. Every time we look at those pictures, we just hound my cousin on how he could let such a woman slip away, but more than that, she was forever in these wedding pictures. The entire thing feels awkward now. I'm not going to subject you or Sam or Sunny to that. It wouldn't be fair."

The bride opened her mouth to protest, but Bane was quick to add, "I appreciate the sentiment and the offer. It's truly meaningful to be invited into your pictures. I've had such a great time with such a lovely couple. But I'm about to pass out and need water. Please excuse me!"

"Oh! Okay . . ."

"I look forward to seeing how amazing the pictures come out, though! See you at the reception, and congratulations!"

With that, Bane patted my stomach as she turned to leave, brushing her breasts against my arm, her eyes flashing up at me.

One. More. Touch.

And I was going to lose any remnant of control I had left.

THIRTY-ONE

Bhanu

The venue, part indoors and part outdoors, had been transformed into a reception while the wedding party took endless pictures on the beach against the majestic colors of a descending sun. The couple would probably be back and forth to capture just the right moment at sunset.

I was content in watching from afar, and happy to have escaped the pressure of being part of the wedding album. We would forget this time soon enough without photographic evidence of our fake relationship ever having occurred.

What a sobering thought, really.

I tried my best to stay in an empty corner. The amount of people and noise was getting to me, and if I didn't act first, then an anxiety attack was sure to happen. But I was really wanting a dance with Sunny. Just one more moment before this all came to an end.

Several people had approached to ask who I was and how I knew the couple, as they'd never seen me around and surely they'd remember someone so . . . beautiful. Purple hair. They could say it. The hair, since not the face, was memorable. Thanking one after another on how lovely I looked was making me more self-conscious than ever. No one, and I mean no one, was as made up as I was except for the bride and her bridesmaids.

Ugh. Diya and her antics.

Oh, well. I was still a princess until midnight, or whenever I decided to wash off my face.

While the wedding party wound down on the last of their pictures, at least for now, the buffet came out. Staff arranged platters of appetizers and drinks on the far table, and I wasn't shy about partaking. I was here for the food, and cake. But I guess I had to wait on the couple for the latter.

I sipped champagne from a flute and eyed slivers of veggies twisted into flowers and thinly cut meats topped with real flowers. There were balls of fruit and sweet rice wrapped in taro leaves. Everything with a toothpick in it for easy grabbing and quick eating.

"Don't fill up just yet." Sunny's Denzel voice was in my ear.

I jumped, almost losing the rest of my drink.

He laughed, his hand on my waist and his mouth near my ear again. Except this time, there was a pause. I could feel the rush of air on my neck as he inhaled, deep and long.

"Did you . . . did you just sniff me?"

"Yeah. I couldn't help it."

I bit my lip. I didn't understand, didn't know how, but that was the sexiest thing ever. His hand on my waist tightened and he took another sniff right as I turned. Our mouths were alarmingly close to each other.

He swallowed, and I stared at his mouth. That perfect, skilled mouth.

My lips parted. I didn't know why. I had nothing to say. Words escaped me. Words didn't exist. What was speech?

"They have the wrapped shrimp still!" someone behind us exclaimed, shattering our trance.

Sunny led me away with a hand on my lower back. "Let's go to our table before we get run down."

He pulled out a chair for me.

"Oh, thank you. Such a gentleman."

"Don't get used to it," he said with a wink as he sat beside me.

Servers had filled fancy stemmed drinkware with ice water while serving wine and tea and probably everything under the setting sun at the bar where a good-sized crowd had already gathered. "Looks like people are about to really enjoy themselves."

"Bunch of drunks." Sunny swerved back to look at me, asking, "Do you want a drink?"

"Are you calling me one of these bunches of drunks?"

"Yes."

I laughed, holding up my champagne. "I'm still working on this."

"Might as well. I don't think they make dragon fruit colada or ube drinks."

"Such a shame."

"Hey!" Aamar said, sliding into his seat as we were joined by the rest of the wedding party.

Of course we were seated at the wedding party table right next to the immediate family to the bride and groom.

I was glad not to be near Sejal, to avoid her glances, whatever they might be. All focus should be on the happy couple. But the truth was, being close to Sunny made everything else disappear. We were floating in a bubble drifting on this moment in time. Cocooned and safe and warm and content.

As soon as the chairs were filled, we immediately stood and applauded when the host announced the newly married Mr. and Mrs. As we took our seats again, the couple commenced with the first dance as photographers and videographers floated around them. The father-daughter dance and the mother-son dance. Then the entire wedding party.

Sunny stood and lifted his hand to me. I blankly stared at it. "Huh?"

"We have to slow dance," he said.

"That wasn't in the rules."

He deadpanned, like really?

I shook my head. A slow dance was fine, but an integral wedding party dance?

"You just hold on to me and sway. Please?" he implored, his eyes soft, his expression pleading. He probably knew how hard it was to deny that face. Maybe that was why he looked grumpy all the time. His lethally handsome expression could take over entire worlds.

I swallowed. From behind Sunny, the rest of the wedding party waited for us, for me. I sighed.

I took Sunny's hand, and he swept me onto my feet. The music started before we merged into the smiling crowd, where each person from the wedding party, as well as immediate family, looked into the eyes of their significant other and moved with the gentle cadence of the song.

To be honest, it was hard not to fall into a sense of romance. The archway of flowers towered over us, the music was moving and smooth, we were all dressed up in our best, surrounded by lovely decor of white linens and roses and lilies, an ocean breeze sweeping through, and Sunny's hand on my waist.

"Thank you," he said, drawing me into him so that our chests were almost touching.

"What are girlfriends for?" I replied, my eyes fluttering away from the intensity of his gaze and to his hands as they took mine and placed them at his shoulders while I tried my best to stay out of the photographer's frames. Once even ducking and tucking my face into his chest and ever so thankful that setting spray prevented my makeup from smearing onto his suit.

"You won't combust, I promise."

Was he sure about that?

As we danced, in what was perhaps the world's longest slow dance, the lights dimmed, and damn if the romantic element didn't kick up a notch. I giggled at the absurdity. Were they trying to make everyone else fall in love?

"What's so funny?" Sunny asked, the corner of his mouth curled as if he found my random amusement amusing himself.

"Nothing . . ."

"But you're still smiling?"

I tucked my forehead against the crook of his neck and he held me closer, our chests now definitely touching. I felt his hands slowly, delicately glide over my waist to my lower back. And then go just a bit lower. I had to bite the inside of my lip to keep from moaning. How was this such a turn-on? How was *he* such a turn-on?

"I think your ex was crazy for leaving you . . ." I found myself saying. *Aloud.*

If Sunny had heard me, he didn't react. Of course, he was pretty good at not reacting. Maybe he didn't care, or maybe I'd crossed a sensitive line. For some reason, I wanted to know if he still had feelings for her. But then what? Would I feel hurt, or would I try to be a friend and talk him through it? Both? What would I say? I'd escaped drama most of my life and stayed out of other people's messes, but for once, I wanted to be pulled into his, if only to help him through it, if only to be this close to him for a while longer.

"Are you okay?" he muttered against my cheek.

"Yes, why?"

"You're tense." He began to move his hands back to my waist, back to a respectable place for two people who had, not too long ago, pretty much hated each other.

"No," I said and guided his hands back to where they had been.

"Okay," he whispered.

His breath crashed against my temple when he asked, "Is this okay?" His hands dipped just a little lower, to the curve of my spine where my butt ballooned out.

"Yes," I whispered back.

"This is, um, very nice." He tapped the top of my butt, and I pressed my lips together to keep from grinning like a fool.

"Ah, you can thank my mama." Thank her genes and good cooking, and those bored days at home doing squats to the beat of '90s pop in front of a rainy window.

"Thank you, Auntie."

I buried my laugh against his neck.

In another instant, the song was over. Sunny left one hand on the curve of my backside and ushered me to our table, pulling the chair out for me once again.

Before he sat down, he slipped off his jacket and draped it around his chair with a sigh of contentment. I imagined he'd been broiling in that jacket.

He unbuttoned his cuffs and rolled his sleeves halfway up thick forearms. And I was shamelessly staring. How was that so incredibly hot? Two veins bulged out of his forearms and my thoughts instantly flashed before my eyes, images of my tongue licking across them.

Okay. *Wow.* Calm down.

"Can you see?" He looked at me from over his shoulder as the couple, still on the dance floor, took a microphone.

"Through that big head?"

He dramatically threw his head back and rearranged our chairs so that we were at an angle, instead of pushed into the table. "Now?"

"Better." I leaned around him.

He gripped the underside of my chair and pulled me toward him, until the gap between us had closed. I clenched his forearm as if the sudden movement would've actually sent me flying off my seat. My knees uncrossed for a second in the jostle. Sunny placed a hand on my bare knee, muttering, "You okay? Gonna survive?"

I leaned toward him, still clutching his arm. I sort of really liked holding on to him, especially when his arm felt so warm and muscular and solid and real and welcoming and protective and basically everything that made my body respond, that made me want to stay attached to him. My thumb felt over the ridge of the veins I'd just been ogling. Yeah. This was ridiculously erotic.

He didn't seem to mind. He didn't shift away. He didn't remove his hand from my knee, either.

We sat like that, turning our attention to the couple as they gave small speeches and thanked everyone. Then their parents and siblings followed with short speeches of their own. Tears and emotions ensued. Pictures were snapped and the crowd applauded, cheered, wiped their own tears, and so on.

What did we do? We didn't move, not even for a single clap where warranted. We were glued to each other and preferred to stay that way. I adjusted my crossed legs so that they were tilted toward Sunny's thigh, which alleviated some pressure off my heels in these shoes. With his hand in place, the movement allowed the hem of my dress to shift up, exposing another inch of my skin. Another inch where his fingers made contact. An inch where his thumb caressed the inside of my knee.

My breath stilled. I didn't understand how such a simple touch could nearly unravel me. I'd had boyfriends and encounters before. Why was this so different? Why was this so fervent?

His thumb started with a quick movement. Maybe a twitch that he didn't mean?

Then it glided back. Okay . . . maybe he was just readjusting to the previous position.

Then it glided back and forth. Slowly. Consistently. Sending an ever-expanding bolt of lightning up my inner thigh until one more stroke sent the sensation shooting to my core.

I clenched my grip around his arm and my thighs. Crap. I didn't mean to. That was definitely out of my control, and now he knew what he was doing to me with this subtle movement that no one else noticed. The room was getting hotter. That breeze wasn't enough. Not by a long shot.

He tilted his chin so that his profile came into better view. Sunny was smirking. He knew exactly what his touch was doing to me. More than that, he liked what his touch was doing to me. Which meant Sunny liked touching me. And that, well, that just turned me on even more.

The couple moved on to the cake.

"Finally," I said, breathless.

Sunny gave me a look.

"What? You know I only came for the cake." I winked and stood as sexily as possible. But first, I leaned into Sunny so that one arm was pressed against his, giving him a good view down the top of my dress. This push-up bra was killing it, and his lingering glance at my display proved it.

"I'm going for the cake," I said. "Want some?"

"I'm here for the cake, too."

I returned with plenty of lemon cake smothered in decadent frosting with a mini yellow orchid. By then, plates full of food had appeared in my absence. But dessert first.

We ate and I listened to others chat, easing out of the conversation to avoid being overwhelmed with the crowds and noise and attention. I could focus on food.

One by one, the wedding party returned to the dance floor, leaving our table empty. They urged us to join them. Sam was even tugging on Sunny's sleeve, and I could tell it was getting harder for him to decline.

"You should go," I insisted. "My feet are starting to hurt. Don't worry about me."

Sunny raised a brow. "Who said I was even thinking about you?"

I knew he was obviously joking, but why did the idea of him not thinking about me hurt? This was desperate, dark water I was wading into, and that was dangerous for a fake relationship. Sure, we were living a trope that played out well in books and movies. But we lived in the real world. This was real life. And as soon as these people were off the island, Sunny and I would go back to being bickering coworkers who lived an hour apart and one of us, perhaps, would resent the other for getting the PM position.

"You should enjoy your friends' wedding. Go. Dance. We're almost over, but that doesn't mean you can't cut out a little early to enjoy what you came here for."

We're almost over. More words shooting pangs through my chest.

Sunny watched me, back to being impassive and thoughtful, quiet. I couldn't gauge a reaction, a sentiment, anything from him. Ah, yes, we were effortlessly creeping back to reality, to what we were before this vacation and what we would return to afterward.

He pressed his lips into a line and looked at my hand before taking it into his own. "Come dance with me."

I squawked out a laugh, quickly covering my mouth as the song changed tempo to something more energetic. "I'm not a good dancer."

"I'm sure you're great."

I tilted toward him. "I'm saving you from being embarrassed."

He tilted toward me. "Embarrassing me is your favorite pastime."

I leaned in even more. "It would be too easy to annihilate your entire reputation with one move. I don't think you're ready for that."

He leaned in even more. "I would love for you to annihilate me with one move."

Why was he so close? So close that his breath smelled of champagne and cake. So close that my lips could almost feel his. So close that he could probably hear my pulse raging behind my ears, my heart beating through my chest.

I sat back, forcing myself to unravel from this fantasy before it entangled me.

I shrugged, teasing at maybe a yes. The truth was, while these events almost always proved to be too much for my anxiety, my body wanted nothing more than to be in his arms.

THIRTY-TWO

Sunny

Bane's shoulders rose in an innocent shrug, and she batted her lashes. I managed to train my eyes on hers, not let them fall to the curve of her neck, where the skin was soft and fragrant, or her collarbone, where the ridge was ripe for a touch, or the swollen mounds of her breasts in this sexy-as-fuck little dress. She knew what shrugging did. She knew that I wanted to look, that I wanted to touch her, to kiss her. And just maybe, she liked knowing that I wanted all those things. Just maybe, she wanted me to.

"Your feet are bothering you?"

She nodded.

"Let me remedy that."

I tapped on her foot, the one swaying from her crossed leg, before taking it and placing it on the edge of the seat between my thighs. She stilled the instant my fingers touched her ankle. I peered up at her, all frozen, watching me, her lips parted, her chest heaving, her hands clutching the sides of her chair.

"Is this okay?" I asked slowly, suggestively. I never wanted to take my eyes off her, not when she looked at me like that.

She nodded, relaxing her shoulders.

I removed her shoe and massaged her ankle, watching her melt into her chair. When I pressed a thumb into her arch, she jerked forward.

"Tickles?"

She shook her head. I pressed harder, and that made it better for her. Her eyelids fluttered when I stroked along the arch to the underside. She gasped, and my attention fell to her mouth. Bane drew her lower lip in between her teeth. My pulse hammered inside my head as I took the other shoe off and repeated.

Mental note: Massage Bane's feet more often. She obviously loved this. Her expression veered closer to last night's territory the way she looked at me, like heated desire itself. Like she wanted me to move up her legs and in between them and didn't care if we were in public.

But we *were* in public.

I settled her feet onto the floor, tucking her shoes underneath the table between us, hidden beneath the shadow of billowing white cloth. "Better?"

She nodded. I was beginning to love the way she looked at me, mesmerized. Hell, I even loved when she looked at me with annoyance. I liked making her react, making her feel something, anything. Best of all, making her look like she wanted me, because I was definitely—despite reason and against logic—wanting something with her. Even if it was just for this ridiculous fantasy vacation. It would end tomorrow, but for now, we still had tonight.

Dancing was good. An excuse to touch her, remembering how she felt, my forehead tipped against hers. Our breaths deepening. The way she gripped the back of my neck, her fingers in my hair. The urge to nudge her head back and kiss her.

But there was weariness in her features. "Are you okay?"

"Yes. Why?"

"You can tell me if this is getting to be too much. The crowds and music."

"I want you to enjoy your friends' wedding."

"At the cost of your comfort? Nah."

Her mouth tipped up into a smile as the music segued into an upbeat song. A very familiar one. *Cake* was playing.

We burst into laughter.

"This is a sign for more cake!" she said, pointing to the desserts table.

I knew what to do. I took her hand and led her to the cake.

"What are you doing?" she asked when I requested two disposable drinking cups and two disposable forks from the staff member managing the table.

The perplexed server gave them to me.

Without waiting to be served, I handed Bane the forks wrapped in napkins, held one cup in each hand, and wagged my brows to her questioning face. Then slammed the cups over the partially cut cake—the bottom, largest tier—and scooped up a big serving in each cup.

Both Bane's and the server's jaws dropped. He probably didn't know what to do.

"Thanks!" I told him.

I turned toward a surprised Bane and urged her back to our table. I handed her the cups, grabbed my jacket, her purse, and her shoes. Facing her, I asked, "Want to get out of here?"

She grinned up at me and nodded.

And off we went into the evening, escaping the party, avoiding sunset pictures, and making the night ours.

Bane was giggling behind me, and I loved hearing it. I wanted to hear more for the hours we had left.

"Do you want your shoes?" I asked from over my shoulder.

"No."

She followed me barefoot across granite halls and smoothed concrete steps leading from the building down to the gardens. Torchlights and large-bulb string lights lit the evening. Cooler air met us as we left the noise and warm bodies behind us.

We slowed down as we passed the pool and found an empty set of beach chairs on a small cliff overlooking the ocean, the lagoon to the left, and the way through the golf course back to the villa to the right.

We plopped down, and Bane twisted toward me. She said with absolute delight, "Cake by the ocean! *Huh?* Another song, you know?"

"I'm not living under a rock." My knee touched hers.

"Are you sure?" She took a bite of cake.

I poked her side and she flinched, but she didn't move away. I took a bite myself, watching her watching the sunset and moving her hair over a shivering shoulder.

"Are you cold?" I asked, draping my jacket around her.

She sank into the garment so that it looked twice as big. It didn't cover her legs. "Thanks." Bane returned to the sunset. "Isn't it beautiful?"

"Yeah."

It truly was. A golden, almost orangish sun floated down past the faraway clouds, transforming the sky with creamsicle and pink and blue. The colors darkened and fading light glistened on the water like a million tiny stars. The ocean looked serene and inviting for once, and not like a beautiful deathtrap.

Bane was still shivering, goose bumps on her legs.

"You're still cold?"

"Eh, it's fine," she said.

"Do you want to go back inside?"

She scoffed and drew the opened jacket tighter around her.

"Come here."

She stared at me as if I'd spoken a foreign language that she couldn't wrap her head around. "Huh?"

I patted my thigh and raised an eyebrow. "I promise I won't bite. Unless you're into that sort of thing."

Her shoulders deflated. "No one's around, you know?"

"Yeah?"

"Who are you faking it for?"

Talk about a punch to the gut. "It's not pretending. I don't want you to die from a cold and then our coworkers blame me."

"Sure . . ."

"I'm not in the mood for a funeral."

Bane guffawed, slapping my arm. I was quick to grab her, pulling her toward me. "Or should I come over there?"

She swallowed, her gaze dropping to my mouth. We were leaning into each other now. It wasn't a far distance to her lips. I touched her knee, the one against mine, and she heaved out a breath. Her skin was cool, riddled with goose bumps. During the day, this area was worse than a sauna, but at night, on the beach, the temperatures dropped.

"You're cold. Come here."

She didn't argue this time. She stood and slipped onto my lap as I placed my empty cup on the ground. I readjusted her a little, asking, "Is that comfortable?"

"Yes. Are you comfortable?"

"I'm very comfortable."

She bit down on a smile and relaxed against me. She was sitting on my right thigh, close to the hip, her legs in between mine, and cushioned against my shoulder and chest. I had one arm around her, keeping the jacket snug against her backside, and the other . . . well, there was really no place to put it except on her thigh. I moved down to her knees, covering them.

"Better?"

She nodded, watching the tips of my fingers tap against her knee. The hem of her dress was a little higher. The section of skin between my hand and her dress had goose bumps. I inched my fingers farther up, a centimeter at a time.

Bane's head dropped against mine. She let out a soft sigh near my ear and I clenched my jaw. My fingers trailed a little higher, exploring cold sections with light grazes. Our breathing escalated. Her chest moved in and out in tempting glimpses beneath the open jacket. Her right hand went to my waist, clutching my shirt.

First, the tips of my fingers disappeared beneath the hem of her dress. Then my knuckles. Until my entire hand was beneath the fabric. Grazing turned into swirls; my fingers digging into her thigh, moving higher and higher, hitting the waistband of her panties. A finger slipped underneath, hooked, and tugged down. Just a little.

God damn, she moaned in my ear. I couldn't take it. I turned my head, nudging her nose with mine so that my mouth could find hers. I kissed her slowly, gently. Savoring every second, every sweet sensation moving through our bodies. I parted her lips with mine, tasted her tongue with mine, inhaled her featherlight groans like they were giving me life.

Bane wanted me as badly as I wanted her.

Bane had fallen into the fantasy as much as I had.

Either our acting was too good, or there was something happening between us. The only question: Was it real, or would it dissolve the second we set foot on a plane?

Right now, none of that mattered. Even if it did, neither one of us cared. Not tonight.

I was vaguely aware of where we were. In the open, on the beach, not far from a fairly well-lit pool and in between torchlights. There was a sidewalk behind us where people wandered by. A toddler shrieked; a dog barked.

Bane startled and pulled away. I immediately withdrew my hand, returning it to her knee. In the dim glow of the torchlight flame, her face was flushed, her lips swollen. I pecked them.

She smiled and ducked against my side, whispering, "We're not alone."

I held on to her waist, asking, "Do you want to be?" My voice had come out gritty with need. There was no lie in it.

Bane pulled away and stood, and for a second, I expected her to tell me to cool off as she finished her cake. Her empty cup now sat inside mine as she slipped her arms into the sleeves of my jacket. She sat on the other chair and went to put on her shoes.

"What are you doing?"

"Have to go past the party to get to the front."

I smirked. "You want to head to the villa or the party?"

She looked at me all sultry and perfect. "Well, I'm not in the mood for dancing."

"You want to head back to the villa . . . with me?" I clarified.

"You'd let me walk back in the dark? Alone?" She pouted and I leaned over and licked her bottom lip. She gasped.

"Breathe," I said against her mouth.

"You make it hard to breathe," she contested, pulling on a shoe.

"Don't your feet hurt?"

"Yes, but I'm not going to walk all the way there barefoot."

I stood and pulled Bane to her feet. She looked so small in my jacket, but the sight of her wrapped in my clothes was an insane turn-on.

I handed her the cups. "How about a ride?"

"What sort of ride?"

I turned from her. "Hop on."

She stepped onto the chair and wrapped her arms around my neck, cups in one hand, her purse in the other, pressing into my back. "Are you sure you want to try this?"

I reached around behind me, quickly finding her legs, and hooked my elbows around her thighs, hoisting her onto my back. Her grip around my neck nearly choked me until I had her adjusted.

"Don't kill me!" she squealed.

"You don't kill me!" I shot back.

"Oh! Sorry!" She loosened her choke hold and kissed the side of my neck. "Is that better?"

My grip around her thighs, skin to skin, tightened. "Are you fully covered back there?"

"Yes, thanks to your jacket. Now giddy-up."

I maneuvered through the sand and followed the sidewalk in the growing dark. We paused at a trash can for her to dump the cups into. We left behind the crowds and torchlights. Ahead was the trail. Above, the stars and a bright moon.

I walked carefully in the dark. The last thing I wanted was to trip and hurt Bane, but I was also in a hurry to get back to the villa with the greatest hope of having the place to ourselves.

THIRTY-THREE

Bhanu

o you want me to light the way with my phone's flashlight app?"
I suggested. If only I could get to my purse without falling off.

"No."

"Don't drop me."

"I'd never do that."

"I dunno . . . seems like great payback for all those times I got to
you at work."

"You're delirious from too much cake; you never get to me."

I took a deep breath, inhaling the lingering scent of Sunny's
shampoo and hair product and sandalwood cologne. I leaned down
and licked his ear, whispering, "Are you sure?"

His hold on my thighs tightened, sending a screaming sensation
of pleasure to my core.

He turned his head and muttered, "If you keep that up, I might
drop you."

I cherished the feel of him. "This is fun. By the way . . . Diya isn't
coming over tonight . . ."

His fingers pressed into my thighs, and I swore he moved faster.

Ahead, villa lights and sidewalks appeared. Waves crashed against the shore and rocks to the left.

"You can let me down," I said, worried about hurting his back.

"Not here."

Even though we'd made it to the sidewalks.

"Okay, now you can let me down," I said.

"Not here."

Even though he was unlocking the front door.

"Here?" I croaked.

He shook his head, even though we were inside and he'd flipped on the lights. The place had been dark, quiet, and obviously empty.

"What's that?" I pointed at the small basket on the counter.

Sunny walked me over and turned, sliding me onto a barstool like it was nothing, graceful and fluid.

He turned into me as I pulled out items from the basket, saying, "It's a gift from Diya. For both of us."

"That's nice of her." He examined the box of decadent local mac-nut chocolates with appreciation.

I riffled through the other items. Local rum cake that was very tasty and quite strong. The small size packed a mighty punch. And underneath that? I picked up the foiled packages before realizing what they were. I hid them behind my back the second Sunny saw.

"What's that?" he asked, peering around me.

"Nothing."

"Obviously something."

"Nah."

"Something so good you don't want to share?"

One hand zipped around my waist, and I twisted away, but his other hand was already behind me in preparation. I held on to the tiny packages. Tightly. My sister was going to kill me with her "gifts."

"Babe. What is it?"

I couldn't help simultaneously melting and chortling at his use of the endearment that still reminded me of Barbie. He couldn't have gone with "sweetie," huh?

With that minute execution of lowering my guard, he tugged on the packages, but I clamped down until my fingers were sore.

"You're so nosy."

Sunny stopped. He stood in front of me, taking up all the space with his legs touching my knees. Then, while keeping this wildly intense eye contact, he nudged my knees apart with his thigh. Slowly. I felt the gentle caress of my dress shifting higher up, his leg sliding in between mine. A tantalizing shiver ran through me.

"Okay," he said with that sensual Denzel voice.

Damn him. I wasn't even trying to fight him.

"Could you do me a favor, though?"

I nodded, unable to form one coherent sentence.

"No wonder I don't wear ties. This thing is getting on my damn nerves." He slipped a finger into the knot, keeping his eyes hard on mine. Piercing. Intense. A challenge. "Seem to have trouble untying this knot."

I swallowed. "Oh . . . do you . . . need help?"

"I think I might." His lips twitched, like he was holding back. Like maybe he wanted to rip that tie off and that shirt and then my clothes.

"You're just trying to get my hands busy so you can see what's behind my back."

"Maybe a little of a lot of things."

I shoved the foil packages into the basket, beneath the rum cake. Sunny side-eyed the basket. A corner stuck out and his lips twitched again. He knew what those were, and by the smoldering fervor in his eyes, he intended to use them tonight.

A tiny voice sounded in the back of my thoughts of how this was a bad idea. We were taking the fantasy vacation too far, but we'd gotten pretty close to too far already.

I took hold of one end of his tie, my other hand at the knot. His fingers moved down my hand and arm, falling to his side. His touch was so light, yet burning.

I slowly pulled down the knot.

Tie off.

He tilted his head to the side, his eyes never leaving mine. "Should we stop there?"

"No."

He edged closer to the seat. His hands slid up my legs, beneath the dress, his mouth on mine to nip and suck on my bottom lip. Then a kiss. And his tongue. His masterful, decadent tongue.

"You taste like cake," I mumbled.

"You taste even better than cake."

I scowled. "What's better than cake?"

"You. The taste of you."

My arms draped over his broad, firm shoulders as he moved one hand to cup my face, kissing my jaw, my neck, my clavicle, down my chest. His other hand went underneath my thigh, gliding back down and lifting my leg up. My other leg followed suit; my ankles crossed behind his waist in the most indecent, depraved way.

He hooked a finger beneath my panties, tugging, teasing. His hand at my neck skimmed lower, his thumb leaving a hot trail. Hot trails all over. So much sensation that I couldn't focus on any one thing. He was doing so much, all at once, some parts slow and agonizing, some parts faster.

His palm sprawled over my chest.

Then his tongue dipped into the bodice. And I nearly jumped out of my skin. An embarrassingly high whimper came out of me.

Sunny smiled against my skin before his tongue darted back inside my bodice. My legs clenched around him. My fingers dug through his hair. I wanted his lips all over me. Everywhere, at once, fast and slow, light and hard, delicate and passionate.

My nerves were coming undone. My body unraveling. And we hadn't even undressed.

That tiny voice in the back of my head tried to shout a demand for me to stop. We were coworkers, going after the same promotion. We bickered all the time. This wasn't real. We were fake. This was a fantasy with a timer ticking down to our last hours and seconds. Like every project I'd ever worked on, there was a deadline, a hard end. It loomed on the horizon. The last of the kanban cards was moving into archives. No extensions permitted.

But that voice of reason was too small, deflating into an echo, overpowered by the intoxication of this man.

Somewhere in between my gasps and his groans—I mean *wow*— I managed to locate the packages beneath the rum cake, hoping they'd fit.

He smirked. "More cake, huh?"

"Is that what you're looking at?" I said, fighting for air.

He took the package, read it, then handed them to me. "I don't know how she knew my size, but hats off to your sister."

Ah, yes. Diya won the competition guessing the size for anything. She was truly gifted.

Without another second to spare, Sunny hoisted me onto his hips, his hands firm beneath my butt underneath the dress, and sprinkled kisses across my chest and throat.

He took a step when I gasped, reaching past him to the counter.

"You're bringing the cake, aren't you?" He nipped my neck.

"I only came for the cake, remember?"

And with that, Sunny took me into the bedroom, closed the door behind us, and tossed me onto the bed, which smelled of him and me and us.

He looked down at me as he unbuttoned his shirt in a way no other man had ever looked at me before. If heated desire could start fires, then this entire villa would be in flames. He looked at me like I was an ethereal queen and there was no other person in existence. Like he would ride or die for me, like he would protect me and uplift me, like he would make love to me in the most euphoric ways . . . like he would bring me ube in the Tacoma rain.

This was a look I'd wanted for so long, but never thought it would ever happen.

No matter what happened tonight, or where we'd return to in a few days, his look, how he melted me, the way his kisses shattered me . . . the bar had been set higher than I'd ever imagined it could get.

There was no coming back from this.

Sunny had ruined me.

⌒·⌒

I'd fallen asleep content and safe and adored.

And I awoke aroused and hungry and desired.

My back was against Sunny's chest when he lifted my hair to kiss the nape of my neck, tugging the sheets lower and lower as his mouth skimmed across my shoulder and down my spine, to my hip and across my waist. I rolled beneath him and immediately face-planted into the mattress because his body weight had created a depression and accelerated my turning over toward him.

He laughed into my stomach. "Are you okay?"

I covered my face because of course that would happen. "I should probably shower."

"Don't you mean 'we'?"

Sunny took my hand and pulled me up and out of bed, leading me into the bathroom. He trailed kisses across my neck and shoulder as we fumbled to get into the shower beneath warm, flowing water.

Skin on skin. *Very* slippery.

Suds. *Lots* of them.

Hands. *All* over each other.

Kisses. *Everywhere.*

⌐∾⌐

Wrinkled as a prune but squeaky clean, I leaned against the kitchen counter, perusing menus, trying to figure out what I wanted. I was in short black shorts and a striped tank top, my damp hair flowing down my back to air dry.

Hmm. An açaí bowl sounded pretty good. Oh! Better yet, a pitaya bowl. The vibrant pink flesh of dragon fruit, as tart and sweet as açaí, turned into a smoothie with macnut milk, honey, and bananas, plopped into a bowl and covered in granola, banana slices, dried goji berries, and a drizzle of honey.

And cassava fritters because carbs were needed after last night, and this morning (forget the fact that I'd had way too much cake).

As per usual, and from heinous habit, I checked my phone. I wasn't sure why, as nothing happened on Sundays. I finally cleaned out an inundated spam folder, only to realize there was a misplaced email.

My company's name, attached to a few extra letters (including HR), glared back at me. Was this the PM results I'd been waiting for? Must've been bad news if they sent an email instead of calling.

Relinquishing any hope and accepting fate, I opened the email. My heart did a little flip as I read and reread the message to make sure I'd understood correctly. A smile crept across my lips. They'd offered me the position. With a significant pay increase compared to what I'd been told. Apparently, they'd held off on making the offer because of a budget increase. They hadn't called because they knew I was on vacation but would be reaching out upon my return.

I laughed. Of course I'd get it, I'd always known! What had I been so worried about?

PM was a lot of responsibility, and I might miss actual UX work. That seemed to be the biggest complaint of PMs. Oftentimes they just wanted to be UXers.

With shaky hands, I reached out to the recruiter at Google with an email about updates, tossing in the fact that I had another offer to at least get a response from them before I made such a big decision. Sometimes, these nudges led to a quick pass, but sometimes they led to action.

I could only hold my breath now, although I honestly wasn't expecting much from Google. Either way, my life was moving forward and out of moss's lethargic reach.

The first person I wanted to tell was Sunny. My smile slipped. Because this meant he hadn't gotten the promotion he needed. It seemed like a hollow victory when I'd been so set on rubbing it in his face.

What did this mean for us? Would he apply elsewhere and leave the company? Until then, if he could even leave, we wouldn't be able to keep up our . . . what were we? Were we nothing? Truly a lie? A fling at best? He'd said what happened here stayed here. But if by some iota of a chance he wanted more, we couldn't be more. I'd be his boss.

Crap.

I willed my racing heart to calm down. Which was worse? Knowing he had no real feelings for me, at least not enough to pursue a relationship? Or knowing he did, and we couldn't do a thing about it unless one of us found work elsewhere?

I tamped down my nausea. I didn't want to know which dead end I was facing.

Diya knocked at the front door and cracked it open like she

expected a ghost. Of course, I'd been expecting her as we'd texted that it was safe for her to return.

"Hello?" she called out loudly.

"Hey, weirdo," I replied, shoving aside all the raw badness churning in my head. I had to stave off anxiety.

She walked in and looked around. "Are you two decent?"

"Yes." Heat surged across my face.

Diya closed the door and meandered toward the counter with two bags, Kimo right behind her with coffees.

"What's all this?" I asked, leaning my elbows against the counter as Diya plated up fresh baked goods.

"Sunny is leaving this afternoon, isn't he?" Kimo said.

"Yes," I replied, saddened by the fact.

"We had to come by to say goodbye and have one last meal."

"Aw. You guys. That's so sweet of you. Most importantly, what did you bring me?" I joked, pushing aside how the truth—or a fake breakup to a fake relationship—would disappoint them.

"I went by your favorite café on the way in."

"Kimo! You didn't have to!"

"He really did it for the coffee and to see Sunny." Diya eyed him. "Bromance in the air."

Kimo shrugged. "I like making friends."

Diya cocked her chin at the ravaged basket. "Get to the bottom of that?"

"Thanks for the chocolates and cake!" I grinned.

Her right brow shot up. "Did you see the bottom of the basket?"

"It was dark when we got back. We sort of just headed for bed. Socializing that much and loud parties really wiped me out." I yawned.

"Uh-huh . . ." She searched the room. "Where's—"

Sunny emerged from the bedroom, one towel wrapped low over his waist, exposing a sexy V-cut, while he rubbed another towel on his wet hair. He froze the second he saw Diya and Kimo, streams of water dripping down his neck and chest.

His eyes didn't linger on Diya, but shifted over to me. I was staring shamelessly because damn! How was I ever going to not mentally undress him during work?

Diya whipped her head back to me, standing in between us, shocked. But only for a millisecond. A giant smile spread across her face as she exclaimed, "Bitch, you *did* finally get some!"

"Oh my god . . ."

Then she had the audacity to whip her head toward Sunny. "You apparently got it right!"

He didn't even respond. No shock or embarrassment or regret. Just a nod, like he knew damn well that he got it right. He backtracked into the bedroom. "I should get dressed."

Diya took out her phone.

"What are you doing?" I went for her, but she jumped away.

"I have to tell Mummie!"

"*Why?* Are you serious?" I ran after her, but that little girl was fast. Always had been.

"She wanted me to call her the second I knew for sure!"

"That we had sex?"

"No! Gross! That you're serious!"

"You don't know anything!"

Ugh, this was bad.

"Diya, stop! Please! Don't tell her anything!"

She scuffled to the other side of the couch.

"Or *I* will tell her you're thinking about marrying Kimo," I spat point-blank, my hands on my hips.

That got her to stop and put away her phone. "You wouldn't."

"I absolutely would. You're trying to tell her something that will make her think I have a solid, long-term serious relationship that could inevitably lead to marriage. That's a big deal. If you tell her that, about something this new, then you better believe she's going to know about you and Kimo."

She shivered like she was shaking off my words. "I'm sure she's expecting it."

"Don't get her hopes up. We don't know where we are, but we're definitely not there."

"Fine. You're right. I'm sorry. It's just . . . we're all *so* excited," Diya said.

"I know," I replied softly, "but everyone needs to calm down."

Having to eventually tell my family the truth was getting harder by the minute. Seemed like telling them that Sunny and I weren't going to work out and leaving it at that was the obvious solution. Although who was I kidding? My family was going to hammer me for details, for any indication of what went wrong and how it could be fixed. They would be on me again, tougher than ever, on how I needed to move forward with my life.

But particularly so because they seemed to adore Sunny, even if they'd known him for only a short while. I couldn't blame them. This Sunny, the *real* Sunny, was particularly likable. And this Sunny was going to break my heart every time I saw him.

THIRTY-FOUR

Sunny

It was extremely touching that Diya and Kimo took the time to bring us breakfast and coffee and to spend one last meal together before sending me off.

I hated knowing they were taking to our lies so well. And worse than that, I hated that this *was* a lie. I wanted there to be an "us" beyond today. But how could I say that, admit it? Would Bane think I was joking? Feel pity? Get uncomfortable?

I thought I was getting better at expressing myself with her. So why was it so hard to just ask her what she thought of us beyond today?

I ate a little of everything that Kimo had been generous enough to bring. I even offered to pay for it, but he wasn't having it.

In front of us was a generous spread of semisweet almond matcha cake dusted in powdered sugar, creamy almond croissants, flaky buttered rolls, bite-size Portuguese custard tarts, apple and fig jam sandwiches, and an ube sweet cream cold brew for me.

Kimo had gotten Bane her favorite—I was honestly expecting an ube latte. Instead, it was a toasted marshmallow chai with home-made whipped cream.

I quirked a brow.

"I know," she said, taking a sip and licking whipped cream off her lips. "Don't denote my Indianness because I enjoy a *chai latte*. Try it."

Sharing drinks had become second nature.

"It's fine," I said after a taste.

"Fine?"

"It's good."

"Why can't you just say that!"

"I just did!"

"Can you guys ever have a conversation without yelling at each other?" Diya asked.

"No," Bane retorted. "Can you?"

A conversation without yelling? But yelling without fighting? This took me back to when Bane explained such an odd thing being part of Diya and Kimo's love language. Had it become something of affection for us, too? Bickering, but in an endearing way?

My phone kept going off with texts, marring this quaint ending to my time with Diya and Kimo.

"Is that important? Should you reply?" Bane asked.

"My sister telling me to have a nice flight home and the group text wondering where we're at because they're having drinks before leaving."

"Sunny!" Bane tugged me out of my chair.

"How are you so strong?"

She pushed against my back. "You can't ditch your friends on this momentous farewell drink!"

"I'd rather stay here," I confessed even as she opened the door.

"Wait." I pressed my hand against the wall above her head, loving how perfectly we fit together. "You're coming, too, right?"

"Just to say goodbye. I don't want to drink with them."

I grinned. But before I suggested what she might rather be doing, she added, "You have to pack and get ready for your flight."

I dropped my head back. *Fuck me.* I didn't want to leave.

"We'll walk with you," Diya suggested, and Kimo agreed.

And with that, we made our way to the hotel lounge, where Kimo gave me a bear hug and Diya clung on to me a few extra seconds.

She said, "Please come back, even if you ditch my sister."

"All right." Bane pulled her away and I said my farewells.

"Hey," I said to Bane.

"Hey." She had a soft smile, but her eyes flickered with a hint of sorrow.

"Are you all right?"

She heaved out a breath. "I'm getting anxious about returning to work."

"Afraid you won't be able to stop staring at me on the screen during meetings?"

"Countdown to reality," Bane grunted when I'd expected her to laugh and toss out a smart-ass response.

I swallowed. "A reality where all this is over?"

"We complicated things," she muttered, averting her gaze.

Well, shit. Was this really the end of us—whatever "us" had been?

"I have to run to the restroom," she announced suddenly.

"Okay. I think the bar is that way—" I started, peering down one of the corridors, but Bane was already walking away.

I waited a few minutes, my thoughts thrashing around on how to accept this as the end. Like unmoving segment attributes that could not be changed without an override. Back to reality. Back to being coworkers. This was what we had agreed to. What happened here stayed here. Even Bane had admitted to being happy in her life just the way it was, and she was not looking to uproot it with a relationship.

The pain taking hold inside my ribs and prying them apart was getting stronger as reality set in. I had known this was coming. I had known it would hurt. But damn, I wasn't expecting to have the breath knocked from my lungs, for my chest to physically ache.

Maya had leaned around one of the massive pillars down the corridor toward the bar and waved me down. I reluctantly walked toward her without Bane. This was the beginning to the end, and I might as well sever myself now. The only problem? Untethering myself from Bane was like sawing my soul in half. And that shit was killing me.

Aamar and Maya welcomed me with a "Hurry your butt up." But as soon as I rounded the pillar, Sejal stepped in between me and my friends. She had her arms crossed in a perpetual state of annoyance, her head cocked to the side, and a knowing smirk that erupted with exasperating words before I could even say hello.

"Why do you look so ragged?" she asked.

"Sejal!" Maya hissed.

"You look like you're sick," Sejal declared.

"Is that concern or an accusation?" I said.

"The latter. You look like you've been caught in a lie, and I know why. It's because Bhanu isn't your girlfriend," she spat triumphantly.

"Stop it," Maya said.

"Are we still doing this?" I asked dryly.

Sejal responded, "I knew it was a lie the moment she said she was with you. Your reaction to her claim, you never having mentioned her, and how Bhanu seemed absolutely oblivious about any of us."

"Could you keep her name out of your mouth?" I said, my voice getting low, agitated.

She harrumphed. "I asked about her when I talked to your parents, and they had no idea you were dating."

"And?" I said, annoyed that she not only had spoken with my parents, but had brought up Bane and my dating life.

"Sejal, please let it go," Maya pleaded.

"There's no way they're *not* dating with that chemistry," Aamar refuted her. "But also, why are we even talking about this? Sunny isn't that guy."

I clenched and unclenched my fists. My friends going to bat for me, wholly believing in this lie. I was turning out to be a terrible friend.

"Not you," Sejal pressed. "You'd tell your parents, especially if you'd been dating this long. She'd absolutely come up."

Pradeep was standing off to the corner, quiet, and I felt as bad for him as I did about lying to my friends.

Sejal had been going on. "I showed them a picture."

I blew out an exasperated breath. "Damnit, Sejal."

"They've never seen her but *have* heard about her from you. One Bhanu. From work. And I looked her up, and yep, it's her. You are such a liar. And a bad one."

"Oh my god," Maya blurted out. "Can you leave him alone? Even if he were lying, which we know Sunny does not lie—"

Crap.

"Why does it matter to you?"

Sejal responded, "Doesn't it bother you that he'd lie to your face and keep it up for days? Even bringing her around on events meant for us, and to the wedding?"

"Sunny is nothing like that," Aamar added. "Please let this go before Sam and April show up."

"Let's call your parents and ask," Sejal said instead, pulling out her phone.

"What the fuck?" I growled, startling her.

"Excuse me?"

I glowered at her. "Excuse you the hell for?" My temper rose. "For making my life miserable?" I'd had about enough. "For calling me out?" The wedding was over, and we'd made it this far without ruining Sam and April's vibes. Bane was already done, so why the hell not? The truth gushed out of me in searing words.

I took a step toward her and snapped, "You want to know the truth so fucking badly? So it makes you feel better that you're always right? Fine. Bhanu isn't my girlfriend. She's just my coworker."

Sejal sneered as if she'd won some imperative game.

I didn't skip a beat, and my next words wiped that snide look off her face. "She happened to be here visiting her sister and was so annoyed by your shit that she blurted out being my girlfriend just to shut you the hell up. All she wanted was quiet, and you came barging in with your demeaning accusations, and unlike you, she's a good enough person to step in to stop—what she calls—toxicity."

Sejal's mouth hung open.

"You got that? She thinks you're toxic, and I finally see it. All you want to do is tear me down. I'm not even in your life, but you sure as hell keep dragging me back in. All for what? So you can knock me down in front of our friends?" I gestured toward a stunned Aamar and Maya.

"I could've pulled you aside and cleared things up, but you'd already opened your mouth and told the entire group. So what was I supposed to do? Tell everyone, when they were so ecstatic at the mere *idea* of me having a girlfriend, and tarnish this week for Sam and April? All I wanted was to fly under the radar, give them a wedding without the tension of us fighting. Then I just hoped I could give them a wedding without anyone feeling sorry for me. So yes, Sejal. It was all a big lie."

I held open my arms, glaring at her. "Is that what you wanted to hear? That I do not have a girlfriend. That a woman had to pretend to be one to save me *this* very awkward moment?"

I looked to a speechless Aamar and Maya, defeated and annoyed and pissed with so many things right now. My voice came out terse when I said, "Sorry I lied. Bhanu is just my coworker, and the entire thing was fake."

THIRTY-FIVE

Bhanu

In the bathroom, all I could think about was our new complicated work situation.

On the way to the bar, all I could think about was Sunny saying, "A reality where all this is over."

It absolutely sounded like a statement. A big, cruel fact.

But what was worse was hearing Sunny say so. I had sidestepped a large, wandering group, who'd forced me behind one of the large pillars wide enough to fit six people across. Turned out, Sunny and his friends were talking loudly right behind it. I caught the last of his words.

Bhanu is just *my coworker, and the* entire *thing was* fake.

My legs nearly gave way. I'd started the entire lie. And now he was confessing to his friends to undo it. It was over. No reason to continue the charade. He'd come clean.

Utter stupidity and naivety rained upon me to have thought there was a chance he'd keep the ploy to himself just in case what we had contained an iota of truth.

I just wished he'd waited until he returned home, or at least after I had said my goodbyes.

Mortification had pinned me into place. Anxiety was catapulting me into true panic mode. The kind where combusting chemical reactions grew tentacles to squeeze my brain. As if saying, "Ha! You thought work and being his boss were bad because you believed you had a chance at a real relationship? Sucker!"

My body was both fire and ice, blistering and freezing. Goose bumps tightened my skin, and my breathing turned erratic.

It wasn't just the mortification. It was the full-faced actuality that these past few days were nothing but a wandering ghost in the timeline of our lives. Surreal and unreal.

Part of me wanted to woman up and take ownership. Part of me wanted to prove to his friends, who'd been nothing but welcoming, that I wasn't some two-faced liar. To at least apologize. But the growing dread of anxiety had deadened my legs and I wanted to crawl into a corner and never see these people again.

I even made it a few steps before Sam and April appeared and excitedly waved. I really hoped they were waving at their friends around the pillar, but turned out they were also waving at me.

"Bhanu! There you are!" April sang as she hurried over.

And with that, Sunny had backstepped and leaned around the pillar. He pinched the bridge of his nose and groaned, "Shit, Bane."

I squeezed my eyes and forced my legs to move forward, to meet the small band of college friends with as much of my self-declared "big UX energy" as I claimed to possess.

My heart was beating out of control with everyone staring at me like I had sprouted horns. The newlyweds had walked into a very awkward mess.

I gave a mediocre wave to pair with my apologetic expression. "Ha. Bane. Get it? Because I'm the bane of his existence. At work. Because we're coworkers."

"You don't have to explain anything," Sunny said.

I shrugged. "We're adults. You all have been very kind and lovely and I hated that I lied to you."

"What's going on?" April asked, perplexed.

I turned to her and said, "I'm not Sunny's girlfriend. I'm sorry I lied. I was trying to get a certain someone off his back and blurted out that I was. And then went with it because I didn't want anyone to give him a hard time or feel bad or tense or anything negative during your week. He really meant to give you a stress-free, blissful wedding."

"Oh. Wait," April said, knotting her brows as if deciphering an algorithm. "That can't be. You two are so perfect together."

Heat crept across my face. I almost told her that we acted so well, but the truth was, I hadn't been acting for a while.

Sejal scoffed from the corner of my eye. "This is really so sad."

She was speaking to Sunny, not to me. I was no one to her. Yet the way she continued to berate him snapped my last nerve. Anxiety and mortification be damned.

I turned to her and said, in my most deadpanned, flat tone, "I did it because you were being awfully cruel to a kind and truly genuine man."

Although I refused to glance at Sunny—I couldn't bear it—I saw glimpses in my peripheral vision of him watching me.

I went on. "I don't know if you're still in love with him or actually this vicious, but you should stop. He doesn't deserve to be cut down by anyone, especially by you, who, no matter what you think, mean nothing to him."

Sejal scowled, but I wasn't done.

"I said the first thing that came out of my mouth because you were scolding him for not having a date. I wanted you to be quiet, instead of ruining my calm because I was sitting there first, and not tear down the best dev on my team who absolutely did *not* deserve that attack."

"You don't know us," she spat.

Oh, hell. She was lucky I wasn't Diya, who would've started with, "Bitch, I know enough."

Instead, I replied, "I know that you *think* you left Sunny because he wasn't good enough, but the truth is that he couldn't thrive around your toxic fumes. Deleterious people create detrimental environments. And you leave a trail of rot in your wake."

"Damn," someone muttered underneath their breath.

I turned to the others and said, "It was truly lovely meeting you. But I'm going now, because this is really embarrassing."

I walked away before anyone could say a thing, so quickly that it could be considered sprinting.

"Bane! Wait." Sunny was right behind me, all the way back to the restrooms near the front of the lounge.

"What?" I said, willing my eyes to stop misting. My face was on fire, and I couldn't bring myself to stop, to look at him.

We were partway underneath the awning between the lounge and the lobby when Sunny took my wrist and forced me to face him.

"I'm sorry," he said.

"For what? It's not your fault. I started this entire ruse." If only he'd waited to tell his friends. Tears prickled my eyes, and I pulled out my phone to glare at something other than his sorrowful face.

"Bane—"

"Don't worry about it," I interjected. "You should get back to your friends for the farewell. I'm sure things will smooth over, and you'll all be laughing about this in no time. See? It wasn't so bad after all, them knowing the truth."

He hadn't released my hand until his phone rang. "I'm sorry. I have to take this. Don't move."

As he answered, I finally looked at him after having blinked away any lingering tears. I forced a smile and said, "No worries. Just leave the key card on the counter when you go."

I walked away but made the mistake of glancing over my shoulder.

Sunny had taken a few steps toward me, his brows furrowed, but he was already on his phone. He was talking to someone, thrusting a hand through his hair.

Sunny didn't follow.

We weren't a rom-com.

We were not a couple.

We were coworkers who got so caught up in the lie we'd created that we ended up sleeping together.

This wouldn't happen again. Ever. Because clearly, we were truly nothing more than coworkers and even a phone call was more important than me.

The probability of any of this mattering to Sunny after a few days, a few weeks, was slim.

What mattered was how my legs wanted to give way from beneath me. What mattered was how my stomach twisted into tight, painful knots, how my heart squeezed a little too aggressively on every beat, how my throat turned sore and raw, how every labored breath pained me.

I swallowed and clutched the strap of my purse. My nails dug into my palms.

Why did this hurt so much? Why did this hurt at all?

My brain screamed that *none* of what Sunny and I had done on this island was real. What had tricked my body into thinking that any of it had been? The fake dating, the fantasy relationship, even the flirting, the touching, the mind-blowing sex . . . it was all pretend. A game we'd chosen to play. A game I'd gotten lost in. And obviously, he hadn't.

Sunny deserved to be at ease with his friends. Surely they'd forgive him and laugh about this together. Sunny deserved to be happy in a real relationship, one where he didn't have to hide or pretend or keep anything locked up.

My parents kept hammering the importance of moving forward, not staying stagnant. For Sunny, the phase of inertia had been truly detrimental. But he seemed ready to leave that behind like he was leaving behind this lie. How wonderful he must feel to have this weight off his shoulders.

Logic must prevail. I mustered up enough sense to stop myself from reacting, enough strength to take an emotional step back.

I called Diya. "Hey, can you pick me up?"

"Sure! Are you done? Is Sunny gone?"

"He's on his way out."

"Are you going to tell me everything about him now?"

I forced a laugh. "Forget him. I have to tell you about my promotion!"

Diya squealed and met me in the parking lot with Kimo in the driver's seat.

Her window was rolled down as she hollered, "We need to celebrate! Kimo's mom is making you a giant ube cake!"

My sister and ube: the best celebration and a cure-all for heartache.

THIRTY-SIX

Sunny

How had life gone from perfect to a shit show? Forget Sejal forcing me to come out like that, and even my friends, who would need a good sit-down to chat about this entire thing, but Bane? I couldn't let her walk off like this.

But then Sheila called, and I had to answer. I couldn't keep Bane there and concentrate on what my sister was telling me.

I knew, like storm clouds writhing overhead, that my weekend of bliss would shatter once reality broke. And reality was breaking hard.

"Papa's in the hospital," she told me, her voice cracking.

"It's going to be all right," I assured, even as worry grew into a hideous, dark monster devouring everything in its path. "I'll be there soon. My flight leaves in two hours."

After telling Aamar and Sam about my dad, they broke off from the group, leaving Maya and April arguing with Sejal, to give me a ride to the villa.

I called Bane on the way, but she didn't answer.

I threw the rest of my things into my suitcase and off we went to the small, open-air airport.

"Are you okay?" Sam asked.

"I'm panicked about my dad. Every time he goes to the hospital for these things, we just expect the doctor to come back and conclude this is the big one."

"He's going to be okay. Your dad is a fighter."

We sat in silence as I texted my sisters for updates and specifics when Aamar said, "For what it's worth, don't feel bad about the lying."

"What?" I asked, derailed from worrying over my father.

"We get why it happened and why it lasted. Don't need to worry about any of that between us."

"Oh. Thanks." A slight reprieve that didn't quite cover the damage I might've done with Bane.

"And for what it's worth," he added, "it might've started out a lie, but it never looked like one."

I frowned.

"Listen. We really like her."

"All of us, especially April," Sam added.

Aamar twisted in his seat up front and said, "We could see how this started, but we can see how much you two are connected. Bro, the chemistry." He whistled.

Sam laughed. "You two were putting me and April to shame."

"Bhanu managed to make you less serious, more in the moment."

"Even April had said it, but man, we saw you thriving and happy like never before. And we've known you for a long time."

Shaking my head, I affirmed, "Doesn't matter. She was just trying to help me out, a generous act. A lie is a lie."

Aamar turned back into his seat. "I don't think either one of you were acting by the weekend. I saw how you looked at each other before the wedding started."

"We all saw," Sam concluded. "Words can lie, my man, but your faces can't."

If only that were true. If only they weren't trying to make me feel better or get my mind off Papa.

⤜ ⑨ ⤛

I went directly from the airport to the hospital in Olympia, where I found Papa in his room, wrapped in a green gown and trying to sit up in bed.

"You didn't have to come straight here," Ma was saying as I quickly hugged her, then my father, in a good, long hug like he might perish any second. "Just another mild stroke."

Mild strokes had their effects. They were still serious. I slept in the chair beside my father all night, forcing my mother and sisters to go home. I helped him get up to use the bathroom, to change positions, adjusted the thermostat, fetched drinks and blankets and whatever else he needed.

"You fuss too much," he said, agitated. I knew he wasn't annoyed with me. He didn't like to be doted upon, feeling helpless and sick and in pain, feeling as if he caused worry in others when all his life he'd aimed to protect and provide.

I let him rant before I stepped into the hallway to get updates directly from the nurse and the doctor, and then call into work to ask for an extra day. Gabrielle was understanding and allowed me to work remotely, per usual, but approved of another day off and missing meetings. She was able to take over where needed.

Then Papa and I chatted about the stroke. He eventually led the conversation toward me, the vacation, the wedding.

"Who was that Indian woman on the boat?" Papa asked as he lay back down.

"Who?" I asked, slowly moving through the TV channels until he told me to stop. "Sejal?"

"No."

"Maya?"

"No . . ."

Of course he'd ask about Bane if Sejal had brought her up first. "My coworker, Bhanu."

He gave a lopsided smile—the effects of the stroke—and my heart ached for him. "The woman you're always mentioning."

"I've maybe mentioned her once or twice."

"Beta, you always bring her up when we ask about work. You talk more about her annoying you or showing off her brilliance than you ever talked about Sejal."

My jaw dropped. I couldn't believe that; my memory wasn't *that* terrible. Yet Papa went on to tell me, in detail, all the times I'd mentioned Bane. And damn. How had this woman infiltrated my life without me even realizing it? I just wished she'd return my calls.

Papa shifted in bed, grunting as he twisted this way and that.

"What do you need help with?" I shot to my feet, pressing the buttons on his bed to raise his head.

"I want to sit in the chair. This bed is giving me bedsores."

I moved the blankets aside, helped him swerve his legs over the edge of the bed, stood with feet shoulder-width apart, bent down, and lifted him by the waist, resettling him onto the recliner. A simple turn and he was in place.

I adjusted his posture with pillows and draped several blankets over his lap and socked feet. "Are you cold? I can turn down the temperature or get warm blankets."

"No, no . . . now sit. And tell me how this woman you can't stop talking about ended up on your boat."

"It's not much of a story," I grumbled, making his bed so that he didn't return to lumps and wrinkles.

"Ah. But you see, the way your face always lights up when you talk about her makes me think otherwise. Even when you're complaining about her, your eyes have a certain life to them. I never saw this when you were dating Sejal."

I sat down, dumbfounded.

"I know I've taught you to always keep calm, but she's had a way of breaking through to you, this Bhanu. I like this better. You seem happier, alive."

"We're just coworkers." Apparently.

Papa smirked. "Is that so? Well, a woman who can light up your face like that should be more. Don't you think?"

"Where is this coming from?"

"Being sick, having another stroke, reminds you that life is short, fleeting. We kept pushing you back to Sejal, but there's obviously some bad things that happened. You can talk to me about it, you know? Anything you want to say. I want to hear."

My father, a stoic man who showed love by feeding us and bragging about us to every uncle in the vicinity, had seldom encouraged me to speak about my feelings.

"I don't want to burden you, Papa. You should rest, not worry about me."

"You think you're a burden? You think your suffering and dreams are burdens to tell me?"

I didn't respond.

"This is my doing. I know. So let me start first, beta."

And for the rest of the night, my father told me how scared he was of getting sicker, of being a burden to anyone, of all the hopes he had for us. And when his eyes misted, mine did, too.

So I told him about Sejal, the true, raw reasons why we broke up and why we'd never make it work, how it felt to have her in their lives when it seemed they wanted her over me, and how I felt when they spoke so intimately with her.

I told Papa about Bane, too, and the fake dating that led to real feelings. For once in my entire life, I spoke openly with my father and vice versa, and damn, it was the best thing in the world. Sharing tears and fears, dreams and hopes, not just for me or for him, but for our entire family.

I eventually helped him back into bed. Since Papa wouldn't be discharged for a few more days, and I didn't want my sisters' lives to be disrupted, I stayed with him all day and again all night at the hospital, going to my parents' house to shower. Despite telling my sisters not to get off track, there they were, cooking and cleaning and doing laundry for our mom so she could stay all day at the hospital, too.

Between taking care of Papa, being there for all of his testing and medical discussions, grocery shopping, running errands, catching up with work to ensure product launch, there was literally no time for anything else.

I'd dismissed Sejal's antics and the PM position.

But I hadn't forgotten Bane. Was she busy? Back to real life without any further thought of me? Ignoring my calls to give me a hint?

Perhaps.

THIRTY-SEVEN

Bhanu

I'd returned home late Monday night and, on Tuesday, dove straight into work to take my mind off Sunny. He'd called several times on Sunday, but there wasn't much else to say. He called a couple of times and texted on Monday. Today, he had stopped. Maybe he just wanted to make sure I was clear on where we stood.

I chastised myself every time I thought a notification was from him. Spoiler alert: Most were from my mom wanting to know when I'd bring him around.

Don't become moss.

I hadn't seen Sunny's face in a virtual box yet, nor was he present at any of the meetings, but I knew he was working because of movement in Jira and Asana.

Attempting to unhinge the tentacles of anxiety, I focused on important things. Like career movement. I wanted to become PM because it was the logical next step, and to prove that I wasn't stagnant in life. But maybe this wasn't it. It seemed that a person should feel less anxious, less unsure, when facing a big decision like this.

There wasn't much time left to waste waiting for Google.

My heart was palpitating when I finally called the HR manager about the PM offer.

"Congratulations on the promotion! As I mentioned in my email, we held off on making an official offer until we knew what the budget increase entailed," she explained.

"Thank you. This is wonderful news!" Yet I kept thinking back to Sunny. Had they offered the job to him first? Had he declined? Of course not. He wouldn't do that, not for a week-away fantasy girlfriend.

"Did you consider anyone else?" I found myself asking.

"We had several applicants and strong candidates, but your skill level and seniority and relations with coworkers and clients are exemplary."

"Was the second runner-up a dev, by chance?"

"Ah, you know we can't discuss that with you."

"Of course." But I knew.

"Shall we begin paperwork?"

Did I want to accept? Did I want to be PM at a midsize company? "Let me think about this."

"Of course. Please let us know as soon as possible."

I hung up the phone and returned to work, glancing at a black box on my screen where Sunny should've been. I found myself missing his face. The way he'd furrow his brows when reading messages, how he'd lean in close to the computer to cross off code, and how goofy his expression turned when I assumed he was watching cat videos.

Biting my lip, I chased away the ache in my chest, knowing time would alleviate the intensity. Slowly, but surely.

After a long, hectic day, I fell into bed glowering at my phone. I should call him, but man, had it been a brutal day with catch-up and deadlines and work emergencies. It was already eleven. Instead, I listened to his voice mails. I loved his Denzel voice and how, even over the phone when all he said was that he wanted to chat, it made my toes curl. His voice was sleepy, gritty in several messages, like he was lying in bed. And my imagination filled with images of his shirtless body barely covered by sheets. Those arms.

I sighed.

Those wonderful pecs and abs and . . . I know, I was torturing myself. This wasn't helping me to get over him, much less forget him.

Fortunately, I'd taken a sleeping aid to calm my thoughts from the still-present anxiety. Before I knew it, my eyes had drifted closed.

∽

The next day, as I studied color-coordinated spreadsheets on the pros and cons of taking this PM position, Google called!

I'd almost vomited from the excitement and fumbled for the phone. Crap. They really knew the meaning of a dramatic resurrection from ghosting. No word for weeks and then bam!

Of course, I took the call with adrenaline raging through my system, my hands shaking, my feet padding against the carpet as I paced my living room, reiterating that I'd just received an offer but wanted to take my time in making the right decision.

They not only made an offer but came in *strong*. I carefully negotiated. With plenty of research under my belt, I knew what to ask for and what I was worth. And Google not only matched my counteroffer but added bonuses on top of amazing benefits.

Well, shoot. I hadn't been expecting this to go so smoothly, but as my parents and Diya had often said, I was worth every penny. When you believe it, companies believe it, too.

Google. No one declined Google; I certainly didn't. Unless Apple came calling, which they had not.

Google offered a UX role, a step back from PM, yet with significantly more pay and considerable prestige. Adding Google to my résumé, should I ever leave, would put me at the top of any candidate list. They were the right move. They were a perfect fit. Not only as one of the best companies to work for, but they had several subdivisions and branches to learn and grow and spread my big, beautiful UX wings.

My entire body was trembling. I couldn't wait to tell Diya and my parents and . . .

I swallowed. I wanted to tell Sunny. I wanted to talk to him, to hear his voice. Would it be weird for me to call? To tell him this news when I hadn't returned his earlier messages? Was that selfish?

Google came with a price, though. Relocation to Seattle. They wanted me in office more than remotely. And while my current company was close enough to Seattle (Renton) that I didn't mind the commute from Tacoma, the Seattle lifestyle was nothing to dismiss.

A big move.

A huge *change*.

Moving forward meant astronomical adjustments for someone who had become settled for so long.

It also meant a colossal tidal wave of anxiety.

THIRTY-EIGHT

Sunny

On Wednesday, the hospital released Papa. I'd meant to text Bane about seeing her in person to talk, because there were things I needed to tell her and it couldn't be done over the phone, but there was a lot happening on release day. Paperwork, detailed discharge instructions, medications to pick up along with recovery-specific items Papa needed, getting him showered and settled, cleaning, cooking, serving, stocking . . .

I was exhausted and stressed, even though he was better. Even though my mother and sisters were here to help. Despite all of that, I took as much of the load upon myself as possible.

That night, I slept at my parents' house. Tossing and turning and walking to their bedroom in the middle of the night to make sure everything was well. Now that things were settled and my levels of stress had simmered, I went to the guest bedroom and crashed. With an arm over my head, I automatically took the phone to call Bane.

But it was nearing midnight. She was probably asleep.

I yawned, my eyelids heavy with exhaustion.

Tomorrow. I would definitely call her tomorrow.

⌒✦⌒

The following day, Papa was feeling well enough to eat at the table with everyone, instead of everyone eating in random chairs around him in his bedroom.

Because there were no secrets between Papa and Ma, our first family dinner together, with my sisters present, Ma looked me dead in the eye and asked, "So when are you bringing Bhanu to dinner, huh?"

I froze in midbite, my sisters gawking.

Papa elbowed me and said, "Go ahead. Tell your sisters about this"—he furrowed his brows as if trying to make out the words—"fake girlfriend with real feelings."

"What is he talking about?" Sheila asked.

"Nothing," I muttered.

"Fake girlfriend sounds like some rom-com plot that you better spill the tea on right now," Sienna pressed.

"And by far the most interesting thing you've ever done!" Sheila added.

I couldn't believe my parents just outed everything to my sisters, but here we were. The house had been so quiet and solemn since Papa was in the hospital. Now, an uproar of laughter, questions, and adamant demands to see pictures tore through our silent woes, bringing joy back into this house.

"I don't have pictures of her."

"I have a picture!" Papa declared.

"How do you have a picture?" I asked as he went for his phone.

"You know we learned to screenshot," Ma said.

And yep, true to her declaration, my mother had taken several screenshots of Bane and zoomed in. Because, as it turned out, not only had Sejal shown them her picture but had flipped the camera once or twice on the boat.

And, of course, Sejal had sent them pictures of the wedding, to which they'd promptly found Bane in a few shots. She might've expertly dodged the official photographers, but not so much the personal cameras.

Bane had not only become friend approved, but family requested.

"Video-call her!" Sienna insisted.

"Absolutely not," I grunted. Not when I had no idea where we stood.

⚭

I'd been pacing back and forth in the guest room, trying to figure out what to say to Bane and why it was suddenly difficult to talk to her. Too many days had passed, and I knew we'd parted in a flustered way. It was like calling a woman a month after the first date. Awkward. Pathetic.

Why hadn't she returned any of my messages? Would she tell me we were back in the real world, where we didn't text or chat?

Hope you had a good first week back.

Did you catch up with work?

How's it going?

I miss you.

Hello.

Hey.

Hi.

I settled on: I hope you're doing well.

Pitiful. Also painful because she left me on READ. Again. Shit. Was she upset with me? Was it about how things went down on Sunday? Or was she as busy as I was?

Yet on this dreary Friday morning when things had settled down with Papa's health and I was able to return to my usual immersed role at work, I couldn't help but sit in my parents' house and stare at Bane during a virtual meeting. My heart palpitated. Indisputably, she still did wild, euphoric things to me. And damn, how I missed her.

She had her hair in a big bun on top of her head and was back in her favorite burnt orange cardigan. I assumed it was her favorite because she wore it every other day. And eating waffles. Just like normal.

I DMd her.

Those waffles look good. You gonna share?

She took another bite, her gaze skimming her screen. I knew when she'd read my message because her mouth twitched. I was dying for her comeback, something along the lines of: *Come over then*.

Instead, she told me to pay attention.

Brutal.

It probably wasn't the best idea to tell Bane, at this point in our quick-death chats, that my family wanted to meet her.

I had to get back to work, delving into Jira and master branches of code, only to be pulled away with a phone call. I had my camera and microphone off but went into an adjacent room to answer.

When the HR manager offered me the role of PM, I was staring at the window, confused. They'd increased the salary to more than what I'd originally intended to ask for, leaving little room for negotiating.

"Am I your first choice?" I asked point-blank.

The HR manager sighed on the other end. "We can't discuss that."

I thanked HR for the incredible offer and asked for the weekend to consider before hanging up. Overcome with dread, I called Bane. Bane didn't answer her phone, so I left a message.

"I just want to make sure that you're okay. Can we talk? I have some things to tell you. I wanted to speak in person, but I'd take anything right now. Call me back."

Maybe DMing through work chat and texting her was overkill, but this silence, this avoidance, this true return to reality . . . hell no. I wasn't having it. Not unless she told me this was what she wanted in crystal-clear words to my face.

Had our company truly not offered her the role? Was she devastated? Had she applied elsewhere? Where would a new job take her? Away from me?

Shit. I couldn't let her slip away, not without a proper discussion. Communication, right?

Sejal and I had diverted to such opposite paths that it was a miracle we'd ever been together in the first place. Our relationship was circumstantial and had fit our needs. It was a relationship of convenience. Our communication wasn't the best. We'd grown apart, and that was fine.

But Bane? She had a way about her that made it easier for me to open up. I *wanted* to tell her things. I *wanted* to do things with her and for her. I *wanted* to be romantic and watch her light up, to push her buttons and get a rise out of her. I yearned for her comebacks and rebuttals. They, for a long time, had put a secret, quiet smile in me. Bane did that, without ever meaning to or demanding it. It just happened. Naturally. Organically. The way designers always said the user's experience through a website should happen, as if they were made for each other and so perfect that they didn't even know it was happening.

Bane and I happened, and I hadn't even realized it.

Bane and I . . . went together like UX design and UX coding. One was beautiful and thought-out, thought-provoking with an interface arousing ideal emotions and actions. The other was meticulous and detailed, seemingly an endless facade of tedious work that brought ideas to life as smooth working interactions.

Bane needed to know how she made me feel, how normal and comfortable, how present and enough I felt. She needed to know how one look from her undid me. How she had my emotions all wrapped up and unraveled at the same time.

Her touch lingered on my skin, in my memories, despite how long it'd been, despite the distance between us. I could still taste her sweetness on my lips, knew the softness of her every curve, memorized the floral and fruity scents of her body tucked against mine. She fit perfectly against me. She was perfect for me.

And she needed to know.

THIRTY-NINE

Bhanu

White miso ramen on chilly days was true comfort. Sautéed veggies with a sprinkle of green onion made it perfect. Comfort foods to calm down my rising anxiety about a new job, a new place, more in-person workdays.

I pulled my knee to my chest and blew on my bowl of noodles. I looked across the screens as I chewed. I ate while I worked, a blanket on my legs and lap, a cardigan around my shoulders, and answered all inquiries before checking on research feedback.

No matter how in the zone I was, my traitorous eyes kept returning to his virtual box. Sunny was sitting there, working, his eyes skimming across all billion lines of code, probably, while moving across multiple screens.

His stare stayed affixed to one section of whatever he was looking at and I tilted my head, slurping noodles. His background was different. Had he moved to a new room?

He looked at his camera before typing. A chat box popped up on my screen.

You've got something on your face.

What! I rubbed my chin and cheek to find sauce on my fingertips. I scowled at the screen, but Sunny simply leaned back in his chair and smirked.

Sometimes I really hated him.

Okay. Not really. It was impossible to hate that playful smile that made me feel so warm and wonderful.

At some point, he'd turned off his camera and muted himself. And then he'd logged off work early. I, however, worked until seven, fully aware that he'd left a voice mail, had texted, and had DMd through work chat. On the one hand, the idea of talking to him made me giddy. On the other hand, he probably wanted to clarify that we should be civil coworkers and nothing more. Thankfully, I was too busy catching up on work *and* doing extra for the weeks ahead so I could leave the company with their best product. Not to mention starting the daunting task of finding an apartment in Seattle without fainting from the price of rent.

It was dark, late, and chilly before I closed all the blinds. I was exhausted by the time I finally found the nerves, and common decency, to respond to Sunny.

> **Bhanu:** We can chat, but maybe later? I'm not feeling well.

Sunny immediately replied.

> **Sunny:** What's wrong?

> **Bhanu:** Been busy.

Sunny: Is that all? Not just avoiding
me?

                              Bhanu: No.

Liar! Well, that wasn't the only reason. Anxiety climbed ever
higher. At least he didn't push for more conversation.

⌒☙⌒

The following morning, I'd drowsily taken a shower and slipped
into fuzzy socks, sweatpants, a frayed T-shirt, and a cardigan
before making coffee and downing ibuprofen for this mounting
stress-induced headache. Finding a place in Seattle, much less within
a reasonable budget, had evolved into a nightmare. There wasn't
much time left before being forced into soul-sucking commutes if I
continued to live in Tacoma. I'd asked for two weeks, and was now
kicking myself for not asking for more time.

I scratched my back and looked through the fridge and cabinets
wondering what in the world I was in the mood to eat. Then realizing
how daunting a task packing would be.

My phone screen lit up with a text.

Sunny: Are you home?

                              Bhanu: Headache holding me
                              captive.

A moment later, as the last drops of coffee dripped into the carafe,
there was a knock on the door. I frowned. Who in the world was knocking on my door? It better be Girl Scouts with cookies to save the day.

I checked the peephole and had to look twice to make sure my eyes weren't playing tricks on me. Sunny was here? Why? No matter the reason, my entire body quivered at the sight of him, at the nearness of him, and just when I'd thought I had this under control.

I checked my phone after the second knock.

Sunny: I'm at your door.

                                          Bhanu: Creeper.

Sunny: 😉

Rebuking jitters never worked; they only got wilder, reverberating against every nerve, snapping them in half. My stomach tied into knots, the kind that sent flutters sweeping through my insides. I swore I was floating away.

I braced for a conversation about how badly we'd behaved and how it could never happen again.

Easy. I was leaving.

When I opened the door, I wasn't prepared to be devoured by Sunny's mere presence. Everything in my peripheral vision blurred.

Sunny stood a couple of feet away. So close that I could smell him. So close that his body heat prowled toward me like a hungry lover. He was tall and broad and took up space in the best way.

He had his hands behind his back, stretching the fabric of his black T-shirt over a broad chest and flat stomach, his chin high so that his hooded eyes were looking down at me with a hint of longing. His hair was its usual disheveled mess, and he was wearing the absolute glory out of a pair of gray joggers—that, um, showcased a bulge that I was well acquainted with. Damn, he looked fine. I couldn't stop staring.

"My eyes are up here," he said in that husky voice, one brow cocked and looking all kinds of smug.

Heat made its theatrical return across my cheeks and neck. "What are you doing here?" Great! I still knew how to use words, but they came out breathy, labored.

"I was hoping to talk."

"Sunny. Really?" I groaned.

He closed his eyes, his expression relaxing. "Damn, I missed how you say my name."

Wait. What? No, don't jump to conclusions! But hope bubbled through me.

"Mmm." He took a deep breath. "Did you make coffee?"

I nodded, wanting him to go back to what he was just saying. Who cared about the damn coffee?

He pulled an aluminum tray from behind his back. A reusable bag hung from his wrist. Sunny watched me as I frowned. He slowly peeled back the aluminum top. Okay. He had me intrigued, I gave him that. I peered over the lip, but he raised the container until I was stepping onto the threshold and on my tiptoes.

"What is that?" I asked, inhaling the sweet aroma of something delicious.

He was going too high now. I grabbed his forearms, careful not to make him drop the contents. His skin was warm, and my body raged. His scent of shampoo and soap and deodorant crashed over me. Our body heat met and mingled around us, and I was about one flirty move away from pouncing on him.

Sunny stilled as soon as our flesh made contact, his nostrils flaring. Just my hands on his arms, but enough to command us. Our eyes locked and I lowered his arms down. Well, actually, he lowered them. At this angle and with those muscles, I could probably hang from his forearms like a monkey, and he wouldn't budge.

I released Sunny so he could proudly reveal a tray of golden tri-
angular pastries with a sheath of glaze and bluish-purple filling that
had bubbled out during baking.

"Blueberry turnovers?" I asked, suddenly starving.

"Ube," he corrected, his voice sleek.

My eyes flitted up. "What!"

He grinned. "Ah, someone's excited."

"You came all the way here, in the Tacoma rain, to bring me ube
turnovers?"

He nodded, as if this weren't a big deal, as if people did this for
each other all the time.

I smiled. "Where did you even find these?"

"I made them."

"Shut up. You did not."

"Come look at the mess in my kitchen and tell me I didn't."

"How . . . where . . ." I had so many questions, but my focus was
pinned to the pastries. "These are for me?"

"If you'd like."

"I'd like."

"And extras." He lifted the bag. "For your anxiety."

"What?" I choked out.

"Chocolate, ibuprofen, heating packs, candles. I don't know. I
read some articles on how to help. Talking, reading, movies, silence, shutting down tech. You might have to tell me what works for
you."

I stuttered, "How—huh?"

"How did I know? I can tell now, from the moments we spent
together, I caught on. I thought maybe you were avoiding me because
of what happened . . . and then I thought maybe you were anxious,
too. Then I saw you on work meetings, and I knew."

"Oh . . ."

No man, including those I'd dated long-term, had ever identified an episode without me saying so, much less from afar, much less brought me comfort gifts to cope.

He explained, "My mom has a lot of anxiety, and she tends to keep it to herself, too. When you told me about your anxiety attacks, I saw her symptoms in you. I always tell my dad to pay attention and be proactive, so here I am. Taking my own advice."

I wanted to swing my arms around him and press him to me, to kiss him with the passion of a million kisses and keep him in my embrace for entire lifetimes. And maybe keep my misty eyes from spewing tears. "Sunny! Thank you. That's so wonderfully sweet of you."

"I'm aware that I'm quite wonderful."

"And now you're back."

He grinned. Oh, how that brilliant smile lit up my entire world.

"I think I should enjoy my ube alone now."

He frowned. "The hell. Are you serious?"

I laughed.

"Smart-ass. How about I come in and we can have coffee and turnovers, and if you want, we can talk? About anything that's on your mind."

I stepped back to let him in. In true Indian fashion, he removed his shoes, toes to heel so he didn't touch them.

He followed me to the kitchen counter, where I poured coffee, asking how he took his. But as I replaced the carafe, I felt his body behind mine. It was perceptible, devouring.

He leaned past me, his arm brushing mine to get the cream, dropping a small amount into a mug. And then a big spoonful of sugar.

"Your teeth will rot like that," I joked, my voice uneven.

Sunny didn't take the mug, nor did he swirl his coffee. Instead, he hugged me. From behind. My entire body went off in flares, and my heart splattered against my ribs with every notion of love and lust and yearning and need.

I instantly melted against him, my eyelids fluttering closed, and inhaled this moment.

In his guttural voice, he said, "I see why hugs from behind are on your list."

His arms snaked around my waist. "I hope this is still okay?" His words came out with a pinch of hope, as if he desperately needed me to say, "*Yes*, we are as we were last week."

I nodded; I couldn't speak, could barely breathe. In fact, my legs were turning to mush, and it was a good thing he was holding me because I might, in fact, melt into a puddle of goo.

His lips were at my neck when he confessed, "I really missed you."

Goose bumps skittered across my flesh at that stupid Denzel voice, even as my body reacted to how my curves fit deliciously against his. "Well, I *am* a delight." How I managed an entire sentence was a miracle.

His body shook with a chuckle.

"Think you can just hug me because you brought breakfast?"

"I mean . . . I did bring home the ube."

"That's cheesy."

"Is it, though? I thought it was sexy."

I turned into him like a mistake that I was happy to make. We were so close, our chests grazing, and his hands planted on my hips. He was hunched over me, his head lowered like maybe he wanted to kiss me.

I stared at his chest, wishing I could call down my big UX energy and just say what was on my mind.

"Bane."

I grunted, lifting my gaze to meet his.

He smirked. "I meant babe."

"What?" I furrowed my brows. I heard his words, knew what he was doing, but my brain couldn't seem to compute, to align data with the value of its evidence.

He took a large breath and exhaled. "I'm a grown man who can't seem to express myself as well as I'd like sometimes."

"True."

"But I'm learning how, and honestly, you make me want to. You make it easier. You made me realize how much I wanted to open up to you during our time together. And those days together were the best days of my life."

His gaze dipped to my mouth for a second before he went on. "You're unlike any woman I've known. You make me different. Better. My true self. You let me shine and you enable me to thrive. We may have started out as a lie, but . . ."

He swallowed, as if maybe he was taking a huge risk by continuing. But I was ever eager to hear him say it. So much so that I had bunched up the sides of his shirt in my fists. "It never seemed fake to me. It was natural to be into you, because the truth is, I've liked you for a long time."

"You always bickered with me," I protested weakly.

"Maybe I was just bad at flirting?"

"Horrible, apparently."

"I think I've mastered it by now." He gently ran a finger across my cheek and tucked wayward hair behind my ear.

I shivered. Masterful indeed.

"I didn't mean for the truth to come out to my friends the way it did, when it did. And I'm deeply apologetic that it embarrassed you and put you on the spot. But know this, my friends adore you."

"Really? After all that lying?"

"They said it might've started out as a lie, but they could see it wasn't pretty quickly. And I wasn't acting after some point. I hope . . . you weren't acting, either?"

I shook my head, the words I'd wanted to say for so long releasing. "It's easy to be with you, Sunny. The lie had become my truth."

He smiled as if my confession had lifted the burden of a million deadlines from his shoulders. "The *only* reason I didn't come after you to tell you how I felt was because my sister called."

"Oh, no. Was it about your dad?"

He nodded. "Papa had a stroke, and we were worried this was the big one."

I hugged Sunny close to me, my hands meeting behind his back. "Oh my god, Sunny. I'm so sorry. Is he okay?"

"Yes," he said into my hair. "Thank you. There wasn't too much damage and he's home. It's why I didn't come earlier, why I'd been away from work. I was taking care of him."

I blinked away tears. Here I was, so stupid thinking he didn't give a crap about me to let me walk away like that.

He pulled away and swiped my cheeks. "Why are you crying? He's okay."

I sucked in a breath and shuddered. "I added unnecessary stress to an already hectic time by not calling back, didn't I?"

"Don't think that."

"But I did. And I could've been there for you while you were dealing with everything. I wasn't. I'm so sorry."

The corner of his mouth tugged up.

"Why are you smiling?" I demanded.

He kissed the tear dribbling down my cheek. "Because you wanted to help me through something so personal. But now, *I'm* going to get a little personal."

"Uh-oh."

"I need to know what happened with the PM position. They offered it to me. Is that why you have anxiety?"

"Sunny! Congrats! I knew they would and it's well deserved."

He pinched his brows together, looking anything except happy. "Where does this leave you?"

"At Google. They made an offer, and I took it."

Sunny lifted me off the floor. "Oh, shit! Big league! Congrats, babe."

I laughed. "Oh my god! Put me down! Were you worried over my job?"

"Of course. I knew they must've offered it to you first, but why wouldn't you take it, and where did it leave you? Hell, now I know. Google came knocking."

"And I threw my hussy self at them. Please tell me you took the PM job."

"I asked for the weekend. I'm going to accept on Monday."

"Congrats . . . *babe*," I said, mimicking his Denzel voice and horribly failing.

He lifted his chin. "So does this mean that you're moving to Seattle?"

"If I can find an apartment. There aren't a lot of places available near work, or ones that are affordable."

"You're not becoming moss."

I groaned. "My mother will be ecstatic, and I know it's the right move. I'm truly grateful. But I only have a couple of weeks before starting work, and the anxiety is getting to me. New workplace, huge company, moving, change. Oh my god, I have to pack. There's not enough time."

"Hmm. Maybe you can . . . crash at my apartment until you find a place?"

Warmth crept up my neck.

He quickly added, "I'm staying with my parents in Olympia for a bit, so the apartment would be empty. If you feel comfortable. It would place you closer to work and give you time to look for an apartment. No pressure whatsoever. And if you like, or need, I can stay with my parents longer until we figure things out. I don't mind."

"That's a lovely and extremely helpful offer." I pecked his cheek.

"But I thought you meant return to how things were, just coworkers. Isn't that what you told your friends?"

"Come here." He walked me over to an empty counter and hoisted me up in one effortless, fluid movement.

I gasped, grasping his forearms as he slipped in between my thighs. Something that did not go unnoticed by him.

Sunny glanced down and a surge of heat ignited between us. "Damn if we don't fit perfectly together."

He pressed his forehead against mine. "I don't want you to think last week was some fantasy and nothing more. The truth is, I've always noticed you. What you're wearing, what you're doing, how you smell. You make it hard to concentrate on anything else. You make me want to ignore everything and everyone and get lost in you. You were always the highlight of my day, even when we were bickering. Days without you are meaningless episodes until the next time I see you. Holding patterns waiting for a CTA to be activated."

"Sunny . . ."

He brushed my cheek, his touch gliding down my throat, inciting a wave of shivers. "I love when you say my name."

My legs instinctively tightened around him.

He inhaled. "I love the smell of you."

I dug my fingers into his sides.

He kissed my neck. "I love the taste of you."

I gave in to the dizzying sensation.

"You are absolutely the most beautiful, intelligent, creative woman I've ever known." He pressed a kiss to my jaw. "You are a goddess."

I gasped, heady, my thoughts blooming with euphoria.

Sunny gripped my hips, adding in that deep, gritty tone, "I don't want to be anything less than a couple. Do you?"

I vehemently shook my head. "I want you."

"You have me."

My mouth crashed against his. My body caved to the need of him.

He wound his fingers through my hair and pulled back. His gaze skimmed from my swollen lips to my eyes. "God damn, I am so fucking in love with you."

"Sunny," I moaned.

"Keep saying my name like that, Bane, and see where it gets you."

"I hope it gets me into bed with you and a tray of ube."

"Then let's go."

I yelped, clinging to him, my legs and arms wrapped around his body, as he carried me into the bedroom.

"I remember which door," he said, walking me into my room.

He gently dropped me onto the bed and backed away. I grabbed the waistband of his sweats and asked, "Where are you going?"

"The ube."

I yanked him toward me and leaned back so that he had no choice except to crawl onto the bed, his body a delectable heaviness pressing down on me.

"Yes?" he teased.

Trailing kisses across his throat, I declared, "I love you, too."

"More than ube?" he jested.

"Let's not get out of hand."

With Sunny in my arms, and new jobs and a real relationship on the horizon, the anxiety of moving forward in life seemed like a wondrous dream spilling into reality. Like adept code changing the user interface to enhance flawless UX, we embraced the perfect design of us.

ACKNOWLEDGMENTS

I had such a blast writing this book! I had so much fun taking you from my old stomping grounds in Seattle/Tacoma to my home in beautiful Hawaii.

Not so long ago, I studied UX design. Those long nights staring at kanban boards, getting "high" on Sharpie fumes while scrawling across endless Post-its, learning that color-coordinating systems are my jam, and losing my crap trying to code from scratch . . . well, it all led to the spark that eventually turned into *The Design of Us*.

Thank you to my amazing editors, Cindy and Angela, for sharpening this story, and to the entire Berkley team. To Taleen (hi, fellow UXer!) for being an early reader.

To my agent, Katelyn, who is hands down the best of the best.

To my husband for planting the seeds of the locale and random things that happened on island that ended up in the book. To all the honu, I adore you so much and try my best to protect you and spread awareness. And ube. Where have you been all my life? I'm madly in love with you.

A big THANK-YOU goes out to all the readers who loved *The Trouble with Hating You*, because your enthusiasm brought this new story to life. Did you catch the Easter eggs? I hope you enjoyed *The Design of Us* and will join me on the next ride!

THE
DESIGN
OF
US

Sajni Patel

DISCUSSION QUESTIONS

1. Bhanu struggles with social anxiety and can get overwhelmed in groups. Are there certain situations where you feel easily overwhelmed?

2. Sunny and Bhanu love to hate each other. Have you ever had an enemies-to-lovers romance of your own?

3. Bhanu loves ube, a popular food in Hawaii. When you travel, do you travel for food as well as destination? What are some of your favorite culinary discoveries?

4. Sunny's father has recently been ill, and Sunny is struggling to share the burden of an ailing parent with his siblings. How do you handle sharing the burden when life throws hardships your way?

5. Bhanu and Sunny find themselves competing for the same job but manage to not let it come between them. Do you think you would be able to do the same?

6. Bhanu is dedicated to her job and struggles to take time for herself. How do you achieve your work-life balance?

7. Despite her feelings for Sunny, Bhanu steps in to pretend to be his girlfriend when she sees him struggling with his ex. Do you think you'd be able to maintain that kind of charade?

8. Sejal seems to thrive on drama and wanted a more passionate relationship with Sunny, breaking up with him when he wouldn't fight for her the way she wanted. Do you consider that passion, or do you think people can show their love without all the drama?

Photo © Sajni Patel

Sajni Patel is an award-winning author of women's fiction and young adult books. Her works have appeared on numerous Best of the Year and Must-Read lists from *Cosmopolitan*, *Teen Vogue*, Apple Books, *AudioFile*, *Tribeza*, *Austin Woman*, NBC, Insider, and many others.

VISIT SAJNI PATEL ONLINE

SajniPatel.com
🐦 SajniPatelBooks
📷 SajniPatelBooks
♪ SajniPatelBooks